## LOVE: NAZI STYLE

Hergett promised himself that he would never again settle for the brutal, loveless sex popularized by the Hitler Youth Movement. But as he looked at Evelyn, the sparse triangle of her bathing shorts, the bold invitation in her eyes, his determination turned to uncertainty, the uncertainty to fire.

"Once you liked me this way." She said it indifferently as she sat down beside him.

Then suddenly she fell back, pulling him down beside her. Hergett pressed her to him violently, as if her body could smother the despair, the helplessness, and the disgust . . .

---

"Dynamic . . . strongly and powerfully written."
—New Haven Register

# MARK OF SHAME

By Willi Heinrich

Translated from the German
by Sigrid Rock

BANTAM BOOKS
TORONTO • NEW YORK • LONDON • SYDNEY

MARK OF SHAME

*A Bantam Book / published by arrangement with
Farrar, Straus & Giroux, Inc.*

### PRINTING HISTORY

*Farrar, Straus & Cudahy edition published June 1959*
*Excerpt appeared in Esquire Magazine May 1959*

*Bantam edition published April 1960*
*2nd printing .................. December 1967*
*3rd printing ............... February 1968*
*4th printing ............... August 1981*

ISBN 0–553–20110–7

*Published simultaneously in the United States and Canada*

---

---

# MARK OF SHAME

# [ CHAPTER ONE ]

The secretary came back for the third time and by now her voice was weak with indignation. The gentleman outside had simply sat down and refused to leave until the Landrat had seen him, she reported.

Six years in office had made of Landrat Schneider a patient man. Looking up at Fräulein von Hessel, he leaned back in his chair. Perhaps the man was from the state government in Munich, he suggested. Fräulein von Hessel did not know.

"All right then, show him in," said the Landrat.

The man waited until Fräulein von Hessel had closed the door behind her. Schneider looked him over. Obviously he was not from the government in Munich, he looked too shabby for that. His cheap, ready-made coat with its sagging pockets was so threadbare that Schneider wondered how the fellow had managed to get past the doorman. The only thing that prevented Schneider from showing his annoyance was the man's self-assured manner. He slouched down in a chair, crossing his legs, and looked around the office with unconcealed curiosity, his expression indicating that he approved of the decor. Impatiently Schneider asked him what he wanted.

"Ah yes," the man took his eyes off an oil painting of the city of Nuremberg and looked at Schneider. "My father sent me to you."

Schneider noticed that he was younger than he had thought at first. He had light grey eyes, a narrow foxy face and tufts of blond hair stood away above his ears. Schneider looked at him disgustedly. It was his opinion

1

that seven years after the war no man capable of honest hard work needed to run around in rags. This opinion reflected in his voice when he coldly told the young man that he couldn't remember ever having heard his father's name.

"Wagner, you say?"

"Ernst Wagner," said the young man. "My father's name is Friedrich. Certainly you must remember him."

Schneider's eyes narrowed. It wouldn't be the first time in his career as Landrat that people tried to remind him of certain names and events which he would be a fool to remember. If this young man was referring to the Friedrich Wagner who had played a part in his, Schneider's past—

"I'm afraid I really don't," said Schneider but added, to be certain: "However, the name does sound vaguely familiar. Wasn't there in the Third Reich—"

He snapped his fingers as if trying hard to remember and watched the young man's face from the corners of his eyes.

The young man grinned.

"You see, you do remember! That's my father, Gauleiter Friedrich Wagner. He told me that he's known you ever since you went to school together."

"When did he tell you that?"

"Two days ago. I was allowed to visit him in jail. You know he's in jail, of course."

"No, that is—" Schneider hesitated and looked suspiciously at the grinning young man. Then he said slowly: "In jail, is he?"

"Yes. It was in all the papers at the time. The denazification board classified him as a major offender and sentenced him to ten years in jail, confiscated his property and all that."

Seeing the young man still grinning, Schneider's soul filled with deep apprehension. He cleared his throat.

"Ah yes, now I do remember," he said guardedly. "Your father hid out in Bavaria for two years and then the police found him."

"They didn't exactly find him," said young Wagner. "Someone denounced him to them. Ever since then my mother has had to struggle along as a cleaning woman. That's why I came to you."

2

"You've come to the wrong person," Schneider said coldly. "Does you mother live in Nuremberg?"

"Yes."

"In the city proper?"

"Yes, in Kreuzstrasse."

"Then you must file a petition with the Municipal Welfare Office. As Landrat I'm in charge only of the rural district. Whatever gave you the idea of coming to me with your problems?"

"I told you, my father suggested it."

"I can't imagine why he would."

"Oh, after all, you were in school together. You see, it's not so much a question of helping my mother, it's a question of helping me. If I had a good position and could earn enough, then she wouldn't have to work. At her age she really can't work any more."

Schneider got up.

"Young man, many women have to work hard all their lives! And as far as you're concerned, you'll have to go to the Labour Office—this office here is not an employment agency."

"I've already been there," said Ernst Wagner. "I've been there four times since I came back from French prison eight weeks ago. But they keep saying they haven't anything for me."

"Then you'll just have to find work for yourself. Every pair of hands is needed for the task of reconstruction. Put an ad in the paper and look through the Help Wanted pages. You're sure to find something, the building industry needs people right and left."

His tone was one of firm dismissal but the young man did not move. Schneider called for Fräulein von Hessel.

"See Herr Wagner to the door, please."

"Just a moment," said Ernst Wagner. Reaching into his coat pocket he pulled out an old, scuffed leather wallet from which he took a piece of paper and pressed it into the Landrat's hand.

"This is the copy of a letter you wrote my father in 1938," he said. "Perhaps you'd like to glance through it before I go."

Schneider stared at the paper. Fräulein von Hessel, who stood dumbfounded between the two men, noticed in alarm that the Landrat's hands began to tremble.

Then the paper drifted to the floor. Before Fräulein von Hessel could pick it up, the Landrat had covered it with his foot and was shouting in a tone she had never heard from him:

"Get out!"

Landrat Schneider was a strong, heavy man with shoulders like a furniture mover. His tightfitting vest nearly burst with the weight of his great belly. Because of the August heat he had unbuttoned his coat and his bald head was pearled over with beads of sweat. To Fräulein von Hessel the sight was a familiar one. What shocked her far more than his roaring voice was his face—a frightened, white distorted face.

When he left the office shortly afterwards, two hours before closing time, Fräulein von Hessel was convinced that something extraordinary must have happened.

The same conviction took possession of Frau Schneider the moment she saw her husband's office car drive up at a time she usually enjoyed a lazy coffee hour.

The Schneiders' comfortable six-room house was in the Nuremberg suburb of Erlenstegen. It was one of Frau Schneider's favorite pastimes to spend the afternoons with her daughter Katharina on the sun drenched porch and to repeat her repertoire of motherly advice. Most of the advice consisted of recommendations which Frau Schneider from the start of her own marriage had failed to follow. She was naturally anxious to prevent her daughter from making the same mistake.

Today the conversation between mother and daughter was interrupted by the Landrat's early return. He came out on the porch with a wild look on his face and threw himself into a chair. Pressing both hands on her heart Frau Schneider stared at her husband beseechingly until he started to talk of his own volition and told her everything.

Frau Schneider then said in a tone she had not dared to use towards her husband in at least twenty years:

"I knew this would happen!"

"If that's all you have to contribute, I can do without it," he said furiously. "Who would have thought this damned letter is still in existence. You did, I suppose?"

4

"Yes," she said drily. "Yes, I did. Ever since you wrote it I was afraid someone someday would turn up with it. Did he at least give it to you?"

"No, that's the point. He said he wanted to see first whether the job I'd give him in the office would 'meet with his expectations.' The impudence of it! And the fellow looks as if he couldn't count up to three."

"Those are the worst," said Frau Schneider. She looked at her daughter who sat at the table, pale and still.

"If you don't get this letter we won't ever again have a moment's peace, neither one of us."

"I shall strangle that blackmailer with my own hands," Schneider said vehemently.

His wife flinched and knocked over a cup. As she put it back tears came to her eyes.

"How can you even say such a thing, Karl. *Guter Gott*, what can we do? How about bringing him here? Perhaps if Katharina and I talked nicely to him he might give up the letter."

"Bring him here! I'm to bring this blackmailer into my own home? Drive him to the door in my own car perhaps? Please, Herr Wagner, after you Herr Wagner, my wife and daughter cannot wait to meet you. That would indeed be the end!"

The thought made him jump up from his chair. He turned to his daughter and shouted:

"Why don't you open your mouth? Do you think this doesn't concern you? If this mess costs me my job your eyes will open, I assure you. But just let him try," he raged on. "To dress me down like a runny-nosed child! 'Let's see if the position meets with my expectations!' I'll be—"

He broke off and fell back on his chair, near collapse with fury and exhaustion. His wife and daughter sat like wooden statues.

At last Katharina stirred. She got up and looked down at her father. It was amazing, people often said how unlike her parents Katharina was. A stranger would never have suspected that they were related. Unlike her parents, who were both tall and strong and getting fatter all the time, Katharina was slight and delicate.

With a characteristic, tired gesture she brushed a strand of silky black hair from her forehead and said:

"You wrote that letter, we didn't. Mama warned you not to do it. If you'd only listened to her."

"If I'd listened to her we would still be where we were fifteen years ago," he said spitefully. "Haven't I done well by you? For whom do you think I did all this? Not only for me, for you! Who's been nagging at me about a house of our own all the time? And when we finally had one, a house for fifty thousand marks, furniture for fifteen, the plot for ten—no one asked how I had managed it. Just move in, the old man will take care of it somehow. Yes, and the old man has taken care of it. But instead of being grateful you now hack away at me."

With a glance at her daughter, Frau Schneider said: "Katharina doesn't mean it like that."

"I know exactly how she means it. She's never appreciated her good life with her parents."

"You've reminded me often enough," Katharina said bitterly. "If you'd let me marry eight years ago you wouldn't have to remind me any more."

Schneider jumped up in anger.

"Are you starting that again? You have every reason to be grateful to your parents for having advised you against it."

"I shouldn't have listened to you," Katharina said. "As long as Klaus was still an officer and wore the Knight's Cross and wasn't wounded you were perfectly happy about it."

"And so? It is our fault that he had to get up and fly on the last day of the war? He never could get enough of it. He wasn't satisfied with the Knight's Cross, he wanted to get the Oak Clusters, too. Instead he got a hole in his skull. As if that were our fault!"

"You've broken his self-confidence." Katharina's voice grew sharp. "You told him it would be irresponsible to marry as long as his attacks might recur. Now he keeps thinking they may come back."

"Of course it would have been irresponsible! It still would be. In the office I get into a cold sweat each time I think he might assault someone again. And he keeps making mistakes in his work. Whoever heard of a Landrat hiring a man who is 90 per cent incapacitated, making him department head and then fighting with district directors, personnel officers and employees to keep him.

6

But no, my daughter knows better. She knows better even than the doctors. You seem to forget that he would still be in the asylum today if I hadn't used my influence for him."

He sounded more and more embittered. His daughter said contemptuously:

"If he were still in an asylum, he'd be there by mistake. He hasn't had an attack in two years, and the doctors say that's the best sign he's all right. And everybody makes mistakes at work. You only used your influence for him because I pestered you so. To talk about him like this now is not fair, but I don't suppose you have any feeling for that sort of thing. The letter to the Gauleiter was also unfair, and that you pandered to the Americans was an indecency, too, when at first you couldn't talk enough dirt about them. You're sitting in a job you couldn't have gotten if you hadn't falsified your questionnaires. That was bound to end in disaster. Whatever this Herr Wagner is doing is no worse than what you've done yourself. I had to tell you that, for once!"

She had already vanished through the door when Schneider stirred from his stupor. He glanced at his wife, then he put both elbows on the table, buried his face in his hands and sat motionless. Frau Schneider got up and went over to him. She pressed her tearstained cheek against his head mumbling soothing words. Schneider finally lifted his face.

"It's all right, Elsa," he said absent-mindedly. "It's all right."

He looked out the window, across the garden to the edge of the woods. Gently he pushed his wife aside, stood up, reached for his hat and, halfway to the door, said in a choked voice:

"My children have never understood me."

The sentence still sounded in his ears when he reached the woods a few minutes later. He ducked behind a bush and from there looked back at his house. Katharina and his wife were standing in the garden. Their attitude expressed so much agitation and concern that Schneider was satisfied. For a moment he was proud of his dramatic exit, but then he thought of Katharina and the disappointment smothered his pride. To talk to me like that, he thought, my own daughter! Pain spread in his chest and his eyes filled with tears. Unable to bear the sight of the two women any longer, he turned and rushed off into the woods.

With clenched fists, muttering wild and incomprehensible curses, he ran around among the trees until a pain in his side finally forced him to a standstill. The physical effort had exhausted his fury somewhat. He walked on slowly, trying to think what he could do about young Wagner. But each time he remembered the fellow's arrogant behavior his fury rose again like a whirlwind and blew apart his painfully concentrated thoughts.

He decided to rest his legs a little before starting home. He found a spot far away from the road, and spread his handkerchief on the ground with some difficulty. When he had finally lowered his massive body and sat with his back against a tree, he felt terribly beaten. He pushed his hands into his pockets and stared unseeingly into the impenetrable green foliage in front of him. Gradually the silence soothed him and he thought again of his family.

Although some of the things Katharina had flung at him made him furious and put him in a righteous and defensive mood, he knew that there were certain things in his life of which he was not proud. For instance, it was not nice, it was not right, that he could not stop himself from being unfaithful to his wife. But what man, he thought, could claim an entirely clear conscience in that respect? He loved his Elsa sincerely and the thought that her heart condition might suddenly take her from his side could stop his breath. He brought her an expensive flower bouquet at least once a week, a habit he had followed since his honeymoon as steadily as he played *skat* one evening a week. And that honeymoon, after all, was thirty years ago—the thought made him proud and sad. During the first years of his marriage he had felt no temptations. But then it started, with a young manicurist—a girl barely out of her teens, but a crafty little beast. Unfortunately that moment of crisis had coincided with a long drawn out illness of his wife. When she recovered, sugar and water had bloated her body into a shapeless mass. The sight of her fat hips, the dull indifference with which she endured his caresses helped Schneider to convince himself that his wife's bad health was to blame for his philanderings. The affair with the manicurist had wakened a passion for young women in him.

Of course, he had always been very discreet. He was quite proud to think that for all these years he had managed to keep his wife's absolute confidence. She was convinced that he, while ruthless in business matters, was the most faithful of husbands.

Only once had there nearly been an accident. Even now, eleven years later, Schneider winced with mortification when he remembered the awful situation in which his son had caught him. Hans had always been a difficult, rebellious child. For weeks Schneider had come home every night with his heart in his throat, expecting his wife to meet him at the door and to fling the story in his face. He had wondered how he might contrive to send the boy away for a while, at least until the incident had faded from his memory, but there was no chance. Anyhow, Hans had kept his mouth shut and this filled Schneider with pride as it proved that the boy had inherited trends of his own character. Nevertheless, he was relieved when the boy came home one day and said he wanted to volunteer for the Wehrmacht. A soldier's life, so Schneider told himself, would make a man out of him and he would come to understand his father's behavior. Frau Schneider did her best to dissuade her son but his father actually encouraged him and finally helped him break the mother's resistance.

In his urge to get rid of his son for a while Schneider had forgotten that something might happen to the boy. Of this he thought only much later and by that time it had already happened.

Ever since then Schneider had suffered. Again and again he would wake up at night, tortured by remorse and pain, desperately hoping that his son was still alive somewhere in a Russian prison camp.

However, he found refuge in his work. It had taken all his cunning and effort to adapt himself to the changed conditions. Katharina's reproaches didn't really bother him—what did women know about these things? It was her attitude that hurt him so. She did not understand how much courage it had taken to succeed in those postwar days. In spite of his bad humor, Schneider could not suppress a thin smile when he thought of it. They had made him fill out three long questionnaires—Fragebogen—and he had perjured himself on all of them. But no one ever found out about his party membership. The Americans had set up this entire denazification machine in such a complicated way that, in the end, they themselves got lost in the maze. Then they turned its execution over to people from whom, already a year later, no dog would accept a bone. In Schneider's opinion this entire, unpopular hubbub would never have evolved if everyone else had used the same method in filling out his Fragebogen as he had. At first it had given him some tremors but then the present government director confessed to him in a confidential moment that he himself had been a party judge during the Third Reich. At the end of the war he had helped destroy the party records with his own hands, he said. Schneider felt safe in his skin again.

Safe, that is, until today. The letter, the damned letter had changed all this. Incredible that Wagner should have kept it all this time! It had been written ten years ago. As a result Schneider's immediate superior in the Ministry was drafted into the infantry and, a year later, killed in Russia.

That had really not been Schneider's intention. True, the man had been in his way. True, his political attitude had been intolerable—he had made it impossible for Schneider to continue looking on in silence. But not for a moment had Schneider wished for anything serious to happen to him. Why did he have to be so stupid, Schneider now thought bitterly, why couldn't he keep his mouth shut? As if talking would have helped anyone! Schneider's bitterness was sincere especially when he thought of the consequences the whole thing might yet have for him.

His behind began to hurt. Clumsily he got to his feet and looked at his watch. In an hour it would be dark. He was pleased that he had stayed out so long. They would be sitting on edge at home. Let them, he thought! He had his worries, why shouldn't they have theirs.

He gave a grim laugh. Keep them coming, he thought, just keep them coming, one blow after another. His son missing, perhaps dead, his daughter engaged to a cripple, a wife with a bad heart, who might not live another year, and on top of it this blackmailer, this damned vagrant, this cursed parasite threatening to destroy with one blow all that had taken a lifetime to build.

Schneider groaned. Mechanically squashing his hat with his hands, he walked on, the tears rolling down his soft cheeks. He did not see the trees or the sky, nor hear the birds chirping above him nor the sound of evening bells, caught up in a tired western breeze, wandering across the hills and woods.

He walked on, his head hanging, a heavy, lonely, unhappy man who all his life had wanted to do so much good and had only rarely done it.

# [ CHAPTER TWO ]

Having warmed up dinner for the third time, and with her husband still nowhere in sight, Frau Schneider became quite hysterical. She told her daughter tearfully that she was ungrateful and impertinent; she could no longer bear simply to sit and wait.

"I'll go and look for him," said Katharina.

"You are my darling child," Frau Schneider gratefully kissed her cheek. "He's probably just walking around in the woods. See if you can find him, you know where he always goes."

"Yes," said Katharina tiredly. "I know." She could not understand how her mother, who should have known her husband better, could be fooled by these antics time and again.

"I hope he's all right," Frau Schneider said tremulously. "You don't think he'd harm himself, do you?"

"I assure you he wouldn't harm himself," said Katharina. "Go and lie down a while, I'll look for him."

As long as her mother could see her, Katharina followed the path her father had taken. Then she took a sharp turn and headed for the nearest street car stop. Twenty minutes later she arrived at Klaus' home.

"Anything the matter?" he asked immediately.

"No." She went over to the window and looked up at the castle. Its towers were dipped in the crimson evening sky. "Is your father home?"

"He'll be home any minute," said Klaus. "They're working overtime again. Listen, is there—"

He broke off. Katharina turned around. He was sitting at the table. She looked at him, at his narrow face with the dreadful scar high on his forehead that looked as if someone had hacked off a piece with an axe and then carelessly patched it back on.

"Yes?" said Katharina.

"There was some trouble at the office today," said Klaus. "Have you talked to your father yet?"

"What trouble was there at the office?"

"I'm not sure. He shouted at that Hessel woman so the entire floor could hear it. They say someone from the government in Munich was there. Has he come home yet?"

"He's come home."

"Must have been a troublesome visitor."

"It certainly was." She went over to the table, sat down and put her hands on his.

"You're crying!" he said in dismay. "What did happen? Nothing serious I hope?"

"I wouldn't be too sure." She reported the afternoon's events. "It had to come some day," she concluded. "Mama and I have always expected it. What do we do now? My head is spinning."

"The idiot!" Klaus said.

Katharina had told him about the letter before. They had agreed never to let Klaus' father know about it. Although he had been as convinced of Hitler's merits as Schneider in those days, he was a decent man and would have been shocked.

Klaus looked at Katharina.

"Have you eaten dinner yet?"

She shook back her hair, a typical gesture of hers which he loved.

"He's run off as usual," she said, wiping her eyes with the index finger. "Whenever he can't think of anything to say he runs away and leaves Mama sitting there. She goes into a panic each time. Let me call to see if he's come home."

She went out into the hall and came back a few moments later.

"Just as I thought. Returned according to schedule. It's the same act each time. He should be ashamed of himself."

"He won't be," said Klaus. "Will you have dinner with me?"

They had dinner in a nearby restaurant and afterwards took a walk up to the castle.

The evening was mild. Below them the city spread with its towers, gables and spires and beyond it at the horizon a gently curving line of hills. To the south a mountainscape of clouds towered like the crags of a ruin into the changing color of the evening sky. It was getting dark. The city started turning on its lights. As if a spark were dancing down the streets, street lamps and neon lights lit up in rows, modern spotlights with five thousand watt beams turned their glowing eyes on crumbling, old, ivycolored walls. From the youth hostel nearby came the sound of singing voices, ancient *Wanderlieder* that had survived through centuries of war and turmoil. The spark ran on and on, across the River Pegnitz, over the town wall, out into the hamlets and the hills and up to the stars until the sky looked like one enormous black lake in which all the lights were reflected.

"What are you thinking of?" asked Klaus.

Katharina had closed her eyes and was leaning back, listening to the songs. It seemed as if her own voice were coming across to her, a piece of the past, a few years of her life returning, wrapped in their sentimental melody.

"Oh, I see." Suddenly Klaus laughed in his old, gay, carefree manner. "They sing it almost as well as we used to, don't they? How long ago that is."

"How very long ago," said Katharina. After a while she opened her eyes.

"Let's go somewhere else. There are so many people here."

Over the battlement she looked down at the town.

"Look at those houses, those thousands of houses," she

13

said. "Some day I'd like to know what it is like to close one's own door behind oneself."

"You can do that every day at home, can't you?"

"I can, can I?" she said. They walked down into the city and stopped before the display window of a furniture store.

"There, that's the kind we wanted—two years ago this cost eight hundred marks," she said, peering at the price tags of a bedroom set. "Twelve hundred—but that's," wrinkling her forehead she calculated: "Why, that's four hundred marks more than it used to be. In two years, can you believe it—"

She turned around. Klaus was no longer behind her. She discovered him, a few yards away, standing at a news stand. Her voice was rough and angry:

"Why do you run away?"

"Look at this," he grinned and pointed to a postcard with a pretty, half naked girl.

"I'm asking you a question," said Katharina. Three sharp vertical lines appeared on her forehead.

Klaus looked at her. In the harsh light of a neon display his face was even paler than usual.

"I didn't notice that you'd stopped," he said. She knew he was lying but she also knew that it was useless to tell him so. Once they had walked through the city every evening, looking at window displays together and discussing what kind of furniture they wanted for their home. Since then much water had run down the River Pegnitz and still no home, no furniture. Instead they went to the woods once or twice a month.

No, thought Katharina, no human being would have the strength and patience to bear this any longer. Not even if you loved a man so much that no risk was too great to marry him, no risk and no sacrifice. But what is the use, she asked herself, why torment yourself, destroying it all and learning in the end that it would have been destroyed even if you hadn't tormented yourself.

She looked down the brightly lit street and remembered when she had walked with Klaus for the first time across the market square. People had turned to stare after the tall, slender air force officer and Katharina had been so proud and excited that she could not finish a sentence, she was stuttering all the time.

Today the market was a wide, naked square lying like a freshly healed wound among the crumbling ruins that had once been handsome patrician mansions and medieval houses, whose ornately laced stone balustrades and steep roofs, graceful bays and pointed gables had been admired and painted and photographed so often that their coquetry had lingered in the narrow little streets like a permanent smile. Today, seven years after the dreadful raids, most people had gotten used to the different picture, to the modern buildings shooting up everywhere and to the naked, open squares where the old burgher houses had once stood. Katharina had not got used to it. Often when they walked together she caught herself glancing at Klaus' disfigured face and remembering how different the city had looked once, the city and Klaus and life.

Suddenly she started walking away from him very quickly. A few moments later Klaus caught her by the arm.

"What's the matter with you?" he panted. "What will the people think?"

"I don't care what the people think," she said. "If I walk too fast for you, don't worry. I'll find the way alone."

"You weren't walking, you ran."

It pleased her that he was so annoyed. His grip on her arm hurt her but she merely said:

"Even if I did run that's no excuse for shouting at me. Let go of me, please."

"As you say." Crossly he put his hands in his pockets. "Sometimes I wonder which of us two is the crazier, you or I."

"It shows how well we fit together." She had decided she wouldn't let him get away this time. A few minutes later, when they reached the city park she said:

"Let's walk through it. It's not much of a detour."

"By all means," he said. "We haven't been here in a long time."

"The last time was in May," she said. "In the old days you took me here every evening, remember?"

"Of course I remember. But later, the deer park was even better."

15

"Later in the deer park you wanted a lot more than in the city park."

"Didn't you?"

"Oh, I suppose. But in the days of the city park everything was much simpler."

"You're not talking about your virginity, are you?" he asked cynically.

"Unfortunately I lost that, along with all those spoiled dresses."

"What dresses?" His face was a blank. Then he laughed. "Oh, the grass stains. You washed those out, didn't you?"

"You can't wash grass stains out of delicate material."

"I'm sorry," he said sheepishly. "Why didn't you ever tell me?"

"Because I didn't want to spoil your fun."

"*My* fun—" He stopped and she heard his heavy breathing. Under the thin shell of her composure she could feel her heart hammering. She had risked it often enough, but each time she felt like someone tightening further the string of a violin that was already stretched to the breaking point. Now he started to talk. His voice had the shrill sound of an electric saw hitting the wood. While she let his burst of rage wash over her, she inwardly admired her own courage. Instinctively her hand touched her neck where two years ago the grip of his hands had been and already half unconscious she had lain under him and watched two men appear and tear Klaus from her. They wanted to take him to the police and it had needed all her persuasive powers to explain to them that Klaus was a disabled veteran who sometimes got overexcited but who had never really intended to kill her.

Then as now they had fought over the same subject. Always they fought over the same subject. And then as now she had provoked him, wanting to punch through his taut shell, to force him to let go and spill out his feelings, his anger, his hostilities. There was always the danger that he might lose control again. But again it seemed she was lucky. The boiler had not exploded, the pressure valve was working fine. She was so relieved, she hardly heard the ugly things he said. She let his rage run down and then pointed out that the other people in the park must have heard every word. Now that he had caught hold of himself, he was very embarrassed. He took her hand and pulled her back out into the street.

"We should have gone across town to the deer park," he said.

"We can still go," said Katharina.

He looked at her surprised.

"Wouldn't it be too late for you?"

"Not today. Today I don't care when I get home."

"I'm sorry," he said. "You know I can't help myself."

"You always say that afterwards."

"I'm truly sorry."

They walked on in silence. They didn't speak again until they got off the street car at the other end of town. As they headed towards the park, Klaus said: "You shouldn't have said anything like that, you know. As if I were the only one who had fun."

Katharina didn't answer.

They had reached the trees and went down a small path they had walked along so often that Katharina could have found it with closed eyes. The thought increased her bitterness and she heard herself say:

"Wouldn't you like it better if there were an easier way?"

"We've discussed that enough." He peered impatiently through the trees. "There, we don't have to go further."

She stumbled after him, her feet caught in a molehill, she ran up against a tree in the darkness and asked unhappily:

"Where are you?"

"Come here, take my hand."

She felt him grip her, pull her towards him and then she was lying beside him on the ground. Underneath she felt the cool earth, knotty roots at her elbows and in her back the sharp pressure of a stone which hurt so much that she pushed Klaus aside and said very bitterly:

"You're murdering me."

"What in the world is the matter with you?" he asked, dumbfounded.

"Nothing." She felt for the aching spot in her back and said a little more calmly: "My dress."

"Take it off, here's my coat, lie down on that."

This time it was a piece of bark that bored between her shoulder blades but she made no further attempt to

17

shift her position. It was no use. The entire wood was full of abominations and she now hated it as much as, at this moment, she hated Klaus whose hands were on her and who said, panting:

"I want you like this, once again like this . . ."

He could have her like this every day if they had their own home, she thought. But the bedroom set was four hundred marks dearer, probably the price would rise even more and so would the rents, everything dearer and dearer and more hopeless she thought . . . the damned, stony ground, if only it were not so hard. And the grass pricking like needles—but, yes, there, yes this is what I like, she told him silently, this is how I like it . . . oh how I do love you, my God, you idiot, I do love you in spite of your crazy head . . . The first time in two weeks—but there you are, she told herself, you made your mistake, you should have held him off until he gave in with his stubborn, crazed head . . . now it was too late, now she was as greedy as he was. What now, what did he want? Oh, all right, that way the piece of wood won't hurt so—my God, but his knees are hard, wait, what is he going to do now—oh no! how does he know these things —finish man, please finish. . . .

"Klaus!"

"I nearly went out of my mind."

"So I noticed. How do you know these—"

"One knows," he said. "Here's your dress—are you cold?"

"Rather."

"The ground is damp." He helped her with the dress. "Cigarette?"

"Yes," she said. "If only my Landrat had seen us now."

"He's done the same thing in his day."

"Oh no, he hasn't."

Klaus laughed.

"You mean because he is your father?"

"No, because he and Mama didn't have to run into the woods."

"Are you starting that again?"

"I shan't stop until we're married."

"It's amazing," he said. "How can an intelligent girl like you be so unreasonable. Where would we live? In

18

your home with your Landrat? If I marry I at least want my own four walls. I've told you that a hundred times."

She nodded with great satisfaction.

"I'm all for that and I've figured it all out."

"You've figured what out?"

"How much money we need. All we have to have is a room and kitchen to start with and as far as furniture goes—you're steadily employed and can get installment credit."

"And pay off two hundred marks a month or more. So we can live on fifty marks a month—"

"Plus your pension. And once we're married I'll get my Landrat to put you in a higher civil service category."

"Oh, sure," Klaus grinned. "I should think he's got other troubles at the moment." He squashed his cigarette and said curtly: "Stop that nonsense!"

Katharina wondered what she had done wrong.

"If that's nonsense," she said, "then what we just did was nonsense too. Then everything we do is nonsense."

"Quite!"

"All right," she got up. "Let's go home then."

Without hesitation and as quickly as she could in the darkness she made her way through the trees. She had almost reached the road when Klaus appeared at her side, put his arms around her and pressed her to him so hard that she couldn't breathe.

"We're talking such nonsense," he whispered.

"You are."

"You provoke me. You should know me better."

"I don't know you any more," she said. "Lately you've made it so difficult for me to understand you. Ever since you came back from the asylum. You can't say I didn't give you time to adapt yourself again. At first we were going to wait half a year, then a year and now it's become two years. How many more?"

"You don't understand," he said unhappily.

"Well, help me to understand. You're cured, otherwise they wouldn't have released you. And if it's merely a question of finances—don't forget that I'm there, too."

"You're where?"

"I mean, I can earn money as well as you can—"

"Just get that idea out of your head," he said, his voice rising. "Either I earn enough to support a family or I won't get married. I just won't stand for my wife having to work. It would show the whole world that I'm not good for anything."

"So that's the reason." For a moment she listened to the silence around them. They might have been the only two people in the world.

Then she said:

"But I know what you're good for—isn't that more important?"

"For nothing!"

"For many things," she said, her voice trembling a little. "For so many things, Klaus. How often must I tell you?"

They held each other tight in the dark. Klaus stroked her slim head.

"You can't exist on that."

"The whole world exists on that."

"Like the lilies of the field—they toil not, neither do they—"

"Klaus!"

"Sorry," he grinned. "I didn't write the Bible. If our Adolf were still here we'd have been married long ago."

"He was a beast," Katharina said disgustedly.

"Because he had the Jews killed?"

"Not only because of that. He started the war, too."

"He had no choice. They practically drove him to it."

"Of course. That's what all the former Nazis say today. Who, may I ask, drove him to it? The French? The English? Or perhaps even the Americans?"

"Well, look at you!" Klaus said cheerfully. "I just talked about that with my father last night. I told him that our own people drove Hitler into the war. What could a little maniac like Hitler do if he's hailed as a new messiah so long that in the end he becomes convinced himself that he is one. Yesterday it was Hitler, today it's some other politician or a movie star or whatnot. There always has to be someone. Call it idolatry or the cult of the personality: in any case it's the flight of the plebeians forward, their flight away from their own mediocrity towards an apparent idol. Don't you see?"

She didn't answer. She didn't think much of his political opinions although, she admitted, at times they sounded impressive. If only he talked with the same passion about music or literature. About politics she knew nothing. And she had never forgotten that it had been to a political meeting that Klaus owed his three years in an asylum. Some derogatory remark had enraged him so that he had jumped on the speaker and, given the time, would have strangled him. He knocked out some of the teeth of one of the policemen who led him away, which didn't help matters. Still, she thought now, what a blessing that they had sent him to the asylum instead of to jail. With his childish sense of honor it would have been the end of him. That was another one of his complexes but one must never tell him, she thought, otherwise he'd go completely and permanently mad.

Walking beside him now she felt the warmth of his arm in her hand and a great gust of tenderness blew away her angry exasperation. She clung to him even tighter, leaned her head against his shoulder and said:

"You're a silly old bear."

"You are silly."

"All right, then I'm silly. When will you take your vacation?"

"When should I take it?"

Katharina hesitated. The idea had occurred to her so suddenly that she had not worked it out. But the thought of being alone with him for fourteen whole days was now so intense that she felt she could not wait another moment. She heard herself say:

"As soon as possible. Tomorrow if you want to."

"Tomorrow?" He sounded much amused. "You are delightful. When I said we should go in June you wouldn't hear of it."

"Mama was sick in bed in June . . ."

"—and then no hint for weeks and suddenly off we go . . . tomorrow if possible. It will take a little while to get permission to leave, we'll have to wait a week or so." He laughed. Her enthusiasm had infected him. Stopping, he turned her around and put his hands on her breasts, speaking into her hair:

"Like this, for two weeks like this and nothing else. And a room with bath."

"And breakfast in bed," she turned her head and

21

kissed him gaily on the corner of his mouth. "I can't wait."

"What if your Landrat finds out—he's sure to block my leave—"

"Nonsense. You simply apply and this time we say nothing about my going until the last minute. I hope we get a room though, it's the height of the season now."

"Well," said Klaus. "It's not my fault we didn't go in June. Your mother would have got well without your help."

Katharina felt something tear a gash in her gay mood. With a quick twist she slipped her breast from under his hand and said aggressively:

"She needed someone to take care of her."

"Why didn't she ask one of her women friends?" he said. "She has enough of them."

It was the timing rather than the subject that upset her so. As if he found pleasure in spoiling every happy mood of hers. The gash was now so wide that all the gaiety inside her was oozing out. Without looking at him she hurried off and did not stop when he called her name. At last he caught up with her.

"Now what is the matter?" he asked uncomprehendingly. "Is it that remark about your mother? Don't be silly. She's worth as little as your Landrat, otherwise she would have taught you better manners."

"I don't want you to talk about them like that," she said coldly.

She had often talked with him about her parents but for some reason this time his contemptuous tone offended her. She thought of telling him so but then she did not want to risk another quarrel. It might upset their vacation plans and she wanted this vacation badly. She wanted desperately to lead a life, if only for two weeks, that bore a resemblance to the picture she once had of the future. She had to feel alive again, alive as a woman rather than a well-bred daughter always living by the dictates of her parents' habits and whims.

The yellow city lights shone sleepily in the distance. They were nearing the edge of the wood. It was very late. Katharina pushed her hand back under Klaus' arm. He was still acting cross. She moved her hand forward until it touched his and, after a second, he pressed it fiercely to his heart. Men, she thought, silly men! All this big, tough talk and yet one small, gentle gesture would soften them at once. It was so simple, so laughable.

She lifted her head. In the dark night, the suburban houses with their naked brick walls had a forbidding, closed-off air. In a way she found them repulsive. She would never have thought that one day she would come to dislike Nuremberg, but she did now. All her memories revolted her now, the good ones and the bad ones. These streets—once she had run through them breathless with curiosity and excitement, once she had discovered hidden nooks and corners that had made her heart beat wildly—now the streets and the corners, it all bored her. With each day she lived here she liked the city less. At times she came close to hating it but she told herself that it wasn't fair. It wasn't really the city itself, it was the fact that in its entire expanse there was not a single square foot of ground under her feet which she could call her own. She had to go away with Klaus, she had to!

# [ CHAPTER THREE ]

Every morning, at eight o'clock sharp, Herr Primelmann, director of the General Administration and Finance Division and Personnel Director entered the gatehouse at the entrance to the Landratsamt. There he settled down to watch the gate and to note in a small book the names of employees who arrived late for work. In some cases he merely put a cross behind an already registered name. Those with five crosses received a little blue note of dismissal. Whenever that happened, Primelmann emerged in a cheerful mood. On less successful days he would remain in the gatehouse for a long time, wearing the peevish expression of a vegetable hawker who's been left sitting on a batch of rotting cabbages.

This morning he was not to be cheered by catching

anybody because the janitor informed him that the Herr Landrat had arrived a quarter hour early and wanted to see Primelmann right away.

Primelmann was too correct an official to be in the least alarmed by this unusual request; he did not need to search his conscience. Whatever he did was always in complete accordance with the Landrat's instructions. When a few minutes later he wished Fräulein von Hessel a friendly good morning, he felt nothing more than mild curiosity.

He did not like arrogant, handsome Fräulein von Hessel but, he thought, looking after her as she went to announce his arrival, would it be better to undress her or strangle her?

Schneider received him sitting at his desk, behind a pile of morning mail. He immediately told Primelmann what he wanted. Primelmann replied him that there were no vacancies at all on the staff. At once Schneider became impatient.

"Somehow you'll find a little niche for him, otherwise you'll have to create one. The man was held as a prisoner of the French until a few weeks ago. You know my point of view: we owe it to our returning soldiers to do something for them. It is a sacred obligation."

Stunned by the Landrat's sharp tone, Primelmann hastened to agree. What has caused his miserable humor, he wondered.

"The man's name is Wagner," Schneider went on in a milder voice. "He'll report to you Monday morning."

Primelmann risked a little conversation.

"I didn't know the French still had German POW's over there?"

"They've made war criminals out of them so they can lock them up indefinitely."

"Incredible!" Primelmann was filled with indignation and compassion. He himself had been locked up by the Americans for four weeks because of his long party membership. The French, he knew, had been even stricter.

"They haven't noticed that times have changed," he said with a sneer.

"They don't want to notice," said Schneider and got up. Primelmann left and Schneider betook himself to

24

the men's room. From there he returned in a state of wrath and called in Fräulein von Hessel to take a memorandum:

"At great expense I have caused modern and hygienic toilets to be installed. During occasional visits I have been forced to notice that the toilets of both ladies and gentlemen are in a condition unworthy of civilized human beings—get that?"

"Yes, Herr Landrat," said Fräulein von Hessel. She had put her pad on her knees and Schneider noticed that she wore no stockings.

She must do a lot of sunbathing, he thought absentmindedly, and went on dictating:

"I must presume enough breeding on the part of all employees to enable them to feel responsible for the hygienic condition of the toilets—get that?"

"Yes, Herr Landrat," said Fräulein von Hessel.

"I herewith appeal to the feeling of solidarity among members of the staff and I hold department heads responsible for the clean and hygienic condition of our toilets. Interoffice memo to all employees, underline the *Inter,* will you?"

"Yes, Herr Landrat," said Fräulein von Hessel, taking a quick look at the clock. "It's time for the district committee meeting."

"I know," he said, straightening his tie. A moment later he left the room with a briefcase in his hand.

From one of the windows in the corridor he glanced down into the yard where a dozen cars stood parked. An unusually elegant sports car attracted his attention. He had never seen it before. He concluded that this must be Franz Leuchtner's new car.

Franz Leuchtner, a brother of the government director and himself a district deputy, was the owner of a large textile factory. During the war Schneider, in his position at the ministry of economics, had done some favors for him. After the war, Leuchtner's brother had suggested Schneider to the American authorities for the position of *Landrat.* Ever since Leuchtner and Schneider had been close friends; they met socially at least once a week.

In one corner of Schneider's paternal heart grew a silent, tenacious hope, feeding on the sweetmeats of pious good wishes for her future, that one day Katharina would give up her foolish objections to Leuchtner's only son. The last time Schneider had hopefully inquired what she thought of young Leuchtner, she had said he was sweet as raspberry syrup. She despised raspberry syrup.

Reluctantly Schneider withdrew his eyes from the sports car and headed briskly towards the conference room where the district deputies waited for him.

He opened the meeting without delay.

"You all know," he said, "that I represent the wishes of the rural communities to the federal government as if they were my own. However, I cannot change federal laws just because now and then they demand occasional sacrifices from a community. The government requires me to create among the communities an understanding for the highway project. The pitchforks of the burghers of Kapfing prevented federal land surveyors from carrying out their duty three days ago. This cannot be tolerated and these farmers will have to answer in court. We're no longer living in the Middle Ages. I must remind you that it happened to have been Kapfing which twenty years ago refused to give up acreage for the Nuremberg-Schweinfurt railway line. The railroad was built anyway, without the Kapfingers, the only difference being that the Kapfingers have to walk five kilometers to the nearest station. Now that the federal government wants to build a direct highway from Nuremberg to Schweinfurt we have a similar case. One would think the Kapfingers would welcome a connection with the main highway system. Think of the tourists, the increased profits for the restaurants, money that will turn up again in the community budget. One must really ask oneself whether Kapfing is in Bavaria or on the moon. Even in Wuerttemberg you don't find that much backwardness and we've certainly seen some extraordinary things there."

"Prussia's worse," said someone.

Everyone laughed. With an understanding grin Schneider said:

"There's no Prussia anymore."

Then he turned to a man who sat stiffly on his chair and took no part in the general laughter.

26

"It appears that burgermeister Wenzel is of a different opinion."

Silence fell as all faces turned toward Wenzel, who pushed back his chair and got to his feet. He was a broad-shouldered man with a strong, rough-hewn face, short hair and large, red ears. During the war he had been master sergeant in a reserve unit. The organization abilities he acquired there were not the least of the reasons why the Kapfingers elected him for their burgermeister.

"The Herr Landrat has felt it necessary to inquire whether the Kapfinger live in Bavaria or on the moon," he said snappishly. "This appears to be a somewhat unwise question because when the Herr Landrat was elected he knew very well where the Kapfingers lived. Before he was elected he was in Kapfing very frequently, much more frequently than in years since then. As Burgermeister I can only say this: we in Kapfing don't want to swallow more dirt thrown up by a lot of automobiles."

"You have one yourself," Schneider interrupted.

"But I don't careen through the village like a wild boar and run over other people's chickens. And as for their leaving any money in the restaurants, we know better. They order a Coca Cola at best, those gentleman drivers. If they want to go from Nuremberg to Schweinfurt, they can go via Bamberg, can't they? It's perfectly ridiculous to say that suddenly they can't go that way any more."

"You completely overlook the fact that during the past five years the traffic has increased tremendously. The Bamberg-Fulda road is overcrowded. And if the zone borders are lifted one day and you have your traffic streaming in from Thuringen to Nuremberg, what do you think is going to happen then?"

Wenzel seemed unimpressed.

"It'll be a hundred years before that happens," he said. "Why should we worry our heads about that now? As far as I'm concerned, all those Prussians can go and hang themselves on a tree. Let them build their road where they want, but not through Kapfing. I can't blame my farmers for using their pitchforks. And if they get thrown into jail for it, well, we'll see the result at the next election. At least I've registered my objections."

Schneider bit his lip. All the district deputies around the table were grinning.

Counselor Klumpp, Schneider's deputy, spoke up on behalf of the federal government and two other deputies spoke against the highway project. A great row ensued. Schneider tried in vain to intercede. Two hours later they were farther from agreement than when they met.

"You're cutting your own flesh," Schneider warned the rebellious district deputies. "I recommend that you look up the federal highway laws, especially paragraph #19, dealing with expropriation procedure."

"This is worse than under Hitler," Wenzel said heatedly. "Those Prussians in Bonn think they can do with us what they please."

"Go and complain to your Bonn representative," said Schneider. "We have as many Bavarians as Prussians in Bonn. Good day."

He took his briefcase and strode angrily from the conference room.

Leuchtner followed him.

"Are you going to call an extraordinary district meeting?"

Schneider shook his head. "Certainly not. I'll send all district members a memo explaining in detail the federal highway laws. And I'll inform Munich."

They were passing the window and Leuchtner pointed down at the sports car.

"How do like it?"

"I thought it must be yours. Never seen this model before."

"I hope not. Custom made for my son—his birthday's tomorrow. You'll come of course for the celebration?"

"Of course. Are we playing *skat* tonight?"

"Naturally," said Leuchtner. "Why don't I drive you home in the new car and pick you up at your house again tonight?"

"Good idea," Schneider said and excused himself to check with Fräulein von Hessel. She handed him the slip containing the names of callers.

"Nothing important," he said after reading it. "Anything else?"

"Here's a note from Primelmann. Herr Langer has applied for his annual vacation."

Schneider reached for the application form. Ordinarily he never saw applications for leave but Primelmann had instructions to inform Schneider about everything that concerned Klaus Langer.

"What day is the twenty second?"

"A week from now," said Fräulein von Hessel.

"Of course. Send it back to personnel. I don't think it will rain tomorrow," Schneider said erratically and returned to Leuchtner.

As they went down the stairs Leuchtner asked what he intended to do about Wenzel.

"Nothing," said Schneider. "They'll bring him around somehow. What makes me furious is that such a creature could be elected to the district committee at all. A stubborn simpleton, a bull from the barracks, an insult to the district assembly. He's a continuous burden for us. I would have kicked him out long ago but I don't know how to go about it. It's just like the Kapfingers to have elected him as their burgermeister! I'd like to turn over that whole community to my colleague in Furth. But that can't be done either."

"That's one of the disadvantages of our democracy," said Leuchtner. "Under Adolf this Wenzel would never have risen above the rank of a master sergeant."

"If only he still were one. It's time we got another Wehrmacht, they will keep these types off our necks."

It took them less than five minutes to reach Schneider's house. He climbed out of the car with trembling knees.

"I hope your son knows how to drive," he said shakily. "This thing works like a jet plane."

"I think I'll order one for myself," Leuchtner said, beaming. "See you tonight."

Schneider watched him tearing around the next curve. A man in his best years, with a sunburnt, energetic face, bursting with force and vigor, the prototype of the successful entrepreneur. But that's no trick, thought Schneider, not if you had a wealthy manufacturer for a father instead of a little railroad official as Schneider had. Sighing he turned and entered his house.

He was greeted by an unusual silence. Usually his wife's voice met him at the door. She would be standing in the kitchen, busily preparing lunch and singing. Most of the time she was singing hymns and, if one weighed sentiment against talent, sentiment won. It would be an exaggeration to say that Schneider was enraptured by his wife's vocal exercises. Often he turned on the radio full force and fled into the garden until dinner was ready and the lower half of his wife's face engaged in a more useful and less offensive activity.

Today, however, he missed her singing. The uncanny silence in the house ate like acid into his consciousness. He saw clearly what effect the fateful letter had on his family life. He must get his hands on it!

He went into the bedroom, hung up coat and vest, exchanged his shoes for felt slippers and glanced into the mirror. He looked awful. No wonder, with all these worries. He took some Eau de Cologne and rubbed it over his forehead and cheeks, massaging the soft skin over the cheek bones until it began to glow. When he could no longer put it off, he finally went into the kitchen.

The small stool on which his wife sat was nearly buried underneath her enormous behind. She was peeling potatoes. Seeing her red-rimmed eyes, Schneider knew she had been crying and his immediate reaction was anger. He touched her cheek with his lips, mumbled something about the weather being hot, asked if there was any mail and wandered around the kitchen, talking all the time. Now and then he stopped at the stove, lifting the covers off the pots and inhaling with seeming delight their various aromas, and asking what good things his Elsa was cooking there. However neither his excessive cheerfulness nor the deluge of talk thawed her frozen attitude. It was only when he mentioned the invitation to the Leuchtner's birthday party that she showed signs of interest. Schneider saw it with relief. He told her about Leuchtner's new car, adding that one could hardly go there empty handed, a birthday present must be bought and, by the way, where was Katharina?

"She's meeting Klaus at the office," Frau Schneider said reluctantly.

He stopped abruptly.

"What? Today? On a Saturday? At lunch time? Well, if that isn't the last straw. What's happened?"

"Ask her when she comes back." Frau Schneider got up, went to the stove and started fussing over her pots.

Her husband looked at her with mean, narrow eyes.

"That's typical of you," he said. "All I have to do is come home a few minutes later than usual and there's another mess. Why did you let her go?"

Her face turned away, Frau Schneider brushed a strand of hair from her forehead.

"I can't lock her up, can I?"

"Nonsense!" His anger grew. "You can forbid her to go. Some day she'll visit him during office hours just to make sure everybody gets the idea!"

He rushed from the kitchen into the bathroom where he rolled up his sleeves and furiously started scrubbing his hands. Then he brushed his teeth but in the middle of it he ran, with the toothbrush in his hand and smears of toothpaste around his mouth, back to his wife. She was sitting at the table, wiping the tears from her cheeks.

"I know exactly why she wanted to meet him today of all days," he raged. "He asked for leave, for next Saturday. And do you know where he's going? To the Baltic coast again, where they lived together last year, probably slept in the same bed, acting like young honeymooners! If it were up to me I'd have told them a thing or two. But no, you with your: Katharina wouldn't do that sort of thing! You've no idea what sort of things she would do! Until she gets pregnant by him, that's what he's counting on, so that we'll have to say yes. And who's going to pay the bill? But this time they're going to have a surprise, I swear. She won't get out of the house if I have to lock every door. Has she told you anything about going away?"

"Not a word," Frau Schneider sobbed.

"Stop blubbering," he said furiously. "You should keep an eye on your daughter instead."

He turned around and disappeared into the bathroom where he slammed the toothbrush into the sink, yanked the towel off the rack and wiped his paste-smeared mouth. Suppressed sobs came from the kitchen. They sobered him a little. He began to regret his temper. Also it occurred to him that he had not brought flowers

31

today. He couldn't remember a weekend when that had happened and he cursed Leuchtner, blaming the man for his own forgetfulness. His wife's continued sobs increased his bad conscience. After a moment he hastily began to dress and then he tiptoed to the door, closing it quietly behind him.

It wasn't very far to the nearest florist. He chose eight red roses and five yellow carnations, but when he learned the price, he changed the order to ten roses and ten carnations. He would have liked to take the flowers with him, but then he remembered he had no car and he would have felt ridiculous carrying them along the street.

"Send them to my house in ten minutes," he said. "But not a minute earlier."

Back in the street he wondered if he could do something else for her. Of course, the butter cream torte! It was his wife's one real passion—she had no other whims of any sort—and her occasional mild tempers could always be instantly soothed with half a butter cream torte. Whenever she sat behind the empty plate, her eyes wore the same, dreamy expression which Schneider had first seen during their wedding night. And today he had forgotten the torte, too!

If he went to a bakery now the flowers might arrive at the house in the meantime and that would never do. He wanted to present them to her personally. Undecided, Schneider looked up and down the street lying empty and deserted in the midday sun. Finally he turned back into the florist shop and gave instructions not to send the flowers for another twenty minutes.

"But of course, Herr Landrat," said the young salesgirl and smiled. Schneider hurried out again. After a nervous glance at his watch he marched quickly across a wide square in the center of which stood a war memorial, showing a young man sinking to his knees with dying eyes turned up towards the cloudless sky. Sweating a little, Schneider reached a street at the end of which there was a bakery. From far off he saw the shutters were down. A sign informed him the shop was closed during lunch hour. Gnashing his teeth, Schneider looked at his watch again and saw he had only fifteen minutes left to reach home before the flowers arrived. It was unbearably hot. He fought the temptation to forget about the butter cream torte. But the tenacity with which he had pursued and reached his goals all his life won out. A few minutes later he was walking back the way he had come, his eyes staring ahead with a fixed expression, his mind irrevocably made up.

Eight of the remaining fifteen minutes he wasted in reaching another *cafe*. It cost him his last reserves of energy. Breathless, his face streaming with sweat, a sharp pain in his ribs, he clambered up the steps leading to the shop and demanded, before he was quite inside, a butter cream torte. Unfortunately they had run out of butter cream torte, they had only cherry torte left and Schneider was not interested in that. He ran out again and ran back to the florist. If anyone had tried to prevent him now from buying butter cream torte, he would have murdered him.

However, nobody tried to prevent him and the same salesgirl waited on him at the florist. She said she was just about to send off the messenger, said it with some astonishment. Schneider's perspiring face dissolved into a happy smile. He told her that, on the way, he had remembered an errand or two, it was all because of his wife and would she please wait another thirty minutes before sending off the flowers. He related all this loudly and incoherently, but he was a good customer and the girl remained friendly and said:

"Whatever the Herr Landrat desires will be done."

It was three minutes to the street car stop. He wasn't taking any more risks now and if he caught a street car right away he could be in town within ten minutes plus five minutes for the torte plus ten minutes back and another five to get home. But he had to catch a street car right away. One more corner then he could see the tracks. The street stretched like rubber, another twenty yards, another five, and there was the corner . . . no street car in sight. Panting, he wiped the sweat off his face, trudged over to the stop and, dropping on a bench, loosened his tie.

The pain in his ribs had grown sharper, he hardly dared breathe because he feared something inside him might tear. He thought: that comes from sitting in an office all day and driving around in a car all the time instead of walking. He would have to cut down smoking too. If only the street car would come. This was a black day if he ever saw one, black as pitch wherever he reached, pitch-black, although he only meant to please them. All of them. In a state of powerless rage he waited another three and a half minutes before the street car came. As he got on he knew that thirty minutes were not enough and he could have slapped himself for not having allowed forty-five. What good was the expensive bouquet if he couldn't present it to his wife in person? Wasted money, that's what it was! A glance at the watch—another fifteen minutes to go. The damned street car crawled like a horse-drawn hearse. At last he got off. Crossing the street he almost ran into a car then he plowed his way through the moving crowds like an icebreaker and landed, completely unhinged, in a bakery.

He had to wait four minutes before the salesgirl turned to him. And the flowers would be sent in six minutes. All is lost, he thought, it is too late, all is lost. Resignation washed over him. Sad and helpless he watched the salesgirl as she carefully put the butter cream torte on a round piece of cardboard, carefully spread a piece of waxpaper over it, tore a piece of wrapping paper from a roll, wrapped it carefully around the cardboard, the torte and the waxpaper and, finally, tied a string around it all with a dainty bow on top.

"Is this all right?" she asked.

Schneider looked at her. He felt that he had never in his life hated a human being so much as this insignificant person with her routine smile on her insignificant face. She repeated the question and he nodded dumbly. Then suddenly an idea came over him like lightning and he asked if he could make a phone call.

When he left the bakery, five minutes later, he did it with the vow not to show his face around that flower shop for at least half a year. But he had gained another twenty minutes, he had bought a butter cream torte and the flowers wouldn't arrive until he was home. He started to whistle.

# [ CHAPTER FOUR ]

Hergett Buchholz put down his suitcase and looked for his ticket in his coat pockets, trouser pockets and, finally, in his wallet. At last he discovered it, handed it to the railway official at the gate and walked through. The people who had been forced to wait behind him were very angry, but Hergett did not see them. He crossed the soot-blackened hall, checked his suitcase at the baggage counter, and then headed towards the huge doors through which the sunlight streamed in great rivers.

Outside he stopped and squinted across the station square towards the *Frauentorgraben*; he saw the castle, the pointed steeples of the old town, the towers and old walls. As he stood there it suddenly seemed to him that he had stood here once before in his life, on the same spot and on a day as hot and clear as this one and inside him there had been the same feelings—everything seemed unspeakably familiar, as if he had come home again at last. For a while he tried to intensify this feeling and stood motionless, like a pile in the water, while the crowd of people washed up behind him, parted and swept past. A snarling voice asked if he had rented the spot on which he stood from the railway administration. Hergett turned his expressionless eyes towards the speaker and was astonished at the rage he found there.

His eyes followed the man who panted ahead with a load of luggage, hailed a taxi and from there sent back a last, scowling look.

Amazement at so much useless and determined hostility brought Hergett back to the reality of the present. He bought a city map at a kiosk and, after studying it in a quiet corner, set off across the station square, heading towards the northern parts of the city. He did not stop once during the whole, long walk and if anyone had asked him to describe the streets through which he was passing, he would have been unable to do so.

He found the house he was looking for in a new, residential area, on the edge of a little wood. It had enormous picture windows, a deep roof and a spacious flagstone terrace that led down to a well trimmed lawn. It made such an impression on Hergett that, for a moment, he wondered if it was the right address. It was. The number was correct and at the small garden gate he discovered a bell and above it Robert's name. Hergett pushed open the gate and walked along the gravel path to the terrace.

It was noon. The houses all around were silent and the sound of faraway churchbells swung through the silence. They reminded him that this was Sunday. Masses of flowers were blooming in the garden, everything looked very well-kept, very elegant. The grass gave out a fragrant scent and water ran splashing into a stone basin at the foot of the terrace.

He reached the terrace and through an open door looked into a large room with friendly colors, modern, overstuffed furniture and a large writing desk. Behind the desk sat a man with his head bent down. As Hergett came in he looked up. His face showed no surprise. He calmly watched Hergett going to a chair, sitting down and wiping the sweat from his forehead.

"How are you?" he asked.

"You've hardly changed," said Hergett.

"Neither have you," said Robert. He picked up a letter opener, played with it and put it down again.

"Thank you. It's only been seven years."

"Twelve," said Robert.

"That's right, too. I was thinking of Russia. In Russia it was seven and it was in October 1940 that we saw each other the last time. That's right, seven and five makes twelve. And Evelyn?"

"She's fine. She's in the kitchen—do you want to see her?"

"No, thank you. I've come to see you."

"She'll be very sorry," said Robert. "Ever since the war she has talked about nothing but you."

"She used to talk about nothing but Hitler. Why hasn't she married again?"

"She's been waiting for you."

Hergett grinned. "How touching of her! That's the sort of thing we used to sing about in the evenings in Siberia. Who told you I was coming here?"

"Nobody."

"My sister?" Hergett asked coldly.

Robert shrugged. "Sometimes women are more sensible than men. I expected you a week ago."

"There were all those formalities—" said Hergett.

"I understand," Robert got up from his chair. "This is also a formality. Excuse me a moment." He went to a door, opened it and motioned with his head. For a second Hergett saw several faces peering over Robert's shoulders. Then Robert closed the door again and returned to his chair.

"My assistants," he said. "On week days my secretary sits there. How do you like the house?"

"Very original," said Hergett. "Was that your body guard?"

"I always did want a ranch type house." Robert smiled and lit a cigarette. "Have one?"

"No."

"All right. How about a drink?"

"How can you sleep with your conscience?" asked Hergett.

"It's a matter of common sense; if someone tells me that a madman is on his way to kill me, it would be silly to do nothing. This is not Siberia."

"That remark about a madman didn't come from my sister," said Hergett.

"I thought it up myself. She advised you against coming here and when you took off anyway she sent me the letter. You should thank her for it. Siberia is bad, jail is worse. And as far as your father is concerned—"

He leaned across the desk and looked at Hergett intently.

"I had nothing to do with it. And when the other thing happened, Evelyn and I were already on our way west, to Nuremberg. It was on May 9th—"

"That's not the issue," Hergett interrupted him. "Of course you saved your skin in time, I know that. You are much too shrewd to let yourself get caught. No one need ever worry about you. But you mustn't underestimate other people's intelligence. It would be your second mistake."

"The second?" Robert lifted his eyebrows. "And what was the first?"

"Denouncing my father," answered Hergett.

"I've tried to explain to you—"

"Oh, I know. I'm not naive enough to expect you to give me a written confession. No one except you had any reason for doing it."

"Really? And what am I supposed to have gained?"

"Afterwards no one doubted your political reliability. You were afraid your good reputation might be damaged and in order to forestall that you tipped off the Gestapo. In July of forty-one my father was denounced, three days later you left the house and almost on the same day Evelyn started divorce proceedings. A neat plan except for one factor."

"And that's you?"

"I hope so." Hergett motioned towards the door behind which the men were waiting. "You might as well send them home. I had plenty of time to figure out how to go about this. Not the way you think, I assure you. You didn't seriously imagine I intended to kill you? I shouldn't have come all the way from Siberia for that!" He got up and looked around the room. "If only you had half as much character as you have money," he said admiringly, "we could be the best of friends. In Vorkuta I always tried to imagine how someone like you lived today in Germany but my imagination was not vivid enough for anything like this. What's the name again?"

"Whose name?" asked Robert and for the first time Hergett noticed a shade of uneasiness in his voice. He looked at him directly.

"Your newspaper. *Voelkischer Beobachter?* No, that was the other one for which you wrote those hurrah-and-carry-on articles under Hitler. This one here is the new one, isn't it?" He went to the desk and looked at a copy of the newspaper.

"Reads almost the same," he said. "I hear you're publishing another paper, too. For former veterans or something like that. Is that right?"

"I wrote your sister all about it," said Robert.

"Yes," said Hergett. "She told me. You wrote her at

least twice a year and you always inquired about my health. She asked me to give you her apologies for never answering. But first of all, life over there isn't easy and secondly there was nothing of interest to report. The only thing that would have interested you would have been some distressing news about my person. Unfortunately it never came to that. How odd she has so little confidence in me—to write you that letter! I've assured her I merely wanted to have a little talk with you. Can I see her letter?"

"Here it is."

"I've never known her to be so confused," said Hergett after he had read the letter. He looked through the open door at the blue sky and shook his head. "Silly girl."

He walked out on the terrace and along the gravel path back to the gate. He had already opened it when some-one called his name. Looking back he saw Evelyn running towards him. While she was running, she tore off her apron and the long hair blew around her head and into her face. She stopped before him, crushing the apron against her breast with both hands, and said:

"Hello, Hergett."

"Hello, Evelyn." His voice sounded strange in his own ears as if it were coming from far away. He had prepared his words a million times for just this moment. But now he said nothing. Her face was close to him, very pale, a little different but not less attractive, he thought. On the contrary, she was goodlooking, damned goodlooking, as a matter of fact. Suddenly he felt that his coat was too tight under the arms and his trousers, too, they were too tight and too short. But they hadn't found anything bigger for him at the reception camp and anyhow he had liked it this way. It was hot in the garden. Radio music came from one of the houses, Mozart or Haydn, once he would have known immediately but in seven years one forgets Mozart and Haydn and many other things he had thought he could never forget.

Evelyn had moved between him and the gate. She stood close to him, very slender, very pretty with her milk-white face, her large moonstone-blue eyes. It seemed incredible that she should be only four years younger than he. He was forty-one. When he first met her she had been twenty-three, no longer a young girl, but now he remembered that she had fooled him even then, as she had fooled him ever after.

He took a step away from her and now he could think soberly again as he had intended to, without sentiment and false emotions. He looked at her hand lying on the gate and he tried to remember how her body had felt at night, when she had come to him. He decided to have a woman at the first opportunity.

"What are you waiting for?" he asked.

Leaning with her back against the gate she looked up at him and said in a low voice: "Perhaps for the same thing."

"I don't believe so," said Hergett. "I'm waiting for you to go away from that door. And you?"

"Well, I—" she hesitated and her voice became nearly inaudible. "I thought you would at least say 'hello' to me."

"But I've said 'hello'."

"Only because I ran after you. If I hadn't run after you, you would have left without a word. You didn't even want to see me."

"I didn't."

"I understand," she said, her voice tightening. "Perhaps in your place I'd feel the same way. I don't want to keep you. I only wanted to tell you how glad I am you're back."

"Are you indeed! I suppose your brother is overjoyed, too?"

"Robert is overworked," she said hastily. "He has so many worries. And then that letter from your sister. Your sister wrote she was afraid you would try to kill him. Has Robert shown you the letter?"

"Yes."

"And it isn't true, I mean, what your sister wrote?"

"He's still alive, isn't he?" said Hergett.

Evelyn bit her lip.

"Listen," she said hastily, looking into his eyes. "He didn't denounce your father, I swear he didn't. Believe me, please. Why should he have done so?"

"I'll find out eventually," said Hergett. "I'm going to stay in town until I do. I've already told him he needn't keep a palace guard around. Nowadays there are enough ways to call people like that to account without having to go to jail for it. You can tell him that."

"You want to ruin him."

"I not only want to, I'm going to. If he's sent you out here to find that out, then you can get away from the door now."

She stared at the ground. After a while she said: "You just don't know the situation around here. Robert is a respected and powerful man. He has connections everywhere. Everyone in town who has a name or position is a personal friend of his. What do you think you can do against him?"

"Leave that to me. Not every public prosecutor is his personal friend. I've been told that since 1945 we have a democracy around here. That's not just a rumor, is it?"

Evelyn lifted her shoulders. Her face was no longer pale but slightly flushed and her voice became contemptuous.

"That depends on how you look at it. We used to have one party and now we have a dozen, that's the only difference. Today things still depend on your having a good friend in the government and belonging to the right party. Wait until you've been here for a while. Things aren't quite the way you think. If you came to Nuremberg just to make things difficult for Robert, you've wasted your time. He won't give you the opportunity, I know him better than you. There is no court in the world that will bother with unfounded suspicions. And how can you do anything except through the law? You can't stand up in the market place and shout: In the Third Reich the publisher of the *NDN* denounced my father! Robert would immediately sue you for slander and then what would you do? You don't have money for a lawyer, you don't know anybody here in town except us. It's a senseless, hopeless plan and I don't want to see you getting yourself into new difficulties after all you've been through. For whom, Hergett, for what? You'll have to put an end sometime to all that hatred and bitterness. There are other and better things in this world, for you, too. For all of us. Am I not right?"

She had talked quickly, in a low voice, and her uplifted face was very close to his. He looked at her mouth and

41

into her eyes. They were moist and tender. And he remembered how she had looked at him fourteen years ago, for the first time.

Hergett had just completed his two years military service and was staying at home, preparing for his entrance exam to Forestry school.

One sunny day, at midday, she appeared, followed by a long row of little uniformed girls, black-and-white chicks, who crowded around the fresh water well in front of the house and then scattered all over the meadow, scaring the forest with their screams.

They were out on a hike, Evelyn explained to him, this was her little Hitler Youth girls troop. He noticed that her face was a trace more beautiful than just pretty. Blond hair brushed back a little too severely but it suited that face, with the large, boldly cut eyes and the generous mouth that had a permanent smile hovering in the corners. She looked handsome in her white blouse and short skirt which, as she sat down in the grass beside him, revealed long, well-shaped, tanned legs.

She pleased him from the first. As they sat in the sun and talked, he learned that she came from nearby Arnstadt where she lived with her brother—her parents were dead—and that she was a province champion in the three hundred meter hurdles. In two weeks she would give up her leadership in the Hitler Youth to become a gymnastics teacher in the G. & S. organization. Being dependent on her brother? No, that didn't bother her. Anyhow, now that she had passed her gymnastic teacher's exam, she would make some money for herself.

He congratulated her. He wished he, too, had his exam behind him.

What exam?

Half an hour later she knew almost everything about him except a few things he did not intend to tell her, such as the women in his past—vulgar, sensuous Eugenie, who finally disgusted him so that he escaped from her into the arms of another one who wanted only to be a comrade and a friend. He asked this one to marry him but while he was in the service she ran off with another comrade who had plenty of money to pay for her camaraderie.

The girl beside him now, a slim-hipped, self-confident creature, warm interest in her smoky blue eyes and insatiably curious about him, was so much of a presence that Hergett forgot the past. Instead he thought of the future and that he wanted to make love to her.

On the following Sunday he did.

That Sunday she wore, instead of a uniform, a light blue dress, tight fitting and cut so low that Hergett could admire her tanned breasts as they walked to the secluded spot in the woods he had suggested for a picnic.

As soon as they were settled she pulled up her dress and said she felt very warm and how silly of her not to have brought her bathing suit. At home she always took sunbaths on her little balcony, without a bathing suit or anything.

She said this very casually and while they were chatting idly about other things, the image her remark had lit in Hergett's mind burned itself slowly along the fuse of his imagination. Eventually he interrupted her gossip about Arnstadt society and asked her in a rather gruff tone why she didn't simply take off the silly dress. She certainly needn't worry that he would learn something new from looking at her.

At once she grew reserved and told him not to play the strong man. She had very definite ideas about strong men.

Perhaps it was time she met a real one in person, he retorted. He certainly could see nothing wrong in making yourself comfortable in a situation like this.

Was that why he was still wearing his heavy coat?

Her sarcasm drove the blood into his head. He unbuttoned his coat, pulled the shirt over his head and threw both into the thick grass behind him with gestures meant to express superiority and contempt and they might have expressed it, too, had they been less hasty and excited.

She smiled but she examined him with the eyes of a veterinary appraising the value of a young horse. Where did he get these terrifying muscles, she asked. Could she feel them just once? It interested her, for professional reasons.

When her cool fingers slid along his arm, feeling the muscles that he, being a man, was flexing conceitedly, perspiration broke out on his forehead. She laughed admiringly. She had never seen anyone built like that.

Well, he said, as he told her before, she had probably never seen a real man.

She laughed again. Your conceit is even bigger than your muscles, she said. Muscles alone don't make a man.

Well, he said, what does?

Her eyes seemed to grow liquid, they fastened on his mouth. Slowly he bent over her and felt the cool fingers digging into his arms. When he let her go, she laughed. Now she was feeling even hotter, she said, brushing a strand of hair away. She was not in the least embarrassed.

Then why in heaven's name didn't she take off her dress.

Only if he turned around.

Of course. He stared at the young pines without seeing anything. He tried to think of something else but couldn't. He disliked himself for what was going to happen—but why? She was making it too easy for him to be pleased, that was it. She was making it too easy for him.

He turned around.

She lay stretched out beside him, a long-legged challenge with some diaphanous little garment covering the eye-catching triangle in the center. Her dress, now rolled into a narrow strip, was carelessly draped over her.

"That is too much," said Hergett.

"What is?"

"That!" His calloused hands tenderly brushed the dress aside. She smiled. She stiffened only when he reached lower.

"Don't!"

He took his time. These fine fabrics were all alike, resilient and so taut that they cut off the blood in his fingertips. Still, it felt like dipping them into a pot of honey. She was smooth-skinned and submissive—slow sliding motions concentrating in an oasis of foam-soft moss.

She had stopped fighting him. But she lay there like a piece of wood, her face averted, offering herself like a prostitute. He went into a sudden manly rage and lost all control over himself.

When he got up, a while later, he was very pale. With bitterness he looked at her expressionless face, at her eyes traveling over him with another long, appraising look. He remembered with scorn that those phlegmatic, outward turned legs belonged to a province champion in three hundred meter hurdle racing.

Rudely he asked her how old she was.

She lifted her indolent eyes, asking why it mattered.

Because, he said, she was acting like a fifty-year-old.

She had twenty-seven more to go for that.

Twenty-three then. Was she perhaps frigid?

No, she said, it was probably just that he wasn't her type.

They would see about that, he said furiously. He would make her scream yet.

She put on a show of astonishment. So one should scream while making love, should one?

Hergett stared at her a moment, then he turned and went off into the trees. When he came back she was gone, so were her clothes. A little later she emerged from the wood, fully dressed.

He had not been careful, she accused him in a sharp, hostile tone. She hadn't passed her gymnastic exam in order to have a baby.

One needn't always expect the worst, Hergett said, feeling guilty and morose. Gloomily he watched while she unpacked the sandwiches and began to eat. When she pushed one towards him he threw it back in disgust. He certainly didn't feel like eating!

She told him not to make such a fuss. If she should indeed be caught with a baby it would be worse for her than for him, wouldn't it? And he needn't worry, she would never marry a man only for that reason.

That's what she was saying now, he said morosely. But how would she feel in another three months?

Three months wouldn't change her, she said. But this was one time when the experience had not been worth the risk!

Each word was an arrow of humiliation well aimed at his masculine pride. He was now in a state where the thought of having to marry her depressed him less than the way in which she was wounding his vanity. When she added that, after all, it depended on the doctor whether or not one must have a child, he felt guilty for having suspected her. He began to degrade himself by trying to make love to her again, asking for caresses which she refused him and trying to pull up her dress. She pushed him away. She'd had enough from that one time!

He dressed in silence. Silently he escorted her back to the station. Then he asked her when he would see her again.

She told him she didn't know. She had a great many things to do in the near future.

Go to the devil, he thought, and left her.

Two months later they were married.


Evelyn did not produce a child. Instead she produced her brother Robert, brought him right into the marriage. She had insisted on that. He needed someone to take care of him, she had kept house for him ever since their parents died in an automobile accident.

Why didn't he get married himself? asked Hergett.

He was too young for that.

Young at thirty-two?

Well, she said, perhaps he was too clever to marry.

Robert was indeed clever. After his first conversation with him, Hergett's father said he didn't want to have anything to do with him. That man, he said indignantly, turns the words around in one's mouth and on top of it all, he's an arch Nazi.

Evelyn, too, disclosed some alarming traits. After four weeks of marriage Hergett admitted to himself that marrying her had been a dreadful mistake. Oh, she was no longer cold and passive in bed. On some days he had the marks of her teeth on his body. But beyond that their marital life consisted of occasional, incidental encounters. She was forever traveling to some meeting or other, with or without her brother, and when she came back she was tired out and cross.

Then she started giving gymnastic lessons.

On sunny days ten to fifteen young girls, fresh as dew and wearing the briefest shorts, flopped around solemn-faced in the little meadow behind the house, hurling imaginary clubs through the air, distorting their unripe hips and finally subsiding into the soft grass at the wood's edge where, to Hergett's complete amazement, they bared their budding breasts and proceeded to do breathing exercises.

When he protested to Evelyn she looked at him with

46

disgust at his backwardness. The lungs had to be aired through, she said. If the sight of the children disturbed him, why didn't he look away.

Hergett said that, for children, they seemed rather well-rounded and predicted that, if his father came upon them, there would be a fearful row.

And there was. After dousing the heated little half-naked creatures with a bucket of ice cold well-water, Hergett's father marched to Evelyn and told her that he would not stand for such indecencies on his grounds. As a result the breathing exercises were scheduled during hours when Hergett's father was away on business.

He was away on business very often now. It pained Hergett to see his father escape from the house where the dirty laundry bulged from the drawers, the furniture began to look as if coated with cement and the kitchen was in a state resembling the aftermath of a banquet. Evelyn did not care. She had neither time nor desire to care about the house. She would sleep late in the mornings, give gymnastic lessons in the afternoon and in the evening go with her brother to meetings.

As time went by, Hergett gave up. The arguments, the strains and disappointments made him closemouthed. His sister tried to cheer him, but she failed. It was his own fault, he said, it served him right.

His father never said a word of reproach. Only once he put his hand on Hergett's shoulder and said, after all, Evelyn was still so young, how could the young people have sense if the older ones hadn't. They wouldn't become sane until this Hitler nonsense was over; it set the people's heads spinning and diverted their eyes from the real values in life. But it would come to an end, he assured Hergett, it would end soon, as surely as day followed night.

He had a way of stating his beliefs that was like writing them on the wall in red letters. Hergett knew that for a man of his father's character the thesis of the individual being nothing and the nation everything was an outrage. Again and again he had to defend his father against Evelyn's and Robert's attacks. Those two believed every word they read in the newspapers.

It was an evening like many others. Hergett and Evelyn

had had a bitter quarrel. He left her sitting in the restaurant where they had eaten and walked home. When he came near the door he heard Robert's voice.

"Nice evening tonight."

He was leaning in the doorway, a cigarette dangling from his lips.

"Where's Evelyn?"

Hergett shrugged.

"Had a fight?"

"Mind your own troubles," said Hergett and started opening the door. Robert quickly grabbed his arm.

"Just a moment." He flung away his cigarette. "This concerns Evelyn. I'm her brother."

"Go on." Hergett stared at Robert through the darkness.

"To make it brief—I don't like the way you treat her."

"Who is treating whom?"

"You've nothing to blame her for. If things go wrong between you and her that is because you, you and your father, are trying to swim against the stream. Evelyn is an idealist, she loves her work—"

"I know," Hergett cut him off. "If she could just ration off a little idealism for us, things might look different around here. I've married a woman, not an exercise machine, and I married her expecting her to do what every decent woman does, namely to care for her man and her house instead of chasing after the butterflies you put into her head. In fact, if you persist in influencing her I'd be insane to stand by and watch this any longer."

"You mean I'm not wanted here?"

"You never were."

"Oh, of course, that precludes further discussions."

His very way of speaking infuriated Hergett. He had the tone of a school teacher and the air of an actor. Although he could not see Robert in the dark, he knew his facial expression by heart. Evelyn said Robert's face was extremely masculine and would fit on any Olympic metal. Hergett suggested that, in order to fit on one, he might comb the waves out of his dark blond hair and shave off the finger-long Lincoln whiskers. He despised the arrogant smile Robert wore on his face like a permanent decoration.

True, he dressed well. He greatly valued a good ward-

48

robe that gave him the air of a man of means. Only when he put on his SA uniform did he suddenly look like just another average citizen, which was probably the reason why he wore it only with great reluctance, despite his otherwise unquenchable party enthusiasm.

He worked as an editorial writer for several newspapers and Hergett estimated his monthly income as fairly high. What he did with all the money, why he never attempted to establish his own home, all this was a mystery to Hergett. He had long wanted to bring out these questions and he detained Robert and asked them now. They were soon talking heatedly and the argument reached its peak when Hergett said that one day he would have to move out anyhow since they would need his room for the children.

"Children? What children? You don't mean your children?" Puffing with anger Robert informed Hergett that if this was worrying him he could stop because, in case he didn't know, Evelyn was unable to have children.

"What are you saying?" Hergett thought he felt the ground move beneath his feet. "What are you saying?"

At the same moment he heard Evelyn's voice behind him.

"It's true."

Hergett turned around.

"What is true?"

She did not answer and glared past him at Robert.

"Well," Robert gave a shrug. "He would have found out some day anyhow, wouldn't he?"

"But not from you," said Evelyn.

"It just slipped out somehow," said Robert, pushing the door open and disappearing into the house.

Hergett looked through the darkness at the white shadow of Evelyn's face.

"So you can't have children," he said after a while. He was amazed how calm his voice sounded.

"No, I can't."

"How long have you known?"

"For two years. I had grippe and then an oophoritis if you know what that is."

"I thought you called that gonorrhea."

"I'd call that a vile remark," she said in a faint voice. He remembered how she had accused him that first

Sunday of not being careful. He could not think through his pain and disappointment.

Loudly she said:

"Hergett, I—"

"Don't put on a performance," he said coldly, looking up at the window behind which his father slept. "You'll wake him up."

"All right," she said whispering. "That I can't have children is only half as important as his sleep. Why don't you go right up and tell him that I'm sterile so he won't have to keep staring at my belly every day. If he's so crazy about grandchildren why doesn't he place an order with your sister? Why hasn't she produced any—is she sterile, too?"

Hergett quickly raised his fist but stopped and went off to his room. He turned on the light. Evelyn followed him immediately. She sat down on her bed and he could see the hatred in her eyes.

"Tomorrow I'll start a divorce," she said.

Hergett was silent. He undressed slowly. He didn't speak until he lay beside her in the dark.

"Have you tried that trick before?"

"No. There were three men. When I told them I couldn't have children they no longer wanted to marry me."

"That's understandable. But to me, of all people, you had to lie."

"Yes." He felt her looking at him through the dark. "You of all people. Because I was tired of being jilted like that. Try to live for years without parents and with a brother who hates to part with a penny."

"Why? He makes enough money?"

"Yes, but when my parents were killed they left a debt. It was a loan that had to be paid back. Robert has to pay it because he had put up the collateral."

"Oh, so that's the way it is." That explained a great deal but at the same time it sharpened Hergett's bitterness. The shock that Evelyn could not have children had numbed him. For the moment the thought of how she had lied to him and misled him was incomparably more painful.

"Well," he whispered, glad that she could not see his face in the dark, "then I'm not surprised at anything.

What luck for you both to have found a yokel like me after all. That's all you wanted, you and your brother. And if I hadn't come to you on my own, if I hadn't, as you so often put it, run after you, you would have told me some day that you were pregnant."

"No, that's not true," she exclaimed. "I told you right away that I did not want a man who would marry me only for that reason."

"Of course," Hergett smiled bitterly. "Of course you said that. Because you knew you'd never be in the embarrassing position of having to prove your broad-minded attitude. I understand. You only had to find someone who gave the impression that he would do the decent thing. Later you could simply pretend you'd been mistaken. Many women have been mistaken that way. That's all there's to it."

"Of course," she said, imitating his tone. "That's all there is to it. And if there's more to it, no one will believe it afterwards." Her voice was muffled with fury. She raised herself on her elbows and leaned over to watch him.

"When I first met you," she said, "I told myself you were different from the others who want a woman only for their bed. Whether you believe it or not, I liked you terribly from the first moment on. Before you came to see me in Arnstadt I wrote you at least twenty letters and tore them up again. I could hardly bear living then. I went to the station three times and then turned and went home again because I told myself I mustn't influence you and that you should find out for yourself whether you wanted to marry me or not. And then when you came to see me, at last, I hadn't the courage to tell you that I couldn't have any children. For the first time it did make a difference whether the man I told it to would run away afterwards. And I've carried it around with me all the time and I was scared someday you'd ask me because I noticed how you and your father were waiting for me to get pregnant. And that's why I didn't tell you because after eight weeks I didn't want to be chased into the street again, like a whore—a whore . . ."

She crushed her face into the pillows and began to weep uncontrollably.

The violence of her outburst stunned Hergett and

for a moment he felt pity for her. But a second later his
bitter disappointment washed away the pity. He was like
his father now, telling himself that the purpose of a
man's life were his children and now that he knew
Evelyn could not give him a child, his thoughts thrust
ahead into an empty void. It was Evelyn's tragedy, perhaps, but he saw it as a sort of malicious disease which
was in the process of destroying his life. He saw it as an
undeserved blow of fate, it made him very bitter. The
longer he thought of it, and the more clearly he re-
called how she had first told him that she might be pregnant, the more indifferent to her weeping he became.
He turned away from her and lay on his side, looking
with open eyes into the dark room. It was already light
when he fell asleep.

They did not mention it again, not the divorce and not
the children. Robert, too, acted as if nothing had happened. The only difference was that Hergett now slept in
the living room. Since his conversations with Evelyn had
been monosyllabic for a long time, his father didn't
notice that they now hardly spoke to each other at all.
Their behavior towards each other was like that of a
ship's crew, forced, in spite of irreconcilable differences,
to stay together until they reached port.

Only once was there another scene.

Hergett came home from forestry school late one Saturday night and was met at the door by Robert.

"I must talk to you at once." Robert sounded so excited that Hergett was alarmed. He put down his briefcase and looked at Robert apprehensively.

"It's about your father," Robert said. "He's taken Jews
into the house. If he wants to cut off his own head let
him at least have some consideration for others. As for
me, I shall leave at once if they don't disappear right
away."

Hergett picked up his briefcase and went to the door.
Looking back over his shoulder, he asked:

"What are you waiting for?"

His father met him in the hall, took him into the living room. Two elderly people were sitting at the table.
They were acquaintances of his father from Ilmenau.

"They're after them," he told Hergett. "I think it's
best for them to stay here until the air is clean."

"They can have my bed," said Hergett. "I've been sleeping on the sofa anyhow."

Between them, that settled the matter. When Hergett went upstairs a little later he was met by Evelyn. Her face was white with excitement. When he tried to pass her she held on to him with both hands.

"You aren't going to keep the Jews here, are you?"

"Do they bother you?"

"It's impossible. Imagine what will happen if the police find out."

"Nothing would happen to you, I'm sure," said Hergett. He went into his room and began to dismantle the bed. He and his father carried it down to the living room. Pale with anger Evelyn was looking on. When they carried up the sofa and put it alongside Evelyn's bed, she kicked it with her foot.

"You're not even consulting me when it comes to my own bedroom," she said, looking at Hergett's father. "You treat any stranger better than me."

"We shall all have to get along," he said with an astonished glance at Hergett. "Haven't you told her?"

"He?" Evelyn laughed angrily. "He never bothers to tell me anything."

"Perhaps you don't give him much occasion to," said her father-in-law and went downstairs to join his guests. Evelyn wheeled around to face Hergett.

"I'm leaving tomorrow."

"Good!" said Hergett.

They were still living in the house, Evelyn and her brother, when Hergett received his draft notice half a year later. He handed it to his father who put on his glasses and read it slowly.

"That's how it started in 1914," he said then. "So I imagine you'll be there when they march into Poland."

"You think it will start with Poland?"

"It started with Austria. Now comes Poland and then all the rest. And no one can prevent it now."

"Perhaps a miracle will happen," said Hergett. His father looked up at him. He had the same eyes as Hergett and this was the first time that Hergett ever saw them grow moist.

Hergett stirred. Thinking of the past he had forgotten where he was. It seemed to him that he had been away a long time, that he had walked an endless road. Now he saw the new house again, the trees and the blue sky above. Evelyn stood before him, unchanged and very close, as if she had stood close to him all this time, during the past twelve years and always.

It was unbearably hot. The sweat burnt in his eyes and blurred his sight. In a blur he saw her face, her sleeveless white blouse, her slender arms, the long tanned legs under the short skirt. How would it feel to touch that now, he thought, after twelve years. Thin panties underneath in this weather, thin panties or perhaps nothing. Nothing at all, he thought stupidly, nothing at all underneath.

His lips felt chapped, his mouth dried out, the coat strained across his shoulders, the shirt stuck to his sweaty skin and certainly there was a bath in the house, with blue or green tiles, cool and soothing, an ice-cold shower over the hot body, a room with curtains drawn, a wide, soft bed and Evelyn wearing nothing underneath. His thoughts were wheeling, he caught himself confusing the past with the present, they began to seem like one, and then he took Evelyn's hand from the gate and forced her aside. The gate had a spring, as he stepped out into the road it slammed shut behind him. He turned and looked at Evelyn. She was on the other side, the fence was between them. Now he knew again precisely where he was and what they had been talking about.

He said: "Robert tells me you've waited for me."

She nodded. Her face was completely white.

"Since forty-five?"

She nodded again.

"Not before?"

"Yes, also before then."

"Since when?"

"That is what I wanted to tell you." She put both hands on the fence and looked at him. Her lips were trembling.

"It was not my idea," she said. "I didn't want the divorce. You weren't here when they came to get your father. They interrogated us, threatened us, Robert got frightened and I—"

"Yes?"

"I am a woman, Hergett. My nerves gave out. Can't you understand that? We'd been sitting on thorns for three years, you only went through one year of it. And when Robert told me I'd have to get a divorce immediately, I fought against it, but he had already prepared everything and when it finally came to it—what could I, a woman, have done? I was scared. I wanted to write you but I was scared about that, too. They might have read the letter. Robert said they were censoring your mail. And later, when I did write you at the camp, you never answered. I know—I know I haven't acted right and I don't want to make excuses, don't think that. I only wanted to tell you how it was and that I didn't like to do it. I just had to tell you, whether you believe me or not."

"There's an excellent chance that I don't." Hergett grinned and walked away.

Back in the center of town he slowed down and began to look at the display windows, studying the prices and stopping for minutes at a time at the intersections to watch the heavy traffic. After a while he began to distinguish the various car models. Among them were some new makes that had not existed before the war. Above all, he was terrifically impressed by the American cars. One of them was being driven by a girl. Fascinated, Hergett stared at her. It was his first encounter with an American woman and when she looked towards him he smiled. Long afterwards, when he went into a restaurant and sat down at a table, he was still filled with a deep satisfaction because she had smiled back at him.

The menu gave him some difficulties; it seemed to be an expensive restaurant and there were many items he could not pronounce. But the liver dumplings he finally chose were excellent. The fat waitress blinked in astonishment when he ordered a second helping. He drank five glasses of beer, ordered a double portion of ice cream afterwards and felt refreshed. He told himself that in the future he would have to be more careful with his money. But today it didn't matter. He had celebrated his reunion with life itself, it seemed to him.

Outside he asked a policeman for the nearest police

station. When he got there the officer shook his head doubtfully.

"It'll be hard to find them without any address at all," he said. He took a fat ledger from a shelf and began to leaf through it. Then he looked up.

"You said the name is Schneider?"

"Yes," said Hergett, his heart beating rather loudly.

# [ CHAPTER FIVE ]

After the official part of the Leuchtner's birthday reception, Schneider became involved in a political discussion with the host's brother, the government director. Franz Leuchtner joined them after a while. When he heard what they were discussing, he put on a grave face and said:

"It's going to explode again, over there. They've been sitting and talking in Panmunjom for a year now; I don't think there's a chance they'll work it out."

"You think they'll never agree?" asked Schneider.

Franz Leuchtner looked at his brother. The government director was a small, insignificant looking man, bald-headed with round, blue eyes behind shiny glasses, and a thin, pointed nose. When he talked he always put his right elbow in his left hand and rested his chin on the extended index finger. He was one of the few people Schneider respected. There was no family resemblance whatsover between him and his brother Franz. A comparison might be more flattering to Franz Leuchtner, but Schneider knew, from listening to both, that the director could out-think and out-talk his good-looking, successful brother in any discussion. Franz Leuchtner might flush with annoyance but he never dared to contradict his brother. Whenever he offered his own opinion, as he was doing now, he always looked at his brother first as if begging for his approval.

"I'm afraid," he said, "they won't agree. And you know

why? The Chinese as well as the Americans have lost prestige in this war. They'll try anything to make up for the loss. They must, to save face. Don't you agree?" he asked his brother.

The director nodded. "Yes, except I'm thinking a little further. Korea was merely the opening move."

He smiled, elbow in hand, the chin balanced on the tip of the index finger, and looked with blue, washed-out eyes at the ceiling.

Schneider looked also at the ceiling and asked:

"How is it all going to end?"

"Don't you know? They'll knock each other to pieces, with little Korean wars at the start and with atom bombs at the finish." He chuckled. "For the first time in their history the Americans have come up against an opponent they can't bluff, neither ideologically nor materially speaking. Korea has shown that the Americans can't win a war without absolute material superiority. After this experience the Russians will see to it that by the time the third world war comes there will be material equality, believe me."

"A bad failure for Washington," Schneider said, smiling. "It's a rather satisfactory thought."

"I'm not really a vindictive man," said the government director. "But I admit, with me Korea went down like a fine glass of brandy. I've waited for that day since '45. Of course, the Americans are still trying to make something out of the Atlantic Pact. They know that without old, much-maligned Europe they haven't a chance against the Russians. But what can they do? France and Italy undermined by Communists, unreliable as allies and choking on their own problems; England is rapidly declining economically, tired of war and prone to compromise. The others: little lice in the fur of Russia when it comes down to it. Who remains? We, the former so-called Nazis and War Criminals! The Defeated, the Beaten ones, in three years at the latest we'll have our Wehrmacht back."

"And then?"

" 'From the land of France to the Bohemian woods we grow our vines'—you know this? No? Fallersleben, who else."

"Well," said Schneider, "but our Western allies—"

57

"You aren't thinking, are you?" Director Leuchtner shook his head condescendingly. "When Rusia and America start throwing atom bombs at each other, what do we need allies for? What we're contracting for now is a marriage of convenience. It's the only way for us to get a new Wehrmacht quickly. You don't seriously think the English and the French feel any friendlier towards us now than they did seven years ago? Nonsense! We're much too well-off again. 'France and England, whose very coasts pale at each other's fortune—' If I have it right— never heard that either?"

"I'm afraid not," said Schneider, glancing helplessly at Franz Leuchtner.

"Why don't you start getting yourself an education," said the director. "And why don't you get rid of the habit of asking superfluous questions. Why wory today what our future allies will do when we retrieve our own property when the day comes. 'The one will ask: What happens afterwards? The other: Is it right? And therein lies the difference between slave and Knight—' This one is Storm, not Shakespeare. Haven't we anything to drink around here?" he asked his brother.

"Whatever you want."

"That's my favorite answer to any question."

While Franz Leuchtner went to order drinks, Schneider excused himself and stepped out on the terrace for a breath of fresh air. The government director was a strenuous presence.

Leuchtner's house, a snow-white villa, lay outside of Nuremberg on top of a hill; it could be reached only by car. The garden was enormous but Leuchtner was already toying with the idea of buying several acres of woodland adjoining the ground behind his house. He said it would charm him to look out the window at his own trees. The wood belonged to a rural community. After they rejected his offer twice, Leuchtner offered them a sum that took the local mayor's breath away. In a few days the decision would be made. Schneider was convinced that Leuchtner, once he had his trees, would never find time to look at them.

Over in the pavilion he saw his wife and Katharina with the other guests. The pavilion was large and airy, it had a beautiful view of the city that lay in the distance below. There was a fountain and enough wrought-iron chairs and benches scattered around to seat everybody. Two maids in white aprons were refilling glasses with cold drinks, the conversation sounded lively. Most of them were younger people, friends of Kurt Leuchtner. Schneider noticed with satisfaction that Kurt was paying a great deal of attention to Katharina.

But Katharina looked openly bored, tearing a paper napkin into little pieces and obviously only half listening to young Leuchtner. Eventually he turned away and began to flirt with another girl, this one a very young thing with an exceptionally pretty face and pointed breasts. She sat gracefully curled up in her chair, her shiny hair was pulled back into a ponytail and she looked meltingly at young Leuchtner. There are too many young people here, Schneider thought. He was afraid that the sight of so much over-ripe innocence might give Kurt Leuchtner ideas similar to Schneider's own.

When he went back inside the house Leuchtner and his brother were in their chairs again, but now there were glasses before them and they were talking a great deal louder.

". . . what we need is the right sort of party," Franz Leuchtner was saying.

"We all know that. Once the right man is found, the right party will form naturally."

"Perhaps." Schneider took a cigar from a box Franz Leuchtner was offering him. "I've never liked the Americans," he said erratically. "I hope we'll see the day when they go back where they came from."

"Oh no," said the government director. "They'd be back from there in a day. I'd rather see them disappear into Siberia."

"You like them as little as I do," said Schneider.

" 'Like them as little' is putting it politely," said the director. "It is well-nigh miraculous how the Americans within a short seven years have succeeded in losing everyone's sympathy. Not just in Germany, also in Italy and Japan and everywhere they went as liberators. Ask a Frenchman what he thinks of the Americans today! And why is this so? I think the answer is simple: lack of tact. Their shirt-sleeve realism is as obnoxious to the gallant

French as it is to the romantic Germans. And they're snobs—they used to act like snobs and if it weren't politically unwise to do so today, they'd still act like snobs. Their attitude towards us hasn't changed since forty-five. The people can sense that. The simple man in the street knows very well that the Americans don't consider him worthy of respect, that they'd as soon spit in his face as shake his hand. The rift grows wider every day, all this alienation, all this resentment will one day lead to an explosion. *Prost!*" He emptied his glass in one draught.

When Irene Leuchtner appeared and suggested that they join the other guests, he agreed at once.

Schneider stopped at Katharina's chair and exchanged a few words with young Leuchtner.

"I've asked Katharina to come along on a trip to break in the new car," the young man told him. "To Garmisch, perhaps, for the weekend."

"The weekend," Schneider repeated happily. "Why don't you start Saturday morning very early before the day gets hot."

Kurt Leuchtner shrugged.

"That's what I suggested. Your daughter doesn't want to go. She has no time. Ever since I've known her I've been getting one refusal after another."

He sounded annoyed. Schneider turned to Katharina.

"What do you mean you have no time?"

"Next weekend I have an engagement," she said.

"With whom?"

Katharina did not answer. Her eyes told Schneider not to go too far. Schneider remembered Klaus' application for a vacation that was to begin the coming weekend. He turned to Kurt Leuchtner.

"My daughter will think it over. She'll phone you."

"I'd be very happy," said Leuchtner. Katharina rose and went past her father, coldly and without haste. A moment later Kurt Leuchtner caught up with her.

"I'll take you home."

They walked to the car without speaking and Katharina slid silently into her seat.

"You dislike me," said Kurt Leuchtner. The corners of his mouth were turned down. "Why?"

"Don't be foolish," said Katharina in a tired voice. "How often must I remind you that I am engaged?"

He looked hurt, like a child seeing his toy taken away, and Katharina had to smile. She didn't want to make him unhappy—after all, this was his birthday.

"You've been engaged for a very long time," he said.

"Yes, and?"

He shrugged impatiently. "You're fooling yourself," he said. "You're the only girl that has ever impressed me. My parents are crazy about you. What do you dislike in me?"

Katharina looked out the window. They had been driving fast. The first suburban houses came into view,

"It isn't your fault," she said. "Probably we're all fooling ourselves. Please let me off here at the street car stop."

"But I—"

"Please!"

"As you wish." He stopped the car and looked at her. "You know how your parents feel about your engagement."

"That's unimportant."

"You shouldn't say that," he said. "Parents do mean well. I don't want to intrude on your private affairs, but you're not happy."

"Are you?"

"Yes."

"You see, then you don't need anything else," said Katharina and opened the door. "Thank you very much."

She crossed the street quickly and got on a waiting street car.

Just as she reached the door, she saw the man. He sat on a little garden bench, asleep, with his face buried in his arms resting on the garden table. He wore a cheap suit, a pair of sturdy shoes and his trousers were too short. You could see a piece of sunburnt leg.

Katharina didn't scare easily. She went to him and tapped him on the shoulder. His head shot up at once.

"What are you doing here?" she asked.

He squinted, drew his hand across his eyes, and rose clumsily. He was so tall that Katharina had to twist back her head to see his face. She liked him. Her voice was less severe when she repeated her question. He had been sitting in the bright sun, his face was damp with sweat. Looking at her with very serious eyes, he said:

"You are Katharina Schneider?"

"Yes."

"I've come to tell you about your brother," said the man. Something inside Katharina tore apart. Her legs turned to water and she leaned against the table.

"He's dead."

"You knew it?"

"We've assumed it," said Katharina. Numbly she looked at him. She remembered that he was tired and had perhaps been waiting a long time. She pushed herself away from the table.

"Shall we go inside?"

"I don't want to be a nuisance," said the man. It was a mere phrase but he said it very sincerely. Katharina unlocked the door and led him into the living room where it was cool and dark. She pulled up the blinds and looked out the window until she was certain she wouldn't cry. Then she turned and asked him to sit down.

"Where did you meet my brother?"

"In Czechoslovakia, on the last day of the war. We were going to make our way through the Americans. At night we tried to swim across the river Moldau. An American guard saw us and he shot at us and he hit your brother. He disappeared."

"Drowned?"

"The bullet may have killed him. It was dark."

"Yes, of course, excuse me." She was crying after all. Her cheeks grew wet, she wiped them with the back of her hand and apologized again.

"My parents kept on hoping," she said. "I didn't. Still, it's so sudden—why didn't you come to us sooner?"

"I was in Russian prison camp. They didn't release us until a few weeks ago and I went home before I came here. My home is in Ilmenau if you know where that is."

"I don't."

"Well, it's in Thuringia, in the Russian zone. I didn't get here until today."

"My parents will be awfully grateful to you," said Katharina her voice quavering.

"I doubt that—in view of what I have to tell them."

"Oh, but yes," said Katharina. "The uncertainty was almost worse. And it's very good of you to take the long trip here to tell us—"

"I had other things to settle here," he said.

"I don't understand, though," said Katharina. "You said you and Hans were shot at by Americans. But you were in Russian prison."

"The Americans delivered me over to the Russians. The whole camp."

"Oh, how dreadful, Herr—"

"Buchholz, Hergett Buchholz."

Hergett put out his cigarette and got up. "I must go. It's time for me to find a place to sleep."

"For heaven's sake," Katharina jumped up. "You can't leave before my parents arrive. They wouldn't understand my letting you go away. Please, stay. You must be hungry, too. And don't worry about a place to sleep —my father will see to that."

Hergett looked at her undecidedly. He would have much preferred not to have to talk to her parents.

"Please," she said. "Do stay, as a special favor to me." She looked at him beseechingly. Reluctantly Hergett sank back into his chair.

"And now I'll get you something to eat." She was out of the room before he could protest. He looked around uncomfortably. Across from him, on the wall hung a family portrait—a large photograph obviously taken towards the end of the war. Hergett recognized the boy in the uniform—it was Hans. The girl beside him must be Katharina, wearing a nurse's uniform. Hergett found that she was much prettier now. The parents flanked the children, both were very tall, stately, the woman in a dark, high-necked dress, the man in a dark suit. He wore a waistcoat and had his right thumb hooked in a watch chain.

Katharina came back. She had changed into another dress and must have cried again, he saw it in her eyes.

"If it's all right with you, let's have some sandwiches out on the porch. Would you rather have tea or beer?"

"In Vorkuta," said Hergett, "we got only tea."

She didn't understand. "What is Vorkuta?"

"A town in Siberia."

"Oh," she said. "Then you must have beer."

While he ate they spoke little. Katharina was astonished to see how clumsily he handled knife and fork. He noticed it himself, put them down and started to eat the sandwich with his hands.

"Out of practice," he said. He was not a bit embarrassed and Katharina liked that. She noticed that his hair was grey, he had a large, well-cut nose and strangely light eyes. His hands were strong with slim fingers showing the marks of hard work. She was pleased with his appetite and when he had emptied one bottle of beer she got another from the refrigerator.

"There are more," she said.

"Thanks. This should be enough. My stomach will have to get used to it all." He wiped his mouth and asked: "May I smoke."

"Don't be silly," she said. "Of course."

He looked out into the wood. "Beautiful place to live, here."

"Yes," said Katharina. "How did you find us?"

"I went to the police and they looked up the register. I didn't know your father's first name, but I knew yours and Hans'. They told me your father was the Landrat. How long has he been Landrat?"

"A number of years. They appointed him shortly after the war."

"Incredible!" said Hergett.

She looked at him sharply. "What's so incredible about that?"

Hergett could have bitten off his tongue.

"Incredible, I mean, I would never have thought that we would have Landraete again," he said, shifting in his chair. "In Russia we have only heard the worst about West Germany."

It sounded pretty convincing to him but somehow he felt that she was still suspicious. She quickly changed the conversation to other matters, asking him about his relatives—the married sister in Ilmenau—the fate of his father.

When she touched that subject, his voice showed that it was painful for him. She would have liked to say a consoling word but could not think of one. The more she looked at him, the more she liked him.

"Will you go back to Ilmenau?"

"No. The Russians are in Thuringia and I've lived with them a little too long."

"Oh, I can understand that," Katharina said warmly. "You must have lived through some horrible experiences."

Hergett smiled. It was the first time he had smiled and his face seemed ten years younger. She looked at him fascinated.

"It depends," he said. "There were some who found Vorkuta quite bearable. I should imagine the Jews under Hitler had worse experiences than a few years' hard work in a quarry. The homesickness was really the worst part. I had the bad luck of being with SS soldiers. They were the most disciplined bunch I ever saw. They went around saluting each other with 'Heil Hitler!' even after two days of no food. There was an officer among them, his name was Fred. He said when he got home he was going to hack the hands off a Jew. The Jew in question was an American officer who had slapped his face during the interrogation. This SS man was completely obsessed by the whole thing. In order not to forget, he cut his own finger and drew the officer's name on the wall with his blood. During the first half year in Vorkuta he ordered his subordinates to stand at attention before the wall each evening and made them sing anti-Semitic songs. Those who refused were beaten up. But as time went by more and more of them got fed up with the nonsense; one day our man had to sing all by himself. He wept, I think with anger. By that time the discipline had crumbled. Too many were dying. We all had dysentery, the Russian woman doctor was helpless. Whoever survived that period survived the rest of the years."

"The SS officer too?" asked Katharina.

"No. He couldn't resign himself to the fact that no one listened to him any longer. He was making a lot of trouble. Then one of his best friends told the Russian commandant that Fred was having an affair with the woman doctor. That did it. They came at night to get him and no one ever saw him again."

65

"But that's—" Katharina fell silent. She was more shocked by the way he talked than by the story itself. This indifferent tone! He must be completely brutalized. She wished she could see his expression but it had become dark in the past half hour. Yet, however dreadful his story was, Katharina was spellbound. She was half convinced she would have been spellbound by his reciting the Lord's Prayer.

Suddenly she heard her parents. The door was pushed open, Katharina saw her father's silhouette in the open door, then the light switched on.

Hergett got up. Even without the photograph on the wall he would have been prepared. Hans had described his father perfectly. The bald, pearshaped head, the tiny mouth between heavy, pink jowls, the short neck and the enormous belly spanning the distance between head and legs like a bridge. Katharina got up, too. Hergett was puzzled at her frosty tone when she told her father:

"This is Herr Buchholz. He's bringing news of Hans."

Before Schneider could say anything, there was a scream. The Landrat was being pushed aside and a woman came rushing into the room.

"He's alive," she screamed. "He's alive."

Hergett looked at Katharina who stood stiff and motionless. Her father didn't move either. At this moment his face looked ill, grey and sagging. The room was completely silent, only the woman's loud breath could be heard. She stood directly in front of Hergett, staring at him with wide open eyes. When he said nothing, she dropped to her knees, clawing at his coat and panting:

"He isn't dead. Don't say he's dead. *Jesus, Maria and Joseph,* don't say it!"

Hergett grabbed her wrists. She was heavy and it took all his strength to haul her back to her feet again. He kept her hands in his.

"I've just come from Russian prison," he said. "In our camp we had a boy about the age of Hans. He was the youngest of five. Two had been killed in Russia, one in France and the fourth over Crete. The father died in an air raid in Munich. And this last one, the one at my camp, died of dysentery. Yesterday I went to see his mother. She didn't even cry. She said she was glad that someone was left to pray for her husband and the boys.

You still have a family for whom you can do a lot more than just pray." He let go of her arm and looked at Katharina again.

"I think I'd better come back tomorrow."

Katharina nodded and went to her mother.

"You have to go to bed, Mama."

Silently Frau Schneider let herself be led to the door. Katharina looked over her shoulder.

"You promise to come back tomorrow?"

"Yes," said Hergett. He turned to Schneider. Schneider had remained standing on the same spot and Hergett noticed that the eyes with which he studied him were cold.

"Who are you?" he asked Hergett.

Hergett was in no mood for further conversation.

"I've introduced myself to your daughter," he said. "Now I want to get out of here."

"You stay here," Schneider declared. "You come into my house, you tell stories that might cost my wife's life in her condition, and you act like a policeman. Plenty of people with missing relatives have been taken in by swindlers. I ask you to prove to me that you are not a swindler. That's all I want."

"That's all, is it?"

"I beg your pardon?"

Hergett pulled himself together. He was furious and it showed in his voice when he asked:

"How can I possibly prove it?"

"Very simple. You were with Hans, you say."

"Why else would I be here."

"What do you know about him?"

"Quite a lot. Almost as much as I know about you," said Hergett.

"About me?"

"Yes. I know that you were a party member, that you beat up a Jew, that you denounced a superior. Your son didn't have a very high opinion of you."

Schneider's face turned ash grey. He felt for a chair and let himself drop into it. Hergett had seen men weeping before, but never like the Landrat. His face remained completely unchanged, only the mouth looked even smaller, like a child's. He made no sound either, he merely wept with the tears wetting his cheeks until he looked as if he had run bare-headed through a stormy

67

rainy night. His arms hung down on either side of the chair as if they didn't belong to him. After a while, Hergett grew bored with the performance. He had no place to stay yet and he was craving for a woman as one craves for a sharp drink to wash something down. He was suddenly obsessed with the idea. He would dig his hands into her breasts and her legs and would think of nothing. For the first time in seven years he would think nothing, just feel and be felt. In Vorkuta the men had come to him at night and he had kicked them away with his feet. He even kept his shoes on for the purpose and he had plugged his ears. Still, he could hear everything that went on in the barracks. A hundred and twenty men, most of them not much over twenty, and seven years without a woman, two thousand and five hundred twenty-five nights. It was a mess.

"I don't know why you're getting so upset," he barked at Schneider. "You must have been prepared for something like this."

Schneider lifted his wet face.

"Tell me how he died."

"He drowned. We were trying to cross the Moldau at night and a bullet from an American guard got him."

"An American," said Schneider. Abruptly he stopped crying, his mouth curled down. "You say an American?"

"Why, would you have preferred a Russian?"

Schneider looked at him distractedly. He didn't seem to have heard him and repeated in a low voice: "So—an American!"

Suddenly he changed into another man. He apologized for his behavior, asked politely that Hergett stay a little longer or, better yet, that the two of them go to a quiet little inn where they could talk over a glass of wine. And as to a place to stay—Hergett needn't worry. He would, of course, stay in their house overnight and had he left his luggage at the station? Dumbfounded Hergett nodded.

"We'll fetch that first," said Schneider. "Sit down a moment. I just want to look after my wife." He was gone before Hergett could object.

He sat down again in a wide, comfortable chair, lit one of the Russian cigarettes he had bought in Vorkuta with his carefully saved rubles, and sighed. Why not stay here for a night—it would save money. Life in West Germany was expensive, he'd noticed that already. He had to find work as quickly as possible, perhaps the Landrat could help him there? He must have connections and influence. It was rather foolish of him not to have thought of this before, Hergett thought, getting annoyed with himself. He might have handled the man a little more gently, not hitting him with the fist in the face right away. Evelyn was right, after all—without connections and money there was little he could do about Robert.

He had no idea what a *Landrat's* position was in public life. Perhaps he wasn't as impressive as the title indicated. But for the moment even the friendship of a well-informed street sweeper was of more value to him than all the prejudices he had brought along to Nuremberg.

He had to put his life in order before tackling the problems that had brought him to this town. He had to find a solid place in life, he must stop drifting around as if he were merely on leave, yet he couldn't get rid of the feeling that he was. Although he had prepared his mind for his return to freedom, he kept feeling somehow embarrassed, as if meeting a woman one remembered only as a young girl. It had been a terrible shock to see Evelyn. He should have waited a few days, settling in the new environment, and he should have prepared himself better for the meeting. He had really acted like a man who, on a steaming hot day and without bothering to cool off, jumps straight into a lake of ice cold water. Schneider's daughter had really finished him. For a man who had slept without a woman for seven years, the sight of her was too much.

The door opened.

"Forgive me for keeping you waiting so long," said Schneider. "My wife is feeling better. She'll prepare the guest room for you. It's upstairs, on the second floor. But now let's get your luggage."

Hergett followed him out into the street where the Landrat had parked his car.

"It's rather small," Schneider said. "As soon as it's got 100,000 kilometers on it I'll buy a bigger one."

Hergett watched him start the motor. He had pushed

the seat all the way back, but still his belly pressed against the steering wheel.

"For long trips I have a chauffeur," said Schneider. "Nowadays with all the traffic it's no longer fun to drive."

"This isn't your own car?" asked Hergett.

"No. It's my official car. You've seen our house—for the money that cost I could have bought fifteen cars. But everything in its time. These prices nowadays! The Korean war forced them up."

"But that's been over for a long while," said Hergett.

"The war yes, not the aftermath. So, there's the station. Let's look for a parking space."

They found one and Hergett got his suitcase.

"Put it in the back," said Schneider. "Now we'll go to a nice restaurant."

The restaurant was in a narrow, dark street and looked very unpretentious from the outside. Schneider seemed to be well-known there, the owner met them at the door and led them to a cozy corner table.

"I always sit here," said Schneider. "Once a week we play *skat* here. It's a nice, quiet place. What would you like to eat?"

"I don't really care," said Hergett.

"In that case I recommend liver with fried potatoes and salad," said Schneider. "Waiter!"

It was an enormous portion and Hergett ate heartily. The Landrat ordered a bottle of wine and filled the glasses to the brim.

"Let's drink to your return home," he said. "I'd always hoped to celebrate this day with my son."

"Well, that's the way things are," said Hergett. He was afraid the Landrat would break into tears again and added hastily: "You can be proud of him."

"He was my son!" said Schneider. "He was still very young and he didn't understand everything. Nevertheless, we were close. Was the food good?"

"Excellent," said Hergett.

"I'm pleased," said Schneider and offered him a cigar. After filling the glasses again, he leaned back in his chair and said:

"Please tell me how he died. And don't leave anything out, I beg you. You needn't be considerate."

"It's not much of a story," said Hergett. Grey-faced, Schneider listened to him, only rarely throwing in a question and when Hergett finished he still sat behind his glass with hanging head. The cigar had gone out. Noticing it, he stubbed it into the ash tray.

"You've done a great deal for my son," he said. "Can I be of help to you in any way?"

Hergett shrugged his shoulders. "You've invited me for dinner, tonight I shall sleep at your house. I'm sorry this happened to your son. If he'd been taken prisoner, like me, I wonder if he would have survived. He was too weak for work in a quarry."

"Yes," said Schneider. "Did many die?"

"Most of them."

"I've heard that," Schneider said, grinding his teeth. "Here in Nuremberg they had the war crimes trials. Completely illegal, judicially speaking, violating the clause of the *ex post facto* law. And they blocked the westward retreat of our eastern armies, leaving them to the Russians. And now they shot my son. . . ."

"I've thought about all these things," said Hergett. "We have only ourselves to blame. We could hardly expect them to treat us with velvet gloves. Without Hitler it would never have come to any of this."

"Without Hitler we would have gone down the river even sooner. Most people have forgotten what this place was like before thirty-three. Then everybody was happy that someone was at last doing away with bankrupt administration and bankrupt politics."

"He did away with a lot more," said Hergett.

Schneider stared into his glass.

"You're bitter, that's only natural. Probably they fed you daily doses of fat lies in your camp. I'm certainly the last to defend Hitler. But as long as you mention his mistakes and errors, you must also not forget his positive sides. And he had them, even if those gutter-bred idiots don't want to know it today. Look at me—am I a war criminal? Because I joined the party in 1937 and slapped a Jew? I'll tell you something—"

He interrupted himself and called for another bottle of wine.

His face had grown very red. He bent across the table towards Hergett:

"When Hitler came to power we were at the bottom, economically and politically. Emergency measures, strikes, bloody street battles between the various parties, demonstrations, unemployment, chaos. The rest of the world could do what they wanted with us. Hitler cleared away all that. He gave us a new economy, a new political system, even a new foreign policy. He gave us back our national self-respect. Suddenly we could be proud again, proud of our history, our culture. Who could blame a decent German for lifting his head higher. I lifted my head high, I tell you, and I am still proud—"

He belched and poured more wine.

He seemed to have become quite unhinged. Hergett began to wonder how he could carry him home. He had stopped contradicting him because it was useless. Grimly he remembered that he had wanted to spend this evening with a woman.

Schneider talked and talked.

"What have the Americans to offer in exchange?" he asked. "Nothing, absolutely nothing. And for that they've smashed our cities to pieces, for that they've blasted our churches, our cultural monuments, the pillars of Western civilization, for that they've turned our beautiful Nuremberg into a rubble heap and on top of all that they've shot my son. If I had known," his voice sank to a whisper. "If I had known that all this was going to happen, I wouldn't merely have slapped that Jew, I'd have beaten him to death. They've broken us, not only from the outside, they broke us from within. They turned the rats loose on us: rats, bought creatures, creatures without a country of their own! It was not only our right, it was our duty as Germans to chase them out of their holes wherever we could find them and you may think about me today as you please, what I did then was not a denunciation, it was an act of patriotism. Denunciations came later, when the Americans were there, when Germans sold Germans to the occupation forces for a carton of cigarettes. And now I'm going to show you something else."

He rose, swaying, shouted for the check and, after paying it, gripped Hergett by the arm. "Come along," he said. "Just come along."

As he headed for the exit his steps were amazingly steady and Hergett wondered whether he had been putting on an act.

Outside, after some fumbling, Schneider managed to unlock the car and slid behind the wheel, his breath coming loud and fast. He drove very slowly on the extreme right of the street, carefully describing a wide curve around each car they passed.

Hergett was looking around curiously. They were passing through an area unknown to him. Both sides of the street were lined by great mounds of rubble, with here and there a ruin sticking out. From some of those ruins shone a single light or two. A few wooden shacks, makeshift shops and living quarters, stood blackly against the dark sky.

"Once that was Karolinenstrasse," said Schneider. "It still has that name, but the name is about all that's left of it. We had 28 air raids, almost 7,000 dead, 40 per cent of all living quarters destroyed. Still, they didn't crush us—not us, they didn't!"

He laughed grimly.

"Today there are again 400,000 inhabitants in Nuremberg and just as many have never forgotten the Americans and their air raids. And they never will forget them!" he cried. Hergett noticed that he was indeed drunk.

They rode on and on. Hergett had the impression that the Landrat was driving around in circles. But then a wide road opened before them, the houses disappeared and flat fields spread on both sides. A few hundred yards further Schneider pointed to the right:

"Congress Hall, they never finished it, just like the March Field; didn't finish that either. And now—look!"

He turned off the big road into another, narrower one that led in a gentle curve around what seemed to be a large lake.

"The Dozen Lake!" said Schneider. "We'll be there soon now. Soon we'll be there, soon, soon!"

"Where on earth do you want to go?" Hergett inquired crossly. It was the first time he had opened his mouth since they left the restaurant. Schneider chuckled.

"One more moment. Do you see, over there, that huge

thing? That's the reviewing stand. From there Hitler gave his big speeches. I'll show you the place where he used to stand. Let's get out."

He stopped the car and, puffing hard, climbed out. Hergett had no choice but to get out too. He watched as the Landrat, with uncertain steps, crossed a broad, tarred road and headed towards a structure of huge dimensions. It resembled an amphitheater, with broad, terraced steps and a gigantic colonnade at the top. From the center of the colonnade a square stone platform jutted out and this was the place the Landrat was heading for. He climbed up the steps and stopped among the gigantic columns: "Come on," he called impatiently. "Come on, will you?"

He waited until Hergett reached his side and then led him out to the center of the rostrum. He put both hands on the stone balustrade and stood motionless, looking across the vast, horse-shoe shaped arena of the stadium.

"Here is where he used to stand," he whispered. "Here, at this place. Like this, he put his hands here, and there where my feet are, his feet used to be. And down there, as far as you can see, they stood, a sea of faces; flags waving, bands playing, they were marching by in rows of thirty, great cheers, happy people, the entire German people–in an ecstasy of happiness. And then his voice: German men and women, German people. . . ." Schneider's voice rose. "German people," he repeated, "German people." He was screaming.

It was shortly before one o'clock and Hergett wondered whether he should shut him up by force or simply go away. He tried to grab his shoulder, told him to stop screaming. Schneider did not stop. He seemed to have forgotten Hergett's presence. He pushed his fists into the air, his body began to shake convulsively, his voice rising to an unintelligible wail. He sounded as if someone were driving a pointed stake into his belly. Then, suddenly, his voice became clear and he called on the dead soldiers to rise from their graves and to liberate the fatherland from its oppressors.

"Oh, poor, unhappy fatherland," he shrieked. "Oh, brothers and sisters. . . ." There was foam at his mouth.

Hergett left him standing there and retreated to the colonnade. From there he turned and looked back at the massive figure silhouetted against the clear sky. Schneider did not stop, he gesticulated with his arms, raged, besought his invisible audience not to give up hope, not to forget their duty towards The Nation.

"We all," he screamed, "we all have sacrificed our most beloved. You gave your fathers and brothers, I gave my son, my only son, on the field of honor, for our imperishable country, our invincible fatherland, our proud German tradition."

His voice echoed across the great, black, empty round of the stadium, it broke against the towering columns and scattered away into the silent space of the star-filled night. Finally it weakened to an uncontrolled sobbing, a painful, childish kind of weeping. His body seemed to grow smaller, he sank to his knees, still clutching the balustrade with his hands. Hergett watched him until the hands slipped down too, then turned and went slowly down the steps. On the bottom step he sat down and looked out into the night. Before the black backdrop of Congress Hall, the lights of the city reflected in the surface of Dozen Lake. The air smelled of woods and fresh grass and Hergett put his face down into his hands. He himself felt like crying.

[ CHAPTER SIX ]

At 8:15 a.m. Primelmann ordered his secretary to bring him a cup of coffee from the canteen and retired behind his desk to study the morning paper.

It contained nothing of particular interest. The opposition accused the government of not doing enough for reunification with East Germany, the government accused the opposition of aiding the Communist cause. In America a new series of atomic tests had begun and the Russians had vetoed something or other. A flood catastrophe in India had cost the lives of an undefined number of people. Primelmann yawned and turned to the local pages. Of the twelve million cubic meters of rubble the war had left behind in Nuremberg, about ten million had been cleared away. The reconstruction work at the castle was making progress, the same was true in the case of the Holy Ghost Hospital. The enormous increase in population threatened to endanger the gas supply and the Germanic Museum had acquired, from a private owner, and for a great deal of money, a bronze sickle the age of which was estimated at three thousand years. A Nuremberg citizen had won 40,000 marks in the football lottery and another one had turned on gas jets during the night and killed himself, his wife and his children. Economic difficulties were suggested as a possible cause. Primelmann shook his head. He turned to the classified ads. Under Capital Investment fifteen loans from two hundred to twenty thousand marks were being sought. Dividends offered ranged from 15 to 30 per cent. Another ad promised five hundred marks in cash to the person who would help find a two-room apartment. Primelmann read this ad twice, then he called the housing office. He had a good friend there who owed his position to Primelmann and with whom he had successfully cooperated before. After the telephone conversation Primelmann made a note in his little book. If all worked out he would make another two hundred and fifty. He could use it. He looked at the clock. It was a quarter of nine.

His secretary, Frau Hansen, came in and asked if he had finished his coffee. She was married to a traveling salesman in gentleman's underwear and had a grown daughter who was just as sharp nosed and flat chested as her mother. Primelmann would have loved to exchange her for a younger, prettier assistant but Frau Hansen was indispensable. She knew everything that happened in the office and she provided him with the information about the private life of all employees, which came in especially handy in the case of those female employees who deserved his closer attention. He was forty years old, unmarried and, except for the beginning of a paunch, a good looking man. If one overlooked the human frailties which his position could not help but bring out, one could not accuse him of any particularly bad qualities. In the office he was disliked only by those female employees he ignored, or those who didn't care for his attentions. The male employees on the other hand could not stand him because he used perfume, and was vain, and their boss. His position of absolute power inclined him to treat all underlings with contempt. Frau Hansen was the only exception. She was firmly protected against any sudden change of jobs by a great deal of knowledge, including that of occasional after-office parties thrown by Primelmann for lady employees in the janitor's office.

At ten o'clock Frau Hansen came in again and announced the visitor whom Primelmann had expected at eight. Without looking up he snapped:

"Tell him to wait in the hall until I send for him."

Ten minutes later Frau Hansen knocked at the door again and said the gentleman could not wait any longer. Primelmann looked stunned.

"Is he out of his mind?"

"I think so," said Frau Hansen. "Shall I bring him in?"

"You might as well."

He received the young man very coldly and without offering him a chair asked him right off what he had learned.

"I have graduated from gymnasium," answered Ernst Wagner. Primelmann looked at his shabby suit, the unkempt hair that grew over his ears. He leaned heavily back in his chair.

"How old are you?"

"Twenty-six."

"Can you type?"

"No."

"That isn't much, then. The Herr Landrat told me that you had just come from French prison."

"That's right," Ernst Wagner smiled. This annoyed Primelmann and he said reprovingly:

"You are here looking for employment, aren't you? The Herr Landrat asked me to do something for you. Did you know him before?"

"He's a friend of my father's."

"Oh, really?" Primelmann looked up. "Your father sent you to him?"

"Yes."

"Where's your father? Also with the government?"

"In a sense, yes."

"What does that mean?" Primelmann asked irritably. "Is he a civil servant or an employee or what?"

Ernst Wagner's grin broadened.

"He's been living at government expense for the past five years," he said. "In jail. Hasn't the Landrat told you?"

Primelmann looked at him with half closed eyes.

"Is that so? Why? What's he done?"

"Nothing at all," Ernst Wagner burst out. Suddenly his face looked very ugly. His hand sliced the air as if trying to break something. "Stop pretending you never heard of him. Wherever I go no one wants to remember him. And before forty-five they all crawled up his ass."

"Just a moment," Primelmann leaned forward. "You're —you're not—" the thought overwhelmed him. "You're not the son of the former Gauleiter Wagner?" he said breathlessly.

"I am!" He sounded proud. Primelmann fell back into his chair, his giggles growing into shouts of laughter.

"The son of—" He gulped, started to cough and squinted with tears in his eyes at young Wagner's hardening face.

"What's so funny about that?" Wagner asked furiously.

"Nothing." Primelmann pulled himself together. He saw no reason to explain his mirth. He could have told young Wagner that he had known his father well, that he had liked and admired him because of his direct, energetic way of doing things and that, at the time, he had felt the Gauleiter's jail sentence as a personal insult directed against him, Primelmann. Under different circumstances he would have enjoyed talking to the Gauleiter's son. But now Wagner was an employee and Primelmann knew what he owed himself and his position.

What intrigued him far more, however, was that the Landrat had been a friend of the former Gauleiter. Schneider, the alleged Nazi-hater, always acting as if he had swallowed democracy with his mother's milk, he of all people! Perhaps Schneider's past was not as unblemished as he himself made it out to be. Perhaps he kept himself so aloof from others to prevent them from learning things about him which might prove harmful to a man in his position. Primelmann had a happy feeling that interesting revelations were in store and he decided to keep his eyes peeled. It would be important to put young Wagner in a strategically placed position. Primelmann had an excellent idea.

He called Frau Hansen in. "You can start working right away, can't you?" he asked Ernst Wagner and went on, without waiting for an answer: "Your day begins at eight a.m. sharp. Lunch hour from twelve to one, work ends at five p.m. Frau Hansen will show you your temporary working place. We may have to assign you somewhere else later on." He turned to Frau Hansen. "Take his data and then take him to Herr Langer."

"To Herr Langer?" said Frau Hansen, sounding perplexed.

Primelmann nodded. "To Herr Langer and Fräulein Huber," he said pointedly. "Fräulein Huber can break him in."

Frau Hansen understood.

"Come along," she told Ernst Wagner.

"In a moment." Ernst Wagner looked at Primelmann. "I want to know how much I'm going to earn here."

"Three hundred and eighty marks."

"Are you joking?"

"What d'you expect? Five hundred or a thousand?"

"At least five hundred," said Ernst Wagner. "Every chimney sweep gets as much nowadays."

"Then why don't you apply for a job as chimney sweep," said Primelmann. "In your job other people start with—"

"I don't care about other people," said Ernst Wagner. "The Landrat promised me a well-paid position."

Primelmann flushed with anger.

"I suggest you complain to him personally when he comes. If you don't like the pay—well, there are plenty of others who do."

He got up abruptly and left the room. Ernst Wagner turned to Frau Hansen.

"I'm going to catch that one yet," he said. "That one and a few others."

"I beg your pardon," said Frau Hansen indignantly.

"You know what you can do to me, don't you?" said Ernst Wagner grinning. "Where's the men's room?"

Frau Hansen stared at him aghast. Then she turned and ran down the hall after Primelmann.

The men's room was at the end of the corridor. Ernst Wagner kicked the door open with his foot. When he came out he inquired of a passing girl where he could find Herr Langer and Fräulein Huber. The girl sent him upstairs to Room 125. Ernst Wagner walked into the room without knocking. There was no one inside. Two large desks stood in the center, a big file shelf covered the wall on the right and in the left corner stood an umbrella stand. The desks were piled high with files, a greasy sandwich lay among them, next to an ashtray filled to the brim with cigarette butts. A woman's raincoat hung on a hook at the door. It smelt of cold smoke, cheese and cheap perfume. Ernst Wagner went to the window. It opened on a large, square courtyard that looked like a prison yard and was completely empty. He felt a sudden draft. Someone had come into the room. He turned around and there was a man with a forehead looking like a piece of raw meat. Probably a grenade splinter or MG volley, Wagner thought knowingly. He slouched back against the window frame and crossed his feet.

"Hello."

"Learned your manners from the Americans, have you?" The man with the smashed forehead sat down at the desk. "You've made a splendid entrance," he said. He lifted the phone and asked for Primelmann.

"Langer speaking," he said. "The man's here in my office. I'll send him—" he broke off, looked at Ernst Wagner and nodded. "All right.

"He changed his mind," he told Wagner. "When I was down there a moment ago he asked me to send you down. Now he wants to wait until the Landrat comes in. What did you do to Frau Hansen?"

"Is she his girl friend?"

"Don't underestimate the man's taste. Besides, Frau Hansen is happily married."

"Is that why she works in this rotten place?"

"Perhaps the happiness is too much for her. What did you say to her?"

"Why do you care?"

"No one has ever succeeded in making her cry. You can cross everyone else in this office, but not Hansen. That was a little stupid if I may say so."

"You may. I told her she knew what she could do to me."

"You told Hansen?"

"Yes."

"My God," said Klaus Langer and grinned. "My God!"

Ernst Wagner grinned too.

"Good, what?"

"Good for Hansen but not for you. Wasn't your father formerly a mason?"

Ernst Wagner's grin faded.

"What do you know about my father?"

"Before 1933," Klaus said pensively, "I'm sure he worked as a mason. In 1935 he became district leader and in 1939 Gauleiter. I call that a career!"

"I can see you were one of those damned officers," Ernst Wagner said disgustedly.

Klaus laughed. "I can't wash it off with lye, can I? Even you can tell. What'll you tell the Landrat when he calls you down?"

"I know what to tell him."

"Blackmail again?"

Ernst Wagner's eyes grew mean. "You know everything, don't you?"

"I'm disabled," said Klaus. "I suffer from over-excitability. If I kill someone they don't put me in jail, they put me in an asylum. Ask the others around here about me. They're always happy to find someone who hasn't heard my story yet."

"You like to brag, too."

"No more than anyone else. I was in an asylum once. It wasn't very pretty and I'm not particularly eager to go back there. However, if you succeed in putting a new Landrat in here, I'll lost my job. With my broken skull I shan't find another one. In that case, I don't care whether I sit in the street or in an asylum. Therefore, with the first foolish remark you make you've had it. And now you can help me sorting out the paper mess there. Sit down on that chair. Just take these files and—"

"Oh, hang yourself," said Ernst Wagner.

Klaus put the file slowly back on his desk.

"Better not say that again."

"I'll say it as often as I please," said Wagner. "Don't

you think I know this is all a pre-arranged act? That fat hog of a Landrat is trying to scare me. But he's come to the wrong address. If he doesn't toe the line, I'll go to the nearest police station and throw the letter on their desk."

"They'd keep you right there," Klaus said coldly. "For blackmail you get jail. You should have gone there before you went to the Landrat; now it's too late. Besides it might mean a new trial for your father. The man he removed at the Landrat's suggestion is dead. He was killed in Russia. That's your father's fault. If the Landrat has difficulties because of this story, so has your father—your father even more so. It would probably mean the end of any parole or pardon."

"You know everything, don't you?" Ernst Wagner said again, but he no longer sounded as confident, and Klaus pushed his advantage.

"I know a great deal about you, too. As the son of a former Gauleiter you are under police supervision." He had just invented that and was satisfied to see that Ernst Wagner fell for it. His uncertainty was now obvious. He left the window and came to the desk, dropping into Fräulein Huber's chair.

"You're all huddling under the same blanket," Wagner said bitterly. "But I'll get you yet. Nowadays one is no longer powerless against people like you."

"No, since the Gauleiters are locked away, one isn't powerless any more. Since then one can open one's mouth again. Unfortunately there are no longer any concentration camps for locking away annoying people. Everything has its advantages and disadvantages."

"I know the disadvantages. I've experienced enough of them. So has my mother. They've treated us like dogs. If it had been up to them we would have died."

"You didn't use to worry about people dying."

"You mean the damned Jews? I've met a few, in France. I'll meet them again some day, but under different circumstances. One of them was on the tribunal that sentenced me to seven years hard labor for war crimes. And all that just because I was on vacation in France when the invasion started."

"Really? A soldier on vacation?"

"Nonsense, I was 18 years old and my father wouldn't

let me join the army. I was with my mother in Cap Breton. You know the place?"

"I've heard of it."

"We had a house there. When the invasion started we were going to start home but my father called and said it wouldn't be necessary. The Americans and English would be forced out of their bridgehead in a day or so. Then suddenly everyone started running. No trains, all streets stopped up. During the day we could make a few kilometers. Then there was an air raid and my mother and I lost each other. She was lucky, an officer took her in his car. But me—the French caught me and I was turned over first to the Americans and then back to the French. When they heard I was the son of a Gauleiter they put me up for trial and gave me seven years. For that the devil can——them crosswise." He made an obscene gesture.

"You talk the way you look. I don't suppose you owned the house in Cap Breton, did you?"

"You don't like the way I talk?" asked Ernst Wagner.

Klaus looked across the two desks into his sullen face.

"Just tone it down around here, will you? And you've nothing to complain about. For a house at Cap Breton you pay at least five hundred marks rent. I'm sure you didn't work those off in seven years in prison."

"The French did exactly the same thing here."

"After us. We started it. You didn't do much thinking in those seven years, that's certain."

"You live and eat the way I had to live and eat for seven years and you unlearn to think! I've done plenty of thinking since I've been back here, though. The same flour bags sitting on top who always sat there. The frustrated would-be-Gauleiters and other sneaks, who always want to be in the middle of the stream but always jump out just in time. Now they act as if they'd never heard of Hitler. The Landrat is one of those fat swine. You know him well, it seems."

"Part of my job. You're really incredible, all of you. First you get rid of everyone who doesn't want to play along and now you want to get rid of everyone who did. One day someone is going to smash your turnip, my friend, if it isn't me, it'll be someone else. Now shut your mouth. Those files contain applications by people who had no stolen houses in Cap Breton during the war, but who lost their legal property through air raids. Whenever you get the applications, you ask the people to come in and check their data to see if it's correct. In the meantime you evaluate the applications—I'll explain that to you. And here is the file case, each community has its own shelf. Remember the names so you won't get them mixed up. Some of them sound very similar."

"Work fit for a moron," said Ernst Wagner. "May I at least smoke?" He was behaving himself now. Klaus pushed a pile of files over to him.

"You may even sing if you want to as long as it isn't the Horst Wessel song."

"You sang that yourself," said Ernst Wagner. He took the files and carried them to the shelves. "Is this in alphabetical order?"

"Yes, from upper left to lower right."

"Isn't there a ladder?"

"Take a chair."

"What a pigpen," said Wagner. "I won't grow old here."

"I hope not," said Langer, looking towards the door. Fräulein Huber had come in. When she saw Wagner she stopped and looked at him over her bifocals. She wore a dark, high-necked dress and black woolen stockings. From her pimply forehead the thin, white-blond hair was pulled back in a tight little knot, emphasizing her long, thin neck. Ernst Wagner paid no attention to her. He had pulled up a chair in front of the shelves and was sorting the files into their various compartments. He continued with his work even when Fräulein Huber stepped up close to him and peered from below into his face. Klaus suppressed a grin.

"That's Fräulein Huber," he said.

"Looks like she's from the Salvation Army," said Ernst Wagner and jumped off his chair. "Any more files to sort out?"

"More than you can handle. Herr Wagner is our new colleague," Klaus told Fräulein Huber.

She nodded, stepping back.

"I've heard of him." She turned to Ernst Wagner asking belligerently, "What was this you said about the Salvation Army?"

84

Ernst Wagner gave her an insolent smile.

"You remind me of one of those—with your glasses and that black dress."

"You're a lout!" cried Fräulein Huber. "Did you hear that, Herr Langer?"

"I heard nothing," said Klaus. "Can't you see I'm working?"

"She can't," said Ernst Wagner. "Her bifocals are out of order."

Fräulein Huber left the room, slamming the door behind her.

"Now where's she going?" asked Ernst Wagner. When Klaus didn't answer, he dropped back on the chair. "I'm always blistering my tongue," he said resignedly. "Everywhere I go with the best of intentions and yet I always end up blistering my tongue. It was the same in France. What do we do now?"

"We wait until the phone rings," Klaus said cheerfully.

"She go to the Landrat?"

"To Frau Hansen, I think."

Sorrowfully Ernst Wagner shook his head. "This is rather thick for the first day. But this time it was your fault. If you'd said a word I would have stopped right away."

"Too late after the Salvation Army."

"Damned," Ernst Wagner said. "But why did they have to offer me anything like her on an empty stomach. I never could stand that kind of fish."

Klaus smiled. "Think of me. Ever since I've been sitting in this hole I've tried to scare her out of here. I'm almost of a mind to have a beer with you this evening. Have you time?"

"For beer always. In France we only got wine, the kind that eats holes in your stomach. I was really longing for a decent glass of beer. Where?"

Klaus hesitated. It had merely been an impulse and now he could not back out.

"At eight at the Rathskeller," he said.

The phone rang loud and long. "There you go," he said. "Shall I say you've gone away on a trip? Langer speaking."

He listened and, with a broad grin, put the receiver back.

"Dear little Hessel. The Landrat wants to see you."

"Hessel, who's that?"

"The Landrat's lady-in-waiting. The loveliest in all the Landratsamt."

"His girl friend?"

"Fräulein von Hessel," Klaus said coldly, "is not a girl friend of anyone. She deserves to be met with courtesy."

"That type I'd like to meet with something else," said Ernst Wagner and betook himself to the Landrat's office.

"Oh, it's you," said Fräulein von Hessel when he came in. "Go right in."

The Landrat was waiting for him looking like a thundercloud.

"What do you think you're doing," he exploded at once. "If you think you can act like a boor around here, you're mistaken. You'll apologize to Frau Hansen at once."

"Not to Fräulein Huber?"

Schneider stared at him, his fury suspended for a moment.

"What do you want with Fräulein Huber?"

"Nothing, I just thought she had complained, too. We've just had a little conversation with her—"

"Who's we?"

"Herr Langer and I."

"Herr Langer—" Schneider stopped, leaning forward with his eyes growing small. "How did you get to Herr Langer?"

Ernst Wagner looked at him. "That's where I'm working. For three hundred and eighty marks. And next to a maniac at that. No, you can have that position. You promised me decent pay and that starts with five hundred marks as far as I'm concerned."

"Who sent you to Herr Langer?"

Ernst Wagner shrugged his shoulders. "What's his name—you needn't pretend you don't know. You won't wear me down this way, not even if you put a second maniac in the room with me."

Schneider closed his eyes and took a deep breath. Then, he pushed back his chair, told Ernst Wagner to wait and, his face stiff with anger, went to Primelmann.

As soon as he opened the door, Frau Hansen and Fräulein Huber shot up from their chairs. Primelmann, rising more slowly, forced a laugh.

"We were just going to see you," he said. "Fräulein Huber wants to make a complaint against Herr Wagner."

"I want to talk to you," said Schneider.

Primelmann paled and sent the ladies away.

"Yes?" he said formally. Schneider propped his behind against the desk, unbuttoned his coat and hooked his thumbs into his suspenders. Then he threw back his head and regarded Primelmann with a piercing stare.

"October first," he said in a hard voice, "I need a new man in the refugee department. The inspector there has reached retirement age. I am considering giving this position to you."

Primelmann turned white as cheese. Never had a department director been transferred to the mere job of an inspector. It would mean the end of his career—and to think of the disgrace in the eyes of the employees—

"I don't understand, Herr Landrat," he said, his voice full of horror. "I've always had your best interests at heart."

"Never mind my best interests," Schneider barked. "You're getting much too independent of late. You have to restrain yourself in the future or else change your job. Who gave you permission to put this young Wagner into the office of Langer, of all people? Haven't I told you emphatically that any personnel changes in Room 125 require my personal permission? The way you ignore my wishes is absolutely unspeakable and I don't intend to put up with it. As long as I am Landrat you'll do as I tell you and if that doesn't suit you, you can say so now. Do you understand?"

He had talked himself into a complete rage and was pounding the desk with both fists. Primelmann had never seen him like that. Shaking with fear and surprise he clung to the back of the nearest chair for support. When Schneider came barreling towards him with his chin jutting out, Primelmann abruptly took his hands off the chair and snapped to attention.

Schneider moved his face up to within an inch of Primelmann's and said, almost in a whisper:

"If I ever catch you setting up intrigues around here, I'll kick you out. Remember that! And you'll put young

Wagner in the welfare office. I don't care what he does there, but I want to be informed where he works, in which room. Is that clear?"

"Yes, Herr Landrat," Primelmann answered hoarsely. "But may I assure you that I was not thinking of any intrigues. I merely thought of sending him to Room 125 because Herr Langer is going on his vacation and when he comes back I would have—"

"I don't care a damn what you would have done," Schneider snapped. "You won't undertake any changes in Room 125, temporary or permanent. Besides, Herr Langer may not go on his vacation. You may have to turn down his application."

"Yes," Primelmann said, confounded. How could he deny the leave without getting into trouble with the employee's council? "Yes, Herr Landrat, of course."

He ran alongside Schneider to the door and tore it open. "Good-bye Herr Landrat," he said.

He wiped his forehead with a handkerchief and went into Frau Hansen's office.

"Well, I certainly told him a few things about his Herr Wagner," he said, putting his handkerchief away. "He'll be transferred to welfare. I've a suspicion about the whole thing. Until I see things more clearly I want you to treat this Wagner like a raw egg yolk."

"Yes, Herr Primelmann," said Frau Hansen.

Back in his office, the Landrat was informed by Fräulein von Hessel that Wagner had gone out. He was hungry, she said, and Primelmann had told him that the lunch hour was from twelve to one. He would return at one.

"Is that what he said to you, in those words?"

"Yes, Herr Landrat."

Schneider's face turned red then white and red again. He went to the window and looked out.

"Call Personnel," he said over his shoulder. "Find out Wagner's home address."

While Fräulein von Hessel was busy on the phone Schneider kept standing at the window. He could feel his nerves giving out and he was determined to clear up the entire situation.

He had considerable trouble finding the street Fräulein von Hessel had written down for him. It was in the southwestern outskirts of the city and it took Schneider half an hour to get there.

The house in which Wagner lived was an old, broken-down apartment building, five stories high. The dirty plaster outside was peppered with holes left by bomb-splinters. The roof must have burnt out during a raid —the outside walls of the top floor were blackened by fire and it seemed covered only with a scrap emergency roof. Some of the windows were boarded up with wood. Schneider looked up the name on the directory of tenants and cursed under his breath. The fifth floor, of course; these sort of people always lived on the fifth floor. On the second landing he stopped to catch his breath. The air in the house was awful, it smelt of unwashed socks, babies, burnt potatoes. Disgustedly Schneider pulled open the small hall window. Below was a small courtyard with a half collapsed shack and a great heap of garbage-littered rubble. A laundry line was stretched across with a few limp pieces of laundry hanging from it. Schneider spat into the courtyard and went on.

The stone staircase ended at the fourth floor. A ladder-like wooden staircase led on from there to the fifth. Schneider looked suspiciously at the crudely nailed boards. He stepped on the first one, bounced up and down a few times and, when it held, panted up the rest of the steps. He came up to a door that had neither a name nor a bell. When he knocked it was opened at once.

Schneider found himself face to face with a woman in a dressing gown. She was between fifty and sixty years old and had a tired, wilted face with sharp lines around the mouth. Apparently she had expected someone else; her whole attitude was one of disappointment and resentment. She moved as if to slam the door in his face but Schneider quickly put his foot inside.

"Stop that," he said rudely. "I want to talk to you. You're Frau Wagner, are you?"

"Who're you?" she asked.

"A friend of your husband's."

"My husband has no friends."

"We might discuss that," said Schneider. "But not here. Don't act like an old maid, for God's sake." He shoved her aside with his belly and was inside so quickly that she could not stop him.

"I'll scream if you don't leave at once." Her voice was shrill with fear.

Schneider pushed the door shut behind him and looked around in the small, dark vestibule from which one door led into a tiny room with slanted walls. Schneider took a few steps and opened the only other door which revealed a larger room that was completely empty except for two wooden crates. The two window openings were boarded up with wood, the walls were filthy and looking up Schneider saw that the ceiling was gone, he could see the wooden beams and rusty sheets of corrugated iron of the roof. He turned back to the woman who stood by the door, clutching her dressing gown at the throat with one hand and gripping the door handle with the other.

"Now I know who you are," she said.

"Good," said Schneider. "Then I won't have to introduce myself. I had thought your son was here. Can we sit down somewhere?"

The woman hesitated, then, shrugging, she went ahead into the small room.

"You better sit down carefully," she said, pointing to the sofa. "The springs are broken."

"Naturally," said Schneider. The sofa was behind a table near the stove. There was a bed and a sideboard on the other side and a closet beside the door. Dirty dishes were piled high on the sideboard. The entire room had a musty, airless smell. When Schneider sat down the springs gave so much he had the feeling he was sitting on the floor. He put his arms on his knees and looked the woman up and down. Her naked legs showed under the dressing gown. They were dirty, mottled with varicose veins, and on her feet were worn out slippers. It seemed inconceivable to Schneider that eight years ago this woman should have had a comfortable villa, car of her own and a high party official for a husband. He felt sorry for her but then he remembered why he had come and asked soberly:

"How do you know who I am?"

"My son described you to me," she said in a hostile voice.

"A nice little crook you've raised yourself there," said Schneider. "Who taught him to blackmail—you?"

"I won't be insulted," the woman said angrily. "I didn't ask you to come here."

"Of course not, your kind usually prefers to work anonymously. It might have been wiser if you'd done the same. And before starting anything like that, you should have calculated the risk."

The woman gave a scornful laugh.

"Risk? For whom? For us? What do we have to lose? Look how we live. My husband is better off in jail than we are here. Risk indeed!"

She leaned forward, her dressing gown falling open, and Schneider could see the flaccid breasts.

"What do you know about the things we've been through," she said wildly. "The humiliations, the insults, the beatings we've taken. And then at the end this trumped up trial just so they could confiscate the money. They even took my last dresses away. And you come here and talk to me about risks. I know better than you who's risking anything around here. This isn't blackmail, this is simply self-defense. Why shouldn't those whom my husband helped once do something for him today? Call it blackmail, I don't care. Let's see who finds it easier to go to jail, you or I."

"I shouldn't let it come to that if I were you," Schneider said in a bored manner. He pulled a cigarette case from his pocket, and put a cigarette in his mouth. "Now let me tell you something." He looked around for an ashtray and, finding none, threw the match on the floor. "I've known your husband very well. We were good friends. When I heard five years ago that he was arrested and then sentenced I was very sorry. I should also be very sorry if the same thing were to happen to his wife and son. I came here to prevent that, that's the only reason. I'm ready, for purely compassionate reasons, to help you as far as I'm able to. You'd certainly be better off that way than if you tried to make difficulties for me. Does that make sense to you?"

"It depends," said the woman. "It depends on what you mean by 'as far as you're able to.' Alms don't help us."

Through the cigarette smoke Schneider squinted at her coldly.

"In your position one can't be choosy, you know. I gave your son a job in my office although there were no vacancies. You can't expect much more. Now, you might get some additional help if you hand over the original letter I wrote your husband. I don't think that's asking too much."

"Perhaps not," said the woman, suddenly becoming affable. She sat down on a chair and smiled a crooked smile.

"How much would you say?"

"Two hundred marks."

The woman's face crumbled, only her nose stood out like a left over ruin.

"You're joking," she said hoarsely.

"Did you expect more?"

She got up. "My son is better at these things than I am. Speak to him."

"I don't want to talk to your son, I want to talk to you. Why don't you tell me at least how much you expected?"

"Well," she said. "I have to get the apartment fixed otherwise the landlord will throw us out."

"Why don't you find another one?"

She snorted. "You think I haven't tried? Where do you find an apartment nowadays without a cash bribe? I need furniture, too. My son doesn't even have a bed. He has to sleep on the thing you're sitting on."

"There are people who live in worse places," said Schneider. "I'll make you one last proposition. I'll pay you three hundred marks and I'll find you an apartment. Will you agree to that?"

The woman was silent. Undecidedly she looked down on her hands. Then she said:

"I cannot decide that alone. I must talk to my son first."

"As you wish," Schneider knocked the ash off his cigarette and used the table to pull himself up. "Think it over carefully. This is a one time chance I'm giving you. I attach to it only one condition: your son must stop behaving so impossibly at the office. If he keeps on acting the way he did this morning, I won't be able to keep him there."

Without another glance at her he left the room and went down the stairs. Before getting into his car he peered unobtrusively towards the fifth floor and saw the woman's face at the window. He was satisfied. As he pushed the gas pedal all the way down and the car shot off with a roar, he congratulated himself. Everything had worked out very well, he was convinced of having left a deep impression.

# [ CHAPTER SEVEN ]

Frau Schneider was in the kitchen, tilting a steaming pot into the sink and pouring off the boiling water when her husband arrived.

He pressed a smacking kiss on her reluctant cheek.

"Feel better?"

"As long as *you* feel better," she said bitterly, carrying the pot over to the table. Schneider trotted after her like a dog.

"You know very well," he said. "I never get drunk any more. Last night was an exception. The news affected me terribly."

"What sort of a father are you?" she whined. "To get drunk on a day like that. I'd like to know what Herr Buchholz thinks of you."

"He's more understanding than you. Where is he?"

"In the living room with Katharina. You might go and apologize to him."

Schneider looked uncomfortably at the door and back at his wife, who was on the verge of tears again. It made him nervous.

"Calm down, for heaven's sake, will you? This won't help Hans now. Please calm yourself." He patted her cheek clumsily and went into the living room.

"Good morning, Herr Buchholz." Schneider held out his cheek to his daughter and she brushed it with her lips.

"Herr Buchholz wants to leave us tonight. We can't let him do that, can we?"

"Under no circumstances," said Schneider, sounding surprised. He felt embarrassed about the previous night and he couldn't imagine that someone who had, by accident, discovered this side of him, wouldn't want to stay around to take advantage of the knowledge.

"Don't you like it here?" he asked Hergett, sitting down at the dining table with them.

"That's the trouble," said Hergett. "I like it far too much. If I stay around any longer, I'll never want to go away again."

"Excellent," said Schneider. He had no objections at all to Hergett's staying around a while. What with his bad conscience towards his wife and Katharina, a guest might help take the poison out of the atmosphere.

He put a great deal of warmth in his voice, and said:

"We've always liked having guests. If you like it here and if you plan to stay in Nuremberg anyhow . . ."

"I don't know yet," Hergett said quickly. "It depends on whether I'll find work here."

"A man like you?" Schneider looked at him benignly. There must be a way of finding him work in the office, he thought. If he put the man under obligation he would gain his confidence and then, if he treated him right, he would have someone upon whom he could rely again. Besides Katharina seemed to like the fellow. This might be one way to divert her attention from Langer. Not that he wanted her to fall in love with this man—for a moment Schneider was alarmed, but then he told himself that, no matter what, at this point, Langer was the greater evil.

He kept smiling warmly across the table at Hergett.

"I think I might have a job for you. How would you like to come to work for me?"

Hergett had been waiting for something like this. He looked at Katharina who was winking at him encouragingly. Today she wore a light, sleeveless dress with a red lacquer belt around the slim waist. Hergett remembered how she had looked the previous night, when she had opened the door for them because Schneider, in his drunken state, couldn't find the key. Her pyjamas, under the hastily belted dressing gown, seemed as transparent as the white skin at her temples. Hergett hadn't been able to fall asleep for quite a while. He looked at the Landrat.

"It's a little unexpected," he said. "And I'm not certain I'm the right man for that sort of job."

"Well, I'm certain," Schneider said generously and then his voice assumed a pained note:

"I'm pleased at your being so modest. My son was exactly like that. And I'm not allowed ever to see him again. Perhaps you can imagine what that means to a father." He lowered his head, sighed, and then continued: "You are the last person who was with him. No no," he said quickly when Hergett made a gesture of protest, "don't contradict me, not now . . . I must finish what I have to say. You came to us in his place and I want you to feel free to consider yourself our son."

He got up and with his face averted hurried from the room, slamming the door behind him.

Hergett looked at Katharina. Her face was a grimace of disgust.

"I'm sorry I couldn't spare you that," she said.

"Lunch is ready, Karl!" called Frau Schneider, carrying a large tureen to the table.

"Green pea soup," she said, ladling it into the plates. "Do you like pea soup?"

"When it's cooked like this I do," said Hergett.

"Hans always liked it best of all my soups. Karl!" she called again.

Her husband appeared a moment later.

"Just had to call the Leuchtners to tell them the news. They were stunned. Tonight they'll come over to express their condolences in person. This is the blackest day of my life," he said to Hergett, pushing the corner of his napkin into the collar. "Do you like green pea soup?"

"Some day I'm going to run away from home," said Katharina.

"It's a wonder you haven't long ago," said Hergett.

They were walking slowly through the sunny, suburban streets towards the street car stop. Frau Schneider

95

had suggested that Katharina show Hergett some of the town. Both had accepted eagerly.

"That's what Klaus always says." Katharina sounded bitter. "But it isn't so easy."

"Who's Klaus?"

"My fiancé."

Hergett nodded; for a moment he saw everything as if through blurred glasses. Then he smiled.

"*Touché!*"

She looked at him blankly. Hergett kept smiling.

"You know," he said after a while. "Your parents are the sort of people who make an invitation so irresistible that if you don't accept, you feel you're letting them down. I don't like to do that. I'll have no choice but to sneak out of the house secretly, at night. I hope you'll help me."

Katharina was silent. Then she said:

"I thought you were going to stay with us for the time being. Has the pea soup changed your mind?"

"I liked the pea soup. And your father is an original."

"Unbearably so. Anyhow if it wasn't the pea soup, what changed your mind?"

He wasn't going to tell her that the mention of a fiancé had caught him in the stomach like a fist. He had accepted Schneider's invitation only because of her—hadn't he? He couldn't see clearly at all. The miserable fact was that he had to depend on someone's charity in this town and that it was Schneider's didn't make it any easier. But he had no other choice, had he? It was disgusting and humiliating. He became infuriated. Without really thinking, he said:

"If you were a man you'd understand."

"Oh, I see." She sounded disappointed. He wanted very much to tell her that she misunderstood him, but his pride stopped him. For a while he walked beside her in silence, annoyed at himself, annoyed at the people they encountered, the many automobiles, the entire noisy carnival. You began to think there had never been a lost war, no three or four million soldiers killed, no bombed cities, those people sitting in the sidewalk cafés spooning mounds of ice cream from enormous silver goblets— they had been sitting there doing the same thing while he was still working in the quarry in Vorkuta and crying at night with longing for home and hopelessness. Katharina asked:

"Do you want an ice?"

"Heavens, no, what gave you that idea?"

"You were staring so."

"I haven't seen anything like this," he said. "It's all so disgustingly matter-of-fact."

He stopped in front of a shop window.

"What are those things there?" he asked.

"Electric shavers," she said. "Don't you know?"

"There wasn't anything like that before the war. How do they work?"

"My father has one. You don't need any lather, no blades or anything. Just run the shaver over the chin or the cheek and it takes it all off. In a minute or two. Would you like one?"

Hergett grimaced.

"Talking like Santa Claus. Seventy marks is a lot of money. But except for that . . ." He found it difficult to tear himself away, Katharina noticed.

"Not to have to lather your face any more, that's really marvelous," he said. "Are you quite sure it's true?"

"Yes," she said. "My father can demonstrate it for you."

"Still, I simply don't understand how it works. Probably the same system as electric hair clippers. But a beard is so much stronger." He could not get over it. Katharina smiled.

"How about the barbers, that must have been a terrible blow for them," he asked.

"I think they'll survive," Katharina said. "With the prices they charge for cutting your hair."

They boarded the waiting street car. As soon as they sat down, Hergett started again:

"It is an incredible invention. No blades! I cut myself every morning."

Katharina laughed.

When they reached the zoo they got off and went in. Hergett was pleased that the animals were left to run free in the large enclosures.

"My father would have loved to see that. He couldn't bear cages. My God, it's pretty around here. Do you often go to the zoo?"

"Not very often," said Katharina. They found a bench in a quiet corner of the park and sat down.

"Wonderful," said Hergett. "Big, old trees and well-trimmed lawns. I'd like to stretch out and feel what it's like to lie in the grass again. We had a fine lawn at home, behind the house, and a lot of old trees. Today some stranger lives there. I didn't even go to see the house when I was in Ilmenau. I didn't want to see it. Now I'm a little sorry I didn't."

"You're homesick," said Katharina.

Hergett pulled his cigarettes from his pocket.

"Would you like one?"

"They're too strong for me, your Russian ones."

"Yes, they have character." He lit one and threw the match over his shoulder.

"I don't know if it's homesickness," he said. "In Russia it was homesickness, at least in the beginning. Then I got the first mail and my sister wrote that my father was dead. From then on it changed to what it is now. Perhaps you better call it sentimentality, or nostalgia. One longs for something that one knows will never repeat itself."

"Doesn't everything repeat itself?"

"No. A woman, perhaps, a meadow with an old tree, or a song but everything—no. When the war started I was twenty-seven. That won't repeat itself, not for you and not for me."

"I don't know," said Katharina. "Perhaps if one could see life again as one saw it then—"

"Yes, but can one?"

"Sometimes I think one can. But it never works very long. Then it slips away from your hand like a cake of soap."

"You see!" said Hergett.

Katharina bent her head, her toes were drawing lines into the sand. Hergett wanted to stroke the smooth skin of her slender neck. He could have touched it with his lips if he had leaned a little closer.

"You're too young to talk like that," she said without looking up.

"It doesn't depend on the years, it depends on the opportunities one has left. What chance does a man like me have?"

98

"Others have started from the beginning."

"I know I'm not the only one. But what became of the others? I'd like to talk to one of them, I'd like to ask if he felt at first as helpless as I do. There were so many of them in Russia but here I can't find them any more. God, was I glad not to have to see their bitter faces again. Now, four weeks later, I miss them."

"You'll get over it," said Katharina, looking at the ground. "The others who came back before you got over it, that's why you can't find them now. You can no longer tell them apart, they've become like the others."

"I don't know," said Hergett. "I can't imagine this happening so quickly. These faces in the street, they're the same faces you saw before the war. During the war they looked entirely different."

"That's the German miracle," said Katharina.

"Perhaps. Over in the Russian zone, in Ilmenau, I didn't notice it as much as here. They've got other things on their minds. They're waiting day in and day out for a solution to the reunification problem, but they don't know themselves how it could be found. And over here you have electric razors and refrigerators with improvements. You can't get these things over there—even without improvements. But you get the armed People's Police and you can't open your mouth. On the other hand, I'm asking myself: what would happen if everybody who was against communism should escape to West Germany?"

"You?" she said. "You of all people ask that?"

"Yes," said Hergett. "It's only lately that I've really started to think this through."

"But you said yourself that you didn't want to go back to Ilmenau."

Hergett nodded. "I know. But perhaps if I didn't come from a Russian prison I'd feel differently. Take my sister's husband. He's working in a 'people's factory' over there. It's swarming with party functionaries and stool pigeons, but he's an engineer and he's making good money, comparatively speaking. Over here everyone makes good money, of course."

"Not everyone; most of them."

"But they don't talk so much about politics, I noticed that in the first few days. They don't talk about reunification either. I've listened to the people in the train.

They talked about everything else except politics. And in the Russian zone the people say over here in the west they haven't the time to worry about reunification because they're too busy keeping an eye on their economic miracle. Well, I don't know, I haven't been here long enough. In a few weeks perhaps I'll know more."

"Perhaps you will," said Katharina. "I'm one of those who don't like to talk about politics."

"Not about reunification either?"

"That's not politics."

"It's something that concerns all of us, but it can't be done without politics. However, let's talk about something else then."

"Yes," she raised her head. "Tell me how you met Hans. I only know you were going to swim across the Moldau with him. He wasn't a good swimmer, my parents don't know that. He and I went to the Dozen Lake often, but he never really dared going in. Didn't he tell you?"

"Yes, he did."

"Then you shouldn't have taken him along," said Katharina calmly.

Hergett bent over and picked up a small stone from the ground. When he straightened up again his face was pale.

"I didn't want to take him along. I told him to go back to the nearest camp. He wouldn't listen to me. He didn't want to go to the Americans, he wanted to go home. I'd have preferred to go it alone but what could I do, he simply came trotting after me . . ."

They reached the Moldau at noon, Hergett told her.

They had just stepped out of the wood into a meadow sloping down to the river when, suddenly, they both saw the American guard. He was standing on the bridge below, staring up at them with his face half hidden by the steel helmet. Hans and Hergett ran back into the wood at once. They thought they heard the guard call out after them, but the noise of breaking twigs and branches as they kept running swallowed all other sounds. They kept running for quite a while, parallel to the course of the river, until they reached the bank. Panting they threw themselves to the ground and peered through the deep hanging branches to the other side. There, too, the woods were thick. The trees on the edge leaned forward, their grotesquely formed branches reaching down to the water like the arms of a polyp. The river was wide. Its current was swift with treacherous whirlpools in the middle and they could hear the water sucking and clawing at the bank as it rushed past. With the trembling, dancing lights on its shimmering back and its unknown depths it resembled an enormous reptile, slithering noisily through the wood. On the other side steep hills bulged their green humps against the sky, blocking out the horizon. What lay behind them the man and the boy didn't know.

They stared across. their elbows propped in the moist ground. The boy's face was still pale from the shock.

"The beast," he said. "The miserable beast!"

His thin lips twitched as if he wanted to cry. Then he said again:

"The beast!"

"The Ami—the American?"

"Who else," said the boy.

"Why?"

"Now we can't get across."

"Of course we'll get across," said Hergett. "We don't need the bridge, we'll just have to swim."

The boy looked at the river, saw the whirlpools in the middle of the stream and measured the distance to the other bank. He began to tremble.

"I couldn't make that. I'm not a good swimmer, and with this current—"

"I'll carry you. You just have to paddle with your legs. I'll help you. I swam across the Dneiper once. It was five times as wide as this brook here and it was in the middle of winter."

"I'd have drowned."

"Many did, three-quarters of our regiment, in fact. But you'll get across this one, don't worry. I'll help you."

"I'm certainly lucky to have run into you," the boy said.

"Well, wait and see. Anyhow, where do you come from? I mean, what's your outfit?"

"I was with the pioneer battalion. We were assigned to your division."

"That's right, I remember. Where's the rest of your outfit now?"

"I think the Russians got them," said the boy. "We were the rear guard and the Russians attacked about an hour after you had finished your retreat. I was on my way to battalion with a message but the Ivans were already there. I could hear them shouting. So I ran away and I kept running for thirty-three hours and then I met you. By the way, what time is it? My watch has stopped."

"I don't know, the Amis got mine."

"The Amis? You were with the Americans?" the boy asked excitedly.

"Yes."

"Tell me about that."

"There isn't much to tell. Our people loaded us on trucks and sent us back towards the American lines. Somewhere in a village they ordered us off the trucks and told us to smash our weapons."

"Smash your weapons?"

"Yes, on the pavement. Some of the fellows actually had tears in their eyes doing that. The general, too. He suddenly appeared and gave a short speech. And then we—"

"What did he say?"

"The general? Oh, nothing much. He thanked us for our contribution to the war effort and said something about the dark powers that had once, after World War I, brought us to the brink of an abyss and would now again crawl from their hiding places if we, the German soldiers, didn't keep our eyes open and resist them as we had resisted the Russians."

"Why are you laughing?"

"Am I laughing? You're imagining things. I've never in my life felt less like laughing than today."

"Me, too," said the boy, looking across the river. "And then?" he asked.

"Well, then we marched another kilometer and there were the Americans. They were lining both sides of the road, standing around with their hands in their pockets and spitting chewing gum in front of our feet."

"Did they do that?"

"Does that bother you? It didn't bother me. Because I was thanking God that the Americans were standing there and not the Russians. The others felt the same way. They even assigned us quarters, those Americans, we were allowed to walk around in the village and the field kitchens distributed the last of their food."

"And then they let you go free?"

"They didn't exactly encourage it. Someone mentioned that we were being turned over to the Russians. That's when I took off."

"I bet that wasn't simple."

"Not exactly simple, but not too difficult either for an old war horse. I had a rough idea of the area and, like you, I kept on walking towards the West, towards the Moldau."

"Until we met."

"Yes. But now I suggest you keep quiet for a moment while I try to figure out how we go from here."

The boy turned over on his back. He was seventeen years old. After several weeks of training he knew how to throw a bazooka at a tank or how to explode a hand grenade. Now he looked into the trees, saw the sun passing over the forest, the dew drops glittering like colored glass beads, and he was so depressed he felt like crying.

And then he actually was crying, soundlessly and stubbornly with clenched teeth, as he often did. After a while he asked abruptly:

"What's your name?"

"You're talking again."

"I only want to know your name," the boy said quickly. "After that I won't open my mouth again."

"Call me Hergett."

"That name suits you very well. My name is Hans, Hans Schneider. From Nuremberg. Not a very rare name, Schneider, is it?"

"Not rare but German. You're eighteen, right?"

"Seventeen."

"That's worse. At seventeen I helped my sister to do dishes and that's exactly as many years ago as you've lived."

"That makes you thirty-four."

"Clever boy. Seventeen years old and knows not only war but arithmetic."

The boy looked at him.

"Where did you get so tanned?"

"I was in Africa before they sent me to Russia."

"Tell me about that," the boy said eagerly.

"Everything in its time. We must rest up for tonight. Take my blanket, I'll use the shelter-half."

The boy stretched out on the blanket. As the day went on it had become hot. Shimmering mosquito swarms were dancing above the water in a bright light that hurt the eyes. The river had turned into a great mirror which caught the sunlight and threw it back in blazing beams. Two dragonflies were drawing strange curves in the trembling air and small, arrow-breasted birds threw themselves with shrill cries into the rippling wall of foliage along the river.

The boy tried to sleep. He hadn't slept for forty hours, he had hardly eaten anything and his feet were sore. He put his hands under his head and tried to doze off. The hard leather of his boots pressed around his swollen feet. Although his eyes were closed the light penetrated every pore of his lids and created an uncertain twilight in his brain in which thoughts and pictures formed and dissolved. He felt the repulsive tickle of ants traveling up his wrists and sat up abruptly.

"I can't sleep," he said. "I keep thinking of having to swim that river."

"We'll swim it together," said Hergett.

"Yes, yes—God, I wish I had your peace of mind. How do you do it?"

"I just don't think ahead."

"That's easily said. As if it were a motor one could switch off at will." The boy sighed.

After a little while he said:

"What do you think about our having lost the war?"

"That it's good."

"Good? You say good? That's—"

The boy bit his lip. Fear and fury fought inside him. He looked across the river to the steep bank rising towards the cloudless sky and a sudden terror turned his indignation abruptly into self pity.

"I wouldn't have thought you were one of those—" he said tearfully.

"One of what?"

"One of those who're glad about it."

He was terribly disappointed. He had been a soldier only for three months but he liked it so much that he could remember even the unpleasant aspects of it without bitterness.

"If you say it's a good thing, that means you don't care."

"I'm sure you know all about that," said Hergett, in a voice that was suddenly different and made the boy feel vaguely ashamed.

The boy waited a while and then said in a conciliatory tone: "You see, it's worse for me. Because I was so glad to get away from home."

"Why?"

"Because of my father. He makes me sick."

"That's very bad," Hergett said.

The boy looked at the river again. The other bank lay trembling in a glare of sun. The day was slowly climbing up the hills. In the forest golden dust sifted through slanting beams of light, ran in broad puddles over shaggy rugs of moss and oozed away under the gnarled roots from which mushrooms burst like hunks of yellow foam. A woodpecker was picking tiny rhythmic holes into the tense silence among the trees.

"I couldn't stand him," said the boy. "Without Katharina I'd have run away a long time ago."

"Who's Katharina?"

"My sister. Six months ago she joined the Red Cross. From then on I really couldn't stand it any more. If she had stayed home I might not have volunteered. She didn't want me to."

"Didn't your parents object?"

"Only my mother. If my father had had his way, I would have joined the army at the age of fifteen. Every day he said it was a shame that no one in our family was fighting for the fatherland. He said the Führer needed every single man, he had confidence in the German people and one mustn't let him down. Actually, father was annoyed that when his colleagues talked about the heroic deeds of their sons he had nothing to say. I couldn't stand it any more, all that talk."

"Why didn't your father join the army and perform his own heroic deeds?"

"He was 'indispensable.' In 1938 he denounced his superior and took his place and became a big man in the ministry."

"How do you know?"

"I saw a copy of a letter he wrote to the Gauleiter. He complained that he, as a faithful follower of the Führer had not been promoted whereas his superior had been a member of the Social Democrats and was discriminating against all the National Socialists. The Gauleiter asked him to his house a few days later. I remember my father coming home that night, drunk, and I had to go and wake up the owner of the store to get two bottles of champagne and he drank those with my mother—"

The boy broke off, thinking of the parents' bedroom next door, their drunken mumblings, like the voices of complete strangers, squeaking mattresses and awful, naked words and he at the door, barefooted, trembling with terror and repulsion and then rushing back into his bed, pulling the blanket over his head but in his ears still the engine noise of those two-hundred-pound mounds of flesh, all through the night and ever after.

"Four weeks later my father was promoted," the boy told Hergett. "Perhaps I shouldn't talk about it. It's awful to say things like that about one's father."

He stated it as a question put there merely to be contradicted. Hergett's silence discouraged him.

"Don't think I'm talking about this to everyone," he said hastily. "Katharina is the only one except you who knows. And I wouldn't have told you if I didn't know I have to swim across that river."

"Still worrying about that?"

"You think I'm a coward, don't you?"

"No, *Kamerad!*"

The boy blushed fiercely. Very quickly, very happily, he said:

"Thank you. And I really haven't told anyone else. But then I must tell you the other story too, the one about the Jew. Do you want to hear it? Or are you against Jews, too?"

"They never did me any harm."

"You sound exactly like Katharina. Actually, I'm not really against them either although in the Hitler Youth we threw stones in their windows. I only did it once but,

106

my God, you should have seen Katharina when I told her about it afterwards. I'll never forget her face. My father, though, thought it was a fine thing. After his promotion he had changed terribly. He didn't want to go to church any more. But, still, when my mother said she wasn't going to church any more either, he made a big scene. He told her that when two do the same thing, it isn't the same, and we should think of the future, too."

"Was he a party member?"

"Yes, but not active, he just paid dues. He never went to those meetings, he said he had too much to do. Now that you ask me, it occurs to me that outwardly he really didn't participate much in the whole thing except once, and that was the story about the Jew.

"It was a Saturday afternoon and we had gone to the movies together, one of those homeland movies, you know, that make people cry. My father always cried too, like a walrus. Everybody could hear him and we were always so embarrassed. When we came out of the movie there was a great crowd. My father asked someone what was going on and the man said 'The synagogue is burning.' Then a bunch of screaming people came running past pushing ahead some other people who had signs around their necks that said 'I am a Jewish Swine.' My mother got scared and wanted to rush us all home but my father wouldn't let her go. He said: 'We have to see this, the children must see how we're clearing away the dirty Jews.' There was so much shouting in the street you couldn't hear your own voice and we were being pushed back and forth. Actually I didn't understand what was going on because I was only ten years old and couldn't look over the other people. But then suddenly my father started shouting and pointed to a man who was trying to run into a house. My father is over six feet tall and he's very fat. It was the only time I'd ever seen him sprint. If the noise hadn't scared me so I would have laughed because he looked so funny. Anyway, he caught the man, that is it wasn't really a man, he wasn't much more than a boy. When we got to him this boy's nose was already bleeding and two of his teeth had been knocked out. I felt terribly sorry for him right away. My mother did too, she kept begging my father to let the boy go because he hadn't done anything, and anyway we should keep out of these things. Katharina tried to talk to him too, but he acted as if he were drunk. He had both hands around the boy's neck and shook him, and spit into his face and then he kicked him away. The boy fell flat on his back and my father kept screaming like a madman, screaming to the others standing around to kill the boy. The last I saw they were trampling on him, then my mother grabbed me and we ran through the streets, past the burning synagogue, back to our apartment. My father didn't come home until midnight. We never mentioned it again, I think he was very ashamed afterwards. Katharina didn't speak to him for four weeks. Today I'm still asking myself how on earth this whole thing was possible. Because if you saw my father, you'd swear he could never do such a thing."

The boy picked up a branch and started poking it absent-mindedly in the ground.

"Anyhow," he said stubbornly, "now you know why I don't like going home."

"Where else would you go?"

"I'd have liked to stay in the army. I was supposed to study economics but now I don't feel like it any more. Not that I'm stupid—you should have seen my marks in school."

The memory colored his cheeks with pride and gave him back some of his childish air of superiority.

"I was the first in my class," he said proudly. "The teachers never bothered to call on me because I always knew all the answers anyhow."

He smiled happily across the river and his oversized uniform seemed to fill up, as his self-respect came streaming back like air into a slack rubber hose, making him, for a moment, seem bigger and stronger. But then he fell together again, as if in surrender before the silent scorn of the river that was smacking at the edge of the bank, staring up at him with poisonous, algae-green eyes. In sudden anger he raised his branch and aimed it at the other bank. Although he put all his strength into the throw, it got not even half way across and he watched in fury as the water closed over the piece of wood and swiftly took it away. His head drooped. Suddenly he no longer cared about anything. His voice sounded tired and indifferent again:

"Today all that studying seems so childish, doesn't it to you?"

"I didn't study, at least not economics," said Hergett.

"What then?"

"Forestry. My father is a forester. Once I wanted to be one too."

"I'd have liked that myself. What do you mean 'once' you wanted to be one. Don't you want to any more?"

"Perhaps. I have to see. It isn't easy to start from the beginning again."

"Exactly. That's why I'd have liked to stay in the army. You know, becoming an officer and so forth. How long have you been a corporal now?"

"Eight years, almost to the day."

"You're joking. A corporal for eight years? I never heard of such a thing."

"You're hearing it now. They drafted me for the first time in 1935 and released me two years later as a corporal. Then they got me again in 1939 for the march into Poland and since then I've been in it without interruption."

The boy shook his head.

"Then I can understand even less why you're still a corporal. Why aren't you a sergeant, a master sergeant even?"

"I would be, if I didn't have a p.u. in my papers."

"What's that?"

"That means 'politically unreliable.'"

"Politically—" the boy sat openmouthed, not finishing the sentence. Then he nodded slowly, as if Hergett had confirmed a suspicion of which he himself had been half ashamed. Finally he said candidly:

"I thought right away that something was the matter with you. That's why you're glad we lost the war."

"Glad isn't the right word. It's like having an accident in which you lose a leg or an arm but still you're grateful to have come off alive."

"I could never feel that way," the boy said. "It was worth too much to me, in spite of everything."

"It was worth as much as we were worth ourselves but all together not enough to make up for the loss of a single one of those men we left in Russia and Africa and France—"

"That's pacifism," the boy said heatedly.

Hergett smiled. Nowadays he could smile whenever the conversation reached that point. Four years ago he would have trembled with rage and frustration. How could he correct the twisted thoughts produced by twelve years of intensive "youth education"?

He leaned forward with the same smile that had so completely disarmed the boy before:

"Do you really know what a pacifist is?"

The boy looked at him stubbornly. He felt stubborn not so much because of hurt feelings—they were quite ready to be instantly soothed—but because he didn't know how to define his fervent objections to pacifism. The longer Hergett smiled at him, the greater his embarrassment became and he finally turned his head away, saying loudly:

"Of course I know. I only hope you do!"

"I do indeed," said Hergett. "A pacifist is someone who tries to hide his inner swinishness behind a so-called ethical attitude. That attitude consists of refusing to take up a carbine and shoot at other people. The difference between him and me is that I've always done what he wouldn't do—which is not to hesitate for an instant to pull the trigger when it came to saving my precious skin. Am I a pacifist or am I not?"

The boy didn't answer and pretended to study the opposite shore. Hergett reached out and pulled him around by a strand of his hair so he could look into his eyes.

"Every one of us has had a tiny chance to pull through," he said. "Those who were heroes and those who were not. There were fewer heroes than other people. But to let yourself be hanged for an 'ethical attitude' without the slightest chance of being saved, to know you've a choice between saving either the ethical attitude or saving the neck—that takes more than either you or I have. And that's why we haven't become pacifists, neither you nor I, nor any of us."

He let go of the boy's hair and smiled at him.

For a while the boy said nothing. Only when Hergett turned aside with a shrug of indifference, did he throw off his last pride and say meekly:

"I'm sorry."

"I'm sorry for you," Hergett told him. "Still, you'll have to go home like everybody else."

"Perhaps I'll join the Foreign Legion."

Hergett looked at him, shaking his head.

"I'm sick of everything," the boy said. "No matter what you say, we didn't deserve an end like this."

"Perhaps the individual didn't. But we've done away with him."

"With whom?"

"With the individual," said Hergett, stretching out on the ground. Beside him the boy's voice went on talking, monotonous and rambling talk as if the end of the war had taken the last bit of purpose away from his life.

"If it hadn't been for the Americans," he was saying, "we wouldn't have lost the war."

"We started the war, not they."

"They spread so much propaganda—"

"Didn't we?"

"I've heard differently."

"We've all heard differently," said Hergett. "Now you better stop this nonsense. Try to get some sleep, you'll need all the strength you have tonight."

The boy saw him looking across the river again.

"Do you think we'll make it?" he asked.

"It's going to be pretty difficult, let's face it. I certainly don't want to persuade you to come along."

"What? What else can I do? Surrender to the Amis?"

"It would be less dangerous for you."

The boy stared at the ground. Some of his defiance had come back in his voice when he said:

"I thought I had already apologized."

"Nonsense. You're much too young to insult me. Also I'm not touchy, in case you want to know. But I must tell you that you're coming along on your own responsibility. And now do what you want."

Hergett spoke more sharply than he intended. His bitterness was directed not so much at the boy as at fate itself. Here, after six years of war, when he should have felt that the worst was over, he found himself in a situation that filled him with more apprehension than any before. He made an effort to control his mood so that it wouldn't further influence his behavior towards the boy. Seeing the depressed face, he said in a more amicable tone: "When two people embark on something like this, they have to be completely frank with each other about it. I didn't mean to frighten you and I haven't changed my mind. With some luck I'll get you across, but you know yourself that in order to succeed we need some luck. One has to catch a little corner of luck in one's hand, otherwise—"

The boy nodded. Hergett's sudden change of mood confused and relieved him. Right now the thought of going to prison camp alone frightened him more than all his other black visions of the future. His heart filled with gratitude. He would do everything Hergett asked him to do, he decided.

"Without luck we would long ago have landed in a mass grave," he agreed earnestly. "I'd rather cross the river and be home in a couple of days than to go to the damned Americans. God knows what they would do with us."

He was getting upset again and Hergett smiled.

"Just make sure and remember these words when you're home!"

He closed his eyes.

The boy yawned, stretched his legs and squinted up into the leafy twilight of the wood. Here and there flecks of pastel color from the sky broke through the even green. The peaceful atmosphere soothed the boy's bitterness. For a while he surrendered himself to a feeling of being safe and protected. He turned over on his side to look at Hergett who lay beside him with his eyes closed. His face was deeply tanned and the boy was impressed with the contrast between the color of his skin and his hair. At first he had thought the hair was grey, but now he saw it was actually an odd salt and pepper mixture with a few lighter strands between. Only the temples were completely white and the boy wondered about that because otherwise the face seemed so youthful. But, peering closely, he could see a thin web of wrinkles around the eyes and in the corners of the mouth. The nose was sharp and big, a little too big, the boy thought, but it went well with the high forehead that was all roughed up by sharp lines.

While he was looking at him, the boy tried to remember the exact color of his eyes and couldn't. They were strangely light and bewildering, it was difficult to stand their stare without wavering. But they inspired confidence, the whole face inspired confidence and the boy thought now that, if he were a girl, he would fall in love with Hergett. The idea made him want to laugh and he wanted very much also to go on talking, although he was getting sleepier all the time.

"What are you thinking of?" he asked Hergett.

"Of home," the answer came instantly. The boy was relieved he had not awaked him.

"I'm just trying to imagine," Hergett went on, "What it must be like to live in hiding, in a little cave, for four years."

"In a little cave?"

"I suppose you could call it a bunker," said Hergett. "Just high enough to stoop in. No windows or anything, just a little periscope hidden with branches. All day in that little cage, you could only move out at night —can you imagine living like that for four years?"

"No," said the boy. He looked at Hergett and it gave him a shock. Hergett's face looked changed, contracted, with white cheekbones from which the flesh seemed to have melted away. The face was like crumbling cement with the eyes like two black crater holes. Then a smile restored the face, it evened the mouth, filled the skin over the cheekbones with color and made the eyes light again. It's only the smile that lights up his eyes so, the boy told himself. And they'd been light all this time. He must have laughed at me all along, he thought. With all I have told him, he must have laughed at me. He felt a surge of childish anger.

"Not only did he have to sit in that hole for four years," said Hergett, "he had to stay alert all the time so they wouldn't find him and hang him. I'd give anything to see him right now. A hundred times I've tried to think of how his face would look the moment he could walk into his house again but I've never been able to. Perhaps that's because he has always reacted differently than you'd expect. We've often tried very hard to make him laugh and how satisfied we were if we brought out only a little, tiny grin! But I'm sure he's no longer able to grin, not even a little."

"Who the devil are you talking about?" the boy asked in confusion.

"My father."

"What's he doing sitting in a bunker all this time?"

"He's been hiding from the Gestapo."

"From the Gestapo?" the boy instinctively lowered his voice and repeated the question, it seemed so monstrous to him.

"From the Gestapo?"

"They've been looking for him over half of Europe, I think. And all the time he's been sitting a few miles from our house in a cave that my brother-in-law and I dug for him."

"Incredible," said the boy. "What has your father done that they're looking for him?"

"He's saved some people's lives by hiding them until it was safe for them to leave the area."

"Jews?" The boy looked aghast.

"Jews and others."

"And you knew about that?"

"Yes, more or less. In 1941 someone denounced him but he got away at the last moment. I didn't find out where until I came on leave three months later. My sister and her husband took care of him, they've been risking their lives day after day."

"That was brave of them." The boy was fascinated. His cheeks were pink and he shifted his position. "I don't think I'd have had the courage in their place."

Hergett nodded. "Thank God they were there to help him. Still, imagine living in that hole for years."

The boy was silent for a while. Then he said:

"He must be quite a fellow, your father."

Hergett nodded again.

"When did you last see him?"

"A year ago."

"You like him enormously, don't you?" the boy asked shyly.

Hergett's eyes were smiling. "You can like a woman or a new bicycle or things like that, but a father—one can only look up to a father."

"Some fathers are like companions," said the boy. "But those are rare. Mine certainly doesn't belong to those. If I look up to him it's only because he's tall. Do you

114

get along as well with your mother as you do with your father?"

"She's dead. I was three when she died. My sister was eight. She can remember her, I can't."

"Oh," said the boy. "That must have been awful for you."

"Worse for my father than for us."

"He never beat you, I suppose, or did he?"

"No, he'd scold us sometimes, but he never beat us. Perhaps we were especially nice children." Hergett grinned.

The boy looked gloomily at his hands. They were slim with pink knuckles and rims of dirt under the nails. His father's hands were thick and fleshy, every week he had them manicured by a girl who came to the house. Once the boy had seen his father putting his hand down the front of her dress and kissing her. The sight had shocked him so much he could not tell anyone about it, not even his mother.

"We were nice children, too," he told Hergett. "But still, he often beat us. When my mother tried to protect us he told her it was the best education."

"Perhaps now and then you deserved it."

"No, not often. I always knew very well when I did deserve it. But most of the time he beat us for nothing. You should have seen it, always the same act . . ."

The trial, with the father enthroned at the table, his face a study of injured righteousness. Beside him the mother in her pathetic, subordinate part, bristling with mother love but too weak to oppose the man who in fifteen disillusioning years had broken her spirits, lined her face and crammed her body full of passions, disappointments and butter cream torte. And before him the children, hands folded behind their backs, and then the interrogation:

"Who broke my fountain pen?"

"I did."

"Come here!"

The humiliation of having to bend over, the hard slaps with a ruler, followed by the warning about the future, inevitably adorned with a suitable proverb or two.

Or, another time:

115

"Who spilled the ink on my desk?"

Silence.

"Did you, Hans?"

"No, father."

"Katharina?"

"No, father."

"Well, I must have done it myself without noticing." Smiling: "All right, children, you may go then."

"In the end," Hans said aloud, "we lied to him all the time. He trained us to lie to him because whenever we told the truth he beat us. Once Katharina stayed away from home for three days with a friend of hers. That worked. After that he never again dared to lay a hand on her. I got all the more, however."

"All this sounds pretty sad," said Hergett. "Have you ever discussed these things with your father?"

"No! What an idea! Anyhow," he hesitated, "anyhow —he probably isn't really worse than others. I know from my friends in the army, they all had pretty similar experiences. Only they didn't mind but I, I get sick over it."

"You're hypersensitive," Hergett said sleepily. "He probably meant very well."

The boy shrugged. He, too, was very drowsy.

They were both stretched out on their backs, looking up at the light green foliage. The sky, a deep, nostalgic blue, shot sheaves of light into the trees and on the other side of the river the hills sat like broad-hipped market women squatting in the midday sun.

Hergett thought of the night ahead. They would have to cross the river by the bridge; they would never get up the steep bank at any other place. They would cross by the bridge but start from a point a little up the river, otherwise the current would smash them against the bridge posts.

He closed his eyes and dozed off. It had already grown dark under the trees when he woke up. The hills on the other side had turned their black backs on the river as if to watch an interesting spectacle on the western horizon, where the sky was still light. The sky was like the face of a sleeping girl, soft night shades in the hair off her temples, the skin reflecting the dying sun in a rosy glow and the red burst of an open mouth sending its warm breath

116

across the river. Hergett's heart ached in his chest, he found himself thinking of Evelyn. Lost in his memories, the hands folded under his head, he watched as the red grew pale, the glow drained away, the face turning first yellow, then grey and finally black. Against the extinguished sky the hills stood blackly, like veiled mourning women.

Hergett waited a little longer, then he woke up the boy. He had to shake him hard.

"It's time to go," he said.

The boy reeled to his feet. Although he had slept deeply, he knew at once with a shock where they were and what was facing him. He gathered his things and swung his knapsack over his shoulders.

"I'm ready," he said.

The march through the black wood was difficult. They tried to make as little noise as possible, but again and again a dry twig snapped under their boots or they would stumble over a root. The wood seemed to have a thousand hands. They grabbed their uniforms, tore at their bags, whipped their faces with swift, treacherous strokes and wrapped themselves around their legs.

"God, if I only had my carbine—" the boy hissed. "Everything would be easier."

His voice was so full of hatred that Hergett glanced at him in astonishment.

"Thank God the days of the carbines are gone," he said. "What would you do, shoot your way home? You couldn't really intimidate the wood with a gun."

"I don't mind the wood, it's those Americans," said the boy. "It's the one thing I agree on with my father. He's always despised them."

"Why?"

"Well—just in general," the boy said stubbornly. His aversion to the Americans was based on stories he had heard at school but didn't remember. As in a distillation process they had dissolved and left behind in his mind a crystallized residue of dislike of all things American.

"Just in general isn't very good, you know," Hergett said reproachfully. He peered up at the sky. Then he stopped, put his bag on the ground and sat down.

"We're going to wait here."

"For what?" The boy's voice was shaking.

"For the moon," Hergett said indifferently.

"All right," said the boy, proud that he had managed to steady his voice.

It was absolutely black around them, they could not even see each other. The boy jumped with fright when Hergett whispered:

"As soon as it grows lighter we'll go across. We should undress here so we won't have to waste time down at the river. And remember, no hasty or unnecessary movements. You'll strap your bag to your chest and as soon as we're in the water you turn over on your back and I take you like that," he knelt up and put his hands around the boy's chin. "I'll hold your head above water and all you have to do is help by paddling with your legs. Understand?"

"Yes," said the boy hesitantly.

They had to wait another hour before the first traces of moonlight filtered through the trees. Gradually the blunt, shapeless mass of hills on the other side broke up into single hoarfrosted silhouettes. Single pines rose like the silver prongs of a crown above the crests and the entire forest, all the way down to the water, filled with rivulets of light from invisible sources. When Hergett stepped forward, he could see the long, slim shadow of the bridge spanning the river. In twenty minutes it would be light enough to see the bridge piles, but they mustn't wait that long.

He told the boy to unpack everything except the absolute necessities. "And when you're through, you get undressed—"

"Undress—you mean completely?"

"Of course. Unless you want to swim across in your long underwear."

With clenched teeth the boy stripped off his clothes and threw them in one heap. When he stood naked, his teeth were chattering.

"Put the blanket around you for now," said Hergett.

He, too, had taken his clothes off. Beside the boy's meager, white body he looked like a moor in the dark. He's built like an Olympic champ, the boy thought, admiringly.

Hergett paid no attention to him, but was busily sorting out the superfluous things from their packs and then wrapping the remainder into a compact bundle. When he was ready he called the boy over, lifted, the big, formless package and hung it by the straps around his chest.

"When we're in the water you put both arms around it and hold it tight. I'll take care of the rest."

"This thing is going to push me under," the boy said tremulously.

"Nonsense. As long as I have your chin between my hands nothing can push you under. I learned that as a child."

They ran down to the edge of the river where Hergett stopped again. There was no sign of life from the bridge. Cautiously he lowered himself to the water and then turned back to the boy, who stood motionless, pressing the heavy bundle to him with both hands and staring across the water.

"Come on," Hergett said impatiently. "Or have you changed your mind?"

"Looks like it's a mile wide," the boy stammered, and started to slide down. He laid the pack across his knees, squatting down next to Hergett. They sat so close that their bodies touched. The boy's skin was like ice, Hergett felt. He reached out and put an encouraging hand on the skinny back while he struggled with the idea of leaving him here after all. Suddenly the responsibility seemed overwhelming, even though the boy had come along by his own decision. Still, by telling him that somehow he would help him get across, Hergett had assumed full responsibility and no one could relieve him of that, least of all his own conscience.

Instinctively he withdrew his hand. His mind was suddenly made up. In an entirely changed voice he said:

"Give me the bundle!"

"What do you want with it?" the boy said astonished.

"Give you your things. You're staying here. Go to the nearest POW camp. If you're lucky, they'll send you home in a few days."

The boy stared at him without moving. But when Hergett reached out for the bundle he quickly moved a yard away and said excitedly:

"What's happened all of a sudden? What's happened? We had agreed that I'd come along."

"I don't want you along." Hergett knew that he was

119

being unfair and it infuriated him. Also the black river looked broader and more dangerous at night. For the first time he felt something like fear. He himself wished now that they were already on the other side. He was rough and cross with the boy:

"With anyone else I'd have crossed over long ago," he said with a violence that took the boy's breath away. "To have your sad figure along doesn't make things easier for me. This is something for men. Five years from now you might be able to try it, provided nature ever does make a man out of you. Now give me the bundle or I'll get it myself."

He had got up and was turning towards the boy. At that instant the boy jumped into the river. It happened so suddenly that Hergett was still standing incredulously on the bank when the boy, caught by the current, was already drifting swiftly towards the middle of the river. Hergett came back to life and swearing, jumped in. The water was so icy that it took his breath away. He reared up to see where the boy was drifting, like a piece of white wood. Feverishly he swam towards him but then he lost sight of him again. At the same time he saw that they were already too close to the bridge to reach the other side in time. He might have made it if he had tried to swim against the stream instead of looking for the boy. He reared up again in the water and at that moment he heard a man shouting and a few seconds later a machine gun barked. At the same time a star shell hissed into the air and in its light Hergett saw the boy, who was spinning like a top towards the left pile of the bridge, smash against it and disappear.

Moments later the swift current had carried Hergett far below the bridge. Half unconscious and with his last bit of strength, he swam towards the shore and scrambled up the bank on all fours. There he stayed, his wet face pressed into the grass, the taste of wet earth on his lips, unable to think or feel.

A few minutes later the American soldiers discovered him. They pulled him to his feet, raised his arms to look for the tattooed blood group number of the SS. The pressure of a pistol in his back showed him the direction in which to go. It led to the bridge. There stood two other Americans beside a jeep which had its headlights turned towards them. The soldiers exchanged a few words and then all four of them looked at Hergett who stood among them with dangling arms. Someone threw him a blanket, he draped it around his shoulders. Everything slid past him as if his mind had turned into a piece of ice. Much later, when he sat between the Americans in the car and someone offered him a cigarette, he opened his mouth for the first time.

*"Danke!"*

"A German," said the man who had given him the cigarette, crossing his legs with a satisfied air. The trip was short. The wood on the left receded from the road and revealed six barracks bathed in the bright light of searchlights. In passing Hergett saw behind the searchlights the barrels of machine guns and American steel helmets. The pistol in his back prodded him out of the car. Three guards marched him through a long, dark corridor and stopped before a door. One of the guards went in and two minutes later returned, motioning Hergett to enter.

The officer behind the table was a Jew, Hergett saw that at once. He turned his expressionless face towards Hergett who was clutching the blanket around him with both hands, presenting a peculiar sight with his naked legs. For a second it seemed as if a tiny smile pulled at the corners of the officer's mouth but the impression was so fleeting that Hergett was not sure. The soldiers who had brought him in posted themselves around him, straddlelegged with their hands behind their backs, looking straight into nothing. The officer put his hands on the table. They might have been the hands of a woman, slim and white, only the fingertips were stained dark yellow with nicotine. Hergett stared at them absent-mindedly, thinking: he didn't even cry out, he never uttered a sound! The boy, the same boy who couldn't swim and who looked as if he would never become a man, that boy passed up his chance to use his voice, to cry out for help. When the guard called out to him, he didn't answer so that Hergett could cross the river unnoticed. A bullet must have got him the way he spun against the pile. The picture sat etched in Hergett's mind. He knew he would never forget it.

They started interrogating him. If it hadn't been for

the uniform, Hergett would have sworn the officer was not an American. He spoke an exquisite, fluent High German without a trace of accent.

Beside him sat a man taking notes. Now and then he sharpened his pencil with a knife and each time he took up the knife he looked at Hergett and ran his thumb along the thin blade.

The interrogation went on endlessly. Again and again he asked the same question: had Hergett been with an SS Division? And if he had not been with an SS Division, why had he thrown away his identification documents? They kept repeating the questions and Hergett repeated the story of how he had lost his clothes, how they had wanted to cross the river and how the boy was shot and drowned with the bag. As he talked, his eyes never left the officer's face.

The officer shook his head.

If Hergett's conscience was as clean as he made it out to be then why did he have to risk his life by swimming across the river at night? Why hadn't he stayed with his company?

"The worst way home is still better than the best prison," said Hergett. "If I had my papers I could show you that I don't have anything to hide. I'm classified as p.u., politically unreliable. The Gestapo have been after my father for years, it isn't very difficult for you to confirm that."

"No, it isn't in an individual case," said the officer. "But you're not an individual case. Every other man who's been brought here tells me the same story. If you had as much character as imagination, you wouldn't be standing here."

Hergett was silent. He was sick of the whole business. He thought of the river and of his guilt and he thought of his father and the now inevitable prison. He was still looking straight at the officer when a voice started shouting outside. The officer went to the window and leaned out. He exchanged a few words with someone, then he closed the window and turned slowly around. For some inexplicable reason Hergett's heart began to hammer. The man at the table was playing with his knife again. He had a colorless face, freckles on his forehead —Hergett stared at the stripes on his sleeve, idly wondering what they meant. When he finally tore his eyes from them, he noticed that the officer was steadily looking at him. When Hergett's eyes met his, he asked:

"Where is Ilmenau?"

It took a moment for Hergett to remember that he had given his home address. For one heartbeat a desperate hope darted up in him and he said, in a high, excited voice:

"In Thuringia, near Erfurt."

"A happy coincidence," said the officer. "Do you know that the Russians will occupy Thuringia?"

"I know now," Hergett said faintly.

"Well, that'll suit you fine. I've orders to turn this camp over to the Russians. Since your home is in Thuringia you couldn't ask for anything better, could you?" he asked.

Hergett looked at him distractedly, his attention tuned to the sounds outside the window. He could distinguish Russian words.

"They're already here," said the officer as if guessing his thoughts. "Aren't you glad?"

Hergett was silent. The officer motioned to the other Americans and they left the room.

"All right," he said then, turning back to Hergett. "Now pull yourself together and admit that the story about your father is a lie, that you've invented it so we'd let you go. If you admit that, I'll take you with us to an American POW camp and chances are you'll be released in a few months. So, come on!"

He waited for a full minute. When Hergett still had not said anything, he said:

"That story was a lie!"

"No!" said Hergett.

With a heavy shrug of his shoulders the officer turned away. A moment later the door opened and the other Americans reappeared, followed by three Russian officers. At the sight of their uniforms a hot stab went through Hergett's chest. He stared at them, not noticing the American officer motioning to his soldiers. Before he knew it, the soldiers had pushed him past the Russians into the corridor and, in the glare of the searchlights, marched him along a barracks wall. Finally a door was opened and Hergett was pushed into a pitch black, foul-smelling room. Behind him the door was slammed shut and he stood for a moment helplessly in the dark until someone touched his arm and asked:

"Who's this peasant?"

Although he still could not see in the dark, Hergett sensed the presence of many people. He said:

"I'm one of you. They caught me when I tried to get across the Moldau."

"Serves you right," said the same voice. "That's what you get for trying to run away, leaving us to eat the dirt alone."

"He's not one of us," said another one. "They've probably sent him as a stool pigeon."

Hergett could feel them moving towards him in the darkness. He stood wrapped in his blanket, wondering if he should drop it to beat them off with his fists, but suddenly the ominous shuffling of approaching boots was stopped by a sharp command.

"Stop it. Have you lost your minds altogether? That's all we'd need, giving the Amis the satisfaction of beating each other up. Bring him over here."

Hergett's arms were gripped, he stumbled over several feet and then stood before the speaker whom he couldn't see, but whose breath he could feel on his face.

"You're one of us?" he inquired. "Which division?"

Hergett answered irately. When the man said that he didn't belong here because he was not in their division, Hergett told him angrily that, after all, he had not exactly joined them of his own free will.

"Yes," said the man. "You've already said that. You should have stayed with your own outfit. Or doesn't that exist any more?"

"It doesn't," said Hergett and he didn't even have to lie.

"That's different, of course." At once the man became very friendly. He invited Hergett to sit down beside him and to tell him in detail what had happened.

"That's lousy bad luck," he said when Hergett had finished. They were squatting on the floor, side by side, their backs to the wall.

"My name is Fred," said the man. "I'm afraid we'll have plenty of time to get acquainted. Did that Jew tell you they're going to turn us over to the Russians?"

"The Russians are already here," said Hergett and told him about the three officers.

"We didn't expect them till tomorrow," said the man. "It seems those vodka pots can't wait to get their hands on us. You see, in case you don't know, we're an SS division. It was a pretty unlucky star that brought you in with us."

"So it seems," said Hergett, mildly amazed that the information didn't shock him more. He pulled a corner of the blanket over his bare legs.

"Hasn't one of you some extra clothes for me? I can't run around in a blanket all the time."

"No, not in Siberia, you can't," said the man they called Fred and ordered someone to bring over his pack.

"Yes, Sturmbannführer," said a subservient voice. Hergett winced. There was the sound of a violent slap and Fred said: "This was the last time!"

"I simply can't get used to it," the subservient voice said plaintively. "For two years I've called you Sturmbannführer."

"If you'd called me that for twenty years, it would still be no excuse. This is just absent-mindedness, nothing else. And I don't intend to have my head cut off because of someone's absent-mindedness. We've agreed that there are no ranks here, we're just SS soldiers. And we'll stick to that—you too," he said, directing his voice back to Hergett. "Don't call me anything but Fred. Here's a set of clothes from me, underwear too. How tall are you?"

"Six foot three," said Hergett.

"By God! Six foot three and not in the SS? Two inches taller than I—but it doesn't matter, the trousers were a little too long anyway and where we're going nobody cares if the jacket doesn't fit. I've cut off the Christmas decorations, so you needn't be afraid they mistake you for a sturmbannführer. But I've left the black tabs to remind those vodka pots with whom they're dealing. They didn't take us fighting! Here."

The clothes were pushed towards Hergett in the dark and he got up to put them on. When he sat down again, fully dressed, he had collected himself sufficiently to be able to thank Fred.

"Don't mention it," said Fred. "You're not one of us, but the SS has always been generous. That's why we're first on the blacklist now, we're first and the others follow. Did that Jew interrogate you too?"

"Yes."

"He slapped my face because I told him my opinion. For that I'll hack off his hands when I get back from Russia."

"You should have told him so he could send you a ticket to America for the purpose," said Hergett.

Fred laughed softly.

"You don't think the Americans will ever return to their country? They won't dream of it. They'll never have such an easy life as they have here. Occupation troops! By God, we know what that means, don't we? And that Jew knows it too. No, he'll stay in Germany as surely as the war would have ended differently if the entire army had consisted of SS troops. And Germany is no longer big enough for him to hide. I even heard his name, I won't forget it either."

"Wait and see," said Hergett. The man's talk revolted him. However, Hergett was wearing his clothes, so he swallowed his comments. But then the other men joined in the conversation and when they referred to the officer as a Jewish swine, Hergett could not stop himself from remarking that perhaps, the Jew was one of those who had lost their entire family in a concentration camp. As soon as he had said it, an icy silence spread through the entire room. Then, almost in a whisper, Fred inquired if Hergett was joking and what he was trying to say.

"I'm trying to say that if we were in his position, we would act exactly the same way," answered Hergett.

The silence spread again until one man burst out:

"Looks like we caught ourselves a real little treasure here!"

"Certainly does," said Fred. Hergett could hear him breathing hard. Then he said in a sharp, commandeering tone:

"Take off those clothes! At once!"

Hergett looked incredulously in his direction.

"Do you mean me?"

"Yes. Because a man like you doesn't belong in an SS uniform."

His voice showed that he meant it. To Hergett the thought of being taken prisoner without any clothes on was, for the moment, rather more awful then prison itself, but he knew he had no choice. If they wanted to, Fred and his men could make life infernal for him.

He undressed and threw the clothes on the floor.

"Here you are. If I'd kept them on, I would never have forgiven myself."

"We understand each other," said Fred. "A swine can't feel at ease in a SS uniform."

"Listen—" Hergett bent forward. He could hardly talk with rage. "Listen, another word like that and—"

"And?" asked Fred. Hergett heard several men getting to their feet and shuffling towards him. He leaned against the wall, naked, and stared into the darkness with wide open eyes.

"Come on," he said. "Come on—"

"Leave him alone," said Fred. "We know with whom we're dealing now. I'm glad he's told us."

"I only told you that you would react the same way if someone had done to your families what was perhaps done to his. I'd like to know what's wrong with that."

"Everything," said Fred. "First of all our families aren't Jews and furthermore we have no use for anyone who feels sorry for those *Itzigs*."

"Because you don't want to be reminded how many you've killed."

"Wrong again," said Fred. "That was others. We were at the front."

"Then I don't see why you make such a fuss."

"I know you don't see. That's why we lost the war, because you people never understood that one shouldn't try to think of ten things at once. As a soldier you have to think only of the immediate issues. And if you insist on thinking about other things, you must remember that whatever doesn't suit you personally, may be beneficial for the whole. In one word, you have to keep discipline. That goes for what we're facing now, too. Either you get used to that, in which case you'll be no worse off than the rest of us, or you don't, in which case I'd advise you to get out of here."

Silently Hergett looked down at him. He wished very much he could see the face of the man. Somehow he couldn't picture him clearly.

"One would think," he said after a while, "that you haven't noticed the war is over."

"It isn't. For us it's only beginning. To get through the coming months one must know how to survive, and why."

"Do you know?"

"I know it by heart."

"So do I," said Hergett and sat down again. He draped the American blanket around his shoulders and, pulling up his knees, leaned back against the wall and closed his eyes.

... "At that time," Hergett told Katharina, "I thought I wouldn't come through it. At night, before they came to get us, I went nearly insane knowing that I was going to Siberia instead of Ilmenau. For a long time I never thought about your brother again. Only later, when I was quite sure I would get through, I remembered him and your name and where his parents lived. I didn't tell you everything because I've forgotten a lot and also today many things sound different than they did then. But I think you can judge for yourself now whether I could have done more for your brother. I don't think I could have. At first I thought I was entirely guilty but later, in Vorkuta, when I thought about it more calmly, I became convinced that this was the way it had to be."

"I'm sure," said Katharina. "This was the way it had to be."

She got up and looked straight into his eyes.

"You must promise me something. You must promise me to stay with us until I see myself that it doesn't work."

"That what doesn't work?" said Hergett. The look he gave her made her blush.

"You know exactly what I'm talking about," she said.

Looking past her at the green grass, the old trees, Hergett remembered what they had talked about before he told her about her brother. Slowly he got up.

"I don't want to have trouble with your fiancé," he said.

"Why should you?" Katharina asked in astonishment.

Hergett buttoned his coat.

"Because I might fall in love with you."

She stared at him. After a moment she asked:

"How long have we known each other?"

"What difference does that make?" Hergett said irritably. "It's happened to other people, you know. Besides, you forget that where I came from there were considerably fewer women around than here."

"I understand. I suppose I'd better give you the house key so you can go out tonight."

Hergett looked at her as if she had drenched him with a bucket of ice cold water.

"Well," he said. "Then you agree that it's better for me to leave as soon as possible, don't you?"

She didn't answer but her expression made him absolutely furious.

"At least tell me one thing," he said. "Why do you want me to stay with you?"

"I don't any longer."

"You see?"

They didn't say another word until they had left the zoo. Hergett went along with a set, clouded face, wondering whether he should apologize or let things go as they were. For the first time in his life he was at a loss as to which was the right and honest thing to do. But he knew now that he was in love with Katharina and it didn't even astonish him very much.

In the street car Katharina said:

"I've some errands to do on the way. Why don't you go on through. You'll have no trouble finding the house from where you get off."

"Of course," said Hergett formally.

She smiled.

"I hope I haven't spoiled your day entirely. At least we've been very frank with each other. Anyhow, you can still stay on a while because I'm going away Saturday for two weeks. During that time you can look for another place to stay."

Hergett forgot his reserve.

"Away? You're going away? Away where?" he asked, greatly alarmed.

"To the coast, with my fiancé. It's his annual leave. I'll probably miss you when I get back. It's so good to talk openly to someone now and then. But I can see I expected too much. This is where I get off. See you at dinner."

She was gone and Hergett looked after her as she

crossed the street. She wore a slim, white, sleeveless dress, the black hair hung in soft curls down her back and she looked like those finely built, confident girls Hergett had seen in a fashion magazine at their house. She never looked back and Hergett's eyes followed her until, like a beautiful white swan, she vanished in the distance. He felt that some of the things that had brought him to Nuremberg had become quite unimportant.

# [ CHAPTER EIGHT ]

As he was leaving the office for lunch, Klaus Langer met Ernst Wagner coming up the stairs. Wagner waved merrily from afar.

"Hello, colleague."

"Oh, you again." Klaus stopped. "I thought they'd thrown you out."

"Because I didn't come back yesterday? They transferred me to the welfare department. But we can still drink a beer together, can't we? How about tonight?"

"I'm busy tonight," Klaus said curtly. Ernst Wagner looked disappointed.

"What a pity. I'm as thirsty as a potato field after a month's draught. I'm going to the Landrat; you too?"

"He asked to see you?"

"I asked to see him! A little family matter that has to be straightened out. However, if your mission is more important I'll gladly bow and stand aside."

"Don't be pompous," Klaus said disgustedly. "I don't want to see the Landrat."

"Well, *bon appetit* then," said Wagner, and with another wave of his hand went on.

Schneider was waiting for him by the window.

"Have you talked to your mother?"

"I talk to her every day," said Ernst Wagner, dropping

130

into a chair. "Next time you pay us a call, I'd appreciate it if you arranged for my presence in advance."

"Get up," Schneider said, looking white.

"You mean me?"

With three steps Schneider was at the chair, grabbed it and, yanking it away, spilled Wagner to the floor.

He jumped back on his feet and glared at Schneider, stunned with shock and indignation. Schneider was straightening his tie, his face beet-red.

"Next time I'll have you thrown out," he said. "You're a lout. You can act like this in your pigsty at home, but not here. Here you'll behave like a decent human being, or else."

"You'll regret this!" said Wagner, panting. He dusted off his coat and trousers with his hands. "You can't treat me like this. And if you think you can get rid of us for three hundred marks, you're mistaken. Five thousand, and not a penny less. And an apartment, too."

Schneider opened his mouth and closed it again. Red rings were dancing before his eyes. His rage was checked by a sudden fear that darted up from his heart. He went to the desk and sat down.

"You've lost your mind," he said, trying to sound calm and wondering feverishly whether he should drive to Wagner's house and take the letter away by force. But the woman might scream, and he wasn't the man to handle that. However, someone else. . . .

His mind was working like a machine, propelling him out on dangerous ground without his being in the least aware of it. His fury at Wagner's insolence, his fear of the disaster if the affair were revealed in public, had become a thick padding against the sharp arrows of his reason. The important thing was to gain time.

He told Wagner once more he would throw him out if he didn't behave, but added in the same breath that five thousand marks was a sum which he, in his position, could hardly raise overnight.

"I shall think it over and discuss it with you in a few days," he told Wagner.

"You're not going to bluff me, you know," said Wagner, slamming the door behind him as he left.

Schneider dried his face with an enormous handkerchief. Then he called his house and asked Hergett to meet him in town for lunch.

Hergett noticed at once that Schneider was itching with some problem, but it wasn't until they had reached dessert that he began to talk.

"There are," he said, "in everybody's life situations where one has to act against one's own conscience. Have you ever noticed?"

"Yes, it happens," said Hergett.

"At your age one understands these things," Schneider said gratefully. "Hans was too young to understand. One doesn't want to harm anyone, one is too decent for that. But if someone becomes a burden to one's fellow men because of his attitude—of course, I don't mean political attitude—then a responsible official has to choose between the lesser and the bigger evil. You know how it was in the Third Reich, one couldn't get anything done through official channels. So I went to an influential friend and asked him, in the interests of my friends and colleagues, to effect a transfer. That was all. The man was transferred and as far as I'm concerned that closed the matter. Confidentially speaking, I've been disappointed that my son had so little understanding—my son of all people."

He drank some wine and paused expectantly.

"People often misunderstand," Hergett said.

"Of course, of course, I'm not reproaching my son, I merely want to set things straight. All I did was—well, file an official complaint on behalf of my colleagues. Now, unfortunately there are people who envy me my present position because I had more luck than they. The luck of course, should be called ability. Today there are creatures who are trying to overthrow our democracy by discrediting people and personalities in public life, undermining public confidence in our form of government. They'll use any dirty ruse to bring this about. They hire strawmen, people who are for sale, and instruct them to put the pistol to one's chest."

Like a cat creeping up on a mouse he stopped for a moment and sat staring into space.

Hergett's suspicion that the Landrat's invitation had some ulterior purpose was confirmed. And Schneider now went on to tell him about the letter and what had happened in the past few days.

"You can imagine the dark cloud this has cast over my family life," Schneider said. "I've no other choice but to pay the five thousand or—"

He broke off, looking straight into Hergett's eyes as if waiting for encouragement to finish the sentence. But no encouragement came. Schneider sighed.

"What would you do in my place?"

"Pay!" Hergett said promptly.

Schneider's face stiffened with disappointment. He rubbed his eyes as if something had flown into them and said, without looking at Hergett:

"From you I'd expected something else."

"What else could I tell you," Hergett said with a surprised smile.

"Are you in favor of aiding these blackmailers by cooperating with them?"

"I'm just looking at it soberly. You want to get your hands on an important letter. If you pay, you'll get it. If you don't, they'll keep the letter and you'll have a scandal."

Schneider winced.

"That's all my political enemies are waiting for," he growled. It dawned on him that with each word he was bringing himself further under Hergett's power and he couldn't bear to think that he might have bared his soul for nothing. With a final desperate attempt to back the conversation out of its dead end, he said beseechingly:

"My dear man, five thousand marks—do you know what that means? I'd give you a fifth of that, outright in cash, if you made me an acceptable proposition. A thousand marks, it would be a little fortune for you."

"Yes, but for God's sake!" Hergett said. "Do you think these people will dance with joy when I come and tell them I want to earn a thousand marks for myself, so please give me that paper?"

"It's only the old witch," whispered Schneider. "You'd have to catch her when she's home alone. A thousand marks, you've never earned so much money so easily."

"Oh, so that's what you have in mind," Hergett gave a short laugh. "Who do you think I am? I'm out of prison, not out of the penitentiary!"

"You misunderstand me," Schneider was beside himself. "I don't want you to harm her. Just be forceful!"

"There's a jail sentence for forcing your way into a home. You're wasting your time."

Schneider's head dropped. He felt like a man who has gone to bed with a woman unsuccessfully. For a while neither of them said anything.

Then Schneider cleared his throat:

"I hope you won't hold it against a man in my desperate situation that he lost his nerve."

"Of course not," said Hergett. "If there's anything else I can do—"

"Thank you very much," said Schneider. The humiliation cleared away from his mind and suddenly he felt ice cold and sober. It seemed to him as if during the past two hours he had acted completely outside his own volition, like a delirious man. Now that he began to realize his impossible behavior he felt a surge of resentment against Hergett without whom, he told himself, he would never have thought up this idiotic plan. He would have to get rid of him as soon as possible. Meanwhile he would find a place for him in the office where he could do no harm. I'll put him with Langer, Schneider thought. Langer already knew everything anyway. And Langer wouldn't be particularly friendly towards a man who lived under the same roof with Katharina. He would arrange for this as soon as he got back to the office. And he would tell young Wagner he would pay him in installments and meanwhile try to think of another solution.

When Hergett returned to his room, later in the afternoon, he found a small package on his table. It was wrapped in red paper with his name scribbled on it. He carefully unwrapped it. Inside was a little box. He opened it—it was an electric razor. He took it to the window, read the instructions, turning it around to study the mechanism, then he plugged it in. Its quiet, whirring noise surprised him. He ran it experimentally over his face and felt the tiny knives massaging his skin. The razor was small, he closed his hand around it. It was humming and it grew a little warm. Hergett felt he was holding something alive in his hand and the thought made him happy. He let it run a while, then he pulled the cord from the plug and laid the razor back on the table.

He noticed a vase filled with long-stemmed dahlias. The same kind grew in the garden below. Who had brought them up here, Katharina or her mother? The razor was from Katharina, he knew. But what should he do with it? He couldn't accept it as a present, it was too expensive. Anyhow, why a present, he asked himself, after he had been so rude to her. He hadn't seen her since she had left him after their visit to the zoo. She hadn't come home for dinner and she had been out all day. Why couldn't he have been more careful with her!

It made him terribly uneasy to think about it. He wandered over to the window and stared at the sweeping landscape with the endless forests that reminded him of Ilmenau, except that in Ilmenau the hills were steeper and the woods were different. Here the soil grew nothing but pines.

Pines with their umbrella-like crowns, like great, thin-stemmed mushrooms standing under the pale grey sky that spread itself everywhere without an obstacle, holding the land like a vast, embracing hand. In the east the grey was running into black. Light clouds sailed calmly over the sleepy horizon, across barriers and boundaries, armed border guards and No Trespassing signs. They sailed into Saxony and Mecklenburg and Pomerania; to Thuringia, to Weimar, Erfurt, Ilmenau. Hergett saw them sailing above the road to Saalfeld with its slender silver poplars, over the St. Nepomuk well and the forbidden private path that was fenced off with rusty barbed wire and led from the Baron's mansion to the fishery. Light clouds were sailing across all the memories and feelings, the rebellions and resignations of his youth, sailing through the dark into the morning and into the dark again where the horizon swallowed them up.

The night opened starry eyes above the woods which seemed to have turned into stone. Moonlight transformed the inky plains into lakes of silver, and in the swamp grass by the River Pegnitz the crickets were chirping.

Hergett closed the window. In the dark he felt his way to the lamp, switched it on, and dropped into a chair. He felt depressed. The highly polished walnut furniture, the warm color shades of wallpaper and drapes, the whole cozy atmosphere of the room pained him becauee he knew that none of it belonged to him, that in two weeks at the latest he would be sitting in another room, without walnut furniture and reading lamp and a gleaming, built-in washstand. With great luck he might find an attic room with a wardrobe, a table and an iron bedstead. And even that wouldn't belong to him. It wasn't much for a man of forty-one. And then this constant feeling of being alone, of having missed the connections, of having to make a fresh start when he felt much more like pulling to a halt, at last. For the first time since he had come he thought that perhaps he should have stayed in Ilmenau. He was still thinking about it when there was a knock at the door and Katharina came in.

She looked at him searchingly and put a key on the table.

"The main door, in case you want to go out tonight."

"I don't want to go out," said Hergett.

"Keep it anyway, perhaps you'll go out tomorrow."

"I don't want to go out tomorrow either," said Hergett.

"And not the day after tomorrow? Why, all of a sudden?"

"I like it here. It's a damned pretty room. When I was a boy I always wanted a room like this. Is the electric razor part of the interior decoration?"

"As long as you live here, yes."

"And later?"

"It's yours."

"You bought it for me?"

"I wanted to give you a present."

"You wanted to make me feel ashamed."

"Why do you say that?"

She wore a white sweater today. In the glow of the lamp her face looked incredibly soft. Hergett's thoughts started to dance like pieces of cork on the surface of his emotions.

"I've apologized to you so often, I'd feel ridiculous if I did it again."

"Don't feel ridiculous," said Katharina. "I can't remember you apologizing so terribly often. You didn't yesterday."

"I saw no particular reason. I think yesterday we were even."

"Is that why you saw no reason?"

"You can drive a man quite out of his mind," Hergett said crossly. "If it's any satisfaction to you, I'll be happy to apologize again."

"Don't twist everything around. I don't know why, but to me it seems that you're contradicting yourself all the time. Don't blame me for your contradictions. Do all men argue like that?"

"I've never listened to other men talking when they were alone with a woman. You should know these things better than I."

"Why, yes," said Katharina. "That's why I've noticed it. For a woman it's very difficult to make sense of it at times. One sometimes feels very stupid."

"Perhaps you don't understand because you've never been alone."

"I've been alone all my life," said Katharina. "I know what you're thinking about but that's another kind of aloneness. For that you need only a house key now and then."

She sighed and picked up the electric razor.

"Have you tried it yet?"

Hergett nodded.

"My fiancé has the same kind."

She put the box back on the table and sat down.

"He was a career officer," she said. "During the war he was a night flier. On the last day of fighting they made an emergency landing and he smashed his head into the instrument board. They operated on him three times. When something upsets him now he goes into fits of rage and attacks people without knowing it—over-excitability, they call it. They put him in an asylum once and they wouldn't have released him if we hadn't pulled every string in sight. Now he lives on whatever my father does for him. But they don't get along any more. If my father could, he'd let him go today. And I can't persuade Klaus to look around for something else. It's difficult for him to concentrate on anything new, he forgets so easily. I've waited so long. Klaus was in the hospital for months after the war and then, when we could seriously think about marrying, this thing happened—he had an attack—and they locked him up. I had to wait another three years until they released him. I've been postponing things and postponing things and now maybe it's all too late. He's become a man without any will power of his own. It would be up to me to carry him along with me if only I had something that would drive me. But, I ask myself—"

"Excuse my interrupting you," said Hergett. "I don't understand a word. You complain about your fiancé and you say you ought to sweep him along but you haven't anything to drive you on. If that's true, what has bound you to him all these seven years—pity, or what?"

Katharina looked at him resentfully.

"A great deal more has bound me to him. But you run out of breath if you have to pull by yourself a cart meant for two horses."

"Then you should have done something about it long ago," Hergett said. "Couldn't you live with Klaus? I mean, marry and move into his house?"

"He doesn't want that. He lives with his father. They get along all right but his father is a little—well, a little peculiar. He's a civil servant and since his wife died he's acquired something like a housekeeper, if you see what I mean. And Klaus, of course, doesn't get along with her. And if she became his stepmother . . ."

"That's unfortunate."

Looking at her expression, Hergett felt sorry for her. His feelings were rapidly changing from admiration to pity to resentment. He tried to think of something to say to help her and at the same time he told himself: why should I? There were limits to his own selflessness, after all. He was a man asked for an act of renunciation that was almost as great as his ability to deny his own self. His own will was helplessly swinging back and forth, like the needle of a compass. But a moment later he told himself that he had already been forced to give up too many things. What did he care about a disabled officer of the former Luftwaffe? On the way to Vorkuta he had learned to defend his own skin. He had learned that people were considerate of others only so long as no personal sacrifice was involved. Once they had nearly beaten him to pulp because he had taken one half-rotten potato too many.

As time went on he, too, had become treacherous and crafty. Crafty and cruel, like an animal fighting for his piece of meat. Those who had not learned this never reached Vorkuta. They were dumped en route and in the end there was enough room in the boxcar for the survivors to stretch their legs and enough potatoes for all.

Now there was more at stake than a half-rotten potato. Hergett caught himself looking around the room and imagining it were his own. In his mind he saw himself going through the connecting door into Katharina's room. Her white sweater would be hanging on a chair, and she had unbuttoned those four big buttons which closed her skirt on the side. The picture etched itself into his mind like a physical pain. He scowled. Why should he act as advocate for a man who meant nothing to him? That man's skull was cracked but he had an advantage of seven years. If he had not succeeded in marrying Katharina by this time it was his own fault, obviously. The chances were evenly distributed, each had been given his own and now they would see which one used his chance best. There was nothing wrong, Hergett told himself, in leaving the decision to Katharina. Of course, he counted on her not being completely indifferent to him. After all, why had she put flowers in his room? Why had she bought the expensive razor?

"I should have looked for a job two years ago," Katharina's voice broke into his thoughts. "That's the one thing I reproach myself for."

Hergett shrugged.

"Why do you waste time thinking about it instead of doing it now?"

"Yes," she said. "You've put that very exactly. Perhaps I need someone who gives me a kick in the—who kicks me," she said hastily, her face getting red because she had almost talked in Klaus' language.

Hergett grinned.

"The other was better. Why doesn't your fiancé do it?"

"He needs someone to kick him!"

Hergett laughed.

"I could say something to that, too, but I won't. What does your fiancé want? Does he want to marry you or doesn't he?"

"He wants to but he doesn't."

"Then he's crazy. He won't find another woman like you in a hurry. If I were in his place I'd make damned sure you wouldn't need anyone else to talk to about me. I'd have married you with the few hundred marks in my pocket and I wouldn't have thought it over for a moment. And I'd never have regretted it," he said fervently.

"You never know that until after you're married."

"Or were."

"Are you—were you ever?"

"Yes, I was. My wife divorced me during the war. It was better for both of us."

He told her about Evelyn.

Katharina looked at him silently.

"Seems we're doing general house cleaning today," said Hergett. "But I'm for establishing clear situations. If you should ever be in the market for another man—"

"A lot would have to change before I'd consider thinking about that."

"Perhaps a lot has already changed?"

"Not with me, it hasn't," said Katharina. "Yesterday you reminded me of how you spent the last years. You must admit that's hardly a good reason for my breaking my engagement to Klaus. Perhaps instead of discussing this any further, you should make use of the house key after all. Now you're insulted again, aren't you?"

"I've no time to be." Hergett grinned. Today he didn't mind at all. "Listening to your tongue I find it even more incredible that your fiancé could put you off so long."

Katharina started laughing.

"All right, that was a neat shot."

Hergett felt the admiration in her voice like a caress.

"Listen," he said. "What if I talked to him?"

"To whom, to Klaus?"

"Yes. I'd let drop, from one man to another, that I'm fond of you. Perhaps he'd show then if he wants to marry you and why he doesn't do it."

"That's not a bad idea," Katharina said, getting up. "Come along. I was going to see him tonight anyhow."

Hergett looked at her incredulously. "Do you mean that?"

"If you meant it, I mean it."

"Well, on your responsibility," said Hergett, unfolding

his long legs. While he put on his coat he waited for her to change her mind, but she didn't. She went into her room to get her purse—he noticed with amazement that the connecting door was not locked.

"Herr Buchholz!" said Klaus. "How nice of you to come. I asked Katharina yesterday to bring you along some day—"

He shook Hergett's hand, ignored his surprised face, and said to Katharina: "I was about to call you. Come in. Both of you."

His room was not large and there were only a few pieces of furniture, all of them old. The chairs were hard and uncomfortable—one sat on them as on a wooden bench. Katharina stretched herself, putting her hands behind her head. Her small, pointed breasts made Hergett's thoughts jump around. He looked away from them to Klaus who was taking a bottle and three glasses from a cupboard and put them on the table. When he had filled them he gave one glass to Katharina and one to Hergett, then he raised his own:

"Let's drink to the late homecomer."

His self-assured manner impressed Hergett. Aside from the ugly scar on his forehead there was nothing wrong with him. Hergett could easily picture him in an officer's uniform. His face was narrow and long, he had dark, almost black hair that was cut very short and his eyes, under the thick brows, looked aloof and knowing. All in all, he was a man who could afford to put off a woman forever without her running away. Hergett grew annoyed at having let himself be dragged into this affair.

Klaus and Katharina started discussing their trip. Katharina insisted on simply leaving Saturday, permission or no permission, but Klaus suggested that she first tell her father. Otherwise there might be a terrible row and he might not have his job when he came back.

"But you know him!" Katharina said angrily. In anger she looked even prettier, much more alive, and the three vertical lines on her forehead hardly mattered. Hergett looked at her admiringly. "You know him, he would only use the occasion to give you a detailed account of all the things he's done for me and for you in the past. We'll just go and I'll write him a card. And if he really throws you out, well, I'm still there. I'll pester him so much that he'll be glad to take you back just so he has his peace."

"What do you think of this girl?" Klaus asked Hergett. "Some day she'll throw her father out of the house and I'll have to support her mother."

"If I were you, I'd have a solution," Hergett grinned back. "If I were you, I'd marry her. I can't understand why you don't."

He was glad when it was out and looked at Katharina who was watching Klaus with a peculiar expression. Klaus stood surprised for a few seconds, then he sat slowly down at the table and looked Hergett slowly over as if he hadn't seen him before at all.

"You're very well informed, aren't you?" he drawled.

Hergett smiled winningly.

"I couldn't help asking Fräulein Schneider why she isn't married yet."

"Why should that interest you?"

"I'm a curious fellow," said Hergett. Klaus looked at him for a long time. Then he picked up the bottle and refilled the glasses.

"I think you're looking for a fight."

"Oh no, that's not true!" Katharina jumped up. Leaning over the back of Klaus' chair, she put her hands on his shoulders and looked across to Hergett.

"Tell him you're not looking for a fight."

"Of course I'm not looking for a fight," said Hergett.

Klaus smiled. He turned his head so that his face touched Katharina's hand. "There's nothing a man wouldn't do for this, is there?" he said.

"Nothing," Hergett grinned. "Especially marriage."

"Quite. But that's on another level. Perhaps some day I'll explain it to you."

"Why some day," said Katharina. "Why not today?"

Klaus stroked her hands.

"Until today it was sufficient that you and I talked about it."

"Until today!" Katharina said.

"Amazing! However, it so happens that today I'm not in the mood for it."

"Too bad," said Hergett.

Katharina saw that she was getting nowhere. She decided to try a different tack.

Looking at Hergett, she said.

"Why? Perhaps there'll be another opportunity. Perhaps in Dahme. Wouldn't you like to go to the Baltic with us?"

"I was just going to suggest the same thing," said Klaus. Ignoring her shocked expression, he reached for his glass, emptied it and winked at Hergett:

"As chaperon. If the Landrat hears that he'll give his blessings to the trip yet." He laughed. "He's worried about his daughter's virtue. Men start thinking about virtue when they no longer have a choice. If you come along as police dog, you'll make yourself very popular with him. What do you say, Katharina?"

She stared down at his head, wishing she could look inside it.

Hergett had watched the whole thing without comprehending.

"If this is supposed to be a joke," he said now, "I think it's one of the worst I ever heard."

Klaus acted astonished.

"Who says this is a joke? This is a serious invitation, isn't it?" he asked Katharina.

She flared up: "Of course, as far as I'm concerned it's serious."

"Then we're agreed," Klaus said boisterously. "Vacation à trois, that's original. Dahme is the ideal place for ex-Russian POW's and people with holes in their heads, isn't that right, Katharina?"

He tried to pat her hand.

"Stop that!" she snapped.

"If you need a police dog," said Hergett, "find yourself one elsewhere. This isn't my sort of thing."

"I didn't say you should come along as a police dog," said Katharina.

"Katharina and I wouldn't consider you anything but a companion," Klaus said soothingly. "Right, Katharina?"

She didn't answer right away and Hergett thought there were tears in her eyes.

"Do you mean this seriously, or what is this?" he said to her.

"I want you to come with us, I ask you to come—please!"

143

"But how much will it cost?"

They added it up for him. It was a lot of money for Hergett, but he had already made up his mind.

"All right, at your express invitation I'm going."

Klaus slapped the table with both hands.

"We'll have to drink to that! For heaven's sake, sit yourself down, girl. Where's your glass? Never mind, I'll get it . . ."

His gaiety seemed exaggerated. Katharina sat down at the table. She looked exhausted.

# [ CHAPTER NINE ]

At noon the next day Hergett went into town and bought a few last odds and ends for the trip—a bottle of shaving lotion, a pocket mirror, sunglasses. On the way back he stopped at the door of a grocery store and looked in. It was narrow and dark with shelves up to the ceiling. In front of the counter stood broad-hipped women with legs like columns and worn-down heels. Bottles, heads of lettuce and loaves of bread were sticking out of their shopping bags. The dull-faced girls behind the counter smiled cramped smiles but their eyes remained bitter. The place smelled of soft soap, herring, white cheese and pickling spices. As he took in the picture, Hergett felt some of his cheerfulness escaping like air from a tire. He felt like a deserter, watching from a safe distance the activities on an army parade ground. This was the ordinary, everyday life—how was he ever going to find his way back into it?

He hurried on. Two women emerged from the revolving door of a *café*.

"You can look all over town," one of them said. "You won't find anything like their strawberry cake anywhere."

"It costs only two thousand five hundred," said someone behind Hergett. He looked over his shoulder. It was a young man in an elegant, double-breasted suit with an arrogant looking girl. He let them pass and looked after the girl. She was wearing white shoes with high, spiked heels. Hergett felt the palms of his hands grow moist. He followed them for a while without noticing what he was doing. The young man kept on talking to her. At one point he put his arm around her waist and the arrogant girl smiled lovingly at him. Hergett looked away. He had lain awake half the night, thinking of Katharina. Remembering, he forgot to watch the arrogant girl and when he looked again they were both gone. Hergett stood in the street, his excitement growing. Brazenly he stared at another girl who was looking into a shop window. Seeing him in the glass she turned around. Her face disappointed him and he hurried away. But other girls kept coming his way, all looking rather alike in their thin summer dresses. Some smiled with their eyes when he looked at them and one slowed down so obviously that he made up his mind to speak to her. But at the last instant something stopped him and he went on walking aimlessly. A little later he found himself in an area that seemed familiar. He looked around curiously. Behind the houses on the right a wood began and a moment later Hergett remembered. His heart was beating fast. He could see Evelyn in his mind, in her sleeveless blouse with her tall, smooth legs that could, when she wished, clasp him like a cat's. She hadn't always wished, but sometimes she had.

He had told Klaus and Katharina about Evelyn and Robert the night before and Klaus had said that Hergett's only chance to nail down Robert was probably through Evelyn. Thinking about it now, Hergett knew how much he wanted to see Evelyn again and now that he had found an excellent reason he lost no time and made the rest of the way to Robert's house almost in a run.

When he opened the garden gate he saw Evelyn lying in a beach chair and reading. She wore a two-piece bathing suit and dark glasses. When she saw him she jumped up, dropping her book. He had forgotten how she looked without a dress and he stared at her as if she were naked. He didn't even hear what she was saying and when she took his hand and led him into the house, he followed willingly. It was only when they were inside that he pulled his hand away.

"Are you alone?"

"Robert is at the office and his secretary won't disturb us." She smiled up at him. "We can go to my room, if you like."

"I do," said Hergett.

He followed her down a long, thickly carpeted corridor with large wicker chairs grouped around a low table. The room to which she took him stopped his breath. One entire wall was made of glass with the woods right outside. The low chairs, the wide bed, even two of the walls were covered with silk. He stood for a while, too impressed to say anything. Evelyn sat down on the bed and looked at him with an indefinable expression in her eyes.

"Do you like it?" she asked.

He turned his head. She sat rolled up on the bed with her legs folded under her. Her light hair was bound up in a bright red scarf. The tanned skin across her flat belly and around her slim waist was smooth and without folds or wrinkles and she didn't need a brassiere for her breasts.

"Typical *nouveau riche*," Hergett said in a strained voice.

She smiled again and stretched out to reach for a silver cigarette case and lighter on the low table beside the bed.

"Since when do you smoke?" Hergett asked amazed.

"I've been smoking a long time. Sit down and take off that thick jacket, for heaven's sake. Is this a new suit?"

"Yes."

"You look marvelous in it."

She was different in some way from when he had seen her a few days ago. However, much as he tried, he couldn't define the difference. She held out the cigarettes and, after a moment's hesitation, he took one.

"Since the money reform everybody is *nouveau riche*," she said. "Even those who had money before the war. How are you?"

"Not quite as well off as you are. But even so, I wouldn't like to change places with you. Are you still doing gymnastic work?"

146

"No, not much. But I still sprint, every morning, two hours through the woods. It keeps me fit."

"Yes, one can see it does. You've hardly changed, inwardly or outwardly."

For an instant the undefined expression in her eyes assumed contours but then it was gone again.

"I'll find us something to drink." She got up and smoothed her tiny shorts. "What do you want, whisky, cognac or wine?"

"I've never had whisky."

"Try it. I like it." She went out and came back with two glasses and two bottles and ice cubes. She poured out the whisky and pointed to the other bottle.

"Soda and ice. You can mix it as you like. I forgot the ashtray."

She got it from another table. Hergett stared at the sparse triangle of her bathing shorts. Suddenly he could feel her watching him. He looked up quickly and saw her face, her mouth half open and moist lights in her eyes. He was annoyed with himself.

"Once you liked me as I am. Why should I change?"

She said it indifferently and sat down beside him. He thought he could see her breasts trembling in the narrow halter.

"If I'd liked you as you are, the train would have run in a different direction," he said in the same, casual manner.

"You haven't changed either."

"I'm glad you realize that. But you could have changed me. I did try very hard until I saw it was no use."

"I've been thinking about that," she said, her eyes moist.

He looked at her incredulously. Then he said with great scorn: "So that's what made my ears ring in Vorkuta all the time!"

He took the whisky bottle from the table, looked at the label and put it back.

"You haven't told me why you never married again. Or has the world run out of fools?"

He was satisfied to see the hard anger in her face and said quickly:

"I didn't mean to annoy you."

"Yes, I know you."

"We know each other."

"Perhaps I didn't want to marry again," she said. The anger withdrew into her eyes. "Why should I marry? I couldn't have a better life than I have with Robert."

"That's true. Still—you're not fed up with men in general, are you?"

"And if I am?"

He looked again at her bathing shorts.

"It's none of my business."

The shorts were held together by a small hook on the side. Hergett took it between his fingers and twisted it a little. He noticed her body stiffening and he let go of the hook.

"When does Robert come home?"

"Not before seven." She sounded disappointed. She got up again, went to the enormous window and let down the blinds.

"Too light for you?" asked Hergett.

"In a few minutes the sun comes around to this side. I can't sleep at night when the room is too hot."

"Sometimes at Vorkuta I couldn't sleep either."

Ignoring this, she said:

"Don't you want to drink?"

"Yes," he said, lifting his glass.

"Wait, how about some soda?"

"I finally want to find out what whisky tastes like. It's a disgrace for a man of forty-one not to know."

When he put the glass to his lips he saw her mouth twitching with suppressed laughter. He held it a moment, then he drank it in a single swallow. He could hold back the cough but not the tears. They squeezed out of his squinting eyes and he wiped them off his cheek with the back of his hand.

"Damned," he said. "This is worse than vodka."

Evelyn could no longer stop herself from laughing.

"Another glass?"

"Of course. Now that my throat's already burned it makes no difference."

He played again with the little hook at her bathing shorts. Pushing his fingertips under the rubber band, he asked:

"You're out in the sun a lot?"

"Yes," she moved closer. "Right now that's my chief occupation."

"Otherwise you've nothing to do?"

"No, nothing much—now that we have a maid."

"That's the life!"

"I'm satisfied." She watched impatiently as he lit a fresh cigarette. Until now he had been following a plan and he was certain he could carry it to the end. He started talking about the house, stroked her legs with his index finger, asked how much her furniture had cost, left his hand for a few seconds on the inside of her thigh, as if by accident pushed his shoulder against her breast, asked how this thing was put together and when she showed him the hidden fastener, opened the halter and closed it again while his mouth touched her neck and one of her ears. Then she pulled his head towards her and bit so hard into his lips that he groaned. She fell back, pulling his head down, and he lay at her side, still on his elbow, but when she moved her body underneath his, he pushed himself up and staggered away from her. This was all still part of his plan, including turning around and looking at her again. She stared at him with her head slightly lifted, her face looking like a white mask with the eyes pushed in. For a second he felt wildly satisfied and more than ever determined to carry out his plan. But as he looked down at her, lying there naked, his satisfaction turned to uncertainty and the uncertainty to fire. And he didn't remember the plan again until after she had rolled off him like a cat and gone out. He stayed stretched out, with his hands under his head, waiting for regret to arrive. By the time Evelyn returned, quite a while later, regret had still not arrived and when she asked how he felt, he said "Good!" and it wasn't a lie.

She had put on a flimsy negligee and sat down on the bed again, looking very contented, very pretty, with her long light hair falling over her shoulders like a fine spun fabric. Smiling, she bent over him.

"Now you must stay here," she said. "We'll go away for a few weeks—somewhere—and when we come back we'll see what ve'll do. I told Robert to give you a job in his publishing house."

"You did?"

"Yes. He's quite willing to."

"He is?"

His sarcastic tone unsettled her. She sat up straight and looked at him suspiciously.

"You wouldn't be foolish enough to turn it down!"

"And if I were foolish enough?"

"Then—" she broke off. For a moment her face hardened but a second later she smiled again and put her hands on his chest.

"Think about it. If you don't want to stay here right away, you can come here every day. You can come and go as if you lived here. I'm almost always home around this time. I hope you like it here."

"Very much," said Hergett. He felt her hands moving down from his chest.

"Once upon a time you weren't so skillful," he said.

"Once upon a time,—" she smiled. Her hands were cool and fine-boned. He moved them away from where they were and said: "Why do you think I came to see you today?"

"I don't know," she said, sounding annoyed. "Wasn't what happened just now a reason?"

"One can get that elsewhere."

She looked at him silently. Then she took her hands from his and asked calmly:

"Why did you say that?"

"Why shouldn't I have said that?"

"If you don't know, you're a bastard," she said in the same, calm tone. "You haven't changed at all."

"You're contradicting yourself. Don't I please you any longer?"

"You're like the others one goes to bed with once and forgets before one's dressed again. I'd rather you went now."

Her calmness impressed him. He knew he had gone too far and gave a forced laugh.

"Expecting anyone else?"

She got up, took her bathing suit and went out. Hergett stayed on the bed, pressing his lips together. When she had not returned after fifteen minutes, he dressed, waited a few more minutes, and finally went to look for her. He found her back in her beach chair. She was wearing the bathing suit again and her dark glasses and she was reading her book. She didn't look up when he came near. He stood beside her chair for a while and when she still took no notice of him, he said:

"I'm going away for two weeks. Perhaps by the time I come back you'll remember whether it was Robert who denounced my father."

"You're an idiot," she said, without looking up from her book.

Hergett grinned.

"I don't care what I am if you'll tell me it was Robert."

She looked up at him. "Even if it had been Robert, I'd be out of my mind to turn over the boat in which I'm sitting."

"You'd merely have to change boats."

"Thanks. Your nutshell isn't safe enough for me."

"Your safety was always more important than anything else."

"I can't swim as well as you can."

"The *Titanic*," he said, "was a very big boat and it went down anyhow."

"Oh, go to the devil!" she said.

Still grinning, he went to the gate, waiting for her to come running after him. She didn't. When he looked back, she was reading. He decided never to see her again.

When he arrived at the Schneiders', the family had already sat down for dinner. Schneider was tying his napkin around his neck. He waved towards Hergett with his spoon, asked how he was and added in the same breath that he had fixed everything and Hergett could start his job on Monday.

"Unfortunately that isn't possible," said Hergett, sitting down. He glanced at Katharina and went on: "I'm very grateful you've arranged everything so quickly, but I've meanwhile decided a few days vacation might be good for me."

Schneider looked astonished.

"Oh? I thought you wanted to start as soon as possible. But if you think it's better for you to wait a while, that's all right with me. I won't push you."

"He's right, Karl," said Frau Schneider. "It'll do Herr Buchholz good to rest a while." She turned to Hergett.

"You must sleep a lot and eat well. We're having rice soup tonight."

"Excellent," said Hergett, remembering that they'd already had rice soup for lunch.

Schneider slurped his soup. He held his spoon in one hand and a handkerchief in the other, drying his face now and then.

"If this heat continues we'll have a water shortage again," he said. "Three years ago we had the same situation. We had to forbid the people to sprinkle their gardens but we ourselves did it anyhow, in the middle of the night. One can't let the plants die, can one?"

"At this time of the year people should live by the sea," said Hergett, glancing at Katharina who turned pale. The fact that she seemed so on edge began to annoy him.

"Were you ever at the seaside?"

"No, but my daughter has been."

"So she told me. I've never been there either. Your daughter liked it so much, she wants to go again. She was kind enough to invite me to come along."

"How—what?" Schneider's hand with the spoon sank down and he stared at Hergett vacantly. "Along to where?"

"To come along to Dahme," Katharina said with determination. "We're leaving tomorrow."

Speechlessly Schneider looked from her to Hergett.

"You want to go to Dahme together?"

"Tomorrow morning," Hergett smiled and turned to Frau Schneider. "It'll do your daughter good. I promise to see that she eats well. How many pounds do you want her to gain?"

"I assume this is a little joke," Schneider said coldly.

Hergett hesitated, then he said: "Of course, I'm only going if Herr Langer comes too."

"Herr Langer!"

"His leave was approved," Katharina said sharply.

"Shut up!" Schneider bellowed.

"Of course, we could go without Herr Langer," Hergett said. Katharina looked at him aghast. Before she could say anything Schneider said:

"Katharina is going away with her mother and myself in September."

"Fine, she can do that too."

"Will you kindly leave it to me to decide what my daughter can and can not do?" Schneider shouted. "I won't discuss this any further with you."

It was a critical moment and Hergett decided to try a different tack. He looked at Schneider with an open, winning smile:

"Please don't think I want to interfere with your family affairs. If I'd known where this conversation would lead us I certainly wouldn't have started it. But, after all, you've discussed even more personal affairs with me."

He turned to Frau Schneider.

"Isn't that true?"

Frau Schneider looked very perplexed.

"I don't know what you're talking about."

"I'm amazed," said Hergett. He looked at Schneider who sat in helpless rage staring at his lap.

"That discussion doesn't belong here," he said tightly.

Hergett nodded.

"As you say. You must understand that I'm disappointed. I've been looking forward to this vacation. And everything is still so new to me, I don't know how I'd find my way around if I were alone."

Schneider was silent for a long while. Then he mumbled: "Well, if that's the reason—"

From the maze of thoughts, feelings and shocks inside him the knowledge arose like a puff of heat from a volcano that he had delivered himself into the hands of still another blackmailer. He bent over his plate and said, trembling with rage:

"If my daughter wants to go with you, go ahead. Herr Langer will stay here, however, even if it means that I have to block his leave."

"He will come along!" said Katharina.

"He will not!" Schneider roared. Katharina jumped up, threw her napkin on the table and rushed from the room. For a moment Hergett and Schneider looked at each other, then Hergett turned and followed her out.

They went to Klaus who received them calmly, patting Katharina's head.

"Calm down, my dear. By tomorrow morning he'll make up with Herr Buchholz and everything will be all right." He grinned at Hergett:

"You've done this very well; he'll never forgive you for having destroyed his faith in human nature, as he'll put it. But he won't show it. I owe this trip to you."

"I wouldn't be so sure if I were you," said Hergett. "He said he wouldn't let you go."

"It doesn't matter what he says. I know him better than you do. After all, he is my future father-in-law."

He gave Hergett a hard, level stare and Hergett bit his lip. Katharina got up quickly.

"Let's get the tickets," she said.

"Let's," said Klaus and smiled.

# [ CHAPTER TEN ]

For the first two days after they got to the seashore Hergett hardly saw the other two. The hotel where they were to stay was filled up and Hergett had to move to another one. Looking out at the sea from his window for the first time he forgot his disappointment that he couldn't stay in the same hotel with Katharina. Perhaps it was even better this way. The thought that he might have had to sleep with only a wall between them and him made him wince. He stayed out of their way, leaving the hotel early in the morning and not returning until dinner time.

When he came into the dining room on the third day, he found a new couple at his table. They hardly looked up from their plates and Hergett overheard the man whispering to the woman that it was nervy to ask them to sit at the table with a stranger. The man was short with cold eyes in a round face. It was hard to guess the woman's age. From a close distance her face looked like an open powder puff with a red dot in the middle. She wore rings on all ten fingers of her hands. After lunch the man wiped his mouth:

"I'm going to lie down a while."

"I want to swim."

"Damned dull place."

"Why didn't you go to Rovigno?" said the woman in a bored, husky voice. The man emptied his glass, smacked his lips and rolled himself off the chair.

"You'd have liked that, wouldn't you!"

Hergett looked after them in disgust. He decided to try to get another table. He finished his meal and lit a cigarette, studying the other people. There were the same faces every day—they bored him. On the other hand, observing them was excellent training for him. He began to learn again how to handle knives and forks, not to cut potatoes with a fork and to open a boiled egg with a spoon. He watched sharply how the others did things and every day he became a little surer.

Finally, he put out his cigarette and went up to his room. He looked out the window. In the morning the sky had been slightly overcast, now a wind had come up and blown the clouds away. The greenish water paled a little and started to throw white waves on the shore. Out on the promenade people with enormous hats and rolled up blankets were heading towards the beach where beach baskets and colored beach umbrellas had been put up. It all looked very colorful, very gay and easy, and Hergett, looking at it, felt a dull rage deep inside him. The silence in the room resounded in his brain and he began to feel strangely pained and restless. He put on beach overalls and left the hotel.

The village was not large. It consisted mainly of a few hotels between which the huts of the native fishermen almost disappeared. There was only one road, coming from the west over the dunes, weaving through the houses and then ending abruptly in the sand. There was no railroad station. One had to walk for an hour to the next town or wait for the mail bus that came twice a day. Katharina had told him that most people came here only for rest and for the beautiful beach. And there was indeed nothing else to come for. The little village with its white hotel façades lay lost in the dunes like a washed up seashell, and Hergett felt just as lost as he avoided the noisy crowd on the beach and headed across the sand. Eventually he climbed up the last row of dunes and saw the sea before him. Walking down to the beach he saw in a flat hollow the naked back of a man with two thin brown arms wrapped around it. So as not to disturb the couple he turned away and sat down at another place on the empty beach.

He felt warm from walking. He took off his overalls and looked at the sea and the steep, blue sky above it. The air was filled with the smell of seaweed, two seagulls sailed lazily through the tired silence, their bellies shimmering like silver. Hergett went into the water. It was cold and drew the heat from his body. He didn't come back ashore until his lips were blue.

Under the white light of the sun the sea moved like a playful animal. A few strands of cloud swam along the dim horizon. After a few minutes Hergett was sweating again. He found the silence among the dunes as unbearable as the silence in his room. Aimlessly he walked on trying very hard not to think of Katharina all the time.

He had not seen her since the morning of the day before when she and Klaus had come over to ask if he wanted to join them for a swim. He would have gone with them but at that moment he had thought of their double room again. He said something about a letter he had to write and they left. He knew this was childish and that Katharina would be disappointed in him. And after all, he asked himself, what had he expected? She had told him very clearly what she intended this vacation to be and if he had hoped for more, it was not her fault. Hergett tried to be fair but he found it terribly hard. When finally he returned to the hotel he had half decided to return to Nuremberg the next day.

In his room he stretched out on his bed, concentrating his thoughts on Evelyn. He never thought of Robert.

While he was eating dinner, Klaus arrived. He smiled at the resentful faces of the strange couple and sat down.

"Sorry, I thought you'd finished eating."

"I got here late," said Hergett, recovering from his surprise. "Where's your—I mean where's Katharina?"

"At the hotel. She's a bit sunburned. I don't think she'll be around again today."

"Too bad," Hergett said disappointedly. Klaus looked across the table at the painted face of the woman. She was busily and with dexterity dissecting the exquisite white flesh of a sole.

"Excellent food here," Klaus said admiringly. "Why don't you eat sole, too?"

"It's not on the menu."

"Aha!"

The man with the woman glowered at them. Then he said to his companion:

"It was your idea to come here."

"I like it," said the woman.

"It's an impossible place," said the man. "You with your ocean."

The woman had finished eating. She lit a cigarette.

"Why don't you leave?"

"Not a day earlier than you!"

Hergett pushed back his plate.

"Let's go."

"Good night," Klaus bowed to the painted woman. "Nice company."

"I was going to change tables tonight but they'd already set my place."

"Her rings are worth at least twenty thousand marks. Why didn't you come over to our place last night?"

"I was too tired," said Hergett.

"Then I'll invite you to a stag evening tonight, I hope you won't refuse."

"Well, I don't feel much like it."

"Wait till you've had a few drinks." He took Hergett's arm. "Let's go. Interesting woman, that."

"The one at my table?"

"Yes."

"Well, it's a matter of taste I suppose."

"Only partly. I know that kind. He's a manager or department store owner and she—didn't you notice her cigarette?"

"It stank."

"Opium or something. She probably needs it to kill her disgust for him. Here we go, over to the right—that's the Pirate."

The building rested on thick pilings right on the ocean. Three sides of it were made entirely of glass and the roof of corrugated iron. To reach it one had to cross a narrow plank. Inside, on the tables, stood red kerosene lamps which were already lit although it was not yet dark outside. Old fishing nets, life belts and large chunks of cork hung from the ceiling. At the bar two men with guitars sat singing. When they saw Klaus their dark skinned faces expanded in broad smiles. Klaus waved to them and said:

"They're Italianos. The place belongs to a real, genuine Corsican. God knows how he ever landed in Dahme of all places. Those are his daughters behind the bar."

Hergett saw two girls with black and red striped blouses and tight black velvet pants. They had red scarves around their necks and their dark hair hung gypsy fashion down around their faces.

Klaus and Hergett sat at a table. Most of the people around were young couples who, if they weren't dancing, were sitting in close embraces. Hergett saw a young man at the table next to them who had his hand on the breast of a girl while the girl, with her eyes closed, nibbled at his ear.

"If it bothers you, look away," Klaus said, noticing Hergett's stare. "I've got used to it."

"They certainly haven't any inhibitions."

"Thank God, no. It's bad enough that they must have inhibitions at home. That's why they come here. So they don't have to play hide and seek for a few days. Our moral apostles maintain that this sort of thing never used to exist, but I maintain that it has always existed. They merely used to hide it behind their bourgeois hypocrisy which makes it worse. What do we drink?"

"I don't care, whatever you say."

"That's wrong. With drinks and with women you always have to know exactly what you want." He studied the wine list.

"Come here, you black witch," he said, looking beyond Hergett. Hergett turned and saw one of the Corsican's daughters. She stood right behind him and he was amazed he hadn't heard her. Then he saw she was barefooted. She had small, brown feet with toenails as red as her scarf.

"How do you like her," asked Klaus. "Doesn't she look like a pirate's daughter?"

The girl smiled. She had unnaturally white teeth, a small mouth with pursed lips and eyes like pieces of coal.

"Won't you make music tonight?" she asked Klaus.

"Not tonight—tomorrow perhaps," Klaus said and ordered a bottle of wine. The girl slipped away and Hergett looked after her.

"Wouldn't that be something for you?" Klaus inquired.

Hergett shook his head.

"No, not in the long run."

"Beautiful, but hot," Klaus leaned back and looked around. "Coming from Siberia doesn't all this seem like paradise?"

"I'm trying to tell myself that."

"And?" Klaus looked at him hard.

"I feel superfluous."

"I don't know what you want—isn't this beautiful here?"

"I suppose it is—for those who don't want to play hide and seek!"

"Ah, now you're being honest—" Klaus was interrupted by the girl who brought the wine.

"I've thought of leaving," said Hergett.

"Oh, now—what do you think the Landrat will say if you come back without his daughter? After you've made up with him, you really shouldn't do that to him."

"I wasn't eager to make up," said Hergett, thinking how well Klaus must know the Landrat since he had predicted his reactions so precisely.

"If it hadn't been for Katharina, I wouldn't have done it," he told Klaus. "The man's mad. I'll be glad when I don't have to see him any longer."

"You're not the only one who feels that way," said Klaus, laughing. "But you can't live together the whole time without seeing him, at least not until you find another job. If it makes you feel any better, think of me. That office makes me as sick as the Landrat does you. If anyone had ever told me that one day I'd end up in a *Landrat's* office—the very word makes me want to throw up. I once figured out that there are at least a dozen offices in which we're kept on a registry card. You start with the citizen's registry, then comes the municipal school office and from then on we're continuously under control. There's the finance office and the passport office because it's no longer enough to have a name and a face, you have to prove you haven't stolen the face, and in the meantime you're fighting around with the rent office and the health office. Then there's the labor office and the welfare office, but perhaps they'll replace those again with the recruiting office and from there it's not far to the funeral office where they'll fill out the last card for the register. That's the education of man into citizen; destroy his illusions about individual life so thoroughly that in the end he's quite happy to let himself be shot in the head for the sake of a patriotic slogan. They have to break his spiritual spine to get him to that point; they do that with repeated shock treatments. Our offices hammer home the man's dependency on the state so long and so often that he ends up believing it himself. If you let the present government disappear and another come in its place, you'd see the apparatus would remain as it is. It functioned as efficiently fifty years ago as it did under Hitler and is doing it again today. A magnificent thing, really."

Hergett had to laugh.

"What do you mean by 'magnificent'? First you tear it to pieces and then you say 'magnificent'."

"I'm trying to be objective," said Klaus, emptying his second glass. "Take the atom bomb—it's magnificently thought out and I admire the work that went into it enormously. But that doesn't mean I think the bomb is magnificent."

"Very interesting," said Hergett. "However, now I want to know why you asked me to come along to Dahme."

"Before I tell you that," said Klaus, "I must have another bottle." He carried the empty bottle to the bar. Hergett watched him talking to the Italians. One of them put a half filled glass to Klaus' lips and he tilted back his head and emptied it.

Behind the bar appeared a swarthy man who was dressed like the girls. He had a sharp, deeply lined face and wore a black bandage over one eye. On his head he wore a red beret. He slapped Klaus on the shoulder, and gesticulated with both hands. The Italians, too, were talking rapidly. It looked as if they were trying to persuade Klaus to do something he didn't want to do. Finally when the two girls joined them and one put her hands on his chest, he turned around, made an apologetic gesture toward Hergett, and reached into his coat pocket. The Italians climbed on their stools. Hergett saw that Klaus was holding a harmonica in his hands now. He said a few words to the Italians and they began to play and sing. Some of the young people applauded and ran to the dance floor. Hergett had never heard the song before. He forgot to listen to the voices of the Italians, soft, somewhat melancholy voices that vanished behind the sounds of the guitar and the harmonica. Hergett, who played the harmonica himself, could hardly believe his ears. The sounds were unbelievably high and clear and sent a shiver over his skin. He caught himself looking through a moist veil, through the window at the sea which, at this hour, had gone to sleep between the horizons. It was getting dark, but far away, where sky and sea melted together, a dart of silver flashed now and then across the water. Hergett told himself that all life and living was subject to a rhythmic pattern, like ebbtide and floodtide, lightness and darkness, and that no one should be presumptuous enough to break this pattern merely because it seemed that of all those who had their little burdens, he had been given the worst.

When Klaus came back to the table, Hergett was determined not to begin another argument with him.

Klaus seemed a little drunk. The scar on his forehead looked fresher than usual in the light of the kerosene lamps and the rest of his face was flushed. Under his eyes were copper colored smudges.

He filled first Hergett's glass and then his own, took a big swallow and crossed his arms on the table.

"So what was it you wanted to know?" he asked cheerfully. "Why did I ask you to come along? When a woman misses a man she thinks too much about him and that's not good for the one who's with her. Does that explain it, or must I be more specific?"

"It explains it," said Hergett, forgetting his good intentions somewhat. "It shows you're not as realistic as you pretend to be. I, for instance, wouldn't dream of taking the men my wife is thinking about along on a vacation. With my ex-wife I'd have had to rent an omnibus."

"Well, in that case you certainly can't compare your

situation with mine. I know that Katharina has no other male acquaintances to miss except you. In order to get it over with I asked you along, that's why."

"I can't say you're stupid," mumbled Hergett, lighting a cigarette at the smoky lamp.

Klaus emptied another glass of wine.

"By the way," he said. "You're not going back to the Eastern zone, are you?"

"I don't know. Two weeks ago I thought I knew."

"Well, now," said Klaus, "you're not trying to tell me that things are worse here than over there. Two weeks isn't a very long time and your experiences certainly haven't been that horrible!"

"No, it's something else," said Hergett. He looked at the dance floor. The Italians were playing a tango and the young couples pressed themselves closely together. "The longer I'm here, the more it seems to me I shouldn't have run away from over there. I know it sounds crazy, but I feel like a deserter."

"That sounds crazy indeed. Why?"

Hergett shrugged.

"It's difficult to explain. My sister and her husband are still there."

"That's no reason. There are hundreds of thousands of people here who still have someone over there and yet they don't feel like deserters. No, you can't convince me by that. Perhaps you're homesick?"

"Perhaps. I've already said to Katharina: everything is so sickeningly matter-of-fact."

"Not over there?"

"I was only there a short time."

"Do you know something," said Klaus. "I have the feeling your change of mind had something to do with Katharina."

Hergett closed his eyes for a moment. It was a well-aimed shot and it hit him broadside. Still, he immediately refused to admit it to himself and he said sharply:

"You're oversimplifying things. But as long as you brought it up, why don't you tell me why you never married her."

"That's as complicated as your deserter's complex. Before I explain that let me get another bottle."

"You're evading me."

"You're talking about oversimplification and you're oversimplifying yourself. Actually, it is simple. I want to marry and I can't."

"Why not?"

"As long as I tell you it's because of exterior circumstances—apartment, money, independence from our Landrat—as long as I tell you that, it's still simple. But the moment you look deeper it becomes complicated. Just a moment—"

He went to the bar for a third bottle, flirted with the pirate's daughters who looked like twins in their costume while the Italians sang a song about *Amore* and the father pirate moved the bandage off an eye that looked as black and healthy as the other and winked at Hergett.

"Now we're all settled," Klaus said to Hergett as he came back. "It's the best thing to do. You have to put a little padding over the sharp edges of existence, otherwise you tear your paws. When I sit behind a bottle, I don't feel the sharp edges—"

"You can't sit behind a bottle forever."

"Not forever, but every time I need it I can."

"That's no solution."

"No, but a compromise. Your wanting to go back to the Russian zone is no solution either. What were we talking about just now?"

"I think we better discuss that some other time."

Klaus grinned. "Now you're the one who wants to evade. I told you I want to marry and I can't." He drank another glass of wine and put it back on the table with a bang.

"Have you ever been inside an insane asylum?" he asked abruptly.

Hergett shook his head.

"Well, be glad! I swear to you the healthiest man would go mad if he had to sit in that sort of place for a year. You were a soldier, perhaps you remember the way the faces of men looked after one or two hours continuous barrage. The shooting isn't as bad as the faces around you. Now imagine you'd have to see those faces not just for a few hours, but for weeks and months and years. In the beginning you fight it, as I fought it and everybody else when they first arrive. You run through the house and through the garden, you run up

163

and down in your room or you sit at the window or on the terrace looking up at the damned blue sky that doesn't care whether or not something is wrong inside your head. After the first week I started raving and shouting. But that doesn't last long. After that you're worn down. You don't shout, you don't run around any more, you just sit in a corner and at night you can hear them in their rooms sobbing and praying and putting their faces in the cushions and whining. The entire house whines, the trees in the garden, the stars you can see from your bed and you can pull the blanket over your head or plug your ears, it doesn't stop until you notice that you're whining yourself and when you've reached that stage, the madness is in your own head. Perhaps you'll understand why I don't want to go back to an asylum, ever."

"I understand that, but I don't see at all what Katharina has to do with it."

"Everything." Klaus wiped the wine off his mouth. "As long as I have her I don't think I'll have another attack. Of course, one is likely to fool oneself, but it helps."

"It helps in what way? It helps never to have another attack?"

"That's what I don't know."

"And because you don't know, you don't marry her."

"Yes. I want to but I'm afraid if I married her it might happen again and then it would be twice as bad for her."

"Yes, now I do understand," said Hergett. "That's why you've been leading her on for years. Because you don't have the courage to admit to yourself that you're a sort of hopeless case. You don't care whether you ruin her life along with yours and that's going to happen, whether you marry her or not. You just want to gain some time for yourself. You know exactly where you stand but you're too much of a coward to draw the conclusions. You simply let it roll and you're probably telling yourself at the same time that you're quite a wonderful fellow. Look around nature. It has its barbaric but sensible laws. What's weak is devoured, what's sick, falls off. It was the same in Vorkuta. During the first years we had two or three each day who couldn't go on. At the end I couldn't feel sorry for anyone any more, I myself had enough trouble surviving. Seven years are a long time. Look at the people in the streets in Nuremberg. Every fifth one has a burden around his neck that is so heavy that it pulls him down to his knees when he's alone. And that happens without their having to denounce all the world as you do."

Hergett had talked himself into a fury. He leaned forward towards Klaus who was staring back at him with rather glassy eyes.

"And I'll tell you one more thing," Hergett declared loudly. "Either you marry Katharina within the next eight weeks or you'll keep your hands off her. Perhaps now you know what you have to do."

"I do indeed!" said Klaus and threw the glass into Hergett's face.

Hergett could feel it splinter. For a second the pain blacked out his thoughts. Then he jumped to his feet and quickly made his way through the dancing couples towards the door. Past the frightened white face of a girl he saw Klaus come out from behind the table. His eyes were like those of a rabid dog, bloodshot and protruding. Hergett turned and shaking off a few fists pushed through to the door. A moment later he was outside. Klaus came after him with dangling arms. He was silent. Hergett turned to the right where the houses ended. As he ran, he tried to keep the same distance between them and when they were far away enough from the houses, he let Klaus come up. All the time he felt the blood dripping from his chin. Then he saw that Klaus had also stopped and stood motionless, looking at him. Hergett waited a few seconds. When he went over to him and slapped Klaus' face with his flat hand, Klaus did not stir, and in the darkness his face looked like a white piece of cloth. Hergett left him standing there and went down to the beach. He felt the blood running down his chin and when he reached for it, he touched a glass splinter. He pulled it from his skin with his nails. Then he washed off his face with sea water. The wound burned like fire and Hergett pressed his handkerchief against it. Without turning once to look at Klaus, he walked back to the hotel.

The next morning Hergett got up early. His wound

hurt very badly and it looked inflamed. Trying to shave was painful. Before he had finished dressing, Katharina arrived.

She wore a red sweater with a deep neckline and yellow slacks that made her look like a boy. Her face was pale and tired. Seeing the wound on his chin she asked immediately whether he had seen a doctor. Hergett said that he had no intention of seeing a doctor.

"But you must," Katharina said firmly. "I'll come back in an hour, by that time you'll have finished breakfast. In the meantime I'll find out about a doctor."

He let her go without further protest. Then he went downstairs for breakfast. The couple were sitting at his table again and Hergett looked around for another free seat. He spotted one in the far corner of the dining room and made his way towards it. Two grey-haired men sat at the table and one looked up at Hergett with an unfriendly face and told him that the empty seat was reserved. He said it in a loud voice and Hergett felt that everyone was staring at him. It was only a few yards to his old table and he crossed them in a furious mood. While he was waiting for his breakfast he avoided looking at the painted woman and her man. At the other table a young girl had joined the grey-haired men. She was yellow haired with a large, provocatively painted mouth and she might have been the daughter of one of the men. After watching her for a while, Hergett was convinced she was not a daughter. She was flirting with both of them. While one was whispering something into her ear, she put her white hand on the other's neck. They acted as if they were on a honeymoon à trois. Hergett was annoyed at their foolish giggles, their affected manners and their fat, conceited faces. He became even more annoyed when the painted woman at the table suddenly began to talk French to her man. Hergett rushed through his breakfast and then, getting up and bowing slightly to the couple, said:

"*Au revoir—monsieur, madame.*"

It was about the only French phrase he remembered from school but of course the two couldn't know that. Their embarrassed faces still cheered him when he met Katharina in the hall outside.

"I found a doctor," she said eagerly. "Just a few steps

from here. Afterwards you can go to the beach with me."

Hergett remarked that the doctor must be an eccentric.

"Why?" Katharina asked blankly.

"Because if the weather is good and one is a summer visitor the place is bearable. But to settle here the year around as a doctor—the man must be sick of life. I couldn't stand it here for more than two weeks."

"You don't like it here?"

"No." Hergett looked across the houses at the dunes with their thin grass and the empty sky above it. "It reminds me too much of Russia," he said. "One's always searching to see a church steeple or a wood."

"All you have to do is get on the bus or walk an hour and you'll have as many church steeples as you want."

"Even so," Hergett said crossly.

There were no other patients in the waiting room. Hergett was relieved. He couldn't stand waiting rooms.

He was waiting for her to mention Klaus. She didn't and as the minutes passed he began to feel her silence like a reproach. He looked at the door to the consulting room and cleared his throat.

"Perhaps someone is in there."

Katharina looked at the door too. "Perhaps," she said.

"I can't stand the smell," said Hergett. "What is it—ether?"

"Probably."

"It might be something else."

"It might be."

Hergett wished the doctor would come. When a day started off like this one nothing much good ever came of it afterwards, he knew.

"How is Klaus?" he heard himself say.

Katharina took her eyes off the door and looked at him sideways.

"Do you miss him?"

"I haven't seen him for a while."

"Not really a while," said Katharina. "When he came back last night he wanted me to go to you. He was afraid you might leave. I told him that you wouldn't leave and that I'd go see you this morning. Ever since then he's been sleeping."

"That's good." Hergett took a deep breath of relief.

167

Suddenly it seemed as if everything had settled back into its old order. "People should sleep a lot more than they do," he said, grinning. Then a thought struck him.

"How did you know I wasn't leaving?"

"Well, you didn't, did you?"

The door to the consulting room opened and someone said:

"Will you please come in?"

Hergett went past a woman in a white coat and looked around for the doctor. There was no one in the room. He turned to the woman, noticing that her face was young and pretty and cold.

"You cut yourself?"

"Yes," he said. "Isn't the doctor here?"

"I'm the doctor. How did you do that?"

"On a glass," Hergett said, surprised.

Her fingers were as cold as her face.

"We'll have to stitch it," she decided. Hergett looked around at the tall glass cabinets filled with medicines like the shelves of a pharmacy. In the middle of the room was a leather upholstered table and alongside it an adjustable, leather upholstered chair. In his mind Hergett saw Katharina and while he was stretched out on the table and the doctor sewed the cut on his chin, an obscene image formed in his head.

Twenty minutes later he carried the image out with him to Katharina whose legs in the slim, yellow slacks looked very long.

She didn't want to go to the crowded public beach and Hergett didn't either. He trudged alongside her across the dunes, sweating under his beach overalls, and thinking of the naked back he had seen the day before and the thin brown arms that had held on to it. Beside him Katharina was talking. She was saying it had been her fault because she shouldn't have let Klaus visit him alone. She sounded very depressed and Hergett made some reassuring remark and put his hand on her back. Through the sweater he felt the upper part of her bikini and the image in his head grew very sharp. He caressed it with his thoughts, he talked without knowing what he was saying and the sweat ran from his chest down his stomach and thighs. He saw the dunes and the sea and Katharina, but he saw everything through the

168

image before his eyes. Once he had seen everything through a piece of bread and he had seen it as clearly as he saw the image now. He had looked at the piece of bread with clasped hands; it had been a big piece of bread, crusty, fresh and aromatic, and behind it a few dozen half crazed men had been stretched out, some of whom were already dead. He had wished the others were already dead, too, so that no one could reach for his piece of bread. He'd sat there smiling at it and enjoying the fine aromatic smell and the fresh, crusty look. It was beautiful, as beautiful as the image before his eyes now. Beside him Katharina continued to talk in a self-reproaching monotone, saying it had all been her fault and that she was terribly sorry about his face and that he had had to have it stitched. He heard her ask what he had been discussing with Klaus and his voice answered by itself because his mind was preoccupied with the image. They stopped and it was pleasant to see through the image Katharina pulling the sweater over her head and dropping her yellow slacks, pleasant and enjoyable to see her sitting down and stretching out on the sand with her long legs, her smooth skin and dark hair shadows under her arms. He saw her through the image as through a badly adjusted lens, with blurred contours. Bending over her he met with no resistance. Her mouth was cold when he kissed her and he tried to push away the upper part of her bikini. She slapped his hands but now he was obsessed by the need of finding out how her breasts felt and they struggled with each other. Through his picture he saw her distorted face and he wanted to put her legs in the position they had in his image. She pounded his mouth with her fists and when he let go of her for one second, she scrambled to her feet and raced off. With that the image evaporated in Hergett's mind. For a moment he sat looking at her sweater and at her yellow slacks. Then he grabbed them and ran after her. He ran very fast and after a few hundred feet he caught up with her and when she didn't stop he pulled her down on the sand. Panting he held her arm. Katharina, too, was panting. She lay with her face in the sand and Hergett waited until he had caught his breath. Then he threw her clothes down beside her and went back to the place where they had been. He picked up his beach overalls and put them on. He didn't see her again until he started walking back along the edge of the water. She was standing in the same place where he had left her, wearing the yellow slacks and the red sweater again. When Hergett came up level, she called his name. He kept on walking. A few minutes later he heard her running after him. He felt nothing, neither shame nor guilt nor disappointment. He kept on walking with big strides and Katharina had trouble keeping up with him.

"Ever since I met you I'm doing everything wrong," she said breathlessly. "I always think I'm doing the right thing and then it turns out that it was the worst I could do. When Klaus came back to the hotel last night and told me what had happened, I wanted to ask you to leave. I'm tormenting you and I'm tormenting myself, but I no longer know what else I can do. Perhaps it's better for you to leave after all. I can't bring myself to ask you to, but I think it would be better."

"I was going to leave anyhow," said Hergett. He had a leaden feeling in his legs, not only in his legs but also in his head and in his arms and he told himself he ought to have a drink. If a man is strung up the way I am, he told himself, he has to drink or he has to go to a whore. To a whore or Evelyn. He stopped.

"Go on," he said. "Go on, hurry up, keep on going."

She looked at him with swimming eyes and whispered: "That's not right, what you're doing now is not right."

"I know. To let me make love to you and then act the wildcat isn't right either. It doesn't matter."

"I didn't ask you to make love to me. I should have slapped your hands right away. I didn't and that's why I've come running after you."

"In order to do it now? You could have saved yourself the trouble. You didn't ask me to make love to you and I didn't ask you to run after me. I don't see why you're still standing around here. Or did you like being made love to after all?"

It had slipped out in anger and he already regretted it when she turned and walked quickly away. At this moment he could have shot himself, but Katharina didn't know that.

Katharina didn't even know she was crying. She put one hand in her pocket and walked faster and faster and in the end she broke into a run. Never in her life had she needed Klaus more than now. When she reached the village street she ran so fast that people turned to look at her.

Klaus was lying stark naked on his bed when she came in. She went straight to the wash basin and squeezed a wet sponge over her face.

"You should get up," she said. "It's time to eat."

When he didn't answer she turned and saw him looking at her with a tense expression.

"Did you hear me?" she asked.

He moved his head. "Yes. Are you hungry?"

"No."

"Neither am I. I'm not hungry and I'm not in the mood to go down. Why are you sweating so?"

"I've been running." She took off everything except her tiny shorts and held her breasts under the cold, running water.

"Must have been a hot conversation," said Klaus, watching her as she dried herself and reached for her dress.

"Come here," he said.

With the dress in her hand she went to him and sat down on the bed. He took away her dress and put his hands around her waist.

"A sad conversation," he said. "Perhaps a good-bye conversation?"

She nodded. Two drops rolled from her eyes past her nose and she caught them with her tongue.

"I didn't intend to have that happen," said Klaus. "I'd rather have him stay. Is he hurt?"

"His chin. I went to the doctor with him. He had to have stitches taken."

"Damned bad luck. Is that why he's leaving?"

"No."

"Because of you?"

"Yes."

"It was inevitable. You were asking too much of him."

"Not more than you of me."

"What am I asking of you?"

She looked down at him.

"Are you tired of it?" he asked after a pause.

"If I were tired of it I'd have gone with him. But you should marry me before I get tired of it. I can't go on like this." She lay down alongside him and cried. "I can't go on like this, Klaus. Help me!"

"How can I help you?"

He didn't understand her but for the moment she thought he could help her and she clung to him very tightly and kissed him and for a few minutes she was happy again.

After a while she said:

"Everything is so complicated. I want to know at last what I'm living for. You're always worrying your head about things we can't change. Let's marry, please, Klaus. Perhaps there'll be even more problems then but one can at least try to solve them."

"You can't separate the problems and our lives."

"Because you've knotted them together," said Katharina. "I don't care to look further ahead than I can see. If people marry they are busy enough worrying about each other. You know, on the train up here I wished something foolish. I wished I'd never have to get off again."

"That's very foolish indeed. Somewhere you always have to get off."

"You don't understand how one can wish something like that?"

"No." He kissed the palm of her hand. "The only train you'll never have to get off from is a different train you'll be sitting in one day. It has no windows and a train without windows is very monotonous. You liked sitting at the window didn't you? Next year—"

"Next year," she interrupted him, "I won't go away on a vacation unless we're married. I'll never go again unless we're married. A lot can happen in a year, but this is one thing I know for certain."

"Is that an ultimatum?"

"I suppose. You can choose between me and your principles. Others have started with less money and they've made it. We've both become lazy, we don't want to face troubles. But that doesn't get us anywhere. Once you're in the water, you have to swim. You only learn it once you're in the water."

"Your brother didn't learn it."

"At least he tried. He had more courage than you and I."

She lay close to him. Suddenly he reached out and crushed her against himself with painful, breathless violence, then she fell away from him and buried her face in the pillow. He stroked her back, tried to turn her around, and when she resisted he became energetic. He thought she wanted it this way and pressed down her arms. Something in her face warned him but he didn't think it possible and when she kicked him with her feet, he was still laughing.

She struggled with him as she had struggled with Hergett. Within a few seconds her feelings had changed from total submission to wild, blind hate. She fought and struggled and when he pressed his knee between her legs, she kicked him away so hard that he fell on his back. With that outbreak her emotions were exhausted. She waited, with closed eyes, for him to fall upon her. She neither wanted to be killed, nor was she afraid of it. After waiting for a while, she opened her eyes and saw him sitting on the end of the bed with his legs pulled up and a distracted expression on his face. Looking at him it seemed inconceivable to her that she had kicked him away. Her immediate feeling was pity and despair. She whispered his name, and when he didn't answer she crawled to him and put her head on his knees and began to weep without a sound. Then she felt his hand stroking her neck. She lifted her face and saw that he was smiling at her. She was so surprised, she forgot to cry. Not even his voice sounded changed when he asked her if she had noticed anything.

"I was amazed last night," he said. "At first I ran after him in my rage, but only a little while, then I was all right. I kept on after him but only in order to apologize. He must have misunderstood that. He came over to me and slapped my face. Then he went down to the beach. The odd thing is that it didn't affect me at all. I was completely calm, as calm as I'm now. If I hadn't thrown that glass I'd really think I'm all right again. A year ago no one could have kicked me or slapped my face."

"It's a marvel," whispered Katharina. "I've always told you you're getting better. You've never wanted to believe me."

He nodded.

"Yes, you said that, but that thing in the Pirate—that shouldn't have happened."

"It would have happened to any man in your place," she said. "That was something entirely different. Every man fights if someone tries to steal his woman."

"If I could only be sure."

"I'll tell you until you know you are: you're healthy, healthy, healthy!" She kissed his face, laughing while the last tears were still running down her cheeks and some of her confidence jumped over to him.

"I noticed it last week at the office," he said eagerly. "When this Wagner was trying to insult me. I don't think I'd have taken that so calmly in the old days."

"Of course not," said Katharina and she was herself convinced. Now that the ugly incident was over and she had overcome her shock at her own behavior, she began to think more calmly and told herself that perhaps it was meant to happen this way, that this had been the only way to prove to him that he wasn't prone to attacks any longer. She felt only a trace of insincerity when she told him about her thoughts and said she had really seen no other way to convince him he was healthy.

"You are the cleverest girl alive," he assured her, laughing. He bent her head backwards so that she came to rest with her back across his legs and when he began to caress her she did not resist him.

Afterwards she felt that things between them had never been so beautiful, and she started making plans for their marriage. She smoked a cigarette with him and they talked about their plans all the rest of the day.

But late at night, long after Klaus had fallen asleep, she lay beside him with open eyes, nourishing a flat, shallow feeling of satiation. She remembered how it had felt when Hergett's hand touched her hip. She hadn't intended it. She had gone with him in order to talk it out with him, but most of what she wanted to tell him had not been said. From the moment they had started across the dunes she had no longer been herself. If he had gone

174

more slowly, if he hadn't right away tried to push away her bikini, she might not have resisted him. She had to admit that she had not disliked his touch. His excitement had, for a moment, infected her and she had felt the sudden urge to help him. Instead, she had slapped his face. And now, with Klaus, she had done almost the same thing. Thinking about it she fell into a helpless mood, no longer knowing where she stood with herself. Although she fought against it, the impression grew stronger that her reaction against Klaus was an act of sudden repulsion. When her physical tension had found no release in his painful embrace, her innumerable humiliations and disappointments had burst open like a boil. With Hergett it had been different. Her desperate resistance was against her own desire rather than against him. It had taken her last will power to run away from him. Inwardly she had wanted him to force her to submit. Of all the insight of the past years, this was the most honest and the most painful to admit and she no longer tried to interpret it any other way. She lay stretched out, her eyes wide open, thinking only of Hergett. Probably he had taken the afternoon train. He would arrive at Nuremberg in the middle of the night. She didn't think he would go back to her parents. The idea of his waiting for the morning on a bench or in the railway station tortured her. She began to cry again and she wished that Klaus would hear it and console her. But he was sleeping soundly. She heard him snore until her own eyes closed and she fell asleep.

## [ CHAPTER ELEVEN ]

When Hergett climbed off the train, he still didn't know what he was going to do. The ride had been long and the train overcrowded. He hadn't slept and his thoughts went around in circles.

Standing on the dark, sooty platform he felt that he

had returned to the starting point of an exploratory journey. If nothing else he had gained experience. All in all he would have nothing to complain of if the immediate future were as clear to him as the present. Katharina and Klaus would not return for another ten days. If Hergett went to Schneider now he would have to give an explanation and that would certainly not tally with Katharina's version. He had no other choice but to wait. He had to solve the problem of living quarters anyhow, but how could he, alone and without connections? There was a waiting list at the housing office and with his empty pockets a hotel was out of the question. But there remained Evelyn. In Dahme he had quite naturally assumed that he would go to her. Now he no longer did. Besides, it was four in the morning, hardly a good time for a visit, especially after the way they had parted the last time.

Hergett went to the waiting room, put his suitcase behind the chair and sat down, ordering some coffee. There were quite a few people around. Some of them slept with their heads on the tables and Hergett became aware of how tired he was. He rubbed his stubbly chin, thinking of the pretty room in Schneider's house. Evelyn's room had been even prettier. It was a damned beautiful place and perhaps she was telling the truth, perhaps she really had been against the divorce and had waited for him all this time. Her words sounded very convincing, especially now while he was sitting in the grey waiting room and thinking of her pretty room. Still, she stuck to Robert. And Robert, Hergett was sure, had denounced his father. Even if he couldn't do anything about that, Hergett could certainly not go and see them again. It struck him how his attitude towards Robert had changed within a few days. A week ago he had been determined to call Robert to account. Today he was satisfied with the intention of avoiding his house. Thinking back over the past days he remembered a few other things and he had to shake his head, asking himself whether he had always been this way. But as he questioned himself, he thought of Robert and Evelyn and even of Katharina and he began to feel like a man treated unjustly. Anyone, he told himself, would have reacted the way he had. He was no worse than anyone else. He was no worse than that fat man at the next table, with his well-fed, Philistine face, or the other one over there, with a silver-grey tie and a dark suit. Hergett looked at them accusingly. They had been worshiping their bellies and building themselves fat homes while he was breaking stones in Vorkuta. They had their women, they had everything else a man could want. They had all been better off than he and Hergett decided that this would be changed in the future. If he wanted to change it though, he would have to do away with scruples—scruples didn't help one, he knew. Certainly not with Robert. Why should he in any way consider Robert or Evelyn? Of course, if he went to see her she would assume he had softened again. Let her think so, then! For the moment he needed her and when the day came when he didn't need her any longer, she'd see her mistake. What else was her bubbling benevolence than the sign of a bad conscience? Why the offer of a job on Robert's newspaper? The moment he'd let himself become dependent on them, they would show their claws again. It annoyed Hergett that they would think him so stupid and his obstinate pride came to the fore. Perhaps he could think of another way out after all. But, much as he racked his brains, he couldn't think of one. He had only fifty marks left in his pocket, one couldn't get far on that. It was all very difficult.

He got up and found the men's room. When he came back, his suitcase was gone. He saw it from a distance and it gave him a sudden feeling of nausea. He asked the people at the next table whether they had seen who had taken his suitcase. They looked at him dumbly and Hergett ran past the tables towards the exit. Just as he reached it someone grabbed his sleeve.

"Just a moment," said someone. Hergett turned and saw that it was the waiter, looking very determined. With a hasty explanation Hergett pressed his wallet into the waiter's hand, and hurried on. But when he came into the hall and saw the throng of people rushing to and fro, he stopped. It was hopeless. The waiter told him that too, when he picked up his wallet at the counter.

"You should have taken the suitcase with you," he said. "Or checked it at the counter. It happens every day. Was there any money in it?"

Hergett shook his head.

"Then you were lucky," said the waiter. "We had one case where someone had ten thousand marks in a stolen briefcase. Go and inform the railroad police, it's to the right when you come out."

"Thank you," said Hergett. He paid for his coffee, took his wallet and went out into the hall again. He still couldn't think clearly. For a moment he considered going to the police but then he told himself that they couldn't bring back his suitcase either. When he thought of the electric razor his eyes actually filled with tears of rage. Since the death of his father, no loss had hurt him so and when he left the station a few minutes later he felt that in losing the electric razor he had also lost Katharina.

Tears still blinded his eyes as he walked the streets without paying any attention to where he was going. At this early morning hour he hardly encountered a soul. The sound of his steps broke against tall stone walls, resounded across empty squares, echoed like a series of small explosions along the narrow canyons of the streets. The upper rows of the windows suddenly flamed up red with the reflection of the scarlet colored sky, then a church steple lit up, the brass ornaments on a door, the gold paint of an old fountain and a little later, after Hergett had walked up a steeply inclining street, he saw the entire town aflame in the morning sun. He looked at the red-tinted silhouettes of the gables, towers and cupolas before him. But he saw, too, the bombed residential areas, the burnt-out walls with their black window caves and he thought of the men in Vorkuta having scurvy, their teeth falling from blackened gums.

In petrified silence the city lay like an enormous cemetery between the horizons. Clouds of vapor rose from its depths, rolled along the banks of the River Pegnitz, past jagged ruins which in the silence of this early morning hour resembled weatherbeaten tombstones; and in the cool light of the morning the façades of the modern office buildings looked like the white marble slabs on the grave of the unknown soldier in Erfurt.

But the city was not dead. Hergett sensed the beating of its heart; its multitudinous noises grew into a dull throb that swelled up in proportion to the blue streaks appearing in the dull grey sky. As if a motor of gigantic power were pumping out the houses, the furrows of the streets filled with life. This was not a festive sunrise like those Hergett remembered having seen in the Thuringian woods. It semed to him he was looking at a marked face, marked by some fatal disease, and he thought he felt the earth under his feet trembling in feverish delirium. The blind eyes of a thousand windows stared up at him, hostile and forbidding, and again Hergett felt excluded and he couldn't get rid of the feeling when he freed himself from the sight and started slowly walking downhill again.

The sleepless night, the stolen suitcase and all his other burdens threw him into a state of indifference and tired resignaton. The streets were full of people with exhausted faces. They all seemed to hurry at the same speed, they looked dull and distracted and no one paid any attention to anyone else. They would have hurried on if a corpse had lain in their way. After a quarter hour Hergett could no longer stand the rush. He left the main street for another, quieter one and thought that perhaps in ten days he, too, would be running; he would run every morning to a certain building and sit behind a desk, eight hours long. His whole life long.

He walked the rest of the way to Robert's house without thinking. He trotted like a horse to its stable and he no longer cared that it was too early for a visit. His head was bent and he didn't notice a car stopping and someone calling his name. Then he looked up and saw Robert getting out of his car and crossing the street towards him. It was a beautiful car and Hergett wondered how much it must have cost. He felt rather embarrassed and overlooked Robert's outstretched hand. Robert smiled without being angry.

"I had to look twice before I believed it. Evelyn told me you'd gone away for two weeks."

"I came back earlier."

"I'm glad. Evelyn is still in bed but I'm sure she'll be glad to get up for you. Nice weather today, isn't it?"

"Yes," said Hergett.

Robert looked past him at the trees.

"The summer is short. Since we live here I don't notice much of it. In Ilmenau it was different." He glanced at his watch, mumbled something about an important conference and, saying he hoped to see Hergett at lunchtime, left.

Hergett went on. Five minutes later he stood before the house. The little gate was locked today. He rang the bell and it was opened electrically. Hergett went along the gravel path to the entrance where a maid in a white apron was waiting for him. She looked him up and down contemptuously and asked what he wanted.

"Madame is still asleep," she said.

The thought that she might leave him standing in front of the door was too much for Hergett. He pushed her aside and went into the hall where he sat down in a chair.

"I'm going to wait here." He almost snarled. "Tell Madame, Monsieur is here."

The girl hesitated, then she disappeared into Evelyn's room. A moment later she came out again and said very politely:

"Madame's expecting you."

Getting up, Hergett wondered to how many men she had said that.

Evelyn sat at her dressing table in a negligée.

"I recognized your voice right away," she said. "I'll be ready in a moment."

"Don't rush for my sake," said Hergett. He looked at the unmade bed. Light blue pyjamas hung over the back of a chair. Hergett put his hand under the thin fabric.

"Clear as glass," he said.

"It's nylon. It's all you need in bed."

"Nylon," he said. "Never heard of it. Why wear anything at all?"

"If you ever see me wearing it, you'll know why."

"I can imagine. You rather love yourself, don't you?"

"If I ever stop loving myself, I'll put on a flannel nightgown." She came over to him, her face looking fresh and good as always. "Two weeks seemed too long, did they?"

She was going at him hard; it was clear she hadn't forgotten his last visit. Sitting down he took off his jacket, threw it on the bed and yawned.

"We can talk about that later. But if you don't mind, not now. I haven't slept for twenty-four hours."

"You look it. What did you do to your chin? Are those stitches?"

"Yes," he said, remembering that the doctor had asked him to come back in a week to have the threads pulled out. "I fell into a pane of glass."

"Oh?" she sounded incredulous but didn't pursue the subject further except to ask whether this was the reason for his not having shaved. When he told her he had lost his suitcase, she shook her head.

"How stupid of you to leave the suitcase standing there."

"It's easy to have afterthoughts. Do you go to the toilet with a suitcase?"

"You said you arrived at four this morning?"

"Four five to be exact."

"From where?"

Her tone annoyed him. It sounded imperious and a shade more unfriendly than he could stand. He got up, picked up his jacket. Evelyn stepped in his way.

"Don't be an ass. Can't one ask you a question?"

"Not when I'm this tired. Don't you remember?"

"One can't remember everything. Give me your jacket."

He hesitated and she simply took it from his hands.

"We've guest rooms," she said. "But if you want to you can sleep here."

"If your maid doesn't faint I'll sleep here."

"Maids don't faint. Do you want a bath first?"

"When I wake up."

"I'll get you a pair of Robert's pyjamas."

"I don't want a pair of Robert's pyjamas."

"As you like. Will it bother you if I stay here?"

"It's your room, isn't it?"

She watched him undressing, then she lay down beside him.

"I'll never understand," he said afterwards. "How a woman who's once been so sick of a man, can be so wild about him again thirteen years later."

"I've explained it all to you."

"That you didn't want a divorce?"

"Yes."

"You didn't let me make love to you for a long time before the divorce," he said.

"Many women go through that sort of thing. It doesn't mean one loves a man less."

"Explain that to a smarter man. I'd like to know what goes on in your head."

"Half as much as you think. Are you back with me?"

"What do you mean?"

"It is as simple as the question."

"And you think with that you can wipe out everything that's happened?"

"Yes," she said. "Just as the war and Hitler and the Third Reich have been wiped out. We've all had to start over again and no one had time to ask what was before. No one said he couldn't go back to his old house because he'd lived in it during the Third Reich. No one has said he'd have to find another profession because he was ashamed to have been a street car conductor or a bank director under Hitler. They've all started again where they left off."

"Where did you leave off?"

"With you."

"That was forty-two, not forty-five."

"It was in the Third Reich," she said. "We all left off in the Third Reich, whether in forty-two or forty-five doesn't matter."

Hergett turned over on his side to be able to look at her. What she said sounded all very reasonable, but perhaps it was too reasonable.

"When two people have been married," he said, "they can no longer fool each other. You have, it seems to me, forgotten a lot."

"Only the unimportant things. I'm going to tell you something, Hergett." She pulled his head close and looked into his eyes. "It wasn't our fault. It was simply that I didn't feel at ease in that environment. Forgive me, I know how you felt about your father. But a woman doesn't want to share her man with anyone. You never cut yourself loose from him. In everything that concerned the two of us you asked your father first before you discussed it with me. No woman can stand that. I felt like a school girl."

"You could have considered all this before."

"It was a mistake. I overestimated both of us. I told myself I could get used to the set-up for your sake."

"I suppose it wasn't elegant enough for you?" he asked scornfully.

"It has nothing to do with elegance. It was simply, to be very frank, too plebeian. I was married to the dust-cloth and the laundry tub instead of to you. I'm just not the type of housewife you and your father had in mind. I was sick, so sick, of cleaning the staircase on Mondays, the basement on Tuesdays, and the study on Fridays. And God help me if I ever forgot anything. You ran your days on such a rigid schedule. All those dear daily habits you wouldn't give up! But those weren't my habits. You asked me to change completely; I was to adapt myself entirely to your way of life. And neither of you ever thought of meeting me halfway, of helping me a little. I married into a family, with all the disadvantages and dependency of such a marriage. I'd never want to go through anything like that again."

"If I remember clearly," said Hergett, "you were quite glad about it at the time. You could bring your brother along. And you hadn't lived as cheaply in Arnstadt as you did with us. If you talk about the disadvantages, you mustn't forget the advantages. There were more than you care to remember now."

"Oh, I'm not forgetting that. And I bore up under it long enough and I would have borne up even longer if it hadn't been for Robert losing his patience. Your father got more and more peculiar as time went on. You couldn't do anything right for him. You weren't home then. From the day they drafted you there was no living with him. There's a limit for every woman, you know. The ideal marriage would be to have a man one likes as much as I like you and at the same time to have a life with a few little freedoms left."

"Like you have now?"

"Yes. Today I have that kind of life, but now I don't have the right man."

"We could marry again, couldn't we?" said Hergett, grinning.

She let go of his head.

"I've thought of that, too. Of course, we'd have to spend some time getting used to each other again first."

"Of course. I suggest a period of, say, ten years. Would that be long enough?"

"Tell me something," she said. "What on earth are you thinking of when you come to see me?"

"I'm asking myself," he said. He remembered that he didn't want to make a mistake and added: "Probably it has nothing to do with thinking. When I married you my brains weren't much involved in the process either. For a woman this should be a compliment."

She laughed, stretching out like a cat.

"I prefer that kind of compliment to any other," she said. "Ever since I've been well off, people keep proposing to me. When I tell them that I can't have children, they all babble about this being the ideal kind of marriage for our age. That's one thing in which you were an exception. How do you feel about that today?"

"The same way."

"Oh? But you must admit it's pleasant not to have to be careful."

"It has its points. Also I've come to the conclusion that I'm too old for children."

"Then it's no longer the same."

"It is, in principle. In principle I feel that children are a necessary part of the whole thing. But one should have started earlier. When I was born, my father was twenty-five. I'm forty-one now and I have enough troubles with myself. It makes me feel queasy to think of the near future."

"Robert says he'll stick to his offer."

"That's not the point," said Hergett. "I prefer my independence. What I need is an apartment. Haven't you any connections?"

"Why? Don't you like it any longer where you are now?"

"One can't always live in a hotel."

"In which hotel?"

Hergett hesitated and looked at her suspiciously. Her question had sounded ironical.

"What difference does it make."

"There are no hotels in Erlenstegen. Don't tell me you've fallen unhappily in love with the Landrat's daughter!"

Hergett whistled through his teeth. "Good work! How did you manage that?"

His admiration was greater than his anger. Evelyn explained that one could get such information for fifty pfennigs at the citizen's registration office.

"I see," said Hergett. "Was the Landrat's daughter included in the fifty pfennigs?"

"No," Evelyn admitted. "But once we knew where you were living the rest was simple. A good newspaper has to know about the family life of the Landrat or else its reporters aren't worth their money."

"Spying on me is hardly the job they've been hired for, is it?"

"No one was spying on you. I just didn't want you to fall into the hands of some strangers who'd cheat you out of your last money. How did you get hold of the Landrat?"

"How did Robert get hold of his publishing house?"

"Oh stop it! If you're too proud to let us help you, you shouldn't have come here in the first place."

"Would you have preferred that?"

"I think I've answered that question," she said coolly. "And I meant what I said. Robert and I have shown our faith in you. You shouldn't do anything to disappoint it."

It was exactly what he had anticipated. In a biting tone he said:

"Are you already appealing to my gratitude?"

"I'm not appealing to anything. I only want to know where I stand with you. I've told you where you stand with me. I respect myself too much for anything else. If you behave again the way you did the last time, you certainly needn't put in an appearance here again. I've managed somehow to live without you long enough and, if you don't come to your senses, I'll make do without you in the future, too. Remember that!"

He watched in silence as she climbed over him and went naked to the closet from which she took a pair of white shorts.

"My morning run through the woods," she said, pulling on the shorts. "Afterwards I take a bath and then breakfast. I do that every morning."

"Even if it rains."

"Even if it rains. You don't notice it much under the trees."

"Very admirable," he said. "What happens if you run across a man in the woods who finds out you're wearing nothing underneath?"

She came over to him and kissed him on the mouth.

"No one has ever undressed me against my will," she said. He tried to hold her but, laughing, she slipped away.

"You were supposed to be tired. Get some sleep."

"*Bon*," said Hergett.

She was gone a long time and he tried to sleep. But half an hour later he felt so wide awake that he had to get up and walk around the room. He tried out the various chairs, examined the innumerable little bottles and boxes on the dressing table, smelled the transparent pyjamas that were still hanging over the back of the chair. When he crumpled them together he could hide them in his fist. Next to the dressing table stood a dainty writing desk. Hergett hesitated a moment before pulling open a drawer. It was filled to the top with letters. He took out a few and started to read. The author of the first one was Walter and Walter complained that he hadn't heard from Evelyn. He reminded her of certain promises and of the hours they had spent together. The next letter was from Walter, too. Then came another handwriting. The name was indecipherable and the letter consisted mainly of words that might have come from a handbook on zoology. Hergett read a few lines, then he put the letters back on top of the others, carefully closed the drawer and sat down on a chair.

By the time Evelyn came back, he had half dozed off.

"Why didn't you stay in bed and sleep?" she asked. Her face was damp and her hair all tangled.

"I was trying to think," said Hergett.

"You're making me curious. But don't tell me anything before breakfast, or I'll collapse with hunger. We can take a bath together."

The bathroom was enormous. Gleaming blue tiles all the way to the ceiling, a big tub, a glass shower stall, two wash basins and mirrors wherever one looked. Hergett was amazed.

He watched her splashing around under the shower. When he went over to her, she pulled him quickly under the ice cold spray. It took his breath away. He swore and tried to get away from her but she clung to him and for a while they behaved like newlyweds.

"Some bath, this!" Hergett said later. "In Vorkuta I spat in my hands every morning and rubbed my face."

"How awful," said Evelyn. She let him dry her and asked:

"Isn't it like making up for the honeymoon we never had?"

"One could think so."

"Promise me you'll stay here."

He looked down into her face. Under her white bathing cap it looked even younger. There was no trace in it of the men who wrote the letters in her writing desk. Hergett felt a fine, razor-sharp pain when he thought of it. An hour ago, when he had read them, he had been indifferent. He took the bathing cap off her head and wound her long hair around his fingers.

"You said yourself that we'd have to get used to each other first."

"We can only do that when you stay here."

"I haven't said yet that I'm leaving."

"Not yet."

"Then give me time. You've had seven years, since 1945."

"Haven't you?"

"No," said Hergett. "For me this is an entirely different situation. I couldn't know then what I know today. We were sitting in two different trains."

"I've always sat in yours, only you didn't notice it."

"Then I need even more time to get used to it."

He said things he did not mean to say. He was saying words that were not his thoughts because he didn't want to do anything that might put an end to the pleasant, comfortable situation.

It was a lie that might trigger off enormous conflicts—he had no idea exactly what kind of conflicts, but his instinctive fear won out, even over the quick regret he had felt at Evelyn's disappointed face. He let go of her hair and said soberly:

"You must understand. I used to be more ruthless. When I saw something I liked I just made up my mind and took it. But if I started again now, there mustn't be a risk."

"The risk is as big for me as it is for you," she said crossly.

"No, it's not. You'll always live with Robert, with or without Hergett. This time it would be me who'd have to leave if it didn't work out between us."

"And the more you talk about it, the sooner it'll get to that point."

"The less you talk about it, the worse it hits you when it happens. I don't want to be surprised again."

"In other words, you're not staying?" she said.

She was forcing him to a decision which a few minutes ago he had thought he could postpone indefinitely. He felt faint. It wasn't so much the unquenchable desire for a woman which he had suppressed so many years, it was the sudden, furious revolt against another renunciation, another injustice of fate—instead of answering he carried Evelyn into her room and pressed her to him as if he could smother all the despair and the helplessness and the disgust in a wild embrace. It didn't help for much longer than the embrace lasted, in fact, afterwards he seemed to feel worse but he said nothing. Evelyn, seeing an answer to her question in his wild love-making, didn't bring up the subject again. She merely smiled and said that it was most strenuous to teach sense to a bull-head like him, especially before breakfast.

Anyhow, it was too late now for breakfast. They could wait half an hour for Robert and have lunch with him. She gave Hergett an electric razor, a new toothbrush and when he reappeared, ten minutes later, fully dressed and freshly shaved, she led him through the house, showing him the guest rooms, the kitchen, the dining room, Robert's bedroom and, finally, the study. There, behind a typewriter, sat a young girl with a long pony tail and indolent eyes that gave her madonna-like face a knowing air. Hergett waited for Evelyn to introduce him to the girl, but she didn't. He had the feeling that there was a tension between them. In the living room she brought it up herself.

"Robert has a weakness for her," she said. "She knows it and is a little saucy. But I'll get it out of her yet."

"He has taste," said Hergett with a thin smile. "Isn't she about thirty years younger than he?"

"Almost. I hope he isn't stupid enough to start anything with her. He has enough others. Would you like a drink before lunch."

"I'd feel very much like having another whisky."

"Poor man, of course. Having worked so hard."

She wore plaid slacks and a trim blouse. Hergett watched her going to the other end of the room to a little bar he had noticed before. Evelyn took the whisky from a glass cabinet behind the bar that was filled with bottles. Hergett asked why the glass panes were so thick. Evelyn explained that the cabinet was at the same time a refrigerator and showed him the refrigeration coils under the glass. Behind the bar there were also an electric grill, a coffee machine and an ice machine. Hergett's eyes were wide with wonder. When Evelyn inquired how he liked the high fidelity set, he admitted that he had mistaken it for a sideboard. She opened the two doors of the set, explained the mechanism to him, pointed out the eight loudspeakers and the built-in tape recorder. She showed him how to say a few words into the microphone and a little later he heard his own voice coming back from all the loudspeakers. It sounded strange and he was so nervous he stuttered. Seeing his face, Evelyn shouted with laughter. She turned on the record player and Hergett stood transfixed, watching the records falling down automatically.

"You're so wonderfully stupid!" Evelyn was touched, and kissed him on the mouth. "Your whisky's on the table."

"In a moment," Hergett stayed in front of the set. "It sounds as if you're sitting directly in front of the orchestra. So natural. How much does a thing like that cost?"

"Five thousand marks or so."

"Dear me! I had just decided to buy one some day, but I'll never earn enough to pay that much."

"Who knows. Robert pays very well. Besides, if you stay here you needn't buy one."

"Is it yours?" asked Hergett.

"Robert gave it to me."

"Very generous," said Hergett.

"He can afford it," said Evelyn. "I think that's him coming now."

Hergett heard the front door slam. A few moments

later Robert came into the room, showing no surprise at seeing Hergett, patted Evelyn's cheek and then shook hands with Hergett.

"How do you like that machine?" he asked cheerfully. "Isn't it amazing?"

"As amazing as the price," Hergett said reservedly.

Robert nodded.

"It's definitely too much money. If they keep on like that we'll soon all be poor again. Can we eat now?"

Evelyn nodded.

As they sat down in the dining room, Hergett had the sudden feeling he had already gone too far. To sit down in Robert's house at the same table with him was an admission of moral bankruptcy. He could tell himself that there was no other way to get at Robert, but at the bottom of his heart he knew his insincerity. To get up now, to leave the house at once, was his last chance. He tried, but on the way from his brain to his legs the command seemed to exhaust itself against a hundred resistances. The sense of great physical comfort was stronger, it weighed down on Hergett like a great, soft fist which became even heavier when he, with dull defiance, called to his mind the pictures of his daily life for seven years. When he thought of them, his present surroundings assumed the powerful attraction of a glowing store in winter whose warmth compensates for unpleasant company. In the course of lunch Hergett managed to suppress his revulsion and even began to talk quite naturally with Robert.

After lunch they went back to the living room. Robert put cigarettes on the table.

"Have you already a favorite brand?" he asked Hergett.

"I'm still smoking Russian ones. There are too many brands here."

"It shows how well off we are. Coming back after seven years in prison, all this must seem like a miracle to you."

"It is one," Evelyn giggled. "The German miracle."

Hergett shrugged.

"One gets used to it quite quickly."

"More quickly, I suppose, than to conditions in the Eastern Zone," said Robert. "You've met the Communists in their own country—are the people better off in Russia than we are here?"

"They're not less content than our people here."

"The horse will eat straw if it gets no hay," said Robert. "But they have the atom bomb today and the strongest army in the world. We have practically nothing. It's a hopeless situation for the time being."

"Which we brought on ourselves," Hergett said bitterly. "Are you still for Hitler?"

Robert waited with the answer until he had lit himself a cigarette. Then he said:

"Hitler was a fact. Once he had started the war and we knew what we were facing if we lost it, we had no other choice but to string along. Not for Hitler but for our fatherland. That we lost the war anyhow was our misfortune. You see what they've done with us. This German miracle is just a materialistic anesthetic to numb the awareness of our national disaster. I'll tell you, the first economic crisis, the first queues of unemployed people at the labor offices and you'll see how much this democracy is worth. Or do you seriously think we'd have succeeded in seven years in establishing what generations before us tried to establish in vain? Democracy!" He laughed scornfully. "Excuse me, but you're confusing democracy and economic miracle. As long as the people can stuff their bellies they'll play along. But woe to us if that ever changes. There are enough people in Germany waiting for the moment."

"And you are one of them?" asked Hergett.

Robert smiled.

"You're making your money by whipping up the old nationalistic feelings, aren't you?" said Hergett.

"My enemies put it this way, my friends maintain I'm an idealist. My God, who cares. I'm addressing a certain group of readers who aren't satisfied with what they can read in the other papers. Above all, they aren't satisfied with the party politics and the ministerial bureaucracy. Politics are made without the people, one simply confronts them with accomplished facts—"

"Was that different under Hitler?" Hergett asked quickly.

Robert shrugged impatiently.

"At least he played with open cards. He told the people what he intended to do. To an extent his policy was constructive. Our present policy exhausts itself in internal party squabbles. The foreign minister's position is more important than foreign politics."

"At least as a voter you can influence the choice of ministers."

"Don't be a fool," said Robert. "The ministerial positions are being auctioned off after the elections. You know what party discipline is? It's people sitting in parliament and saying yes or no in a bloc, depending on what their party requires them to say. Those who revolt don't end up in a concentration camp any more, but at the next election they're off the list of candidates. All that goes under the pseudonym of democracy. The voter must be satisfied with a deputy who obeys his party leaders as blindly as he used to obey Hitler. You must admit the difference isn't really overwhelming."

"No," said Hergett. "Not the way you put it. If you want to see the difference very clearly, however, you have to go to Ilmenau."

"Dear old Ilmenau," Robert smiled sentimentally into the cigarette smoke. "We've often talked about it, wondering how things look there now. Evelyn even wanted to go there a couple of times. I advised her against it."

"I was actually homesick sometimes," said Evelyn. "But Robert thought it was too dangerous."

"Not for people with a good conscience," said Hergett, grinning slyly. Robert looked up quickly.

"I thought we'd closed that subject once and for all."

"We have to discuss it once more first," Hergett heard himself say although there had been quite different words on his tongue. It always broke out of him so suddenly that he was himself surprised by it. He looked at Evelyn who made no attempt to conceal her anger. She got up abruptly and he thought she was leaving the room. But she merely got three glasses and said, when she came back, into the tense silence:

"Why not? If Hergett thinks there is something left that needs to be discussed, then we'll simply discuss it."

"A real democratic attitude," Hergett said sarcastically, watching Robert who hesitated a moment and then adopted his mood.

"I've no objections. All right then, what's the question?"

Hergett put out his cigarette. He had already lost his impulse and said:

"I suggest we discuss it some other time. We have enough time."

"I think so too," Evelyn said relieved. "What do you want to drink?"

"Whisky," said Hergett. "I've got used to it now."

When Robert left, a short while afterwards, Evelyn sat down on Hergett's lap and put her arms around his neck.

"It seems you still don't know what you want."

Her mouth was very close and he kissed her.

"One doesn't digest as fast as one eats," he said. "What do we do with the leftover day?"

"Come along, I'll show you." She took his hand and led him back to her room. He stayed with her the following night, and had breakfast in bed with her the next morning.

"We should go away for a while," said Evelyn, "to Lugano or some place like that."

"I wish we could go to Ilmenau," said Hergett, hardly listening to her. "Perhaps I'm silly, but I think that nowhere in the world are there any woods as beautiful as in Ilmenau. I've been all over everywhere since the war started, and, except in Africa, there were plenty of woods elsewhere but none like those in Thuringia. I don't care for flat country, it always makes me feel as if the sky could come crashing down at any moment. It was the same in Vorkuta, one could see too far. In Ilmenau you saw woods on all sides."

"In Lugano you can see woods, too," Evelyn said impatiently. "Sometimes I have the feeling you'd like to go back to Ilmenau to live."

"Didn't you like it?"

"Certainly, Hergett. Certainly I liked it. There were many things there I'd like to bring here if I could."

He looked at her. There was not a shadow of insincerity in her face and as he caressed her breasts, streams of memory released themselves. The great, never answered questions of his youth, the unfulfilled ambitions of his working years, the friendly banks of his life between which his hopes had drifted like glowing sails. In the treacherous radiance of his past memories, all his bitterness, all his hardness and disappointment dissolved. The world had changed, the people had changed, but this was still here. Love and tenderness, devoting your life to the other and the recovery of your self. And Ilmenau, too, was still there. His woods, his meadows, the small lakes where he had dreamed his dreams. The rivers were still running as they used to, the church bells were still ringing through the same old streets, and the mountains, green glowing domes of his childhood, had not lost their secrets.

Hergett looked down at Evelyn's face. The face of his wife, familiar in all its lines, each expression reflecting his own emotions. She was a piece of his own life and she had been closer to him than any other human being he had ever known. She knew his tricks in bed, she knew the words that broke out of him in moments of the highest excitement, she knew the kind of ties he liked and how primitive he could be. She was the only person to whom he needn't pretend and having her beside him again gave him, in his lostness, the feeling of having returned to himself. Half forgotten images rose before his eyes, memories of a wheatfield in the summer, of a rainbow, the falling of leaves in the fall wind when the fog had lain over the empty fields in melancholy silence. Never anywhere had he been more intensely aware of the seasons. And nowhere, it seemed to him, had he been happier than in Ilmenau. Never and nowhere. And Evelyn was part of Ilmenau, a recaptured piece of warm, living past. He took her face between his hands and wished that she felt the same way he did, that she—if he asked her now—would go back with him to Ilmenau. At this moment, this, as he felt, solemn and never to be repeated moment, the fear that she might again disappoint him contracted his throat. But then he asked her anyhow and she could hear by his voice how deadly serious he was. Cautiously she drew his hands from her face, held them, and laughed uncertainly.

"Don't tell me you actually want to go back to Ilmenau to live, Hergett?"

"Why not?"

"No one goes back to the Eastern Zone once he's managed to get out. It's insane."

"Oh? Insane?"

"Yes, I'm very sorry, but it's true."

"So if I tell you that I'm going back, then I'm insane?"

She took her time answering.

"Everyone of us has a certain image of what his life will be like," she said slowly. "This life here," she gestured around the room as if she could scoop it up in her hand. "This is roughly what I imagined my life to be. I couldn't be without it again. I told you there are many things in Ilmenau I'd like to bring here if I could and that's the truth. I would like to take a trip there with you. But to stay there, no Hergett, that you can't ask me to do."

"Of course not," he said more soberly. He felt less disappointed than he had expected. Thinking it over he had to admit that he would probably not have considered going back even if Evelyn had agreed. It had been a question asked out of principle and Evelyn's answer, no matter how it turned out, would have had no effect on their life. He was acting like a man asking a woman to sign a vow of fidelity without having made up his mind whether he wanted to marry her.

As the days went by, the carefree, unproblematical existence affected Hergett like a narcotic drug, not strong enough to numb his consciousness completely, but putting him into a state of calm indifference from which he awakened only when, on the fifth day, Evelyn pressed a banknote into his hand. It was a hundred mark note. Hergett gave it back and said it was out of the question.

"Why?" said Evelyn, astonished. Since he had not really thought it out, he shrugged, but she persisted:

"You must have a reason for not taking money you need."

"First of all I don't need it and secondly it's enough that I'm living in your house. Let's not discuss it any further."

"But I want to discuss it," Evelyn insisted. "What difference does it make whether you take money from me now or in two weeks? One day you'll have to take it anyhow."

"I don't have to take anything. Have I ever said that I want money from you?"

"You can't live on love alone, you know. You can pay me back later, when you get a salary from Robert. If we've remarried by then, you don't even have to do that. Don't be so terribly stubborn. Don't you see how ridiculous you are?"

Of course I'm ridiculous, Hergett thought, everything is so ridiculous one could die laughing. It's ridiculous that I'm sleeping with her, living with her, going out with her, drinking coffee with her, and counting the days until Katharina comes back. Five more days, you idiot, he told himself, five times twenty-four hours and you've made it. She won't even shake your hand when she sees you again. He grinned, thinking that when he left Evelyn he'd have twenty marks left in his pocket. It was so hopelessly ridiculous, so terribly idiotic, that he at once began to ask himself why he wanted to leave her at all. He no longer needed to fool himself. He'd slept with her because he'd been crazy for a woman, had lived in her house because he had no money to live elsewhere, and had sat at the same table with Robert because he was tired of coping with new problems. There was no longer any argument with which he could convince himself of more admissible motives for his actions and he told himself that, if he wanted to preserve a residue of self-respect, he should talk to Evelyn honestly now. She sat in a chair opposite him with a very determined expression in her face. He looked at her, searching around in his mind for an explanation and finding that he had none. It seemed to him that all he had done in the past weeks had happened without his own volition, as if he had as little influence on the course his life had taken as a piece of wood that is thrown up on the beach by one wave and carried off again by the next. It was hopeless.

He went over and sat down on the arm of her chair. She moved away slightly and looked up into his face.

"Let's talk this over sensibly," he said. "I've been in Nuremberg twelve days now. That is not, you must admit, a lot of time either to get settled, or make important decisions. If you remember my motives for coming here originally and what I've done instead, you have no reason to be dissatisfied. Haven't I asked you for time?"

"You didn't ask for time before going to bed with me."

"Should I have?"

"Let's not talk in circles," she said impatiently. "After all, there has to be a basis for all this. Either we're both seriously interested in getting back together, or one of us is not. Then he should tell the other, so that the other can draw his own conclusions. And if you are seriously interested, then I think you don't have to make a fuss about the money."

"Perhaps I don't know yet whether I'm seriously interested."

"Then you'd better find out before I lose my patience."

She slipped out of the chair and left the room. She didn't come back for lunch. Hergett spent two hours writing to his sister and then took a walk through the woods for many hours. When he finally returned to the house, he half felt that his period of living there was coming to an end.

To his surprise he found Robert in the living room. He stood at the window, smoking a cigarette.

"Been out walking?"

Hergett nodded and stopped undecidedly.

"Evelyn came to my office today," said Robert, and went to sit down at his desk. He picked up a paper, looked at it and held it out to Hergett.

"Read this over. It's a draft for your contract with us. The starting salary is five hundred marks with a yearly increase of one hundred until you reach eight hundred, then we can renegotiate. I hope you'll be satisfied with that. Why don't you sit down?"

"No, thank you." Hergett took the contract, read it paragraph for paragraph and then put it back on the desk.

"You should have asked me first," he said. "One doesn't draft a contract until one has reached a basic agreement."

"I thought we'd reached that."

"A mistake. We haven't said a word about a contract."

"Well," Robert smiled benovolently, "the preparatory negotiations were handled by Evelyn, I gather. Aren't you satisfied with the contract, do you want a better one? By all means, say so, I told you this is just a draft."

"In other words: you'd pay even more."

"It would be unusual," said Robert. "We have our salary ranges as do all other businesses. But among relatives one can discuss such matters."

"Among former relatives."

"Let's say future ones. I assume that the, well, that your improved relations with Evelyn haven't fooled me into drawing premature conclusions. She told me this noon that you've reached an agreement."

"That's not the way I remember it. Where is she?"

"Evelyn?" Robert looked at the door. "She should be here by now. She had to do some shopping. Anyhow, we don't really need her. It isn't the first time we've talked to each other without her."

He put down his cigarette holder and rested his chin on his hands.

"I'm not trying to fool you and you aren't trying to fool me. We've never tried to fool each other, we've always told each other frankly what we thought and although there was often more honesty than love in it, we didn't do badly that way. At least there were never any misunderstandings between us. Let's keep it that way. I tell you very frankly that if I had any influence it wouldn't have come to this renewal of your relationship with Evelyn. It goes against my feelings, in a sense it goes against my morals. Please, let me finish. I know what you're going to say. Since my parents were killed I've felt responsible for Evelyn and I think I've done more for her than my parents ever could have. It was I who encouraged her to marry you when I saw how crazy she was about you. She isn't easy to handle, especially not since her operation. No one in the world knows better how badly she's suffered. She was, if I may say so, my trouble-child all my life. So naturally when your marriage went so badly I reproached myself for having encouraged it. For me a divorce was the only solution for you two, after the first few months. If I hadn't been so handicapped financially, I'd have pressed for one much earlier."

"I'm glad you admit it at least," Hergett said bitterly.

"Yes, I'm sorry, but that's the way it was. Evelyn became nervously sick in your household. I'm sure she told you. Today the situation is a little different. Even if you remarry, she'll be independent and she needs that. You'll never make a meek little housewife out of her, she isn't the type. I frankly don't know what goes on in your mind, whether you actually, as she thinks, still like her, or whether there are other motives behind it. You can tell her that yourself, I don't want to meddle. I told her she's in the process of making an enormous mistake and that ends my part for the moment, I'm afraid. She's outgrown me slightly in the past years, she no longer listens to me the way she used to. As I said, I don't know what goes on in your mind, but I know what goes on in hers. Unfortunately, I've never succeeded in talking her out of this fixation that she has to make up for something as far as you're concerned. She talked herself into that and when the Russians got you, it made it even worse. It's become a sort of complex with her. You're probably, in her eyes, some sort of childhood idol persecuted by fate. Anyhow, whatever it is, I don't really care. If she thinks she can be happy only with you and no one else, she'll just have to find out by experience. But let's get that over with quickly. I'll try to help her as best I can. Here's the contract, as soon as you've signed it you can start with us. When you marry, I'll give you the two guest rooms for your own use and you can decorate them any way you like. I'll give Evelyn the money for it. Considering my basic opinion of the whole thing, you must admit that this is the utmost I can do. Or don't you?"

"Yes, yes." Hergett could see everything almost clearly now. He looked at Robert.

"If what you say is true, then Evelyn's reason for wanting to marry me again is pity."

Robert lifted his hands. "Pity, sentimentality, a guilt complex, who knows? Perhaps a little of everything. Believe me, she's too old and experienced for love with all its excesses. After all, she hasn't lived here as if this were a convent."

"No, the place hardly looks like one. There's one thing, Robert: I've told you often enough why you're not my type. What's the answer in reverse?"

"I could say a lot about that. To sum it up very briefly: you're the son of your father."

"That was straight," Hergett said approvingly. "I have a business suggestion to make. Give me five hundred marks, then you're rid of me. I'll pay it back to you as soon as I earn money. The only thing that prevents me from spitting in your face is my empty wallet. This isn't a disgrace, it happens to many people, but without money one doesn't get very far."

Robert's eyes narrowed.

"Are your feelings for Evelyn included here?"

"No. I'll think about a remarriage, but not here. I'm not independent here. For such a decision one needs time and I don't want to fool either her or myself. After all these years a few more months won't matter. As soon as I know what I want I'll get in touch. It would be much easier if you didn't exist."

"It's hardly my fault that I do," said Robert, smiling, and opening a drawer to take out a checkbook. "You can have a thousand if you want."

"Thanks. Five hundred is all I need."

He watched Robert writing out the check and carefully drying it with a blotter.

"Now just a little note for my files," said Robert. "I think we'd best put it that I've given you a loan without interest, to be repaid at some indefinite date. All right?"

Hergett nodded. When he put his name under the note, he noticed from the corner of his eye that Robert was smiling contentedly. He put the note in his desk and handed Hergett the check.

"There, now you're able to spit in my face."

"I've already done that," said Hergett, "in my mind. As soon as I have found a permanent address I'll write you so you won't have to bother the citizen's registration again."

"Evelyn did that. I'd rather you wait until she comes. Otherwise she'll think I scared you away."

"Which indeed you did. I'm still too much of a squarehead not to react to this sort of thing. With your talent you won't find it difficult to put all the blame on me."

Robert got up.

"I must admit I'm surprised. You've changed your attitude very quickly indeed."

"This is the place to learn it," said Hergett. "Now all I need is a briefcase. I'll return it to you."

"That's not necessary, there are enough briefcases here."

Robert left the room and came back a moment later.

"Here you are, genuine cowhide. It was a birthday present, I've never used it."

"I'll pay you for it," said Hergett. Robert shook his head decidedly.

"It didn't cost me anything. Please take it. If there's anything else you need—"

"No, thanks," said Hergett. "I'll go upstairs and pack."

He finished packing in five minutes. Before leaving Evelyn's room he turned and looked back. He found it much harder than he had thought and he left quickly. Robert sat at his desk again. He looked up smiling.

"Already?"

"I haven't as much property as you. One more thing, Robert. You know me well enough to know that a promise from me is a guarantee for you. I promise not to take any steps against you. I only want to hear from you whether you did it."

"Whether I did what?"

"Whether you denounced my father. I just want to know."

"All right." Robert stopped smiling. "It was self-preservation. They would have caught him one day anyhow. Then they'd have hanged us all—me, Evelyn, your sister and her husband, all of us. I had no choice."

With brimming eyes Hergett looked into his indifferent face. Then he turned and went over the terrace, through the garden out into the street. It was half past six and there were many people in the street. They were rushing like those he had seen the morning of his return from Dahme. They had a hard day behind them and were anxious to get home.

[ CHAPTER TWELVE ]

Hergett went to a hotel and again he found himself sitting in a strange room and again it had a table, a closet, a chair, a night table and a bed. It wasn't a very good hotel. Broad cracks ran across the ceiling, the table-cloth had brown stains and the bed looked as if the sheets had not been changed for weeks. The window opened on the dark shaft of a court which was so narrow that he could see directly into the opposite window.

Hergett drew the curtain and lay down on his bed. Robert had denounced his father and Evelyn was Robert's sister. She would never leave her beautiful room. Through the slits of her blinds the sunlight had fallen in broad, warm strips and she had smelled wonderful when she came from her dressing table. He couldn't get tired of touching her. Now someone else would touch her. Robert would tell her what to think of a man who let himself be paid off with five hundred marks. It was all very clear. Wonderfully clear, Hergett thought, grinning up at the cracked ceiling. You handled this very well, he said aloud to himself, you've handled this very well indeed. Very respectably. Very, very respectably. Your father would be proud of you. One may stumble, he always said, but one must never fall. And you didn't fall, no, not you! You've shown character, you even accomplished what you set out to do. Not all of it, but most of it. You heard from his own lips that he was the one. Self-preservation. He saved your sister, your brother-in-law, even your wife from the gallows. And now he's loaned you five hundred marks and given you a fine brief-case. Isn't he a wonderful fellow? Hergett grinned. Yes, he's a wonderful fellow and you're a pig, a sex-obsessed little dog who hasn't anything in his head but women, women, women.

He got up and peered at himself in the mirror above the wash stand. The blind glass reflected his face in a strained grimace.

"You poor idiot," he said. "You poor, respectable idiot."

The next morning he asked the reception clerk where he could find a furnished room. The man made a face as if Hergett had asked him for a loan.

"That's very difficult," he said. "Go to the housing office, or better yet put an ad in the paper."

"Good idea," said Hergett.

After breakfast he went to the newspaper the man had suggested. The ad cost eight marks and was to appear the following morning. For lunch he went to a cheap restaurant. His depression had been replaced by a nervous restlessness. He felt like someone standing at a street crossing and not knowing which way to turn. His actions and thoughts were strangely detached from his past, as if overnight a crack had opened inside him and there was now an unbridgeable gap.

After lunch he took the street car to the zoo and walked around for hours, trying to visualize Katharina beside him. He sought out the bench where they had sat and remembered the talk with her. Closing his eyes he could see her face before him and he had to smile when he thought how aggressive she had been. That Langer would never marry her. Hergett knew the type. A mixture of white knight and beast of prey. One of those who'd tasted a little too much blood, who'd pulled the trigger too often to give up easily. In the end they always did give up, with banners fluttering in the wind and in losing still feeling like victors because they capitulated only before themselves, before their sense of responsibility or whatever they called it, but they capitulated nevertheless. And deep inside Katharina had resigned herself to it. Of all she had said, he remembered most clearly her remark that she lacked the strength to endure it much longer. What woman in her place would have played along for seven years? She was magnificent, unique, and he couldn't understand how Evelyn had succeeded in pushing her, however temporarily, out of his mind. The sister of the man who had denounced his father! The woman to whom he owed all the bitterness and disappointments of his life so far. She probably thought herself quite magnificent, too, because she had waited for him seven years. Four of them in a mansion, as a pampered lady of the world, who could afford lovers and vacations in Lugano! And then to complain about his father, the proletarian household, having been married to the dustcloth. . . . The sister of an informer.

Hergett knew that he was being unjust. He knew that to get away from Robert he had to accept the money. He also knew that he would never forgive himself for it.

He looked across the well-trimmed lawn to the great old trees. They stood singly on the light green space and above them the sky was blue as if the shadow of a cloud had never crossed it. It was a view to grow homesick on and Hergett thought that lately he'd been getting homesick a little too often. All he needed to think of was the hotel room, the awful airshaft, and he was ready to climb into the next train. Except for Katharina, nothing kept him here. He got up and started walking back into town. He didn't take a street car because he thought that if he tired himself out he might be able to endure his room.

He walked briskly but his mind was in a state of apathy. He saw a woman coming towards him with her head lowered. Just before she reached him she looked up. Her face was most attractive and her great, dark eyes studied Hergett with interest. After they passed each other, Hergett noticed that it hadn't caused any reaction in him. Since he had left Evelyn, he hadn't consciously looked at any woman. He didn't even feel the desire to sleep with one. Even when he thought of Katharina, he did so without any sensual feelings. It was as if his dammed up desire had broken through the dam and left an empty indifference behind. His feelings for Katharina were clean and without sexual desire, but he had a burning urge to see her again.

He turned towards the center of the town. The towers and walls stood out against the moon-bright sky like the contours of a great castle and the moon's light sifted a blue-white glow even into the darker streets. Hergett walked more slowly. He had time and it didn't matter where he went. The vivid picture of Katharina's face in his mind changed the city into a stony garden. With each step he took, it scattered its lights towards him like bunches of colored flowers. He saw the crenelated walls, the slender towers rising like silver poplars above the black bulwarks, and in all the corners and nooks he imagined Katharina's face, he met her at every crossing and when he sat down on a bench to rest, she sat beside him. For the first time he felt a deep affection for the town. It seemed as if he had looked into its heart and the town had smiled back at him. It was Katharina's smile and it stayed with him until he returned, late at night, to his hotel and the darkness of his room engulfed him like a deep, good sleep.

His ad in the paper remained unanswered. On the third day he followed the advice of the girl at the newspaper and put in a repeat. He had no hopes, however, and left the offices feeling very depressed. In the street he stopped and stared distractedly into the swarm of automobiles, street cars, bicyclists that poured like a torrent through the narrow gorge of the street. He wondered whether he should go back to the hotel for lunch or go to a restaurant when someone from behind put his hands around his eyes.

Hergett turned around. At the first moment he didn't recognize the grinning man's face but then it went through him like an electric shock.

"That's impossible," he said breathlessly. "Ansberger. Fat and round and bouncing! How did you get here?"

"That's what I was going to ask you," said Ansberger. "Buchholz!" They laughed and slapped each other on the shoulder.

"You're the first one of the crowd I've met again," Hergett said, overwhelmed. "Don't tell me you're living in Nuremberg."

"You don't remember? Ever since I was born. I've told you often enough."

"I forgot, I completely forgot."

Hergett saw the people staring at them. He pulled Ansberger aside and they looked at each other again, grinned, shook their heads and then Hergett suggested a drink to the reunion.

Ansberger looked at his watch.

"Half past twelve—can't make it. My little woman is waiting with the lunch. I have another suggestion, come along, you can eat with us. Or do you have a little woman somewhere who's waiting with lunch?"

"I'm not married."

"Congratulations! Where do you have your car?"

"Car!" Hergett laughed. "I was released from Russian prison six weeks ago."

Ansberger's eyes grew wide.

"You poor bastard! I didn't know that. Ever since that shrapnel splinter in 1944 I've been away from it all. Imagine, I was in the hospital here when the Americans came in. What a circus, I'm telling you. Come along, I've

205

my car up there in a side street. Didn't you live in Thuringia before?"

His good memory surprised Hergett. While they went to his car, he told Ansberger his story.

"Of course, I couldn't stay forever with these Schneiders," he said. "At the moment I'm looking for a room. I've put an ad in the paper but no response yet."

"Rooms are scarce," Ansberger nodded. "You see how it looks here. The Amis have smashed up half the town. So, there's my car."

Hergett whistled through his teeth.

"Look at that! You don't seem to be doing too badly."

"God, one manages. I took over my parents' business. Stationery and such. It does pretty well. Wait, I'll unlock it for you."

"I'm still stunned," Hergett confessed as they drove to Ansberger's apartment. "I really hadn't thought of you in years."

"But I've thought of you. You'll laugh, but it isn't four weeks since I last told my wife about you again. How long were we together in Russia?"

"One and a half years at least. Ever since I joined your outfit. That was in Witebsk."

"Of course." Ansberger laughed. "I remember noticing your face right away. You looked as if you'd just come from a summer resort."

"Africa was a little hot in every respect for a summer resort."

"So you let the Russians catch you after all!" Ansberger shook his head. "How did you manage to do that?"

Hergett told him.

"Those pigs," grumbled Ansberger and through the open window spit at a bicyclist.

"It's just like the Amis. But their trees won't grow all the way up to the sky either. The Russians will see to that. There, that's where I live. The shop and the house are mine. I just had it renovated. My parents help a little in the store, but I do most of the work. Let's go through the store."

Hergett looked at the house. It was four stories high and looked rather garish with its white plaster front. The store had five large show windows and was very spacious. Inside a few customers were being waited upon by sales girls in brown smocks. Ansberger spotted a teenage girl who appeared to be waiting. He excused himself and asked her what she wanted to buy. She told him and he smiled.

"Oh, I have something very special for you in that line." While he went behind the counter Hergett had a chance to look him over. His blond hair had grown very thin in the past nine years but the face had remained the same. It was a little rounder with deepened lines, but the hooked nose still hung over the small mouth that always looked as if the lower lip were engaged in devouring the upper. Altogether the face looked greedy and Hergett tried to imagine it as it had looked under the steel helmet. He had never liked Ansberger especially and he rememberd well the day when he was wounded. It had been raining and a cold wind was whipping across the flat land. They had run across a muddy field towards the edge of a wood with Russian tanks carrying infantry behind them. On the way Ansberger had collapsed with exhaustion and Hergett had kicked him in the belly to bring him back on his feet. Then they had run for another hour through the wood, through the veil of dry leaves which the wind blew before them until they reached a clearing where they stopped to cool off their burning lungs. Later they had run on through the woods and again across a field and another wood and then they ran up a bald hill from where they had seen the towers of a city in the misty distance. They dug a hole on the slope in which the water rose knee deep, and everything had been so dreary and hopeless they had wished to be dead. In the evening Ansberger was wounded. Hergett had not thought he would ever see him again. He had not missed him either. But this unexpected encounter in Nuremberg, where he was happy to know anyone at all, had overwhelmed him. He watched Ansberger talking to the teenager.

"It's the best there is," he said. "You'll get a six months' guarantee with it."

The teenager pouted.

"I don't like the shape."

"You surprise me," Ansberger leaned over the counter and looked down the girl's bosom. "This shape is very fashionable. If I had enough of them, I could sell a hundred each day."

"It's too black," she said. "Haven't you one in green or blue?"

"Not at the moment. But black is always very distinguished. Most people ask for black mechanical pencils. The color fits into every purse."

"I need it for school," she said shyly.

"It fits into every school, too. I sell it especially to the gymnasiums. You're in a gymnasium, aren't you?"

The teenager blushed. "Yes."

"Then I would definitely advise you take this one. Have you any other wishes?" He smiled engagingly and started to wrap up the pencil. When he returned to Hergett, he wiped his forehead.

"That's the way it goes all day. The plebs are so stupid, one could sell them a fountain pen for a pencil. This is the way to my apartment."

Hergett followed him up the stairs and a moment later came face to face with Ansberger's wife.

"My old war comrade, Buchholz," he said. "I told you about him only four weeks ago."

Hergett looked into a pinched face with colorless eyes, knife-sharp lips and protruding cheekbones. Her hand felt cool and moist. He withdrew his own quickly and said something about not wanting to cause undue extra work.

"Nonsense!" Ansberger patted him on the shoulder. "For an old war comrade of her husband my wife will do everything. Come into the living room."

While they were waiting for lunch, Ansberger explained that his parents lived on the next floor.

"It wouldn't work in the long run, living together so closely," he said. "They have their ideas and I have mine. Lisa, too." He smiled. "She has a weakness for Italy, by the way. Italy and the French Riviera. She's crazy about them. In June we traveled through Italy for two weeks, almost down to Sicily and then back up to Genoa, over to Nice, up to Paris and from there back to Nuremberg. That was some trip, what Lisa?" he said to his wife who came in with a soup tureen.

"Next year I want to go to Spain," she said, blowing a strand of hair from her face.

"You may. With the new car even."

"You want a new car with the one you've got?" Hergett asked in astonishment.

"Lisa wants one. Since the husband of her friend has the new Mercedes she's at me all the time."

"Our old one already has forty thousand kilometers," Frau Ansberger said as if it were a personal insult. She looked at Hergett.

"Have you been to Spain?"

"No."

"They say it's beautiful," she said, ladling soup into his plate.

"You mustn't forget he's just come back from Russian prison," said her husband. "What those poor devils had to go through! But, well, we had a lousy enough time of it after 1945 ourselves. Be glad you didn't have to live through that," he said, turning to Hergett. "Horrible, horrible, I tell you. No butter, no meat, not even enough bread. For a sack of potatoes you had to make ten trips and stand in line for hours. Those were lousy days, what Lisa?"

"I've gone through a lot," she nodded. "Today, the men don't want to know about it any more. They wanted to eat and we women had to see where we got it."

"We know, we know," Ansberger assured her noisily. "We fought through it together and we've survived it together. For that we're better off today. Right, Buchholz? My God, man, do you remember that damned position before Armenskaya? My God, that time I really thought the Russians had us." He turned to his wife. "Russians, Russians, wherever you looked and we in the middle. I at the MG—giving it to them, once, twice. Buchholz beside me throwing hand grenades like rotten eggs. Did we tear a hole into them, what? Just think of it! The real stuff we were, don't let anyone tell you differently. That was real war! Pity we lost it after all. No one will ever get me again. Next time let the others do their bit, those half-baked ones, they haven't an idea what our generation went through."

He went on in this vein for some time and, when they finished lunch, he offered Hergett a cigar. His wife took off her apron and sat down with them. Hergett had to tell how he had left the Eastern Zone.

"You see," said Ansberger, "reunification here, reunification there. Of course, as a German I, too, say reunification. On the other hand I'm asking myself, should we risk all that we've built here since forty-five? Our government is pretty sensible in that respect, I must say. Here in West Germany we're well off today, better than before the war. Look how much a worker earns today. Reunification—that'll take care of itself in due time. I'm only afraid of one thing, namely that one day the opposition will take over the government. I don't trust them across the road. We businessmen don't want any experiments, we want a reliable government that keeps our currency stable." He turned to his wife. "He told me he's got a position at the Landrat's office."

She gave Hergett a bored look. "You're lucky there. In those offices you earn well."

"I don't think that is so," Hergett said disgustedly. "I've talked with some employees there."

"Those people are never satisfied," retorted Ansberger. "It's the unions behind them and behind the unions the Communists. For heaven's sake don't listen to what these people tell you. You're not married. As a single man you'll make out beautifully. I'm a businessman; I know."

Hergett moved his head impatiently. "It's not a matter of making out, it's a matter of getting started. I've no apartment, no clothes, only what I'm wearing on my skin. How many thousand marks do you need for an apartment like yours? As an employee at the Landrat's office you'd never have made it."

"We all had to start from the beginning at one time," Ansberger said reservedly. "Of course I earn more than an employee. But for that I've more expenses."

"And more worries," his wife spoke up. There was open hostility in her voice. Hergett looked at her briefly. Probably she was afraid that he was trying to borrow money from her husband.

"I think everyone has the same amount of worries," he said very coldly, and turned to Ansberger. "I'm glad for anybody who has been successful. Anyhow, it was good to meet you. You'll have to go down into the store and I have a few errands to take care of."

Ansberger protested. "Work doesn't run away. We have so much to talk about, my God. Whatever became of the company commander—that long stick—for years I've tried to remember his name."

"I don't remember it either." Hergett wanted to get away. He had enough of the two. If he hadn't eaten at their table he would have left immediately, but he forced himself to stay another half hour. To his relief the woman, after yawning several times, went out. She had an angular figure with fat legs and he tried to visualize her driving through Spain in her new car. When Ansberger looked at his watch, Hergett grabbed the opportunity to take his leave. He didn't see the woman again. She had, as Ansberger said, gone to take a nap.

"To keep beautiful," he smiled. It wasn't clear how he meant it. "Come back soon. If you have an apartment, let me know where. I'd like to help you a little but there's nothing free in our house at the moment. But, here, I must give you something at least."

He reached for his wallet and Hergett was about to open his mouth when he saw that Ansberger merely took out a business card.

"If you want to call me some day, it's all here," he said.

Out in the street Hergett tore the card into tiny bits. He had the taste of bitter almonds in his mouth.

He spent the rest of the afternoon struggling to compose a note to Katharina. He tried to tell her what had led up to the incident on his last day in Dahme but it all sounded nonsensical and contradictory, it wasn't even convincing to himself. In the end he merely wrote her a few lines, telling her his hotel address and asking her to get in touch with him so he would know what he was to tell her father. He took the letter to the post office immediately. Tomorrow was the date of her return. The thought made him too restless to sit still. He decided to go to the station and see at what time trains from the coast would arrive. There were so many possibilities that he decided his plan of watching their arrival from a hidden place was impossible to carry out.

He ran around the town for a while and that night he slept so badly that he felt completely battered the next day. He sat in his hotel room hour after hour, imagining Katharina opening his letter and reading it. He went to the desk downstairs and left word that he was expecting a telephone call. He went out into the street to wait for Katharina. But no one appeared and it became dark outside and in his room. He didn't dare to go out for dinner for fear a message from her might arrive in the meantime. He stood at the window and stared down the dark, narrow shaft, trembling with impatience. In his chest an aching knot grew to a weight that almost stopped him from breathing. When he could not stand it any longer, he went downstairs and bought himself a bottle of whisky for twenty marks. He lay down in his clothes on the bed and drank until he no longer felt the ache in his chest and no longer knew where he was and who he was. And so he fell asleep.

Katharina woke him up. He opened his eyes several times and each time saw her standing at his bed. Eventually he knew that it was no dream but his head hurt so that he closed his eyes again. Then something wet dripped into his face. He sat up, his hair over his face, unshaved and stared hazily at Katharina. She was holding a wet towel in her hand and her face looked as if she were laughing and crying. She took the towel to the sink and hung it on a hook. Hergett looked down at his wrinkled suit in which he had slept, saw the half empty whisky bottle on the floor, and next to the bed a tray with his breakfast. He wondered how it had got there. The process of thinking caused such pains in his head that he stopped and stared again at Katharina instead. Her face was sun tanned. To him she looked unearthly beautiful, like an angel who had lain on a sunny cloud for four weeks. With bated breath he watched as she went from the sink to the window, pulled open the curtain and then came over and sat down at the end of his mussed up bed. He could not get rid of the fear that this was merely a dream. He remembered writing her a note and he remembered the long, bad day yesterday. It seemed like a miracle that she should be near him now, so near that he could feel the warmth of her body. He wiped the hair from his face with both hands, shook his head a little and laughed but his voice sounded rusty as if it were coming through a drain pipe, so he quickly fell silent again. In a daze he got up, went to the sink and held his head under the water rubbing his face till it burned. Then he dried himself, combed his hair and

212

brushed his teeth endlessly. All the time he kept glancing at Katharina in the mirror. Her face was turned towards him. She still looked as if she were both laughing and crying and he did not know what to make of it. All this time not a single word had been said and the silence in the room was becoming unbearable. It was a relief when Katharina finally opened her mouth and asked why he didn't shave, too, while he was at it. There was no trace of irony or anger in her voice. Hergett stopped in the middle of the room.

"If it doesn't take too long for you," he said helplessly.

"I have time," she said.

He went back to the sink and started to lather his face mechanically, without a thought in his head. Katharina appeared beside him.

"Where's your electric razor?"

He didn't know what to tell her at first. His sleepiness had disappeared and his headache was fading. With his returning ability to think, the thought of the condition in which she had found him horrified him. It took him a while to pull himself together enough to answer.

"It was stolen."

"Where?" Katharina asked, shocked. "Here in the hotel?"

"In the station." As he shaved he told her of the incident in broad detail, like a man who is happy to bridge an embarrassing moment with a gush of words. Katharina listened in silence. She had walked to the window and stood with her face turned away. After a long pause she asked:

"Why didn't you go back to my parents?"

"I couldn't," Hergett said bewildered. "I didn't want to get you in any new trouble. I thought you could tell them I'd stayed with you in Dahme."

"How could I? I didn't even know where you were. You might have written me a note to Dahme."

Seeing that she was right, Hergett shrugged.

"It was because of your fiancé that I didn't write you at Dahme."

"You don't say! I hadn't remembered you as being so considerate."

Hergett scowled.

"Did you come here to reproach me?"

"What did you expect? A declaration of love?"

"Please," said Hergett, "I had every intention of apologizing."

"What good does that do me?" Katharina said calmly. "My parents expect me to bring you home for lunch. It's past twelve—"

Past twelve! So the chambermaid must have been in, too—she must have had a nice impression of him. Hergett sat down on his bed and looked at the floor.

"I'll tell you something, Fräulein Schneider. I'm not going to your parents' house again."

"Why not?"

"Because—I'm sick of it. You can take that sort of thing if it's your own father or father-in-law, but this way—what for? Why? It's too much of a strain for me."

Katharina nodded.

"I understand. You can say it. I can't. Not for the moment, anyway. Have you enough money for the hotel?"

"Enough for another two weeks."

"And then?"

"I'm looking for a room. Perhaps I'll be lucky."

"What if you're not?"

"I don't know," said Hergett. "Perhaps then I'll go back to Ilmenau, perhaps somewhere else. We'll see."

She came over and sat down on the bed again.

"Is that my fault?"

"What?"

"That you want to go back to Ilmenau?"

"Would it matter to you?" Hergett asked.

"It would if you did it because of me."

"Why do you worry about it?"

"Please answer me."

Hergett looked through the open window at the dark backyard. He remembered it was Sunday and he remembered the Sundays in Ilmenau, where you sensed Sunday the moment you woke up. The poplars were more silvery, the hills seemed greener and even the air, it seemed to him, had smelled more festively. He looked at Katharina. Her dark, shining eyes regarded him earnestly and he thought he saw a change in them. He had the urge to tell her that there was nothing in Nuremberg to hold him back except her, but his pride stopped him. He said that if he went back some day it would certainly not be because of her.

"Have you seriously considered it?" asked Katharina.

Hergett lifted his shoulders.

"One thinks of many things. For someone like me it makes no difference where one starts—in Nuremberg or elsewhere."

"That may be," said Katharina. "But Ilmeanu! I don't understand your wanting to go back there—you must have a reason for it!"

"Perhaps I don't know the reason myself." He looked broodingly down at the floor. "I'm sure there is a difference between this side of Germany and theirs but I don't know if it's big enough to make up for the other things."

"What other things?"

"My God, would you find it easy to leave Nuremberg?"

"Very easy. I don't like this town. I'm so tired of it in fact that sometimes I'd like to run away. I'd run to another country for a place of my own."

"Even to the East Zone?"

"No," said Katharina, "that's different. When I hear East Zone I think of the Russians. I don't like Russians."

"I know them better than you do," said Hergett. "There are good ones and bad ones, just as with us."

"I feel differently. I've heard only bad things about them. I've told you once I don't care about politics. But I have something against the Russians and you can't talk me out of it."

"I don't want to talk you out of it," said Hergett. "I'm only asking myself what's going to happen to us if we don't finally end this. If you ask me—long ago I stopped putting all the blame on the Russians. I don't even owe those seven years in Vorkuta to the Russians, I owe those to quite different people, and some of them are back in charge and no one gets excited about it. Why should they get excited? They told us in Camp Moschendorf that Hitler had killed six million Jews. I still haven't met anyone around here who's excited about that. We always scream when someone steps on our feet. What's this grudge your father has against the Americans?"

"Why?" asked Katharina. "What brings that up?"

"Judging from his words he seems to despise them."

215

"It's friends that talk him into it," Katharina said hesitantly. "The Americans arrested a lot of them after 1945 because they were in the party. They never forgot that."

Hergett nodded.

"But they'll forget all about Hitler. Oh, well, over in the East Zone they sometimes forget that they aren't Russians. I think we are the most forgetful people in the world. As far as I'm concerned, I don't give a damn. Perhaps that's a mistake. I used to get a little mad now and then, but no more. If I want to salvage anything for myself from this messed-up life, I can do it only by dismissing everything else from my mind. On the other hand, you can't blame me for wishing that one could go from here to Ilmenau without crossing a border. I've already told your fiancé that, no matter how stupid it sounds, I feel like a deserter. Today even more than two weeks ago. When I see how dissatisfied the people are here, I think of my sister on the other side and how happy they would be if their standard of living were even half as high as ours here. Please don't be offended, but Klaus is one of those dissatisfied ones. No matter how justified the criticism, you can't always look at the negative side in life. I wonder how a woman can listen to that for years without losing her mind. I'd lose mine, I know."

He waited a moment and when Katharina said nothing he felt for his cigarettes and lit one.

"It's not my business, of course," he said, blowing the smoke through his nose. "You must know how much you can stand. Every man goes through those stages as Klaus has. I'm revolted at the thought of having to sit in an office. But that's not the point. The point is that one copes with the revulsion and gives some sense to one's work and a name to that sense. I don't know yet how I'll christen mine. I'd like Katharina best. Do you like the name?"

She didn't answer. Instead she looked at her watch.

"What do I tell my parents?"

"Tell them I can't make it. As soon as I have an apartment I'll report to your father in the office. I hope he won't change his mind. It's harder even to find a job than to find an apartment."

"I don't think he'll change his mind." She got up.

"How long do you think you'll go on proposing to me?"

"As long as I can," Hergett assured her. He carefully put down the cigarette in the ashtray and took Katharina's hands into his own.

"My personal opinion is that you won't marry Herr Langer," he said softly. "He may be able to lead a party or be a parliamentary deputy, perhaps he might even start a revolution somewhere, but making a woman like you happy—that he can't! One day you'll come to me and tell me that I was right. I'm not one of those men who go to pieces if they can't get a certain woman. I shan't go to pieces because of you either. I merely think it would be a pity."

"What would be?"

"If we didn't get together. There are moments when a man breaks through all barriers. Ten days ago in Dahme was such a moment. I'm sorry that happened. Give me a chance to prove to you that my feeling for you is more than the usual thing. I've gone somewhat off in the wrong direction, and that's not surprising when you consider that the whole world has gone off in the wrong direction. But I tell myself one needn't go along with the world's madnesses to the end, that there must be a point somewhere at which one remembers oneself and remembers what life has left us. It isn't much at the moment. But two people, I think, two people together could do something with it, don't you think?"

"You're proposing to me again."

"I told you I would keep on doing that."

"It's no use, really," Katharina said tiredly. She freed her hands and looked out the window. "Klaus and I've agreed to marry at Christmas."

"That's not the first time," Hergett said.

"This time it's serious. He has the money we need to get married. You're not one of those men who go to pieces over a woman and I'm not one of those women who let a man go to pieces. Klaus needs me."

"If he needed you he'd have married you long ago."

"He was waiting to fulfill a certain condition. He didn't want to marry before. Now that he's finally fulfilled it, I can't leave him."

"Is that your only reason?"

Katharina said nothing. He saw her mouth beginning

217

to move. Then she turned and rushed from the room. Hergett made no attempt to hold her back. He stayed sitting on the bed. One should get him back into an asylum, he thought.

# [ CHAPTER THIRTEEN ]

It was one of Schneider's Sunday habits to turn on the radio at ten thirty and listen to a religious program. He ought to do something for his soul, he felt. In 1937 he had for good reasons decided to leave the regular Sunday attendance at church to his wife. After the collapse however, he had come to the conclusion that it might be beneficial for his future career if he returned to the flock. But the anti-clerical tendencies of the party to which he belonged made it seem advisable not to profess his piety too visibly. Also, his wife could no longer cope with the strain of an hour-long service. She started to complain about the hard benches, the continuous collections and the penetrating odor of incense. This would not have kept Schneider away from church. On the contrary, he loved the smell which, mingled with the aroma of hot wax, woke in him dim childhood memories. And church had never bored him. He found it most diverting to watch the other people, especially the female element in the devout crowd. In addition, however, it was true that in recent years the occasional stirrings of his conscience had begun to increase. He was by no means convinced that the sinister prophecies of the church, regarding the fate of a fallen soul, would actually come true. Yet, the very thought that there might be something to it, inclined him not to break off all bridges leading to an after life. The regular Sunday broadcasts were an excellent solution. After all, he told himself, quite rightly, this way it was much easier to concentrate on the actual service.

This Sunday, however, Schneider hardly heard the pious sounds emanating from the radio. Katharina had arrived the previous day. Schneider was surprised how glad he was to see her back. But then he learned about Buchholz—that he had returned from Dahme ten days ago but had not got in touch with Schneider—and it threw him into a turmoil. Katharina didn't know where he was at first, but later in the day a special delivery letter had arrived for her and she told her father that Buchholz was staying in a hotel and she would go to see him the next morning.

Now Schneider had been sitting in a state of suspense for an hour, waiting for Katharina to come back. While he absentmindedly watched his wife setting the table, he thought for the hundredth time of the evil things Buchholz might do to him if he wanted. He was as dangerous to him as young Wagner. Schneider sighed. He had to clear up the whole affair as quickly as possible, he would give young Wagner the money in one batch and get the letter! Once he had the letter no one could do anything to him. Neither Wagner nor Buchholz nor Langer. In Schneider's mind the three had melted into a single unit. Their common knowledge of the letter made them a common danger. He couldn't say which of the three he hated most, but he was determined to get rid of them all, as soon as he could do so without taking risks.

At last Katharina arrived. Schneider saw at once that something was wrong. He asked her why she hadn't brought Buchholz along but she didn't answer until her mother repeated the question.

"He didn't want to come along. I couldn't persuade him."

"I can't understand him," Schneider said. "Hasn't he told you why?"

"He says he can't live with us forever. As soon as he's found an apartment he'll come to the office and start working."

"Is that what he said?"

Katharina nodded.

"Now, that's understandable." Schneider, greatly relieved, turned to his sad-eyed wife. "He just doesn't feel at home with us. As a young man I wouldn't have moved in with a strange family either. As soon as he comes to the office, I'll talk to him."

He turned to Katharina who sat silently at the table. "Did you have good weather up there?"

"Yes."

"No rain?"

"No."

"It was nice here too," said Frau Schneider. "I hope you didn't stay out in the sun too much. I read somewhere it isn't healthy. You didn't gain weight either. On the contrary. Don't you think she's thinner?" Frau Schneider asked her husband.

Schneider was about to say something mean but he controlled himself and said instead:

"Yes, she's thinner."

Looking unobtrusively at Katharina he imagined her making love with Klaus. With great effort he suppressed the rage that welled up in him.

After lunch he called Franz Leuchtner and asked if he could come over that afternoon. Leuchtner told him he was just about to call him because he wanted to show him a surprise.

On his way Schneider wondered what kind of surprise Leuchtner would have. He hoped it was something pleasant because he wanted Leuchtner to be in good humor.

Actually five thousand marks shouldn't mean much to Leuchtner. Schneider could have borrowed them from the funds which were at his disposal at the office—in his nervous state he had actually considered it at one point—but he thought too highly of himself to take such a step. He was a conscientious official and the idea of spending money, not his own, for private purposes was so shocking that he couldn't bring himself to consider it seriously even if he soothed his conscience by telling himself that sooner or later he would pay the money back. He preferred to borrow from Leuchtner.

A maid led him into the garden, where Franz Leuchtner was in the process of explaining to his son how to handle a golf club. He had built himself a golf course a few weeks earlier, ostensibly for his health. He welcomed Schneider effusively, grabbed him by the shoulders and turned him around.

"What do you see?"

Schneider looked blank.

"I see your garden."

"And further on?"

"The fence, or what?"

"And beyond the fence?"

Schneider turned around.

"You've made it!"

"Right," Leuchtner said boisterously. "This morning, on a Sunday, they called me. The wood belongs to me."

"Congratulations." Schneider shook his hand. "It's taken long enough. How much did you have to fork over?"

"He didn't even tell us," said Kurt Leuchtner. He wore dark blue slacks and a white shirt. Schneider looked at him benevolently.

"Business secret," Franz Leuchtner said cheerfully.

Kurt Leuchtner turned to Schneider again.

"How is Katharina. I've been waiting to hear from her for three weeks. She said she'd call me."

Embarrassed, Schneider tugged at his tie. "She would have called but there was one thing after another—I'm sure she'll call you next week."

"I'd be glad," said Kurt Leuchtner.

"We'd all be glad if she came around more often," said his father. "A marvelous girl—intelligent and full of spirit."

"Just like her father," said Kurt Leuchtner.

"Oh, thank you." Schneider was flattered. When a moment later Kurt Leuchtner excused himself and went back to the house, Schneider looked after him with moist eyes.

"He reminds me of my boy."

"You're not over it yet, are you?" said Franz Leuchtner.

"Would you be—in my place?"

"No. I don't know what I would have done. Come on, have a drink with me."

As they walked up to the house he started talking about the wood again.

"I feel like a country squire now. It was the only thing lacking. Except for a daughter, perhaps. Too bad my wife didn't want another. Well, it's not us men who have to give birth to them."

"Thank God. I got sick just watching."

"I didn't, I was drunk."

As soon as they were settled on the terrace with their glasses, Schneider went straight to the point.

"Listen, I want to talk to you about something. I've hit a little bottleneck there, because of my house. It's ridiculous because I do have credit, bank and savings bank. But one doesn't like to use it, especially not in my position. It immediately creates talk. You know, people like us can't have a hole in their sock without its being written up in the papers. The house cost me—"

"How much do you need?" Leuchtner interrupted yawning. "Ten—fifteen—?"

"Good heavens, no!" Schneider said shocked. "Five thousand. I could pay it back within, say—"

"Say nothing. Your bank account number is sufficient. Just a moment, let me write it down."

Schneider looked lovingly at his unconcerned face.

"You can count on me for the rest of my life. I'll do the same for you some day—"

Leuchtner laughed.

"I certainly hope you won't have to. *Prosit!*"

When Schneider climbed into his car two hours later he was more determined than ever to prevent a marriage between Klaus and Katharina with all means at his disposal. He whistled loudly all the way home. He was once again very satisfied with himself.

Sitting in the street car on her way to Klaus, Katharina thought again of Hergett. She knew now that she liked him.

She was staring out the window, almost missed her stop, and walked the last stretch to Klaus' house without knowing what she was doing.

"Trouble at home?" Klaus asked.

"Why?"

"You can't fool me," he said. "I can tell by the tilt of your nose."

They sat down on the shabby sofa and for a moment Katharina closed her eyes.

"Coming home is always the same," Klaus said morosely. "One shouldn't go away in the first place. Last night when I came in here I felt like turning right around and leaving again. The entire vacation isn't worth this misery. What did they say at home?"

"The usual. Have you a cigarette?"

"Here." He held out the pack and watched her drawing the smoke deep into her lungs. "Did he make a fuss?"

"No, not really. But Mama has talked a streak all afternoon. It wasn't decent to travel with a man one isn't married to. She seems to be afraid that 'something happened.' "

Klaus laughed angrily.

"As if we'd have to travel to Dahme for that. They actually seem to have convinced themselves that there's nothing between us. Sometimes I really doubt their sanity."

"Mothers think differently from other people."

"Especially yours. Was there anything else?"

She knew he was thinking of Hergett, but she couldn't talk about that yet and answered:

"No. That is, they started talking about Leuchtner again, of course. I couldn't wish for a better husband, etcetera etcetera."

"They really want to procure you for him, don't they. I must have a look at the fellow someday."

"Save the trouble. He's just a brat."

"No wonder, with all that money. I've picked the wrong father. When I think that a week from now I have to go back to the office, I could throw up. I could get drunk all day long."

"You promised me you wouldn't."

"Well, I'm sober, aren't I? Let's go out and eat."

In the restaurant Katharina said very little. She noticed Klaus looking at her now and then. He had ordered apple cider.

"If I'd ordered one glass of wine, there would have been more to follow. But for you wine might have been better."

"Why?"

"It might have cheered you. You're extremely taciturn these days. I've noticed this before. Is anything the matter with you?"

"Nothing is the matter with me."

"Good, so I don't have to worry. Haven't you heard anything from Buchholz?"

His direct question bewildered her. She took her glass in her hands, turning it around, then she said:

"I saw him this morning."

"Oh?" He inspected his cigarette. "You're telling me rather late in the day. So he didn't go back to your house?"

"No."

"Where did he go?"

"To a hotel." Katharina's voice was muffled. "He's looking for an apartment. When he's found one, he'll come to the office and start work."

"Were you with him long?"

"I didn't look at the clock."

"Approximately how long?"

"Really!" Katharina said irascibly. "You ask as if I owed you an accounting. We're not married yet."

Klaus looked at her surprised.

"By all means, I'm not trying to push you. As far as I'm concerned we can wait a few more years."

"I believe you!" She felt that she was losing control and said, a little more calmly: "I refuse to discuss it. That subject is settled between us. Unless you've lost your bit of courage again."

"Courage," Klaus snapped back. "What's that got to do with courage. Who's responsible if it doesn't work out, you or I?"

"Neither one more than the other," said Katharina, glancing at the next table where an elderly couple sat. She reached for her purse. "We'd better talk outside."

"By all means," Klaus waved to the waiter and paid the bill. As soon as they were out in the street, he started again. "Typical woman stuff, they can never think an inch beyond their own noses. They—"

"Stop it," Katharina interrupted furiously. "I'm so utterly sick of your eternal complaints. Apparently it doesn't occur to you that a woman would like to hear something else now and then, something that gives and doesn't only take away. If life were the way you paint it, I'd jump from the Sinwell tower. Always complaining and criticizing—women, men, the church, politics and God knows what. In many ways you're exactly like my Landrat. He's only happy when he can tear down everything."

"Are you through?" asked Klaus. His cynical tone set Katharina's blood burning.

"Please don't treat me like a school girl." She was almost shouting. "Perhaps I know less about many things than you, but that is not the point for a woman. I do know the things that matter. You are discontented, through and through. If you don't try to change sooner or later, I'll have to get used to the idea that it isn't necessarily my inescapable fate to marry you."

"Perhaps your inescapable fate is called Hergett?"

He stopped and when Katharina walked on, caught her by the arm.

"All this is rather sudden," he said. "The poor POW from Russia, the poor refugee from the Eastern Zone. We have enough of that kind running around here. Who knows what else has driven him over here? He wouldn't be the first who had to beat it over there and then shows up here as a political refugee. I'd like to hear what his divorced wife has to say to that. She had her reasons for leaving him, I'm sure. Suddenly they've all hidden Jews during the Third Reich. There've never been as many Jews in Germany as they've allegedly hidden. The way they talk it seems I was the only man in all of Germany who didn't hide any Jews. At the same time you only have to listen around to hear that today they all again wish the Jews would go to the devil. Do you know what I think about your Buchholz?"

He snapped his fingers. "This! His stories sound too beautiful to me. The father chased by the Gestapo, the wife leaves him for political reasons, the former brother-in-law a super-Nazi and informer. That's the kind of fairy tale they impregnate the spies with before they send them over here from the East. And you fall for it, of course, you let him soften you, let him tickle your tear glands. I suppose he's awakened your mother instinct. How he'd love to cry on your bosom. Or has he already?" He asked scornfully.

Katharina looked into his angry, distorted face. Then she freed her arm and said with unnatural calmness:

"I didn't know you were so mean."

"Of course!" Klaus drew up his lip. "I am mean. I am discontented through and through. I criticize, I'm crazy and I'm mean. And all that because of some vagrant showing up here. But all right, run after him if you want. You'll come back to me when you're normal again. Because at this moment I doubt that I'm the one who is crazy!"

He turned brusquely and crossed the street with long steps.

Katharina looked after him until he vanished from the lighted circle of a street lamp into the darkness. Then she turned home. Her teeth were clamped into her lower lip and she walked slightly stooped, as if she carried a weight on her shoulders. She walked all the way home.

Her parents heard her come in. She opened the door to the living room to wish them goodnight and immediately closed it again and went upstairs.

The Schneiders looked at each other confounded.

"What is the matter with her?" said Herr Schneider.

"I think she's been crying," said his wife. "She acted funny this afternoon. I asked her what was wrong and she said she had a headache."

"Odd." Nervously Schneider folded up his paper. "There's something wrong. You don't think she's pregnant, do you?"

Frau Schneider gasped.

"Karl! *Jesus Christus,* how can you think such a thing?"

"It wouldn't amaze me," Schneider said. "You don't think they spent those two weeks counting their beads?"

He looked up at the ceiling where they could hear Katharina move.

"I had a funny feeling the moment she came back. If I only knew. . . ."

"I simply don't believe it," said Frau Schneider in despair. "We've brought her up so carefully. And she's no longer a child."

"Exactly! Exactly because she's no longer a child. She knows more about these things than we do. If I'd gone away on vacation with you before we were married, your father would have cut off my hands. Wherever did you see anything like this when we were young? And I of all people must have such a daughter. What do you think the Leuchtners would say if they knew? What an opinion they'd have of us! We wouldn't dare go near them any more."

"I don't care what *they* say," said Frau Schneider. She

had recovered from her shock and decided it was time to defend her daughter.

"They say nothing when their Kurt goes away with a girl for a week end. He has another one each week."

"How would you know?" Schneider said furiously.

"How would I? They tell everyone themselves. And you've talked about it too. The things that boy's done already! Who knows whether he'd stop once he's married. They certainly needn't put on airs. Look at his mother, how she runs around. As a married woman with a grown son I'd be ashamed to run around in those half naked dresses she wears. I didn't wear that sort of thing even as a young girl."

"Because you didn't grow up in a city," Schneider said. "If it were up to you she'd wear a black dress summer and winter. I know you've got something against her."

The reference to her rural origins hurt Frau Schneider. "I've nothing against her," she said offended. "But for her age she behaves very loosely. They think because they have so much money they can get away with anything. It's certainly not decent."

Schneider, who had been pacing the floor, stopped. It was not the first time that she had attacked Irene Leuchtner. He looked disgustedly at her fat face, at her barrel-shaped body with the mass of flesh seeming ready to burst the dress and he said spitefully:

"So, that's not decent! But you've been letting your daughter roam around with this fellow Langer for years, and then when I try to stop it you jump at me, that is decent, is it? You have some highly distorted views, my dear, I must say."

"I've done all I could. What can you do when she likes him. You can't do anything by force. She's too old for that."

"We'll see about that. I can imagine what she likes about him. But others can do that, too. The Leuchtners made it very clear today that they wouldn't object to a marriage between the two. As soon as I've got that letter in my hands, I'll start a new tune!"

"What's the letter got to do with it?" Frau Schneider asked blankly.

"Everything. It's obvious that Klaus knows about that affair. He's capable of talking about it. Once the letter doesn't exist any more, he can tell what he wants. I'll stuff his mouth."

Frau Schneider sighed.

"That letter, it'll be the death of me yet. I can't sleep at night any more. When will he give it to you?"

"He'll give it to me, don't worry!" Schneider said confidently. "I'll have it in a week at the latest."

The thought soothed him. He went to the bathroom, brushed his teeth and went to bed. When his wife came to the bedroom, he had recovered his cheerful mood.

"And actually I don't think she's pregnant," he said, yawning. "That's the only thing you can say for the man. He's sure to have so much experience that there won't be an accident. Katharina isn't his first one, I assure you. Those soldiers, they slept with everyone, they had another one in each town and the officers even more. In his uniform at least he looked like someone."

"You were the one who pressed for an engagement," said Frau Schneider. "You can hardly reproach the child."

The reminder made Schneider uncomfortable. He said irritably:

"What could I do once she had started something with him. Should I have stood by and let the people talk about her? I didn't know him as well then. In the office they call him the maniac. And it's getting worse with him. One day he's going to kill Katharina in one of his crazes."

Depressed, Frau Schneider looked up at the ceiling. She had pulled the sheet up to her neck and said, after a while:

"I've often been afraid of that. But she says he'll have no more attacks. Perhaps it's been cured."

"Nonsense! Once a skull is cracked, it stays cracked. You can't repair that. How is this going to be cured, you tell me?"

"I don't know about those things."

"Not even the doctors know about those things. If someone is crazy, no one can help him. No surgeon and no psychiatrist."

"But nowadays they can do everything."

"Not that, they can't," said Schneider. Under the blanket he emitted a loud sound and Frau Schneider said:

"Really, Karl!"

"It's that potato soup tonight," Schneider said apologetically and turned over on his side. "I'm dead tired. Good night, Elsa."

"Good night, Karlie," said Frau Schneider and switched off the light.

Schneider heard her sighing and stretching out her legs. He thought of his newest conquest, Rosa. She was only a waitress, but he didn't care. You couldn't tell that when she was naked. He'd have to see her more often. A few more years and it would all be finished. He was fifty-four now, really not very old. But one could tell. Thinking back it seemed that the years had raced past as if he had spent his life on a conveyor belt that had carried him on so fast, he had hardly had time to reach out for anything along the way that he liked. The women he thought of as flowers standing alongside his way had lit flames in his heart and their presence had been like a continuous flow of wine. Today it seemed to him that instead of all the flowers he had seen, only a thistle had been left in his hands. The world had changed with every year. At first he had felt its colors, later its contours and now, after he had seen through most of the illusions in his life, he saw only its skeleton. He wished often he could see the world as he had seen it before but even the attempt ended in sentimentality, in painful memories of un-used opportunities, hours he had missed, and encounters that would never recur. Even his professional ambitions had faded. As often before, he caught himself trying to imagine against the washed-out background of his sleepiness the pictures which had been before his eyes all his life. Sometimes he saw himself as a leader of the people on the shoulders of an enthusiastic crowd. Then again, to use an earlier image, as the commanding general of the German Wehrmacht, at the last second and at the head of his divisions, freeing the encircled VIth Army at Stalingrad. His favorite role, however, was to make himself invisible and to appear like an avenging God whenever the interests of his country required it. But he realized he would have to be satisfied with whatever he had achieved so far. Only one thing he could not swallow: the unconditional surrender with its catastrophic consequences for Germany. It was his most fervent wish to live to see the Americans and Russians, on whom he put most of the blame, paying for it. It seemed to him as if his life which, as he saw it, was unalterably tied up with the fate of his fatherland, would thus have a crowning finish. It was often the last thought before he fell asleep.

# [ CHAPTER FOURTEEN ]

"I've changed my mind," Schneider told Ernst Wagner the next morning in the office. "You'll receive the remaining 4500 marks tomorrow. Bring along that letter."

"You'll get that only when we have an apartment," Wagner said quickly. "I haven't heard anything about *that* yet."

Schneider picked up his telephone and asked for the housing office. He exchanged a few words with the department head, then he put the receiver down.

"You'll be notified tomorrow at the latest when and where you can move in."

For a moment Ernst Wagner stood undecidedly. Then, when Schneider took no further notice of him, he turned around and left the room, rubbing his chin with a worried expression.

Schneider, who had pointedly turned his back, looking out the window, rubbed his hands and was about to sit down when something caught his attention. He looked out the window again and saw Hergett walking through the entrance gate. Schneider chuckled and stepped back to his chair. This wasn't a bad day at all.

The moment Hergett turned from the bright street into the dark passageway he instantly regretted that he had not waited a few more days before reporting for work. The harsh voice of the janitor, who sat like an owl behind his window, asked what he wanted. Hergett felt exactly as when he was first drafted into the army and had passed the scowling guard to enter the barracks ground.

His cheerful mood vanished. Yet the day had started so well. There had been an answer to his ad in the newspaper and he had gone directly to the address. The people's name was Walters, she made a nice impression. For the room they wanted fifty marks a month. It was comfortably furnished, had a wash stand and a separate entrance. He even had a letter box of his own in the entrance hall. Hergett had come to a quick agreement with the people. He had got his things from the hotel and had afterwards gone to lunch. The decision to start at the office that same afternoon had been made because of Katharina; he wanted her to know his new address as soon as possible. He didn't dare call her because her mother might answer and to write another letter would have seemed somehow silly and persistent. This way he hoped she might learn his address from her father or from Klaus.

The Landrat greeted him with a great show of heartiness.

"So there you are again," he boomed, shaking Hergett's hand like a pump. "I hadn't counted on you so soon."

"Neither had I," said Hergett. "I found a room."

"Congratulations! What's the address?"

He noted it down and kept his pencil in his hand, playing with it.

"We were very disappointed that you didn't come back to stay with us. But you'll come around now and then, won't you?"

"If you want me to."

Schneider smiled.

"Katharina tells me you stayed in Dahme only for a few days. Didn't you like it?"

"No, not much."

"Oh," said Schneider. The explanation didn't satisfy him at all. He opened his mouth to ask another question but thought better of it. Instead he said:

"I'm glad you're back, anyhow. I put you along with Herr Langer. Since you already know him it'll be easier for you to get used to everything." He put the pencil down. "I hope you'll like working with us."

"I hope so, too," said Hergett. He had expected a

lengthy conversation and felt baffled and a little uneasy when Schneider took him to the door, shook hands and turned him over to Fräulein von Hessel.

"Please take Herr Buchholz to Herr Primelmann—he's informed."

Primelmann took down his personal data and then told Frau Hansen to show Hergett to Klaus Langer's office. When he came in Klaus looked up with an expressionless face.

"This is Herr Langer," said Frau Hansen, who was secretly in love with Klaus. "Herr Langer this is your new colleague, Herr Buchholz."

"We know each other," said Klaus. Frau Hansen looked stunned.

"You—really? How?"

"Herr Buchholz was the Landrat's guest for a few days."

"But that's—" Frau Hansen broke off, looking from one to the other. When neither of them said anything she deflated and, with a reproachful look at Klaus, left.

Hergett looked around the gloomy room.

"Very cozy, what?"

"Very!"

"*You* seem to like it," said Hergett. "You told me you had three weeks leave."

"I couldn't stand the boredom," said Klaus. "You in your hotel room couldn't stand it either, I suppose."

"Dear me, word does get around fast, doesn't it?" Hergett laughed. "However, since this morning I'm living somewhere else. I found a room. Not far from your house."

"Congratulations."

"Thanks. Tucherstrasse 12 is the address."

"Doesn't interest me."

"It might interest Fräulein Schneider," Hergett said coldly.

Klaus looked down at his hands. "You wrote her your address once, why don't you again. Or would it give you special satisfaction if I told her?"

"I'd be much obliged if you did. Writing is such an effort. Who is Frau Hansen?"

"Why?"

"On the way up she told me an entire novel about your virtues and qualities and what a marvelous person you are. If I hadn't known you I might have believed it. Is she the secretary of the personnel director?"

"Yes."

"He seems a pretty nice guy."

For the first time Klaus grinned.

"You wait. It won't take you long."

"What won't?"

"Getting to know friend Primelmann. He'll show you who you are in this place: a recruit with his ass pulled tight to attention. If you ever relax you get a bad conduct mark and after three bad conduct marks you're up for—"

"What are you trying to do—frighten me?"

"I wouldn't take the trouble. But as one old front soldier to another—"

"Never mind that gibberish," said Hergett. "Better tell me what I'm supposed to do around here."

"Keep an eye on Fräulein Huber so she won't stab you in the back," said Klaus. "Furthermore you can help me sort out the afternoon mail. Requests on one heap, complaints on the other. They'll have to get you a desk."

"Who's Fräulein Huber?"

"Our sexy secretary. She's downstairs in the registry looking for the files I lost. She'll hate you for crowding in on us. How do you like your new apartment?"

Hergett didn't answer.

"Apparently not," Klaus said tenaciously. "You should have stayed at the Landrat's house."

Hergett looked up from the stack of mail Klaus had pushed over and said furiously:

"Mind your own affairs, will you?"

"Why so agitated?" Klaus grinned. He hadn't heard from Katharina and he feared Hergett might meet her again in the evening. "You should be glad that I'm concerned about your welfare," he said scornfully. "One knows what one owes a poor POW just back from Russia. On the other hand, you can't be as poor as all that. If you were how could you have traveled to Dahme with us and you certainly couldn't have afforded to stay in a hotel there. I never knew our returning POW's were treated so generously. Or have you any other sources of income?"

Hergett suppressed the urge to punch him in his grinning face. He leaned back in his chair and looked at Klaus coldly.

"Suppose I had some."

"I'm sure you do," said Klaus. "There are plenty of people like you coming from the East Zone who have more money in their pocket than we can earn here in five years."

"I don't know anything about that." Hergett didn't understand what Klaus was trying to say. "Why so complicated? There are people around here who don't mind helping a man in an emergency."

"Then you must be more talented than I," Klaus said slowly. "I've never found any. You're not talking about the Landrat, are you?"

Hergett hesitated. He had a sudden inspiration. Quickly he said:

"Is that the only person you can think of?"

He saw in Langer's face that the arrow had hit.

"You're not seriously saying that—"

"I'm not saying anything," said Hergett.

Klaus stared at him. He didn't doubt for a moment that Hergett was talking about Katharina. And he was convinced now that she had gone to see him after he left her the previous evening. In a furnished room. The thought went like a red hot iron through his head. He said with a voice that was muffled with rage and disappointment:

"It fits you. Probably you're even proud of yourself. I suppose you know what one calls a man in that line of work, do you?"

"I don't know, but I wouldn't advise you to annoy me," said Hergett.

"Keep your advice. There's a special expression for—"

Klaus broke off and looked at the door. Fräulein Huber came in and went to her desk. She acknowledged Klaus' introduction of Hergett with a dry little nod and a moment later she was deep in her work. Ever since the incident with Ernst Wagner she had talked to Klaus only about business and only when she had to. Klaus did not mind, her former chattiness had been worse.

Lighting a cigarette, Klaus noticed that his hands were shaking slightly. He pressed his lips together. All of his thinking, ever since the night before, had been centered on the thought that it might be too late, that he might be in the process of losing Katharina. All these years this possibility had never really occurred to him. Oh, he had thought about it now and then, but the thought seemed to leave him curiously indifferent. Only now he realized that his indifference was actually the conviction that Katharina would never let it come to that. It was the same as with dying. You flicked your wrist at the thought all your life but when you were actually confronted with it, you were suddenly neither prepared for it nor resigned.

To lose Katharina, Klaus knew now, would be as unbearable as a return to the asylum. He had to marry her, he had to marry her as soon as possible. That's why he had come to work a week early. He had to change relations with his future father-in-law. He had to prove to Katharina that he was serious about marriage by removing Schneider's objections once and for all. He would remove them by rendering Schneider a service— an invaluable service. He would get the letter away from Ernst Wagner, somehow.

He noticed Hergett ogling Fräulein Huber. Klaus' mouth curled down. Let's watch him try charming this one, he thought. Hergett, noticing his look, grinned back. Then he turned back to Fräulein Huber.

"Have you been working here long?"

"Why does that interest you?" she asked. Hergett noticed that she lisped slightly.

"I try to get along with my fellow-workers and I like to know a little about them. Besides you don't look as if this were your natural vocation. I bet you have artistic ambitions."

Fräulein Huber blushed.

"I?"

"One can tell by looking at you," Hergett said at random.

"I play the organ," Fräulein Huber confessed bashfully. Hergett acted delighted.

"A coincidence. I love organ music. You play in church?"

"Yes."

"I must listen to you some day. I imagine it is hard for a woman. Isn't it strenuous for you?"

With each one of his words Fräulein Huber's face grew brighter. Now she smiled at him with her thin, colorless lips and with a quick gesture made sure that the tiny knot of hair in the back was straight.

"I've been training for a long time," she said. "We have a brand new organ now, with a mechanical register, *Tremulant,* if you ever heard of it. If you feel like it on Sunday—I play all morning, from eight to twelve."

"You're an idealist," said Hergett. "I'm fascinated. Some day when we have time you must explain to me how an organ works. I have a little knowledge, but not more than a Sunday driver has of his car engine. Do you have an electric winder?"

With flushed cheeks Fräulein Huber nodded. She explained a few details about the mechanism, while Klaus listened with a grim face. Fräulein Huber was in raptures, the soulful looks she gave Hergett would have made a rock perspire.

Since they were obviously merely trying to annoy him, Klaus decided to ignore them. He set his jaws and concentrated on his work. He and Hergett did not exchange another word all afternoon.

In the evening Hergett sat in his room, watching the night spreading before the window until the last bits of light had been absorbed like drops of water by a sponge. He sat for hours, hoping Katharina would come. But she didn't. The silence brought the past to life. He remembered evenings in Vorkuta when they had lain on their hard planks, no longer able to think or talk about anything because all their talks had ended in a dull homesickness. And while he thought of it, and remembered how many turns into the dark his life had taken before he was ever given a chance to really start it, he asked himself whether it could be that now, when he thought he had finally found a beginning, he should have to pay for it with an even greater loss. It seemed to him that all that had happened to him, all his longings and privations, had had only one purpose—to lead him to Katharina.

Just as he went to bed it began to rain. In the chestnut trees before the window the rain rattled down like hail. Hergett remembered that he had no coat. Everything comes together, he thought bitterly.

The next morning Hergett overslept. It was bright daylight in his room when he woke up. Still half asleep he stumbled out of bed and looked aghast through the window where the rain came rustling down through the chestnuts in broad even streams. Since he had no watch and the overcast sky gave no hint as to the exact time of the day, he dressed feverishly. Just when he put on his jacket, his landlady appeared at the door with a tray.

"I heard you were up," she said. "I'll have to bring your coffee now because I must go to the store."

Hergett interrupted her to ask what time it was.

"Just after eight," she said. "Did you sleep well—"

"Eight! I'm supposed to be there at eight!" Without looking at her shocked face he stormed from the room, jumped down the stairs and out into the street where he ran on in spite of the rain. He made it in ten minutes and arrived at the office completely drenched. Someone called him from the entrance gate but he paid no attention, chasing up the stairs, taking four steps at a time. He felt the stares of Klaus and Fräulein Huber on his back when he went to his desk. Sitting down he pulled out his handkerchief and wiped his face dry. His trousers stuck soaking to his legs, he lifted them by the creases, beat the water from his jacket and glanced up at Klaus who was watching him with a thin grin around his mouth.

"What did you do, fall into the Pegnitz?"

Hergett cursed between his teeth. The telephone rang. Fräulein Huber answered it.

"*Jawohl*, Herr Primelmann," she said and looked at Hergett. "You're to come to the personnel office right away."

Hergett got up silently. On the way he combed the hair out of his face. Primelmann kept him waiting for ten minutes. Then he called him in and looked him up and down.

"In my life I have seen many extraordinary things," he said frostily. "But that an employee arrives a quarter of an hour late on his second day is unusual even in my experience. If that happens again during your try-out period you can go home right away."

"Perhaps I may explain—" Hergett began but Primelmann cut him off.

"Thanks. If you leave your home in time you arrive at the office in time. Go back to your work."

Hergett clenched his fists and went out. The conceited, arrogant, damned bastard, he thought. Treating one like a schoolboy.

Back in his room, Klaus looked up and grinned:

"What did I tell you?"

Hergett cursed again.

In the evening they left the office together. Out in the street, Klaus stopped and looked up at the sky.

"I think the good weather is over," he said. "Weren't you sorry to have left Dahme so early?"

"Not sorrier than you were," replied Hergett.

For a moment they stared at each other with undisguised hate. Hergett made a movement as if he wanted to shake off something, then he turned and crossed the street.

As he walked home he thought of the gloomy office building with its dark corridors and many doors, the plain desks in the white-washed rooms. When he imagined that he would spend every day in those surroundings from now on, a hollow, empty feeling spread inside him and filled his mouth with bitterness.

He reached the street where he lived. It had two rows of old houses that looked as if the only reason they had not fallen down was that they were leaning against each other. His house had a pointed gable, tall narrow windows and an elaborately carved door. The Walters family lived on the second floor and Hergett climbed up a wooden staircase that groaned under each step. There were two entrance doors, one of them Hergett's own.

He unlocked it and saw at once that things had been changed since morning. In the morning there had been only one chair, now there were two. Also a different bedspread was on the bed. And two new pillows on the sofa. The water pitcher on the wash stand had been filled and his toilet articles, which he had left on the table wrapped in a towel, were neatly lined up on the shelf.

Hergett looked around and it occurred to him that for the first time in thirteen years he actually had an apartment of his own again. Only a furnished room, but anyhow, his own room. The thought forced a smile into his face.

There was a knock at the door and Frau Walter came in. She was a tiny, lively lady with snow-white hair and red spots on her cheeks. She brought him two glasses and asked if there was anything else he needed.

"Just ask me, any time," she said. "Our previous gentleman always did. He was a student. We were sorry he had to leave. Before that we had never rented a room. The room belonged to our son. He was killed in France."

"I'm sorry to hear that," said Hergett. "Was he your only son?"

"Yes. He was twenty-one years old. We wouldn't have rented the room though, except—may I sit down?"

"Of course," said Hergett. "By all means."

With a sigh she sat down on the sofa and said:

"We have our business in the Konigstrasse. A renting library. Two years ago the house was sold to a lady from Stuttgart. It isn't a nice house any more, very old. Right next to it a shoe firm has built a modern shop with marble fronting down where the show windows are. What does our new landlady do? She goes to the other side of the street, looks at the two buildings and then she comes into our shop and says we'd have to put up marble facing too. My husband told her we hadn't the money. We lost everything with the money reform and rental libraries don't bring in much. People don't want to read books any more, they want to buy automobiles and radios. But try and explain that to a person like our landlady. She only said she'd have to give us notice if we didn't put up the marble facing. So what could we do? Ten thousand marks my husband had to pay. We hadn't all that money and had to take a loan. That's why we're renting the room now. All our savings are gone and we have debts too now. It isn't nice any more in this world.

People have no consideration for each other any more. If you want something to read, tell me. Of course, you needn't pay for it."

"That's kind of you," said Hergett. "Thank you very much."

"Don't mention it. And if you have any other wishes—"

"I'll let you know," Hergett said smiling. Frau Walter wished him a good night and left. For a while Hergett sat staring into space, trying to imagine what the woman from Stuttgart looked like. He thought it was the same thing everywhere.

He didn't know how much time he had spent sitting there when there was a slight knock at the door. Thinking it was Frau Walter, he got up and opened the door. He stiffened with surprise. It was Katharina. She looked past him into the dark room.

"I hope I didn't wake you."

Hergett couldn't speak. He shook his head and groped for the light switch.

"Oh, but that's very cozy," she exclaimed and entered the room. "You even have a sofa." She turned around. "Why were you sitting in the dark?"

"I like sitting in the dark," said Hergett. His voice was an octave higher than usual. As if the sound of his own voice had broken his paralysis, he woke up to an eager and unnecessary liveliness. He ran senselessly around the room, pushed a chair closer to the table, straightened out a table cloth and asked Katharina three times please to sit down.

"I'd like to take off my wet coat," she said.

"Of course," he said in confusion. "Please forgive me."

He rushed to the closet, took out a hanger and helped her out of her coat. Her umbrella he put into the washstand which he emptied first. When he finally sat down on a chair he didn't know what to say, he was so happy.

She was wearing a soft, gray dress with a broad leather belt. Her face, he thought, looked a little pale but it suited her. Everything suited her, one could not think of changing any detail without damage to the whole effect of it.

He laughed.

"You have this devilish habit of always coming when one least expects you."

"There was a letter for you," said Katharina. "It came eight days ago. I asked my father for your address."

"Must be from my sister," he said, watching her take the letter from her purse. "Do you mind if I read through it quickly?"

"Of course not," she said. He opened it and glanced through it. "Not bad news, I hope," she said.

"No. They write that they got my letters and that they're glad I found a place with you. Also that they finally got a new apartment. Until now they had only two rooms. The new apartment, they say, is big enough for them to have me live there." He smiled. "With or without a wife."

"Your sister seems to be very fond of you," Katharina said in a low voice.

Hergett looked at the letter in his hands. "Ever since my mother died she's sort of taken her place."

"You must tell me about your family some time," said Katharina. "And about Ilmenau. I haven't really a picture of it in my mind."

"I bet anything you'd like it," Hergett said eagerly. "And there aren't any Russians in Ilmenau. They are over in Erfurt. God, Ilmenau! Imagine a landscape with thickly wooded hills with narrow valleys and clear little streams and then imagine a small town with very old houses and churches—that's Ilmenau."

"It sounds very romantic," said Katharina.

"It is. Once it was a winter resort. When I saw Nuremberg for the first time it reminded me a lot of Ilmenau. Ilmenau also started with a castle. But it is more beautiful, the landscape is. And it only has eighteen thousand inhabitants. One doesn't feel so lost there."

Katharina looked at his flushed face.

"I might fall in love with a place like that," she said seriously. "If only it weren't in the Eastern Zone. It's easier for a German nowadays to go to Australia or America than to Ilmenau. Even if, as you say, there are no Russians in Ilmenau, the Communists are repulsive enough."

"They speak the same German language we speak," said Hergett, "One day we'll have to get together with them again, one way or the other, and it would be good if by that time we'd learned to put what we have in common above that which divides us."

"You're contradicting yourself," said Katharina. "Three weeks ago you told me you had come here because of the Russians. Now suddenly you're trying to belittle that and say there aren't even any Russians in Ilmenau. Every day you read in the newspapers that so and so many people escape from the East Zone each month. Why do they do that if everything is as harmless over there as you make it out to be?"

Her suddenly sharp tone unsettled Hergett. He thought he could see open suspicion in her eyes. He took his sister's letter into his hands again, looked at the beautiful, clear handwriting, and said as calmly as he could:

"They're not escaping here because of the Russians. I know why they're coming here. But I'm not one of those. If I hadn't had a couple of errands here, I might never have thought of leaving Ilmenau again. I've survived Hitler and Stalin, I'll survive the German Communists too. But once I was here, the thought of staying was more obvious than that of going back. I wanted to look at this business in the West and I did."

"And now you're disappointed?"

"No, that would be an exaggeration. Although I do think the people here don't quite seem to know what they want. They don't seem to know what to do with a democracy. But otherwise . . ."

"Yes?"

Hergett smiled. "For someone who hasn't any money in his pocket there's as little to buy here as in the Eastern Zone. I'm certainly not a Communist. I think you and I, we've lost so much time through the war that we can afford to think for once about ourselves."

"I already told you I'm not interested in politics."

"But you're afraid," said Hergett. "The entire world is afraid of the Communists. Just as it was with Hitler. He would never have come that far if the world hadn't been so afraid of him. At any rate, you'll meet more Germans than Communists in Ilmenau and if things really didn't work out, it's just a short jump from Ilmenau to Nuremberg."

"What on earth are you talking about?" Katharina asked.

Hergett quickly reached across the table and took her hands in his.

"I'm talking about us. Perhaps I can't put it as beautifully as others, but if you married me it would be like starting my life from the very beginning again."

"In Ilmenau?"

"It doesn't have to be Ilmenau. Perhaps it would be simpler for me there, even if that doesn't sound logical. But I could imagine getting back into my old profession again if you went with me. But, as I said, it needn't be Ilmenau. With you I'd have the courage to start afresh wherever you want to be. Please try it with me. You'll never have to regret it."

For a long time Katharina looked at him. Then she gently freed her hands and said, in a low voice:

"I'll think it over."

It was more than Hergett had expected. He leaned forward.

"I won't press you. You must know very clearly what you want. And you mustn't think that you have to go to Ilmenau for my sake. My view is probably different from yours. I have people there who are waiting for me. They'd receive you as happily as they would me, I know, and after two days I'm convinced you'd feel at home. But it is a little more than that for me. For me it is half my life I spent in Ilmenau."

"Three weeks ago," said Katharina, "you wouldn't admit you were homesick."

"True. I've only become really aware of it during the past few days. I've even thought that it must have something to do with you."

"With me?"

"Yes." Hergett laughed a little. "It's hard to explain. When I look back I feel as if of all my former life only the frame was left, it's like a destroyed picture. Without a picture it had lost its attraction. When I imagined how you would look in that frame, it started to look again as it did before."

"You've said that very beautifully," Katharina said quietly. She sat for a few moments looking down. Then she got up. "I must go now."

Hergett did not attempt to persuade her to stay. He

helped her into her coat. When she put her hand in his, he said:

"Now I'll wait for you every evening."

"You'd better not do that," said Katharina. "You promised not to urge me."

"If I'm waiting for you, I'm not urging you."

"Yes you are, in a different way. I wanted to ask you something else."

"Yes?"

"Did you do anything about your brother-in-law? I mean the one who lives here?"

"No."

"And you're not going to do anything about him?"

"I've other things in my head now," said Hergett, looking into her eyes. She blushed.

"I'm glad. Tell me, Hergett, how many kilometers from here to Ilmenau."

"Oh, about—" Hergett broke off. He realized she had called him by his first name and he stared at her breathlessly.

"Don't you know?" she asked.

"Yes." With some effort Hergett restored his thoughts to order and his voice sounded very strange when he said:

"About a hundred and eighty."

"That's all?" Katharina shook her head in surprise. "I always thought it was much further away. A hundred and eighty. With a car it would only take three hours to get there."

"If it weren't for the zone border."

"If! I never knew before how awful it is, that border. It sounds over dramatic, I know, but it's like a trip from which one doesn't return."

"You can always return if you want to."

"You think so?" she said. "Tell me, Hergett, how long do you think that border will be there?"

"I don't know."

"You don't think that one day it'll disappear?"

"As soon as I'm in Ilmenau with you I'll believe in everything again," Hergett said solemnly. Then he took her face into his hands and kissed her gently on the lips. Then he said: "Even in myself."

For a moment he felt her pressing against him but before he could hold her, she was at the door. He watched her as she went down the stairs. On the bottom step she stopped and looked up at him, smiling. Then he heard the front door slam. Stiff-kneed he walked back to his bed and sat down. Later he saw that she had forgotten her umbrella.

# [ CHAPTER FIFTEEN ]

Ernst Wagner did not come to work Tuesday. On Wednesday morning Landrat Schneider asked Fräulein von Hessel to call the Welfare department and find out if he was absent again. To his relief Fräulein von Hessel reported that Wagner was at his desk. He told her to send for him immediately. The Landrat paced restlessly up and down; he had had a bad night. When Wagner came in he asked him why he hadn't come to work the day before. Ernst Wagner acted astonished.

"But you said we should look at the apartment."

"And because of that you don't show up for a whole day?" Schneider snapped. "Your mother could have looked at the apartment alone."

"It interests me as much as it does my mother," Ernst Wagner retorted. "If I take off a day the Landrat's office won't go bankrupt."

Schneider bit his lips. He controlled himself with an effort and sat down at his desk.

"Have you the letter with you?"

"No."

"No! Why not? I told you to bring it along."

"Not until I get the money."

Schneider reached into his jacket, took out his wallet and extracted a bundle of banknotes. Ernst Wagner stared at the money, a greedy expression on his narrow, foxy face.

"Here's four thousand five hundred marks," said Schneider. "You already have five hundred. I didn't bring a check—I don't want to lose any more time. You have the apartment. Now go home and get me that letter."

"Couldn't you give me the money right away?" asked Ernst Wagner.

"When I get the letter," Schneider said firmly. "Not a second sooner."

"Well, then at least let me have two or three thousand —the rest on delivery."

Something in his expression made Schneider suspicious. Coldly he said: "Out of the question. You can be back in an hour. Then you'll get the whole sum."

"You won't get the letter until we have an apartment."

"But you have an apartment."

Ernst Wagner shook his head.

"We don't like it. First of all it's too far from the office and secondly it's too small. And it doesn't have a bath. Without a bath we don't want it."

For a minute Schneider stared at him. Then he got up, went to the door and opened it. His face was unrecognizable when he said:

"I'm giving you five seconds, then I'll throw you out. Without the letter you needn't come back here."

"You better think that over," Ernst Wagner said hastily. "I merely wanted a decent apartment and—" He stopped and watched with fearful eyes as Schneider closed the door, turned the key and put it in his pocket. Before he could turn around, Ernst Wagner bolted towards the door that led into Schneider's anteroom. Ignoring Fräulein von Hessel's astonished face, he walked past her out into the corridor and straight into Primelmann's office.

Primelmann lowered his morning paper.

Posting himself before the desk Ernst Wagner drawled:

"You may give your Landrat a message from me. If he hasn't sent the money to my apartment by two o'clock, I'll take the letter to the police."

"What letter?"

"Ask your Landrat," said Ernst Wagner and slammed the door behind him.

Frau Hansen's disturbed face appeared in the door.

"What on earth," said Primelmann, "do you understand any of this?"

Frau Hansen shook her head.

"We'd better tell the Landrat right away."

"Of course, that is . . ." Primelmann fell silent. He had an instinctive wish to stay out of this. What letter —why had the fellow come to him, why hadn't he told Schneider directly? It was all very queer and he was better off out of it, he was sure. Besides, what reason had he to protect Schneider from troubles? On the contrary.

"We better keep our hands off this affair," he told Frau Hansen. "I've a funny feeling about all this. You don't want to get yourself into trouble, do you?"

"For heaven's sake, no," said Frau Hansen, looking shocked. "I want my peace. I'd be glad if I never saw that impossible person again."

"Exactly," said Primelmann. "He's probably insane. No normal individual would act like that. We simply don't know about anything, that's all."

Frau Hansen returned to her desk.

After exactly two hours and twenty eight minutes she had reached the point where she would have suffocated if she couldn't have shared her information. As soon as there was a chance, she went to Klaus Langer.

Frau Hansen had a weakness for Klaus Langer. She found him fascinating-looking and she admired him greatly for having been an officer and a bearer of the Knight's Cross. Also his affair with the Landrat's daughter gratified her vivid, romantic imagination. When the other employees laughed about Klaus' engagement to Katharina Schneider and predicted an unhappy end to it, Frau Hansen proclaimed ringingly that they would marry. Thus the outcome of the affair had become something of a prestige question for her, personally.

She decided to tell Klaus about the incident not merely because of her voracious enjoyment of gossip, but also because she vaguely felt she could thus contribute to an improvement of relations between Klaus Langer and the Landrat.

She motioned Klaus to come to the door and told him in hasty whispers of the incident.

Annoyed at their secretive behavior Hergett looked up and watched Klaus' face changing color, but although he tried, he caught nothing of the conversation. Only at the end, when Frau Hansen turned to go, did he pick up a few words:

". . . after all, I'm not doing this for the Landrat, I'm

doing it for his daughter. I'll phone you the address."

With that she left. Klaus went back to his desk, took a file, opened it and concentrated on its contents. Glancing at the letters on the cover, Hergett saw that he was holding it upside down. From that moment on Hergett forgot about his work. The phone rang. Quickly Langer reached for it and, taking a pencil, jotted down an address on a slip of paper. Hergett got up and walked past Klaus, peering over his shoulder and memorizing the address. He went to his coat, which hung at the door, pretended that he was searching for something in the pockets, then returned to his desk.

Klaus Langer sat motionless, staring at the slip of paper with the address. Then he folded it carefully, glanced at his watch, and began to clean up his desk. A moment later he got up and left the room. Fräulein Huber gave an indignant little cry at this unusual act. But before she could recover from her astonishment, she had a new surprise. Dumbfounded she watched as Hergett rushed to the door, took his jacket off the hook, and disappeared into the hall.

He caught sight of Klaus half a block away and slowed down to follow him unobserved. When he had heard Frau Hansen mentioning Katharina, fear had cut off his breath. His decision to follow Klaus Langer was merely an instinctive reaction to the thought that, while he sat in the office, something might happen outside, something that had to do with Katharina.

Now he was intent on remaining unseen by Klaus. But when Klaus stopped at a street car stop Hergett decided to give up the childish hide-and-seek and went over to him. The rain had stopped during the morning, but the sky was heavy with clouds and the streets looked empty and grey. Across from the street car stop was a little park with a few trees. A cool wind blew the first yellow leaves down into the street and left them lying on the wet asphalt like sad little children's faces.

"What are you doing here?" asked Klaus. His voice sounded calm and betrayed no surprise whatever. Hergett could not suppress an uneasy admiration. He looked at Klaus' expressionless face, with the scar on the forehead, and grinned.

"You guess!"

Klaus turned and walked away from him. When Hargett followed, he stopped and asked coldly:

"What do you want—to spy on me?"

"If I wanted to spy on you I'd have fixed it so you wouldn't have seen me."

"Go away," said Klaus, his voice sounding a trifle less calm. Hergett didn't move. Klaus started walking away, but Hergett kept up with him without any effort.

"This is just a waste of time and energy," he said cheerfully. "I'm a very good, tough marching man. I'll march alongside you, if need be, for two days without food. Even faster, watch it—"

He took such enormous strides that Klaus fell back. Hergett stopped and waited for him to catch up.

"That's no disgrace," he said companionably. "You're not as well trained as I am. First of all I was in the infantry and you in the air force and secondly you've hardly had any exercise in the past seven years while I was on my feet all day. Why don't you want me along? Anyhow, even if you did succeed in shaking me off I might as well tell you that I'd reach your destination on my own—Kreuzstrasse 8, isn't it? Shall we go on now?"

Klaus stared at him open mouthed.

"Who told you that?"

"I peeked," Hergett said, smiling. "You keep making mistakes. You're not half as smart as you think."

"You dirty bastard," said Klaus and spit in Hergett's face. Hergett turned pale. He quickly raised his arm and Klaus, bracing himself for the blow, blinked his eyes for an instant. When he opened them again, Hergett was wiping the spit from his cheek with his sleeve.

"We'll discuss this later," he said. "It was the stupidest thing you could have done. Shall I go alone to Kreuzstrasse?"

Klaus didn't answer. They went on to the next street car stop. During the ride they did not exchange a single word. By the time they got off, Klaus had come to the conclusion that he could not get rid of Hergett. Perhaps it was even better to have someone along who might cover up for him. As they entered the house, Hergett glanced at the name plates in the entrance and his eye fell on the top one. He began to see things a little more clearly.

He climbed the stairs after Klaus and stood behind him while he knocked at the door until it was opened.

"I'm bringing the money," said Klaus and pushed past Ernst Wagner into the dim hallway. Hergett followed him.

"You alone here?" asked Klaus.

Ernst Wagner was dumbstruck with surprise. He looked at Hergett who was leaning with his back against the door and asked with concern:

"What does he want here?"

"Same thing I want," said Klaus and went into the living room where Frau Wagner was standing, her face pale. Klaus surveyed in one glance the little room then went out into the hall again and looked into the other empty room.

"Now, there's a nice conference room," he said with satisfaction. He went over to Wagner and hit him on the mouth with his fist. Stunned, Wagner sat down on the floor.

"That was just a little down payment," Klaus said soberly. He grabbed Wagner by the collar, dragged him up and pushed him ahead into the empty room where he stood with his back to the door. Ernst Wagner ducked and ran towards Klaus. He was half a head shorter, and Klaus hit him with both fists between the eyes. Wagner stopped as if he had run against a tree. He reached for his nose which had started to bleed, then he went at Klaus again who kicked him in the stomach. Ernst Wagner found himself sitting on the floor again.

Klaus turned to Hergett. "Get me the old woman," he said.

Hergett went in to Frau Wagner. She hadn't seen the action in the other room and when Hergett came to her she was still standing on the same spot.

"Nothing is going to happen to you," said Hergett. "Come along."

She didn't move. When Hergett reached for her arm, she drew back. "Don't touch me!" she hissed.

"You're a bad mother," said Hergett. "Your son needs you, I think."

She rushed past him to Klaus, who was watching Ernst Wagner trying to get back on his feet.

"What do you want from him?" she screamed. Klaus waited until Hergett was in the room, then he closed the door.

"The letter." He turned to Wagner who was looking at him balefully and fingering his nose. "Where do you have it?"

"I'll never tell you," Ernst Wagner said in a tight voice.

"We'll see about that," said Klaus and slapped his face hard. Before he could slap him again, Frau Wagner threw herself between them.

"Leave him alone," she cried and turned to her son: "Tell him, why don't you tell him?"

Ernst Wagner shook his head.

"I'm not telling him anything. If he touches me again I'll scream so loud the entire house will hear it."

"You'll scream only once," Klaus said calmly. "You'll scream exactly as long as it takes me to draw this across your visage." He unbuttoned his coat and took off his broad leather belt. Holding it in his right hand, he said:

"All right, start screaming."

Ernst Wagner changed color. His mother now turned determinedly towards Klaus.

"He can't give you the letter. The letter doesn't exist any more."

"Shut your mouth!" Wagner shouted.

Klaus raised his eyebrows.

"What's this?"

Frau Wagner laughed hysterically.

"What I said. My husband burned it before he was arrested. When I told him—"

"I told you to shut your mouth," Ernst Wagner panted. She gave him an angry look.

"I've shut my mouth long enough. If you'd only listened to me. I told you this wouldn't work."

She turned back to Klaus.

"When I told my husband in jail that Schneider had become Landrat, he remembered the letter and rewrote it the way he remembered it. He told me to take it and go to Schneider with it and ask him to help us. I couldn't do it. My husband then said to wait until Ernst came back from prison."

Klaus exchanged a look with Hergett.

"You don't really think I'm going to believe you?" he said to Frau Wagner.

"I don't care whether you do or not," she said contemptuously. "As far as I'm concerned you can turn the entire apartment upside down. If my husband had kept those letters, a lot of other people would have been in trouble. He had an entire crate full of them."

"Where did he have them, here, in Nuremberg?"

"Yes."

"And when he fled, he burned them?"

"He only burned them when they came to arrest him. He'd hoped he might use them again."

"For blackmail?"

Frau Wagner was silent. Klaus looked at Hergett.

"What do you think? I can't imagine our Landrat falling for such a crude swindle."

"With his bad conscience . . ." said Hergett. He looked at the woman.

"Where's the forged letter?"

"My son has it."

"Give it to me," said Klaus. Ernst Wagner reached hesitantly into his coat and pulled out a wallet.

"Give me the wallet," said Klaus.

"The wallet doesn't concern you," said Wagner and stepped back. Klaus hit him across the face with the leather belt. Ernst Wagner let out a wild scream and covered his mouth with both hands. The wallet dropped to the floor. Before he could bend for it, Klaus had retrieved it.

"Want any more?" he asked. Frau Wagner pushed her son aside.

"Haven't you enough yet?" she hissed at Klaus. "You know what you wanted to know, don't you?"

"I want to know what's in that wallet," said Klaus and examined it. There were three hundred-mark bills, a couple of bank slips, half a dozen pictures of nude women and an identification card. Finally he found the letter. He unfolded it and read it, then he put it in his pocket and handed the wallet to Frau Wagner. Seeing the hundred-mark bills and the nude photographs she gave her son a dark look.

"It seems to be true," Klaus told Hergett. "I know the style of our Landrat. I'd swear he never wrote this letter. I just don't understand why he didn't catch on to the swindle."

"He never really looked at the letter," Frau Wagner said scornfully. "He was so scared, he dropped it at once. My son picked it up and put it back in his pocket."

Klaus grinned. "I think we can go now," he said to Hergett.

He put his belt on again and straightened out his clothes. Then he looked at Wagner.

"Don't ever dare show your face again in the office," he said.

Wagner didn't reply.

When they were out in the street again, Hergett gave a short laugh. "That's a joke."

"A good joke, in fact," said Klaus.

For a while they walked in silence.

"Where did you learn this sort of thing," asked Hergett.

"In the air force."

"Oh?" said Hergett. It sounded skeptical and Klaus looked at him.

"You don't believe me?"

"It was a little too professional," said Hergett.

"Nonsense. With this fellow it wasn't difficult. He's a coward, it was just a matter of the proper treatment. At the asylum we had that type, too."

"You treated them too?"

"Sometimes, when they went wild. The attendants were grateful if one took over some of their work and it was good for the self-respect. You didn't act stupidly either."

"Just a walk-on part," said Hergett. "What would you have done if I hadn't been there?"

"I'd have lost even less time," said Klaus, and looked at his watch. "It's after lunch. We can go to the Landrat right away."

"You can go there alone," said Hergett.

"Don't act the modest man," said Klaus. "This time I want you with me. I need a witness."

"For what?"

"For a certain eventuality," said Klaus.

Fräulein von Hessel looked surprised when they came in.

"I don't think the Herr Landrat is free now," she said. "What do you want to see him about?"

"About the letter," said Klaus.

"I beg your pardon?"

"About the letter of—it's enough if you tell him it's about the letter," he said impatiently.

Fräulein von Hessel picked up the telephone and repeated what Klaus had said. Then she nodded and said they could go in.

Schneider sat straddle-legged behind his desk and looked towards them with ill-suppressed excitement.

"What's going on?" he asked hoarsely.

"This might interest you," Klaus said and put the letter on the desk. "It's forged. The original doesn't exist any more. Perhaps you'd like to read it over again."

Schneider felt his brain beginning to churn. He stared first at Klaus then at Hergett then at the letter. The lines swam together before his eyes. He read it three, four times, opened his mouth and closed it. Then he pushed himself up from his chair and walked with uncertain steps to the window, a hot, glowing onrush of thoughts and feelings threatening to burn up his insides.

Klaus watched him expectantly. When Schneider remained silent, he said: "We were in his apartment. His mother confessed that her husband burnt all his letters. Then when he heard you'd been made Landrat, he rewrote the letter from memory. You should have looked at it more carefully."

Schneider did not reply. His brain was as if paralyzed, with his thoughts whirling around crazily. Yet gradually he began to see and feel a little more clearly. His first thought had been that he had made an enormous fool of himself. Yet at the same time he sensed a chance, an equally enormous chance which the situation offered to him if he did not lose his head altogether. When he turned around his face was completely controlled.

"You say you were at Wagner's home?" he asked Klaus coolly.

Klaus nodded.

"Herr Buchholz and I."

"When?"

"About an hour ago."

"Who told you to go there? There must have been a reason."

Klaus looked at Hergett who was leaning against the door with his hands in his pockets.

"There's been a reason for a long time," he drawled. "What does it matter? The main thing is that you know where you're at with regard to the letter."

"I've known that for weeks," Schneider said coldly. "What you're telling me there isn't new to me. I've known all along that this letter was forged."

Klaus turned pale.

"That's a dirty lie," he said loudly. "I can prove to you—"

"What did you say?" Schneider took three long steps away from the window and stood before Klaus with clenched fists. "You'll withdraw that remark at once."

"I certainly won't," Klaus snapped. "If you claim you've known this, then you're telling a dirty lie."

Schneider stared at him with bulging eyes, then he slapped him on the cheek. Klaus staggered back against Hergett who was now taking his hands out of his pockets. He could have held Klaus and for a second he was going to. Then he remembered that Klaus had spit into his face, and he thought of a few other things, of Katharina for instance and his messed up life and all the things he had had to take during the past seven years—he thought of all that and watched motionless as Klaus jumped upon the Landrat in a blind rage. He turned and as he was opening one door and walking out, Fräulein von Hessel was coming in through the other door. She screamed so loudly that they could hear it down the entire hall. Hergett had walked about twenty steps when he began to feel sorry, but now it was too late. As if an earthquake had burst open all the doors, people with shocked faces came running from all directions, and without having to see it Hergett knew what was happening now. He was back in his room, staring blankly at the empty chair of Fräulein Huber, when he heard the shrill wail of police sirens and shortly afterwards the sound of hobnailed boots rushing up the stairs. Then everything became silent. Hergett sat a while longer, but finally could not stand it any more and went towards the door. Before he reached it, it was opened from the outside and he found himself face to face with a young man who stared at him curiously and asked whether he was Herr Buchholz.

"I am," said Hergett.

The young man was embarrassed.

"Herr Primelmann has sent me," he said after a little pause. "He wants me to tell you that you may go home."

"Home?"

"Yes."

"Dismissed?"

The young man shook his head violently. "You were only here temporarily, so they couldn't dismiss you. It's just that they don't need you any more."

"Interesting," said Hergett.

He walked out. In the hall and on the stairs stood many employees, talking excitedly. One could see how happy they were at the interruption.

When he got home, Hergett wrote an urgent note to Katharina, asking her to give him a chance to talk to her. If she could not come, she should write him where to meet her. He mailed the note at once, thinking that for some reason he was counting on a letter from her rather than on her personal appearance. He had been completely without emotion all afternoon but now he felt a dull repulsion rise inside him. Twist and turn as he might, he could not rid himself of the feeling that he had dirtied himself.

He stayed in bed late the next morning. His state of mind matched the overcast sky before the window. It took an effort to get up at all. While he washed himself, Hergett tried to figure out how much money he still had. It wasn't much, he knew, enough for three weeks at the most.

He sat down at the table and counted his money. It was even less than he had thought. He looked at it for a while, then took two bills and put them away into the back compartment of his wallet. He needed only enough for one ticket. For Katharina it would be too dangerous

to cross the zone border illegally. Once he was in Ilmenau he would get her an entry permit.

The rest of the morning he spent sitting idly in his
room. He watched the rain beating down on the chestnuts and his thoughts moved steadily around one point,
like a wheel around its axle. It was the most difficult, the
most frightening question he had ever asked himself
and by afternoon he had not yet found an answer as to
what he would do if he should never hear from Katharina again.

Eventually Hergett put on his coat and went out into
the street to look for the mailman. It was time for the
afternoon delivery, but he had to wait for almost an hour
before he spotted the mailman coming out of a house.
He walked towards him to ask whether he had a letter,
but did not go through with it for fear the man would
say no. The mailman was disappearing into the next
house now—two more and he would reach Hergett's. The
street was almost deserted. A man on a bicycle was tread-
ing his way forward into the beginning dusk. Hergett
waited. He saw the mailman coming out of one house
and going into the next. He was a small man. Under the
vizor his face looked self-important and he moved with
the slow, comfortable gait of a man who knows that in
his old age he will be taken care of and secure. It
seemed an eternity before he came out again. Hergett
moved a little to the side to let him in and looked at the
mailman's hands, but they were concealed by a rain
cape. He looked at Hergett suspiciously, then he went
inside and Hergett could hear the sound of the mail
being distributed in the boxes. He merely had to turn
around to see if he had put anything in his own box
but again the fear that he might not have prevented
him. He was still standing in the door when the man
had long since gone on and he was asking himself what
on earth stopped him from looking to see if he had a
letter. It is ridiculous, he told himself. It is ridiculous,
the way you behave. If she hasn't written today, she will
write tomorrow or the day after or she will come herself,
or devil knows what. It is really ridiculous, he thought,
but he felt his heart hammering and he kept standing
there and the longer he stood, the less courage he had

257

to face disappointment. At long last he found that he was acting like a moron. He pulled himself together and, turning, went with long, determined strides into the foyer. It was already too dark, so he pressed the light button to see. And then he stopped and blinked and looked again and it was no mistake, there was something in his mailbox. Feverishly he began to search for his key, he unbuttoned his coat and went through all his pockets but then he remembered that he had the key in his room upstairs, and he ran up the stairs four at a time and returned with the key. The moment he unlocked the mailbox, the automatic hall light went out. In the dark he took out the letter, walked up the stairs in the dark, and in his room he stopped and looked and saw right away that he was holding the announcement of a lottery in his hand. He stared at it a while, then he spread his fingers and let it drop to the floor while a giggle rose in him, a giggle that grew into a hysterical laugh. Great heavens, he thought, great heavens. He put his face in his hands and stood as if in the dark and then the thought came to him that he might go to Katharina and wait for her in front of her house.

It was dark in the street and it had begun to rain again. The street lamps blinked sleepily down on the wet asphalt. From some of the roofs the water came rattling down on the empty sidewalks like showers of hail. Hergett walked swiftly and twenty minutes later he reached Erlenstegen and Schneider's house. The blinds were down in most houses, including the Schneiders', and Hergett could not see if anyone was home. He stood on the other side of the street and looked across, his uneasiness increasing. He now reproached himself for not finding out whether Schneider had been hurt in the fight with Klaus. It had been stupid simply to run away and not bother about anything. The more he thought about it, the more worried he became. Finally he could not stand the uncertainty any longer. He crossed the street and hurried to the entrance door and felt for the bell in the dark. The shrill sound of the bell rang out into the night. Hergett rushed away from the door, and a few yards away he stopped and pressed himself against a dark, wooden fence from where he looked back breathlessly.

Nothing moved in the big house that stood huge and black in the rain. Hergett wondered if he should try again when at last he saw the door being opened and light falling into the garden. A second later he saw Katharina. The outline of her body showed clearly against the lighted hall and it seemed to Hergett as if she were looking directly at him. He pressed himself against the damp, cool wood of the fence and didn't dare to breathe. She's seen me, he thought, she's surely seen me. He closed his eyes and a minute went by while he felt his heart in the tips of his fingers. Then he could not stand it any longer. He opened his eyes and saw that the door was closed again. He moved away from the fence and with his hand kneaded the skin over his heart because it seemed to hurt unbearably. Then, suddenly, there was another sound. It came from Schneider's house again—the door opened and Katharina stepped out. She wore a light raincoat with a hood and looked up at the sky. Hergett stared after her as she crossed the street and vanished into the dark. For a while he could still hear her steps coming quickly and rhythmically through the rain, growing fainter and fainter and finally disappearing. Hergett wiped the rain from his face. Suddenly his thoughts were functioning again—if she were coming to him, he had to go to the apartment before her. He raced off, through a side street, jumping across puddles, panting and praying that he would reach the street car stop before her. He did and when, ten minutes later, he got off he cursed himself for having gone to her house. Had she left a moment earlier he would have missed her.

He dried his wet face, combed the water out of his hair and thought that he would have to buy a hat. But that, he hoped, he could do in Ilmenau. He sat on the couch, his elbows on his knees, his chin in his fists and listened to the rain. Time passed and he grew first impatient and then, gradually, resigned. She had gone elsewhere, probably. Still, he might look down the street once more. When he opened the door she was standing there. For a second they looked at each other, shocked. Then with a tired gesture Katharina brushed her hood off her head and said:

"I was just about to knock."

"You needn't ever knock to come to me," said Hergett. She went past him and he noticed that she did not offer him her hand. Neither did she make a move to take off her coat. She stopped in the middle of the room and looked around:

"Have you my umbrella?"

Her voice sounded cool and distant. Her face, too, was different, with rings under her eyes and hard lines around her mouth. Hergett went to the closet and took out the umbrella. He kept it in his hand and said:

"I noticed too late that you had forgotten it, otherwise I'd have run after you. Don't you want to sit down?"

"No." She lifted her eyes and he saw they were reddened. "You know that Klaus is in jail?"

"I don't know anything," said Hergett with an empty feeling in his head.

"They took him yesterday," said Katharina. "It is certain that they will put him back in the asylum. My father is in bed. Klaus beat him almost to pulp. What's worse, Klaus doesn't say anything. He doesn't defend himself. My father claims he suddenly attacked him and you were standing there and then you left the room. Is that true?"

For a while Hergett was silent. Then he said:

"Do you know why we were there?"

"My father didn't say."

"I'll tell you. The letter was forged."

"Which letter?" she asked. "The one they tried to blackmail him with?"

"Yes."

"Who said that?"

"The blackmailer himself. We were in his apartment."

"You were—who? You and Klaus?"

"Yes," said Hergett.

"I don't understand," she said perplexed. "Did you plan to do that?"

"He didn't want me along at first, but I went anyhow."

"And then?"

Hergett hesitated. He was not sure whether he should tell her all, but then he did anyway and concluded:

"Of course your father didn't know that the letter was forged. He couldn't know."

"Perhaps he did," said Katharina. She sat down on the

260

edge of a chair and looked at the floor and thought. "The last few days he was much more composed," she said.

"I think it's out of the question," Hergett said. "Why wouldn't he have told you then?"

"I'll ask him. But it makes no difference now."

"I wouldn't say that. I'm wondering how one could help Klaus. If I went to the police and told them—"

"What would you tell them?"

"That your father provoked him."

"After he provoked my father first. It isn't just my father—Klaus injured two other people who were trying to hold him back. It seems to me almost as if he'd done it intentionally. He knew he'd go back to the asylum after the slightest incident. He was only out on parole."

"If the police hear—" Hergett began but Katharina interrupted him.

"—that my father denounced someone in the Third Reich? You wouldn't help Klaus with that either. The only one who could have helped him was you."

"I don't see how—"

"You didn't answer my question before," Katharina interrupted again. "Was it true that when Klaus attacked my father you walked out?"

Hergett looked into her eyes. They were as hard as her voice. He searched for a credible explanation but found none. To gain time he said: "What do you want to know from me?"

"I told you twice," replied Katharina in the same, hard voice. "You're strong enough to've been able to cope with Klaus. You could have held him back. Instead you walked out. Why did you do that?"

"Why shouldn't I do that?" said Hergett. "Am I his governess?"

She looked at him in silence. Then she got up and said in a low voice: "You needn't have done that, Hergett. I had decided to go with you to Ilmenau. Now I can't do that."

Hergett nodded bitterly. "You're making things easy for yourself. All you needed was a good reason. If this is the only reason why you don't want to go with me now, then you've never seriously intended to go."

"This is how cheaply you think of me?"

Hergett did not answer. He knew that his words did

not express his true thoughts. But he refused to seek the blame for it all only in himself. Besides he thought that Katharina was overdramatizing the whole thing.

"How I think of you I don't have to tell you. I only think you're blaming me for an accident that has been, according to all I've heard and seen, in the air for a long time. That it happened just now isn't necessarily my fault."

"It's all our fault," Katharina said tonelessly. "But that's not the point. It's enough that I have to reproach myself. If in addition I were married to a man who could have saved Klaus from the asylum, it would be twice as bad. Don't try any more, Hergett. If I ever marry I want to be able to look my husband in the eyes and I can't look into yours any more."

She went quickly to the door and was gone before he could say anything else.

He stood rooted. His face was as white as the plaster wall. Then he ran after her. He didn't know why he ran after her because he could think of nothing else to tell her. But he couldn't help it. In the street he saw her, about fifty yards away. He saw her light coat and began to walk behind her, slowly and without thinking and without wanting anything. He pushed his hands into his pocket and felt the rain burst on his skin, soaking through his clothes and shoes, he had to brace himself against its force as if he were walking through underbrush. But he hardly noticed it. He was numb with pain and he told himself it serves you right that it happened this way, this way and no other. He shook his head and giggled a little without knowing it. He walked on and then he started to wonder why he didn't simply go to her and tell her that all this was nonsense, the thing with Klaus, too, who would never have made a good man for her. Nonsense too, for him to be running after her through this damned rain while she had the umbrella and was waiting for him to come to her. And he said: "That was funny, your telling me a little while ago that I needn't try any more when you know so well how much I love you and that everything I'm doing is being done for you, too." And he felt her pressing his arm and saying: "Of course, I know that."

"It really is funny," he said consoled. "It's funny that

two people who love each other as much as we do walk through the street one after the other as if they were afraid to look each other in the face. We can't have that," he said, "you know it as well as I do that we can't allow two people to walk one after another, two who love each other—" his thoughts became confused. Crossing the street he stepped into a big puddle and the water splashed up his clothes. With his sleeve he wiped his wet face and thought if it would only end, if it would only— and there, ahead of him, walked Katharina, her slim back bent a little. Once he came up so close that she would have seen him at once if she had stopped. But she didn't stop and he held back a little until the distance between them had increased. Then he continued after her, thinking that it was senseless. Yet as long as you are running after her so senselessly, he told himself, why don't you simply go to her and never mind what she'll say or do or think. And don't ever imagine that you can impress her with your damned pride because, he asked himself, what would it have cost you to say simply you hadn't the time to hit him over the head because they were already on the floor before you realized what was happening or else you walked out only to get help because you weren't strong enough to cope with a man run amuck. Nobody, he thought, can ask you to be so stupid and merely in order not to lie, stand back and watch how everything is going to pieces—*finis*—*kaputt*. The thought so terrified him suddenly that he stopped and gasped for air. Ahead of him walked Katharina. He saw her fighting against the rain, against the wind that had arisen and was hurling clouds of dripping darkness into the narrow canyons of the street, above which the sky had collapsed leaving only a yawning black hole where the roofs ended. He was still thinking why there should be no other possibility than the one that, at this moment, shocked him so, and why, in the name of three devils, he could not do something that would cost him merely a small lie, a few cheap little words, and his eyes never left Katharina who had walked quite a distance away from him by now. A little later, the darkness washed her black waves over and around her and she disappeared at the end of the dark canyon, disappeared once and for all, although he had only needed to walk a little faster to hold her. And he still had found no answer to his question. With hanging shoulders he stood in the rain that was slapping his face with cold fists, coming down in roaring cascades from the roofs and strewing a forest of tiny fountains on the hard pavement. Then he started to grin. It was not until twenty minutes later, when he lay stretched out on his bed, that he stopped fooling himself and until he fell asleep it gave him an idiotic and painful satisfaction to feel the water run out of his eyes.

# [ CHAPTER SIXTEEN ]

The next morning he woke up late. He no longer felt any pain, his head was strangely clear and filled with one thought only. He dressed, packed his belongings into the briefcase, wrote a note to his landlady and hurried out of the room.

It was no longer raining. He had no idea when the next train was leaving but he moved with the precision of a man who is about to start a carefully planned business trip and must not lose a minute. Only once he stopped at a store and looked at the display. He went in and bought an electric razor. It was the same model Katharina had given him. For his sister he bought a small coffee machine and for himself a flashlight. The electric razor, he decided, he would give his brother-in-law. Except for the two bills he had stashed away in his wallet, he had almost no money left now. He watched the friendly salesgirl wrapping up the things and then put them into his briefcase. The salesgirl went to open the door for him and said: "Please come back and let us serve you again."

"I certainly will," said Hergett. It was starting to rain again and he hurried to the station where he bought a street map of Bavaria at the kiosk. After studying it for a while he decided to take another route across the zone border this time. He went to the ticket window and bought a ticket to Hof. From there he would have to walk about two hours. The next train, he was told, was leaving in an hour. With his last eight marks he went to the station restaurant and ordered the most expensive lunch: roast venison with potato dumplings and bilberry compote. He ate heartily, drank a glass of wine, and felt very satisfied, very detached from everything. He remembered his stolen suitcase and looked around for the waiter who had held him back at the door but he didn't see him anywhere. Perhaps it was his day off, or he was sick, or had died in the meantime. Who knows, thought Hergett, who knows. He smiled to himself and then it was time to pay after which he had one single mark left. He held it in his hand when he went up on the platform. The train was already there. It had only four coaches but they were practically empty. Hergett had a compartment all to himself. He put down his briefcase and, as the doors were being closed, he lowered the window and leaned out. On the platform stood several people in identical postures with identical expressions of hidden pain in their faces. They held kerchiefs in their hands and waved. They were still waving when the train had left the great roofed hall and rolled over a maze of tracks and switches northward into the cloud-hung day. It rolled past single houses, little gardens and patches of wood, across a bridge beneath which the dirty water of the Pegnitz flowed. Hergett leaned further out the window. The pointed towers of the Lorenz Church rose clearly visible above the roofs, and further back the mighty basilica of the Frauenkirche stood against the dark ruins of the castle. A little to the left of it, just there where the big woods began, lived Katharina. Hergett swallowed. He wiped his eyes with the back of his hand and kept on staring out the window until the silhouettes of the city flattened and melted into the veiled horizon. Only then he turned back to his empty compartment and he said:

"Are you sad?"

Since no one answered he sat down on the bench and murmured:

"I'm sorry that you didn't come along, but what could I do?"

And since Katharina remained silent, he bent over to her and whispered:

"Actually I didn't want to leave at all."

Later he told himself he'd gone mad.

It was dark when he got off the train at Hof. During the train ride he had again studied the map and determined his route. Since he didn't want to cross the border too near the autobahn, he had decided to cross near Muenchenreuth. It was about twelve kilometers north of Hof in a woodland that stretched all the way to the border. From there he would walk another fifteen kilometers to the autobahn and hitch a ride. He estimated that it would take him about six hours in all to make his way. If he started off at once, he would get there by two o'clock in the morning and could rest a while and wait for the dawn.

He slid his map into his coat pocket, made sure he had his flashlight, and left the station. Out in the street he asked the first man who came along about the way.

"Muenchenreuth," said the man. "Not on foot, surely?"

Hergett smiled condescendingly and told him that he was a good walker and would make the twelve kilometers easily.

"It'll take you three hours at least," said the man and described the road he should take. Hergett thanked him. It took him half an hour to pass the last houses and reach the road leading in a straight line into the darkness. The rain, which had intermittently stopped during the train ride, was starting again with a thin drizzle and the landscape on both sides of the street was almost invisible. The further away Hergett walked from the town, the fewer people he met. Once he encountered a man on a bicycle who called out something Hergett didn't understand. He didn't care anyhow, he had only his road in mind and as he strode along he didn't think once of Katharina. He moved past black clusters of trees, through dark villages, like a machine and he was obsessed with one single thought: to get to Ilmenau as quickly as possible.

After about an hour's march he reached a bridge. In spite of the darkness he could detect the broad bands of the autobahn beneath. He looked for the headlights of cars but it seemed there was no traffic at all. Hergett went on. He had to watch sharply now. Two kilometers behind the bridge a small road branched off to Muenchenreuth. On the map it was marked with a thin line only. Hergett suspected that it was a country road. He kept close to the right edge, walking along the black wall of a forest. After twenty minutes he noticed a gap in the forest. He beamed his flashlight at it and saw a small path. According to the map it should lead in a northeasterly direction and Hergett cursed the rainy weather that made it impossible to orient himself. He told himself that this must be the right way; anyhow, he would find out soon enough. According to the map he should come upon a village after ten minutes.

Between the trees it was so dark that he could find his way only with the help of the flashlight. The rain wet his face in a steady fall. Also his arms hurt from carrying the heavy briefcase. He broke off a branch, pushed it through the grip and carried the stick on his shoulder like a carbine, with the briefcase resting on his back. After a few minutes the wood ended abruptly. In the darkness he could see the blurred outline of a few houses. When he reached the first one a dog started barking furiously. Hergett walked faster and after a while the barking stopped. A little later he reached Muenchenreuth. In order not to rouse another dog, he walked around the village through a sodden field and reached the edge of the wood that ran from Muenchenreuth north to the zone border. He knocked the loamy mud from his shoes and went into the fringe wood. According to the map there should be a little brook somewhere around, and hilly land from here on. Until now Hergett had noticed the difference in altitude between Hof and Muenchenreuth only in his legs because the darkness hid even the nearest hills from sight. He suspected that Muenchenreuth was at the bottom of a valley, at least it seemed as if he had walked steadily downhill during the past twenty minutes or so. Hergett felt his way along the trees, a safe distance away from the edge of the wood. Luckily there was little underbrush and he made good time. He was beginning to wonder where the small brook was when the ground beneath him dropped sharply. He beamed his flashlight down and saw a narrow gorge at the bottom of which water was shooting along between great boulders and stones. The other side rose just as steeply and then there were woods again. What was beyond the woods didn't interest Hergett. He now merely had to follow the brook and he could cross the zone border with his eyes closed. He unshouldered his briefcase and lit a cigarette. He was confident now. Soon he would be across and in a couple of hours he would reach the autobahn—not the autobahn of the West German Federal Republic, but that of the German Democratic Republic of which Katharina had been so afraid.

For the first time since he got off the train at Hof the memory of her overcame him with a violence that clamped his body together like a spring and caused a burning pain inside him. He threw away the cigarette, jumped to his feet and picked up his bag. Then he walked on as fast as the darkness allowed.

He slowed only when the ground began to rise. The effort of climbing distracted his attention and he was almost glad about it. But as time went on, it became worse. He had clearly been mistaken in the nature of the terrain. When he felt his way towards the gorge again and directed the beam of his flashlight downwards, he saw that it was now nearly three times as deep as before. Carefully he stepped over a fallen tree trunk. He tried not to use the flashlight and when he did, he held it close to the ground so that no light would fall upward. According to the distance he should have crossed the zone border by now, but he knew that the toilsome climbing, the continual obstacles in his way, had taken a great deal of time. He was forced to stop at ever shorter intervals to calm his lungs and he had given up trying to keep alongside the gorge all the time. The mountain showed him the way and when he finally felt the incline flattening he was so exhausted that nothing could have induced him to change direction. Anyhow, he was convinced now that he had made it. The trees were less thick here and the higher he had climbed, the lighter the air had grown although here, too, the rain continued to spray into his face. He changed the briefcase into his other hand—the method with the stick had proved too troublesome—and went on. Suddenly he felt a road under his feet. Hergett stopped and closed his eyes, trying to orient himself by instinct. If he was right, the little path should be leading from west to east. It was about two yards wide and in good condition. At least it looked and felt like a forest road that is used a great deal. The temptation to walk along it a while was too great, Hergett could not resist. He followed the road for about two hundred steps when he came up against the contours of a house. It stood a little off the road and when Hergett approached, slowly and apprehensively, he saw that it was only a hut with three walls. The fourth side was open. He went inside and switched on his flashlight. There was a bench, the floor was scattered with scraps of paper and empty cigarette packs. Hergett picked up one and looked at it. Then he picked up another and eventually he found a wrinkled page of a newspaper, flattened it and looked at the large advertisements. Shock and disappointment made his forehead sweat. The newspaper was from Hof, the cigarettes he knew from Nuremberg. He had miscalculated the distance or, what was worse, had lost the direction. For a while he didn't know what to do. He sat down on the bench and tried to bring some order into his thoughts. If he had really lost his way he would have to wait for day and re-orient himself. Perhaps it was better to cross when it was light. Just before daybreak—the thought cheered him a little and he felt happy to have a roof over his head in this weather. You should be glad to sit in a dry spot, he told himself. For an old soldier you act mighty peculiar, one must say. He opened his briefcase and took out some bread he had taken along from his lunch. Then he took all the papers that might be of danger and burned them with a match, keeping only the letter which his sister had written him to Nuremberg. He read it once more and then pushed it into his coat pocket. After that he lit another cigarette and stretched out his legs. The sound of the rain made him very sleepy but he fought the sleep, shaking his head now and then, and getting up a couple of times.

The hut opened up towards the road and he could overlook it for a stretch in the same direction from which he had come. One could distinguish little in the darkness and except for the blurred contours of the trees on both sides there was nothing much to see, but then Hergett did see something after all. With one jump he was on his feet and reached for his briefcase. On the road two men came walking towards the hut. They had lamps with strong spotlights which they alternately switched on and off. But it was enough for Hergett to see that they wore uniforms. He began to run. First he ran down the road a stretch and when the two began to shout after him and switched on their spotlights he turned to the right and ran blindly down the mountain. He didn't feel the branches whipping his face, not the painful impact when he ran against a tree, he was solely obsessed with the idea not to be caught and when the incline grew steeper he braked his speed with a couple of zig zag jumps, holding his briefcase before him like a shield. Then he got caught in something and he stumbled while a hot pain shot through his legs. He threw his shoulders forward, his face crashed down into moist leaves, and he tried to kick his legs free. He realized he was caught in barbed wire. The briefcase had dropped from his hands but he had no time to grope for it. Behind him he heard the two uniformed men shouting and with a wild kick he freed himself, stumbled to his feet, and chased on, feeling the blood run down his thighs. His only thought was that he now had the zone border behind him. He saw the precipice just as the ground disappeared under his feet and he fell down about thirty yards and lay with unnaturally distorted limbs.

The two border guards found him. They shone the lamps into his face and the taller of the two knelt down beside him and searched through his pockets.

"Is he dead, Alfred?" the other asked in a tight voice.

"You try and jump from up there," said Alfred morosely. He had once been an employee in a transport firm that had gone bankrupt after the money reform. Then he had joined the border police. The other's name was Otto. He wanted to become an officer and was nineteen years old. He raised his eyes to the sky and shook his head.

"The idiot. He must have seen the barbed wire. What did he run into the quarry for?"

"Must have had a damned bad conscience," said Alfred. He had found the letter in Hergett's coat pocket and looked at the address.

"He wanted to cross over," he said. "The lettter's from the zone. Doesn't even have any papers on him."

"Probably one of those Communists."

"May be, but this is a Nuremberg address. If he wasn't a Communist we may have trouble. Next thing they'll say its our fault that he fell down there."

"Damned, yes!" said Otto.

"You remember how it was with that other one. His mother acted as if we'd murdered him."

"Damned, but what do we—"

"Psst!" Alfred quickly switched off his lamp. "What was that?"

They stared fearfully into the night. But it was so dark that they could not see the two policemen from the East Zone who stood twenty meters away on the edge of the wood with their machine guns uncocked.

"Someone coughed there," said Otto.

Alfred lowered his voice to a whisper. "They must have heard us shouting. Are we too far over?"

"No, the border goes through the center of the quarry."

"If he'd only dropped over on the other side," whispered Otto. "A few more meters and he wouldn't be our business any more."

"Grab his legs," Alfred said quickly determined. "We'll drag him across."

They hung their carbines over their shoulders and dragged him a little ways across the quarry.

"That does it," Alfred said, panting. "They'll find him tomorrow morning." He put the letter back into Hergett's coat and said: "If he were one of us, but this way—"

"Come along," Otto urged nervously. They ran back and stopped again.

"Didn't someone yell just now?" whispered Otto.

"Nonsense, he won't ever yell again. And if so, it's none of our concern."

"All Communists, anyway," said Otto. They hurried off.

The two policemen waited until they had disappeared. Then they stepped out of the wood and went over to Hergett.

"Those rascals," said one of them. "Did you get that?"

"They're trying to hang another one on us," said the other. His name was Gunther. They were brothers. During war they had served in the infantry. In February 1945 their parents were killed by a bomb in Dresden. Since they had no longer a home, Paul and Gunther had joined the East Zone police after they were released from the army.

"Next thing they'll write in their newspapers that we killed the fellow," said Gunther.

"Shall we report it?"

"I don't know. Let's see what kind of papers he has." They read the letter and looked at each other.

"Apparently he wanted to come over to us."

"Should have stayed where he was," Gunther said glumly. He was the older one and had no desire to get mixed up in the affair.

Paul nodded. "He probably noticed that it's better over here. Can't read the sender's name."

"But the address. Buchholz care of Schneider, Nuremberg Erlenstegen. Actually he isn't our concern. Those in Nuremberg can come and get him. You know how the Old Man is. If we report it we'll be ordered to drag the corpse up the hill. There's at least two hundred pounds of him. Those crooks knew exactly why they laid him down over on our side. What time is it?"

"Half past three."

"At four o'clock our turn's over anyhow. You know what? We'll take him back over there. If they can be smart, so can we. He's their business, not ours."

"Good idea," said Paul relieved. When they lifted Hergett off the ground he began to moan. They were so shocked, they dropped him at once.

"My God, he's still alive," exclaimed Paul.

Gunther wiped his hands off on his coat disgustedly.

"I never would have thought . . ." he stared down on Hergett. Then he said, "I don't care. I want to go home, into my bed. By the time we'd have dragged him up he'd be dead anyhow. Come on, grab him."

He was heavier than they had thought and they had trouble dragging him even those few meters.

"So, there!" said Gunther. Panting he straightened up. "Imagine if we'd had to carry him up the hill."

"Couldn't have done it, just the two of us. What do we do with the letter?"

"Leave it on him otherwise they won't know who to notify. Man, does he make a noise." They looked at Hergett whose moans had grown louder. "I remember one of us howling like that in France," said Paul. "He had a shot in the belly."

"He's as good as dead," said Gunther. "Come on, man, into the woods." They ran off.

When it grew light, Hergett was still moaning. But he wasn't found until two hours later when a border patrol, led by an officer, came upon him.

The room in which he was lying had a high ceiling. Next to his bed he saw a woman in a white coat who had her fingers on his wrist. It bothered him. Later he noticed that the door was white too. Everything was white, only the floor was dark. He had noticed that before but he didn't know when. Now and then the door opened and a man looked in. Then he disappeared again and Hergett looked at the cracks in the ceiling and the contours of the lamp. Only the fingers on his wrist distracted him a little. Later Katharina appeared before him. He remembered that she had been here once before with a mouth without color and eyes that didn't look at him. This time her mouth had no color either and Hergett thought how dreadfully changed she was. She sat down on a chair and asked in a low voice:

"How do you feel today?"

"Fine," said Hergett but he didn't hear his voice.

"You'll be well again," said Katharina and did not look at him. Then another voice said, "You must go now."

Katharina nodded. She leaned over him and he saw her face large and close above him. It bewildered him and he closed his eyes but opened them again right away and looked after her as she went to the door. There she turned and said something he could not understand. But he wanted to give her pleasure and acted as if he had understood and smiled at her. Then she was gone. Again he felt the fingers on his wrist. They were so cool he felt them to his bones. He would have liked to tell the woman to take her fingers away but he hadn't the strength. Through the window a beam of sun fell on the floor. For a while Hergett watched the tiny dust particles in the light and he tried to count them. But there were too many and they were changing their position rapidly all the time so that his head grew dizzy. Also the coldness had now crept from his wrist up into his shoulder and he felt it move across his chest. He began to tremble. If she doesn't take off her hand I'll scream. But that, too, he forgot quickly. He looked again at the beam of sun and it seemed to him as if the light had grown dimmer. The dust particles appeared to change their color. They turned first grey then black. This alarmed him and he thought: how odd! Now it already seemed as if he were seeing everything through dark glasses. The coldness had spread through his whole chest and a little later he could feel it even in his brain. And just at that moment he saw Katharina again. As if her picture had chased the fingers away from his wrist he felt the coldness disappear and he thought he could hear a few quick steps in the distance, a door slamming, then he was walking out with Katharina and she put her arm through his and asked:

"How long do you think you'll go on proposing to me?"

"As long as I can," Hergett answered and smiled. In the air was the smell of seaweed and the sea moved sluggishly along the coast. Two sea gulls sailed slowly over the dunes, their white silver bellies gleaming in the sun.

"Imagine a landscape with thickly wooded hills," said Hergett. "With narrow valleys and clear little streams and imagine a small town with very old houses and churches—that's Ilmenau."

"It sounds very romantic," said Katharina. "I'll think it over."

Hergett was very pleased, but suddenly he stopped and Katharina gave a cry of terror. Before them, so deep that Hergett could not see the bottom of it, opened an abyss and when he looked over to the right, his heart missed a beat. Across the dunes a man came running directly towards the abyss. In spite of the distance Hergett could see that it was Klaus Langer and he yelled at him to stop. But Klaus Langer didn't hear him and Hergett ran towards him. He was still a dozen steps away when he saw Langer disappear in the abyss. But then he noticed that the abyss was moving closer to him although he was standing still. He opened his eyes wide in amazement, hearing Katharina's voice calling his name. But the abyss came running towards him like a voracious animal with wide open jaws and it was beneath him so swiftly that he was still uncomprehending when he lost the ground under his feet. He fell so long that he felt nothing when he hit the bottom because by that time he was already dead.

It was a Saturday.

Herr Primelmann had turned to the last page of his morning paper when his eyes grew round with surprise. He rushed to Frau Hansen with the paper in his hand.

"Read this," he said breathlessly. "Engagement notice of Fräulein Schneider and young Leuchtner. And I had no inkling—"

"Neither had I," Frau Hansen was aghast. "This is in today's paper?"

"Read it," he gave her the paper, tugged nervously at his necktie and said: "I must congratulate the Landrat at once; if I don't he'll be insulted."

"Of course you must," said Frau Hansen, shaking her head. "He really kept that a secret. Well, the poor thing has deserved it. She's waited long enough. It's almost a year now since that thing with Langer."

"More than a year. She can be glad it happened this way. Someone who goes and cuts his wrists with a razor blade is pretty soft in the head." He looked at his watch. "I'll be back in a moment."

Schneider wore a dark suit this day and received Primelmann benignly.

"What good thing is on your mind?"

"If you'll permit me," Primelmann said with dignity, "I should like to offer my congratulations on your daughter's engagement. I just read it in the paper."

Schneider smiled sentimentally.

"Yes, thank you. Yes, we are going to celebrate a bit today."

"So the wedding will be soon?" Primelmann asked boldly.

"In four weeks at the most," answered Schneider. "My future son-in-law wants to work for two years in the firm of one of his father's friends in South America. So of course he wants his wife along."

"Oh! But that will be hard on Fräulein Schneider. So far away from home!"

Schneider's face darkened a little. The whole thing had been Katharina's idea. She had persuaded Kurt Leuchtner to leave Nuremberg with her. Kurt's parents had finally agreed, and it was the one bitter drop in Schneider's cup of happiness.

"She's no longer a child," he said curtly and went on to discuss a few office matters. Finally he reminded Primelmann to do his duty as a voter on the following day.

"You know what's at stake," he said warningly.

"Of course, Herr Landrat. Reunification is at stake."

"Germany is at stake," said Schneider and nodded good-bye. Shortly afterwards he called Fräulein von Hessel.

"I'm leaving earlier today. If there's anything—I'll be at my house until one o'clock."

"I hope you have a wonderful time," said Fräulein von Hessel smiling.

Down in the courtyard stood his new car. It had cost ten thousand marks and although it was an official car, Schneider considered it his personal property. He wondered if there was anything else he should get. They had bought the engagement presents three weeks ago. The celebration was to be at the Leuchtners' house—Schneider's own was too small for the number of guests invited.

Since his wife was going to get enough butter cream torte on this day, he bought only flowers. Leaving the shop he noticed the election placard of another party. It was pasted to a gatepost and one corner was loose. After making sure that no one could see him, Schneider tore it down quickly and crumpled it with his feet. Traitors to the fatherland, he thought contemptuously, traitors. He carefully put the flowers into the car and slid in behind the steering wheel. Before he started the motor it seemed to him that he was hearing music from somewhere. He rolled down the window. Now he could hear it clearly. It was probably one of the propaganda trucks of his own party. They were playing the old military marches and Schneider's eyes grew moist as cold and hot shivers ran alternately down his back. Imperishable, he thought, Germany imperishable! He was filled with a big feeling.

## ABOUT THE AUTHOR

WILLI HEINRICH is a German novelist whose specialty is the look, smell and sound of military defeat. He came by his competence honestly and bitterly as an infantry officer in a fearfully mauled German division that bit deep into Russia and withdrew its remnants in broken retreat. He was born in Heidelberg and received his education in German grade and trade schools. He is also the author of *The Cross of Iron* and *Crack of Doom*. His hobbies are chess and fast cars. He lives in Karlsruhe.

# Join the Allies on the Road to Victory
# BANTAM WAR BOOKS

These action-packed books recount the most important events of World War II. Specially commissioned maps, diagrams and illustrations allow you to follow these true stories of brave men and gallantry in action.